TRANA MAE SIMMONS

LOVE SPELL NEW YORK CITY

LOVE SPELL®

February 1994

Published by

Dorchester Publishing Co., Inc.
276 Fifth Avenue
New York, NY 10001

If you purchased this book without a cover you should be aware that this book is stolen property. It was reported as "unsold and destroyed" to the publisher and neither the author nor the publisher has received any payment for this "stripped book."

Copyright © 1994 by Trana Mae Simmons

All rights reserved. No part of this book may be reproduced or transmitted in any form or by any electronic or mechanical means, including photocopying, recording or by any information storage and retrieval system, without the written permission of the Publisher, except where permitted by law.

The name "Love Spell" and its logo are trademarks of Dorchester Publishing Co., Inc.

Printed in the United States of America.

*To my own hero, Barney,
without your support, it couldn't have happened.
And to Rob Cohen, Debbie Byington,
and Candice Kohl, thanks for everything.*

Bittersweet Promises

Chapter One

February 13, 1866

The door on the general store slammed open and the stagecoach driver clumped across the board walkway, halting at the edge to bite off a hefty chaw from his newly purchased tobacco plug. One of the coach horses pricked its ears and snorted out a steamy cloud of breath as it turned its head toward the voice.

"Danged fool passengers," the driver grumbled around the bulge in his cheek. "Got nothin' better to do than sit inside and rest their legs and backsides, while I ride up there in the weather. Then they 'spect me to be their lackey and carry their bags back to the hotel, just 'cause I didn't stop there an' let them out!"

"I heard that!" Shanna pushed the door she had caught in midswing open farther and marched after the driver. "I'll report your insolence! Don't you think I won't!"

The driver rolled his eyes and shook his head before

he turned around. "You an' that boy can carry your own bags. Don't look to me like there's a derned thing wrong with neither one of you."

Realizing her little brother had followed her outside didn't calm Shanna's anger a bit. "Our passage money entitles us to your assistance in handling our baggage. Every other driver we've had on this trip gave us that courtesy."

"Yeah, well those other drivers probably didn't have to wait an extra fifteen minutes in the morning for you to primp your face. You put me behind schedule, and now I gotta make up the time."

The driver climbed into his seat as Shanna glared at him indignantly. Fix her face, indeed. All she'd been trying to do was at least get her upper body washed and her dress changed. She darn sure hadn't lingered over that breakfast of half-cooked oatmeal.

"You're a disgrace," she finally spat at the driver as he reached for the reins. "I'm going to make that report in writing, not just verbally. I'm also going to tell the company how rude you were to Toby and me at the way station this morning and ask them to discipline you."

"Won't do you no good," the driver said with a sneer. "Coach lines can't hardly get drivers these days, 'specially ones good with a gun—an' I am. The lines are makin' money 'cause all the train tracks was tore up in the war, an' they ain't about to fire me just 'cause I won't haul your blasted bags to the hotel. Should've brought your fancy-pants maid with you if you wanted someone to wait on you hand an' foot!"

He spit a glob of tobacco juice over the side of the coach, and it spattered on the step to the walkway, just below Shanna's feet.

Shanna instinctively jumped back, her face contorting with fury. "You . . . you barbarian! I hope every one of your darned horses goes lame before you get to your next stop and you have to walk fifty miles!"

The driver pursed his lips again, then thought better of it. He released the brake and picked up the whip, cracking it over the team's heads. The coach surged forward amid a jingle of harness and plops of pancake-size hooves, leaving Shanna nothing to yell at but the rear of the departing vehicle.

Angrily, she swept her skirts up and, avoiding the glob of tobacco spittle, climbed down to the second step. With her fist half raised, she suddenly realized how ridiculous she would look to her nine-year-old brother if she shouted the words pushing at her throat. Lord, that would be some example for Toby!

Instead, she gazed up at the sky while she breathed deeply and tried to smooth the fury from her face before she looked at Toby. A biting wind chilled her cheeks and the bank of purple-black clouds scuttling overhead foretold yet another blizzard on the way, perhaps as bad as the other two storms they had encountered on their journey.

For just a second, she felt a stab of sympathy for the coach driver, who had to fight to keep his schedule in the inclement weather. But she quickly shifted her concern to the horses. That old coot could freeze for all she cared.

"Shanna, are you gonna stand there all day?" Toby asked.

Shanna gave a start and finally dropped her arm, unclenching her fist and lifting her skirts again. "I'm coming, Toby," she said as she climbed the steps. "You must be freezing."

"Yeah," Toby admitted. "And I thought you were freezing there for a minute. You looked like you were gonna run after the stagecoach; then you just stood there like you couldn't move. You sure looked funny."

Shanna made a valiant attempt to overlook Toby's

giggle, smoothing at her cloak and searching in her pockets for her gloves. Trying to appear nonchalant as she pulled out her gloves and worked her hands into them, she turned so she could glance up and down the street. Luckily, she only saw vacant hitching rails, even in front of the two saloons on down the street.

She breathed out a sigh of relief. The inhabitants of Liberty, Missouri, appeared to be taking shelter from the approaching storm. She didn't see even one other person on the boardwalks who could have witnessed the spectacle she had made of herself.

Liberty, Missouri. Good grief, she hadn't even known there was a town called Liberty in Missouri until a few weeks ago.

Cody Garret stepped out of the telegraph office on the opposite side of the street. A satisfied smirk creased his full lips as he stuffed his copies of the telegrams he'd just sent into the pocket of his sheepskin-lined coat.

He'd told Aunt Bessie a search would be useless. No woman of sane mind would travel very far through the war-ravaged South right then—especially for the paltry salary he could offer. Now maybe Bessie would quit being such a pain in the as . . . neck and hoist her elderly fanny back out to the plantation—and he could get a decent, woman-cooked meal for a change.

The half of cinnamon-laden apple pie and two glasses of milk from the well house he'd eaten for breakfast that morning hadn't really satisfied his appetite. But it was better than wrestling that black monstrosity of a wood stove into coughing up an edible meal. Aunt Bessie would definitely not have approved, though.

Cody's smirk dissolved into a wry grin. Twenty-five years old, a widower with a small child, and a war behind him, and he still cringed at the thought of a censuring look from his elderly aunt.

Bittersweet Promises

A flash of sunlight caught the corner of Cody's eye. He briefly glanced at the cloud-laden sky, then realized his mistake. Across the street he noticed what seemed to be the only other two people in town braving the frigid weather.

He didn't recognize either of them and gathered they had arrived on the stage. And he sure as hell would have remembered that woman if he'd seen her before. Or at least that shining blond hair—the only bright spot of color in the stark winter day.

She bent down and tucked the little boy's muffler more securely around his neck, and Cody sighed in disappointment when she straightened and pulled the hood of her cloak forward with a graceful movement.

Lucky man, whoever that woman belongs to, Cody thought to himself as she walked over to the carpetbags sitting outside the store. And most definitely female. His mouth quirked in appreciation of the swaying gait that the long, woolen cloak couldn't conceal as she trudged slowly up the walkway.

"Probably headed to the hotel," Cody murmured. "Reckon I ought to go over there and offer to help with those bags. The one that little mite beside her's carrying is almost as big as he is."

A gust of icy wind hit Cody as he stepped down into a street still muddy beneath a thin crust forming in the cold air. He glanced overhead as he grabbed his black Stetson and clamped it more firmly over his chestnut hair, then stopped abruptly when he dropped his gaze from the sky and found another sign of life in town.

Three riders—mounted on blooded horses the like of which Cody hadn't seen around town since before the war—rode slowly up the street. Long dusters flapped beside their stirrups and hats pulled down almost to their noses shadowed their faces. A glimpse of movement in the alley beside the bank caught Cody's attention, and he could barely detect the outlines of two more horses, standing just far enough back to be almost invisible from the street.

Cody's senses sharpened and his eyes narrowed. His skin crawled with the same feeling he'd had the day he avoided a well-concealed ambush on his company during the war, and the hair on the back of his neck actually prickled. It took him only a split second to measure the distance between the woman and the bank.

Trusting his instincts, Cody leapt back onto the walkway and pushed open the telegraph office door. His voice cut through the quiet office. "Ed, go out the back way and find the sheriff! Tell him to get over to the bank!"

"What's going on, Cody?"

"Whatever it is, I don't like the looks of it. Have Dan bring his rifle and deputies!"

Ed scrambled from his chair, his face strained with worry. "Cody, all my money's in that bank."

"So's mine and everyone else's in the county," Cody said grimly. "Move!"

Ed ran for the back of the office as Cody slammed the door. Despite the biting wind, he unbuttoned his heavy coat and slipped the loop from the handle of his six-gun as he angled across the street. Maybe he was wrong. Hell, he hoped he was wrong, but he'd rather look like an overly cautious fool in front of Dan than a gullible one.

Glancing up the street toward the bank, Cody saw the three horses now riderless and a fourth man he hadn't noticed before sitting in his saddle, holding their reins. The woman and child were approaching the land office, the last building before the alley beside the bank. And the bank was between them and the hotel.

"Ma'am!" Cody called, though he had little hope his voice would carry over the wind. "Ma'am, wait up a minute!"

Bittersweet Promises

Shanna stopped and frowned, puzzled at the slight sound that had broken into her concentration. Peering over her shoulder, she saw a tall, broad-shouldered man hurrying up the street in her direction. He wore what she had come to think of as working clothes the farther south she traveled—a heavy coat, denim jeans and boots. But even at this distance she could tell his denims fit much better than those on most of the men she had encountered—or maybe his body was just better proportioned.

He wasn't close enough to make out the features on the face beneath the hat brim, but one thing she could tell. The man's boots were sinking in mud and clumps of other matter left behind by the horses, spattering clods of muck on the denims, which tightly encased his muscular legs. Obviously, she sniffed to herself, they didn't have street cleaners here.

Shanna shrugged and placed a hand on Toby's shoulder to urge him forward again. The man couldn't be calling her—she sure didn't know anyone in this town.

She didn't particularly care about meeting the people in this town, either, especially if they were anything like that ill-mannered coach driver. It was just another mindless stop on her and Toby's journey, and right now the promise of a soft bed and hot bath at a real hotel urged her onward.

"Ma'am!" came the voice again. "You there with the child. Wait up!"

"Shanna, I think that man's talking to us." Toby twisted from beneath Shanna's hand and looked out into the street. "Do you think he's a cowboy?"

"Hum?" And a hot, well-prepared meal. She hoped that hotel had a decent cook. She didn't even want to think about what might have been in the half-congealed stew served at the wayside stop last evening.

Shanna halted again and glanced behind her. A tired sigh escaped her lips as she retraced a few steps and

15

reached down to take her little brother's small hand in her own. Wasn't she ever going to get to the hotel?

"Come on, Toby. It's freezing out here and I can't wait to soak in a hot bath."

"But, Shanna, it's not Saturday," Toby grumbled as he obeyed the tug on his arm and followed his sister.

Cody glanced at the lone rider holding the horses once more as he climbed the steps to the walkway. The man straightened his slouched shoulders and shifted nervously in his saddle, his head swiveling from Cody back toward the bank window. His hand swept his duster behind him, then rested on his six-gun.

Cody reached for his own gun, dropping his arm before he could pull it from the holster. Jesus, that woman and child would be caught in the cross fire if shooting started.

Just then, five more riders emerged from the trees a few hundred yards from the edge of town, riding their horses at breakneck speed toward the bank.

"Hell and damnation," Cody muttered. "Hurry up, Dan."

Where the blue blazes was the sheriff? Cody cautiously started after the woman, keeping his eyes on the lone horseman in case he pulled his gun, but realizing there wasn't really a damned thing he could do about it as long as that crazy little fool and her small companion were in the line of fire. Why the hell didn't she realize she was walking straight into danger?

"Typical woman," Cody growled under his breath. "Got her mind too full of feminine poppycock to notice the devil if he swished his tail right in her face!"

"Stop right there, lady!"

Shanna's carpetbag thudded on the walkway and her panic-stricken eyes centered on the black bore of the pistol the man on horseback aimed at her and Toby from across the alley. Frantically she tugged Toby's small body close to her, her terror warring with the need to protect her brother.

"P-put that gun away!" she demanded. "What in the world do you think you're doing?"

The gunman's eyes flickered to something behind her, and the pistol barrel shifted slightly. "You!" he shouted.

The pistol barked and Shanna screamed. Splinters of wood sprayed the arm of her cloak when the bullet buried itself in the wall at her back. Hysterical with fear, Shanna stumbled backward, pushing Toby behind her.

"Stay still, lady," a voice hissed. "For God's sake, don't try to run. He'll shoot you and the boy both!"

The sibilant warning terrified Shanna further, but she bit down on her lower lip, stifling her next scream and clogging the terror in her throat. Behind her, Toby whimpered and Shanna's fingers tightened on his arm until he quieted. Ever so slowly, Shanna swiveled her eyes away from the pistol barrel toward the voice. The mud-spattered figure of the man who had been crossing the street stood a bare yard from her, his hands in the air, a dangerous glint in his eyes and his body tensed.

"What's going on here?" someone shouted out in the street.

The man on horseback jerked around in his saddle, and the pistol cracked again. The young man running at them clutched his chest and crumbled to the street. His scream of agony was drowned by the rebel yells issuing from the throats of the riders on the five galloping horses, now a scant 50 feet away.

The instant the gunman turned his back, Cody flung himself forward and grabbed the woman and child. Another shot rang out as Cody's shoulder shattered the land office door, his momentum forcing the three of them through the opening. Diving behind the front wall, he carried the other two with him, partially breaking their fall with his own body.

"Stay down!" he ordered. He wrenched his gun from the holster and knocked out a bottom pane of glass. The hammer landed with a dull click when he pulled the trigger, and the cylinder jammed tightly when he thumbed the hammer again. He cursed and grabbed the cylinder with his other hand, but it refused to revolve.

A barrage of shots shattered the top windowpane. Cody instinctively dropped over the woman and child to shelter them from the falling glass, shoving the useless six-gun back into the holster. The woman grabbed his neck in a stranglehold with one arm, little whimpers of fear puffing her breath against his neck while she tightly clasped the boy in her other arm. He had to get them to a safer place.

"What the hell's going on out there, Cody?"

Cody loosened the woman's arm enough to turn his head toward the wizened figure barely poking his head over the wooden counter bisecting the room. "A gang of men are robbing the bank, Tom!" he called. "My gun's jammed! You got a rifle back there?"

"Hell, yeah. But I'm not going out there. That's the sheriff's job!"

Cody pried himself free from the woman's arm and stiffened his arms to raise his body a few inches. Shaking his shoulders, he flung shards of glass from his coat and gazed down at the frightened faces beneath him. Two identical pairs of terrorized blue eyes met his.

"Listen to me now," he said grimly. "When I get up, I want you two to keep low and crawl across the floor. Go through that gate beside the counter and take shelter with Tom. You'll have to be careful of the glass. Do you think you can do that?"

The heart-shaped face of the young woman triggered some buried memory in Cody's mind, which he immediately disregarded when she shook her head frantically and rolled away from him, the little boy in her arms.

"No!" she cried. "We're safer here behind this wall!"

Cody grabbed her chin, turning her face to him. "Damn it, I don't have time to argue! Those bullets can penetrate this wall. If you don't want to get that boy killed, move your ass!"

Shanna gasped in understanding and tore her eyes away from the hypnotic brown gaze, cold now with anger and frustration. She scrambled to her knees, pulling Toby with her. When the man's hands circled her waist, urging her forward, she squeezed Toby's hand and rose into a crouch, scurrying across the floor. Toby stumbled awkwardly beside her, while the masculine bulk behind her protected them both from more bullets.

New shots in the street gave the three figures impetus as they scrambled through the wooden gate. Cody administered a final shove to Shanna and Toby and looked across them at Tom.

"That rifle. Where is it?" Cody demanded.

"In the closet." Tom swung his head toward a closet door behind him, but made no move to reach for the doorknob.

Cody shot him a disgusted look and started for the closet. The woman gave a sob beside him, and he hesitated when she cried out, "Toby. Oh, God, Toby, you're hurt!"

Cody looked down to see the young boy cuddled in the woman's lap, her blond head bent over the small palm cradled in her own. Blood poured from around the piece of glass embedded in the boy's hand.

"I fell on the glass, Shanna," the little boy whimpered. "It hurts!"

The woman reached for the embedded glass with shaking fingers, then gave a moan of dismay. She pulled her hand back and shook her head.

"Please. Get it out, Shanna," the boy cried, tears streaming down his face.

Cody glanced at the closet door, then back at the boy. Outside in the street, men shouted and horses neighed. The rifle he needed to help defend the town was only a couple feet away. But his immediate concern was for the child, who was only a few years older than his own daughter.

Cody jerked a handkerchief from his denim pocket and sat down by the woman. Tenderly he reached for the young boy's hand and held it firmly while he pulled the glass out and threw it aside. He probed the wound further, assuring himself there was no more glass in it, and the boy gave a gasp of pain. But when Cody scanned his face, the boy shot him a gutsy grimace through his tears.

The remaining panes of glass in the land office window rained onto the floor and a bullet thwacked into the wall above them. Damn it to hell! There was a bank robbery going on out there—and they were stealing *his* money while he knelt here tending this boy!

Cody stifled the urge to shake the woman—to remind her that she should be the one caring for the boy. Instead, he grabbed her trembling hand and thrust the handkerchief into it.

"Wrap his hand for now," he growled softly. "I've got to get out there and help Dan."

When Cody started to pull his hand away, he felt the woman's fingers curl around his own.

"Be careful. Please," she whispered when he glanced up from their clasped fingers.

"Yeah. Yeah, I will," he returned gruffly, surprised at how deep the tender concern in those blue eyes touched him. He gently pried her fingers free and took a steadying breath before he crept to the closet door.

Carefully he reached for the doorknob, wrenching his

hand back when the wood just above it splintered from yet another stray bullet. After an unconscious glance over his shoulder to make sure no splinters had landed on the woman, Cody groped for the knob again and swung the door open, reaching inside for the rifle propped in a corner. With it in his hands, he retraced his path to the front window.

Cautiously Cody raised his head, aware that the noise in the street had diminished. The band of robbers was near the edge of town, the main body of horses galloping in a bunch while three men strung out behind covered their retreat. Quickly he flung the rifle to his shoulder and snapped off a shot. One of the fleeing bandits twisted in the saddle, but the rider closest to him reached over and pushed the man forward, onto the horse's neck.

Cody instinctively reached for the lever on the rifle before realizing it wasn't the Spencer repeater he'd left in his saddle scabbard. The last horse entered the trees beyond town, and Cody stared down at Tom's single shot rifle. If he hadn't been distracted by the boy's injury, he'd have had time to search for the reloads in the closet. He gave a grimace of disgust and tossed the rifle aside. There wasn't anything left to shoot at now.

He stood and stared out the broken window until the sheriff emerged from behind a horse trough on the other side of the street. A barber's apron covered Dan's chest and white lather obscured half his face. The two deputies stepped out of the doorway in the building behind the sheriff, wisps of smoke curling from their rifle barrels in the frigid air. One of them ran down the walkway toward the sprawled body in the street.

"Y'all all right over there, Cody?" the sheriff called.

"Yeah, Dan, go ahead and get Doc for that man out in the street."

"We been trying to get to him to see how bad he's hurt, but there were too many of them," Dan replied.

"They kept us pinned down so we couldn't even get off a good shot at any of them. That poor son of a gun hasn't moved since we first spotted him, though."

"Where the hell is everyone? Why didn't they help?"

"Inside shaking in their boots, I reckon," Dan said scornfully. "Can't say as I blame them, I guess. That bunch meant business!"

Cody shook his head and turned from the window, striding to the counter to check on the woman and child. He found them huddled together, the woman's head bent protectively over the boy in her arms. For just a second he glared down at the woman, resenting the fact that his need to protect her and the child had interfered with his aiding Dan—perhaps catching the robbers in a cross fire. Almost every penny he had in the world was in that bank, all of it earmarked for the needs of his daughter and aunt.

It wasn't her fault, he reminded himself just as quickly, realizing how absurd it was to blame the frightened figure on the floor. It was those damned cheap bullets— the only kind available after the war—that had jammed his six-gun.

"Are they gone, Cody?" Tom's strident whisper broke into Cody's concentration.

"Huh? Oh, yeah. Yeah, they're gone," Cody replied with barely a glance at the old man. He laid a gentle hand on the woman's shoulder instead of the tousled curls the hand strained toward. "It's safe for you to come out now, ma'am," he said in a voice softened with consolation in an attempt to ease her abject fright.

Shanna clutched Toby even tighter, still hearing the echoes of shots and men's shouts in her mind. "No," she moaned with a shake of her head. "They'll kill us. I can't let anything happen to Toby."

"Ma'am, please," Cody soothed. He gripped her arms and tugged upward, but she resisted the pressure, still shaking her head. "It's all right now,". he reassured her again. "Come on out of there so we can check the boy's hand a little better and make sure you're all right."

"Shanna." Toby struggled in Shanna's grasp. "Shanna, you're crushing me." He managed to get his uninjured hand free and swatted at Shanna's shoulder. "Shanna, let go!"

Shanna lifted her head a fraction of an inch and stared down into Toby's face. "Hush, Toby. There's men . . . and . . . and guns. They shot at us! I'll take care of you. I promised you I always would."

"Ma'am, the men are gone," Cody repeated.

"Don't you hear him, Shanna?" Toby insisted. "He says they're gone. Come on, Shanna. Let go so I can breathe."

Slowly Shanna loosened her hold on Toby and glanced up at the man standing over her. He gave her an encouraging nod and almost at once a good deal of her fear left her as she studied his warm brown eyes for a brief instant. She allowed Toby to rise to his feet, grabbing his arm in a firm grip when he tried to move away from her.

"No! You stay right here with me, Toby!"

"But, Shanna, I wanna go see what happened out in the street. There's probably all kinds of dead bodies out there! If we don't hurry, they'll carry them off before we get to see them!"

"Good Lord," Shanna breathed. "You're not going anywhere, Toby. You mind me and stay here!"

"She's right, son," Shanna heard the man standing over them say. Keeping a tight hold on Toby's arm, she pulled her legs under her and awkwardly stood up. The man gripped her shoulders to steady her, his touch gentle, yet firm.

"Aw, some big sister," Toby grumbled under his breath. He scuffed the toe of one boot against the floor as he gazed longingly at the front of the land office. "I still wanna see."

"That's enough, Toby." The hands on her shoulders fell away and Shanna glanced behind her at the broad male chest. She had to tilt her head back at an ungainly angle to see the face above the wide shoulders. He stood so close she could smell the open-air scent of his coat mixed with the masculine after-shave, and reassurance flowed from the velvety pools of eyes set in a ruggedly handsome face.

A woman could rely on a man like him. The thought sprang unbidden into Shanna's mind as she found it difficult to tear her gaze away. Trust him with her life, as indeed she and Toby had just done. She cleared her throat to force her voice past the last lingering terror in her chest.

"Toby and I owe you our heartfelt thanks," she said earnestly, wishing she could somehow think of stronger words to express her gratitude. But she was still struggling against the slowly receding fright and guilt over dragging Toby into the middle of a shoot-out. At least, that was what she told herself it was when she fought the urge to fling herself into those protective arms once again.

Abruptly, Cody sucked in his breath and stepped back, the memory surfacing again, demanding his acknowledgment this time. My God, how could he have missed it before? Even the clear Yankee accent lent credence to the nagging suspicion trying to claw its way up through the fast crumbling layers of resistance in his mind.

He quickly jerked his hat down over his eyes, though a corner of his mind told him she couldn't possibly know him. When he tore his eyes away from her puzzled expression, he glanced down at the child by her side. It couldn't possibly be....

Sensing his change of attitude, Shanna gasped and

Bittersweet Promises

moved protectively between the man and Toby, drawing the walnut-hued inspection back to her own face. Fighting the thought that this man might be more of a threat than the entire gang of bank robbers, and confused at the sudden stab of hurt the cold look on Cody's face sent through her, she drew herself up to her full height and eyed him warily as she tried to edge past him.

"Excuse us," she said in a tight voice when he thrust out an arm to block her path. "We need to get to the hotel."

"Who the hell are you?" he growled deep in his throat.

Chapter Two

"Did you get a look at any of them, Cody?"

Cody dropped his arm, tensed into a rigid barricade to keep Shanna from passing and wrenched his eyes from Shanna's bewildered, mud-smeared face to Dan standing in the shattered doorway of the land office. He rolled his shoulders, loosening the tension, immediately glad for the interruption.

"Not a good enough look to identify anyone," he admitted, his mind adding the silent words, 'at least for sure.' He'd deal with that other, nagging suspicion about the woman later. "They had their hats low and collars up," he told Dan instead. "And those last five who rode in wore bandannas. The horses shouldn't be hard to recognize, though."

"Yeah, if we've got anything around here that can catch them after all those Jayhawker raids during the war," Dan said in disgust. "You ready to ride? My deputies are gathering a posse."

Bittersweet Promises

Cody strode across the littered floor, resolutely pushing aside the shattered look his rash demand had left on Shanna's face. "How much did they get from the bank?"

"Cleaned it out. Don't have a count yet. I'll be back in a second with your horse."

"Toby, stop!"

Cody instinctively grabbed the back of the little boy's coat. He lifted Toby off the ground, ignoring the boy's cries of outrage. Toby's legs spun like windmills and his hands balled into fists as he tried to reach over his small shoulders.

"Let go of me!" Toby demanded. "I wanna go see what happened!"

Cody's lips tightened in impatience and he barely kept himself from shaking the struggling figure. Wasn't he ever going to cut loose from these two tenderfeet and go after his bank account?

He started to turn and thrust his twisting burden at the woman, but stopped when he glanced out into the street. An uncompromising look stole over his face and he dropped Toby back to his feet. Taking a firm grip on the slight shoulders, Cody forced the boy to look toward the small party of men Dan had joined.

"All right, young'un," he said in an icy voice. "Is that what you want to see?"

Shanna's face blanched when she followed Cody's gaze. Two men bent down to pick up the prone body of the young man who had drawn the robber's attention away from her and Toby, allowing them to escape almost certain death. Blood soaked the front of the man's jacket, and his head lolled on his chest when the men lifted him by his feet and shoulders. A black-clad man stood and picked up a medical bag by his feet, shaking his head sadly.

For just a second, Shanna's mind superimposed the quick glimpse she'd had of the young man running toward them over the still, dead body. He had been still alive at that moment—such a brief second ago in time. Now he was lifeless, his future gone—somewhere was a mother who would waste away in grief when she got the news, as Shanna would have had the body been Toby's.

Cody knelt behind Toby and shook the boy's shoulders. Despite the whimpers emerging from Toby's throat, Cody kept the boy's face pointed at the scene in the street.

"Is it, son?" he asked again. "Did you want to see some dead bodies? Sorry, but we've only got one to show you today. Maybe there'll be more next time."

Toby's small frame shook with a sob, penetrating Shanna's dazed senses and tearing at her heart, shocking her back to the realization that her very-much-alive little brother was suffering a brute manhandling. Anger flared and she surged forward, reaching for Toby.

"Get your hands off him! Give him to me!"

"I'm not done yet," Cody said as he turned Toby around to face him.

"Oh, yes, you are," Shanna gritted through clenched teeth, her fist balled in case she had to make her point in a more violent manner. "Just because you protected us a minute ago doesn't give you the right to push my little brother around! Leave him alone, or I'll have you arrested!"

Cody tossed her a brief glance. The dangerous glint in his eyes clashed with her pugnacious stance, quelling Shanna in her tracks. Then he ignored her and pulled Toby's small fists from his eyes, where they tried to stem the tears running down his cheeks. Blood and moisture soaked the handkerchief bandaging Toby's hand, reminding Cody of how bravely the little boy had tolerated the pain from his wound.

"I want you to remember this day, son," Cody said in a softer voice. "There's nothing exciting about men killing

Bittersweet Promises

other men. And on top of that, a lot of good people lost their life savings today. If we can't catch those robbers, the people who had money in the bank will be wiped out. Do you understand what I'm trying to say, or am I going to have to take you out there for a closer look?"

"Y-you bully! You sorry b-bastard!" Shanna sputtered, her courage returning now that she didn't have to contend with that obdurate stare. "He's only nine. I suppose it makes you feel proud of yourself to terrorize a young boy!"

"Boys grow up fast out here," Cody said without taking his eyes from Toby's face. "Between the hard living and the war, a lot of them don't have much of a chance to be children. In fact, you both better start thinking about the consequences of your actions around here before you go blundering into more danger. And"—Cody finally allowed himself another look at the outraged package of fury hovering on the brink of a full-fledged assault on him—"you didn't think I was such a *bastard* when I kept both of you from stopping a bullet!"

Shanna fumed in rage, unable to rationalize a suitable retort to the unerring truth of his last statement. She gathered her courage again—at least enough to brave the black thunderbolts of the man's eyes—when, to her amazement, Toby straightened his shoulders and looked directly into Cody's face. He sniffed loudly and wiped his coat sleeve across his nose.

"I'm sorry, sir," Toby said in a cracked voice. "I thought it would be like the pictures in those penny books my friend Eddie has. It's not. It's awful."

Cody sighed and stood up. "Real life's very seldom like it's painted in some trashy book, son. Remember that, will you?"

"Yes, sir," Toby replied. "I will. And . . . and thank you for protecting my sister and me. It . . . it could have been one of us who got killed."

Cody reached down and gave Toby's shoulder a comforting pat before he pushed him toward Shanna. "Go on over to your sister now. We've got some robbers to catch."

"I hope you get 'em."

"Me, too."

"Cody, I've got your horse here," the sheriff said from behind him. "We've got to ride. That snowstorm's gonna cover their tracks pretty quick."

Cody turned and took the reins Dan held out to him. Disregarding the stirrups, he mounted the dun stallion from the walkway. He checked the stallion's movement for a moment and glanced over at the blond woman. An icy-blue gaze met his, and he pulled his Stetson down another inch over his eyes before he reined his horse around to follow Dan.

Driven by the rising wind, the first pellets of hard snow hit his face beneath the shelter of his hat brim. He glanced overhead at the thick black clouds and knew without a doubt the robbers had planned their getaway well. There wasn't a chance in hell Cody and the others could catch them before the snow obliterated their trail.

But he'd much rather be out chasing the bandits in this frigid weather than frozen beneath the arctic-blue gaze of that little boy's sister.

Cody shivered from a feeling totally unlinked to the wintry weather. Undoubtedly his hunch about the woman would turn out wrong. The downtrodden gossamer angel described to him would never have braved his male ire or let a profanity pass her lips. The dog-eared photo he had seen years ago had still been clear enough to show the wistful expression on the woman's face, completely opposite from the mystical daggers shooting at him from Shanna's eyes. At one point, he'd even had to consciously will himself not to throw up an arm to ward the daggers off. Besides, she was much too young—and the boy himself had told Cody she was his sister.

Damn, she was beautiful, though. He gripped his reins tighter in an effort to still the tingle in his fingertips at the remembered feel of her skin. Blue-eyed blonds had always been his weakness—delft-blue eyes and porcelain complexion had been what first attracted him to Nancy, his dead wife. That had to be what stirred him about Toby's sister—the promise of fragile femininity that her coloring implied.

Shanna's outwardly delicate demeanor covered fire and grit, however, and he'd never cared for independent, outspoken women. Women should be sheltered, cared for, pampered. In return, they made a man feel taller than a mountain and able to easily accomplish the most difficult tasks. A woman had no business traipsing around the country alone, without a man to keep her safe from danger.

He'd felt that masculine competence for only a few moments around Shanna, protecting her and the little boy called Toby from harm, even at the expense of losing the money he had deposited in the bank. She damned sure didn't appreciate it. Hell, he couldn't have done anything different—wouldn't have left her in danger even if he'd known in advance how she would turn from a soft, appreciative lady into a barely restrained spitfire.

Women, Cody mused to himself, urging his stallion into a canter when he realized he was falling behind the posse. He was better off keeping his thoughts centered on his lost money, instead of recalling how Shanna's quick personality change had brought to mind his encounter one spring with a feisty palomino mare determined to elude capture. That mare had never become a satisfactory saddle mount, and it had only settled down when allowed to run free in the pasture next to his father's chestnut stud, Copper.

But the pair of them produced offspring unequaled in the state—at least after the colts were caught and trained. That usually happened only after the mare came into heat again and dropped her overprotective vigilance of her current colt.

Someone else would have to stand stud to that palomino mare back in town. Cody leaned down into the shelter of his dun's neck as the frigid wind whipped by him. He'd done all that could be expected of him. Besides, both ice and fire in a woman were contradictions he didn't care for. Intriguing, definitely—but only in passing.

Shanna waited until the last rider from the posse rode out of sight before she relaxed her angry stance and looked down at Toby. When he quickly ducked his head to hide his tremulous gaze, Shanna's heart melted, and she reached out a hand to brush at one dirty cheek. She couldn't bring herself to scold him again. That man had done a good enough job of that—too blasted good.

"Toby," she said quietly in an effort to calm the indignation still seething in her mind, "let's get in out of this weather and find a better bandage for your hand."

Toby raised his head hopefully. "You . . . you're not mad at me, are you, Shanna?"

Shanna hesitated, then decided to be honest with him. "Yes. Yes, I am, Toby. But I don't think there's anything I could say to you that would be more effective than what you've just seen."

Shanna knelt and pulled him close. "Toby. Oh, Toby, you're going to have to learn to listen to me out here. It's not like back in New York. Remember, we talked about this time after time before we left."

"I remember," Toby said solemnly. "And I'm really trying to be good. Honest I am."

Shanna nodded and hugged him before rising to her feet. "I know you are, Toby." She stared up the deserted street again, giving herself a little shake when she found her eyes watering with strain as she stared at the trees behind which the posse had disappeared. She had to get Toby in out of the cold. But her eyes fell on the dark spot where the young man had lain, now quickly being covered with blowing snow.

"Oh, God," she said around a shudder. "Maybe we should go back. Maybe this was the wrong thing to do."

"No!" Toby grabbed her hand frantically, tugging on it, forcing her attention back to him. "No, Shanna! We can't go back. He'll send me away and I couldn't stand it. You promised you wouldn't let him do that. Please, Shanna. Don't make me go back there!"

"Toby, calm down. I didn't mean it. I was . . . I was just thinking out loud. We'll stay together, Toby, no matter what it takes."

"Cross your heart?"

Shanna resolutely fixed a sincere gaze on her face and drew an X across her chest. "I promise, Toby. Cross my heart and hope to die."

"Sh-Shanna?" Toby asked in a quavering voice. "Do you think our promises to each other would be just as good if we left off that last part?"

"About hoping to die?"

"Y-yeah."

Shanna squeezed his small hand reassuringly. "I'm sure they would be. Now, do you think we can find our bags? I hope they haven't gotten damaged."

"There they are." Toby pulled his hand free and pointed at the land office wall.

Before Shanna could move, the grizzled little man from the land office stepped out the door. "Here, I'll help you, miss. Well, my, my. What have we here?"

Shanna blushed violently when Tom bent down and picked up a sheer object from the walkway. The lacy chemise dangled from his gnarled finger, the fine quality of the silk garment showing through despite the mud spattering it. Shanna saw several other of her more intimate garments spilling out of the carpetbag, which had popped the clasp when she dropped it.

"Ain't this purty," Tom said with a soft chuckle. "Why, I bet ain't a woman in town's got anything this nice."

Shanna jumped forward and swiped the chemise from his hand. Ducking her bloodred face, she bent down and stuffed the chemise and other lingerie back into the bag.

"That wasn't very nice of you, mister," Toby said. "Men ain't supposed to make fun of all them geegaws women wear."

"Aren't," Shanna corrected as she snapped her bag shut.

"Yeah, men aren't supposed to do that," Toby said. "Don't you know that, mister?"

Tom chuckled loudly and patted Toby on the shoulder. "You're right, son. Men ain't—aren't supposed to make fun of such as that. I apologize, miss. Guess this young whippersnapper's got better manners than me."

"I ought to have good manners." Toby gave a long-suffering sigh. "Every time I turn around, Shanna's telling me don't do this or do do that."

Tom threw his head back, a loud guffaw erupting from his wattled throat. "Well, son," he said when he could control his laughter. "Like you heard a minute ago, things are different out here. Best you keep that in mind. And I sure hate to have to be the one to tell you this, but you might need to learn a whole different set of manners out here than what you're used to."

"Oh, no," Toby said around a groan. "Is that true, Shanna?"

"Good manners are the same anywhere, Toby," Shanna replied in a stiff voice, picking up her bag. "And I don't need *anyone* butting his nose into how I'm raising you," she continued with a cutting glance at Tom. "Get your bag and let's go on to the hotel. It's freezing out here."

"'Pologize again, miss," Tom said with a shrug. "Just tryin' to be friendly. Want some help with those bags?"

"We can manage, but thank you for the offer of help with the bags." Shanna started off down the walkway, with Toby following a step behind her.

"We got a good laundry in town that can clean your stuff, miss," Tom called after her. "But I'd make sure they use something besides that lye soap they usually wash things in, if they do your things."

Shanna straightened her shoulders and ignored him this time, her heel taps ringing loudly on the walkway as she marched away. She glanced quickly through the shattered windows of the bank as she passed, catching a glimpse of a white-haired man sitting slumped on a chair inside, his head cradled in his hands. Toby slowed his steps beside her and craned his neck to see through the broken windows, and she firmly placed her free hand against his back to urge him onward.

At the hotel door, Shanna hesitated. "We'll have to sign a register in here, Toby. Do you remember the name we're going to use?"

"Uh-huh," Toby confirmed. "It's Allen. You said it sounded enough like Alstyne that we wouldn't forget it, but we should drop the Van part of our name so P-Pop couldn't find us."

Toby sniffed back a short sob and tugged on Shanna's hand when she started through the door. "Shanna. Shanna, can I . . . ."

Shanna stopped and knelt again when she saw the tears threatening in Toby's blue eyes. She cupped his small shoulders in her hands. "What is it, Toby? Does your hand hurt? I can carry both bags."

"No. I can carry mine. I just . . . Shanna, can I still call him Pop? You said. . . ."

"Oh, Toby." Shanna wrapped her arms around him and pulled his head into her breasts. "I don't know. It's . . . it's something we'll have to talk about later."

Toby buried his face for an instant, then stepped out of her arms and gave a manful sniff to control his misery. "I'm all right now, Shanna," he managed to say. "It's just so much has happened since Mama d-died."

"I know, darling," Shanna said as she stood. "And you're being awfully brave about all this. I promise, we'll get things worked out."

"Just so *you* don't leave me, Shanna. Just so you promise *you'll* always be with me."

"I promise, Toby. Cross my heart and . . . cross my heart."

Shanna pushed open the hotel door, and they stepped into the welcome warmth inside the lobby. Looking toward the desk on the far side of the room, she found it empty, but a small bell sat on the edge of the desk to call the clerk to the front. Shifting her carpetbag to the other hand to relieve the strain on her arm, she walked across the lobby.

"Liberty," she heard Toby say beside her.

"What, Toby?"

"Liberty. That's the name on the front of the hotel. I saw it when the stagecoach passed by. Is this town called Liberty, Shanna?"

"Yes, Toby. We're in Liberty, Missouri."

"You never told me where we were going."

"No, I guess I didn't," Shanna murmured distractedly as she tried to decide whether to use the bell or to wait for the clerk to appear. She hated to shatter the silence of the quiet lobby by ringing a loud bell, but she wasn't prepared to wait much longer for that bath. And she ached for some privacy to sort out her confused emotions concerning the events of the past few minutes, not the least of which was why she had reacted so violently to that man's change in attitude toward her.

At first, she had felt drawn to him, almost sensing a haven in his strong arms where she could pour out the nightmarish anguish and frustration of the last few weeks. Then he had turned on her, demanding her identity and muddling her thoughts, and the fear that he knew her true identity had raced through her mind.

Her initial yearning was only the result of her exhaustion and gratitude, she told herself. She would have felt grateful to a man with a potbelly and bad breath for rescuing her and Toby. That the man who saved them had a trim waist she had to rigidly keep from flinging her arms around and a muscular chest she could have buried her face on very willingly—

"Is that something else we'll talk about later, Shanna?"

"Hmm, Toby?" And his breath had definitely not been sour—more like a hint of a spring breeze on her cheeks when she had turned around to get her first decent look at him.

"Where we're going. Will we talk about that soon?"

"Yes, Toby." Shanna tilted her chin decisively and reached out to tap the bell. Darn it, no matter how blatantly masculine he was, the man had shown his true character when he tried to discipline Toby.

While she waited for the clerk to answer the ringing summons, Toby's words slowly sank into Shanna's preoccupied thoughts, and she determinedly pondered them in an attempt to keep the other unwelcome reflections at bay.

What the heck *were* they doing in Liberty, Missouri? Despite the hundreds of miles they had already traveled, this might be just the start of another long, dangerous quest, and what would she do if she placed Toby in danger again?

They could so easily have been shot. And almost worse than that—if anything could be deemed worse than a sure, quick death like that suffered by the young man in the street—was the fact of their rescue by that stranger with the quicksilver personality. Admittedly, he had risked his life to shove them inside the land office. If he hadn't, there might only be fading blood spots on the wooden walkway to mark the fact that she and Toby had passed through Liberty, Missouri.

But she wasn't going to think about the stranger. . . .

Shanna shivered as she also tried to push the vision of twin blood spots away, and her toe tapped impatiently while she waited for the desk clerk to respond. She owed that man more than she could ever repay, she acknowledged to herself. Why, when she attempted to express her gratefulness, had he done such an about-face and possibly even traumatized Toby with his ill-conceived attempt at punishment? What unmitigated gall he had, forcing Toby to look at that dead body. Who did he think he was, acting as though saving their lives gave him the right to offer unasked-for discipline to a child not his own?

She couldn't even recall his name, she realized, not too unhappy with that fact and still trying to ignore the nagging persistence of his memory in her mind. She would probably never see him again, since she didn't plan on staying in Liberty very long. And what the heck were they doing in Liberty, Missouri?

Shanna slipped her hand into her cloak pocket, caressing the letters left by her dead mother, and the feel of them effectively brought her critical predicament to the forefront. As before, the remembered words in the letter addressed to her didn't bring much comfort, and she almost wished she hadn't probed into her mother's things after she'd died.

But what else could she have done? Even Shanna's father didn't know about the secret drawer in Diedre Van Alstyne's writing desk—the drawer where her mother allowed Shanna to hide childhood treasures. It was a place only she and Shanna should know about, Diedre had insisted.

How close she had always thought she and her mother to be. How could her mother have withheld such a terrible secret from her? Recalling the final bitter face-off with her father, Shanna confronted the fact that he had known all along. So many things had become clear after she read the revelations in the one letter, even the probable reason her father always treated Toby, who was his son and heir, as though he were an unwelcome presence in his life, no matter how hard Toby strived to win Christian Van Alstyne's love.

Shanna, darling. Please don't hate me.

Shanna fingered the open letter in her pocket, running her finger along the jagged edge. She knew its contents by heart; the first few words burned into her mind. At this point she didn't know if she hated her mother or not, but she couldn't let her confusion overshadow her love for her small brother. She shied away from the distinction her mind tried to form and reached out to give the bell another firm tap, hoping the noise her action prompted would put an end to the racing thoughts in her mind.

Shanna, darling. Please don't hate me. The words from her mind chased the echoes of the bell around the lobby.

Chapter Three

"Hold your horses. I heard you the first time!"

The door behind the desk opened and a young man only a few years older than Shanna emerged. He walked to the desk and removed a pair of round glasses from his suit pocket, settling them on his nose. Staring at the two mud-spattered figures before him, he gave a haughty sniff.

"And just what are you doing in here?" the clerk finally asked.

"Obviously, we would like a room," Shanna shot back at him, outrage at his imperious stare clear in the tone of her words. No one had ever dared treat her with such disdain!

"We don't accept unaccompanied women at this hotel," the clerk informed her. "Perhaps you might try Mrs. Clark's boardinghouse a couple blocks over."

"In case you haven't noticed," Shanna said angrily, "there's a blizzard starting up outside. I'm not about to

Bittersweet Promises

drag my brother two more blocks in that wind and snow. I demand you give us a room!"

"Impossible," the man said with a nonchalant shrug. "Besides, we're full up."

Good Lord. Was every man in this blasted town a dunderheaded dolt who thought a woman should bow to his superior masculine gender?

"You're lying," Shanna spat. "There are several keys hanging on that board behind you."

"Some of our guests prefer to leave their keys here, rather than carry them around with them. I repeat, we're full up."

Shanna leaned across the desk and glared at him. "And I repeat, you're a liar. You just don't want to rent me a room because I don't have a man with me!"

"Perhaps," the man admitted, refusing to be daunted by the frosty-blue depths of Shanna's eyes. "But I have strict orders from the owner. Unescorted women only cause trouble in a hotel of our class."

"Trouble!" Shanna said with a gasp. "What possible trouble could a woman and child cause?"

"Are you a widow?" the clerk questioned.

Shanna frowned, taken aback by what she felt was an incongruous query on the clerk's part. "No, I'm not. And what on earth does that have to do with my getting a room?"

"If you were a widow, an exception could be made. But since you're not, the rule stands. Women do not travel alone, especially women your age, unless they . . . ah. . . ."

Suddenly what the clerk was hinting at dawned on Shanna. Her voice rose in astonishment and indignation.

"Are you insinuating that I'm a loose woman?" she demanded, completely forgetting about Toby's young ears taking in her every word. "A . . . a. . . ." Shanna searched her mind for the words her mother would never explain to her. "A barfly . . . a *tart?*" She spat the last word at him, a look of fury on her face.

"Either remove yourself from these premises, or I'll fetch the sheriff!" the clerk shouted back across the desk. "We do not tolerate your ilk here!"

"The sheriff's out with the posse! Give me a key, or I'll come around there and show you my ilk!"

"Dear me, Perkins. What in the world's going on here? I started downstairs to see if we'd had word from my nephew, and here I find you and this lovely young lady caterwauling at each other loud enough to disturb every guest in the hotel."

Shanna glanced toward the new voice to see an elderly lady leaning over the banister of the first landing, an amazed look on her face. Blushing furiously as she realized she didn't know how long the woman had been standing there—or what she might have heard—Shanna dropped her eyes to the floor as the woman moved down the stairway.

An uncomfortable silence filled the room, broken only by the older woman's footsteps and the clerk's shuffling feet as he tried to decide whether to stand his ground or escape through the door behind the desk again. The clerk started to turn toward the door, but one glance at the face of the elderly woman now approaching the desk put an end to any thought of flight.

"I asked you a question, Perkins," the woman said as she stopped beside Shanna. "Melinda's taking a nap up in our room and I won't have her sleep disturbed. What is this shouting match all about?"

Shanna glanced over at the woman in time to meet a pair of bright brown eyes. Snow-white, carefully curled hair topped the worn and wrinkled face, which held an expression of assurance that the explanation she had requested would be forthcoming immediately. Still embarrassed, Shanna dropped her eyes to the bodice

Bittersweet Promises

of the neatly pressed black gown the elderly woman wore. Shanna's experienced gaze found several faded and patched places on the gown, but she could tell it had once been a quality garment.

"I apologize, ma'am," Shanna said quietly, forcing herself to overcome her discomfort and look back at the woman's face. "My brother and I need a room, and this man insists we aren't of good enough *quality* to stay at his hotel."

The elderly woman's brown eyes narrowed dangerously as she turned to the clerk. "Is that true, Perkins?"

"Mrs. Garret, just look at them," the clerk babbled. "Why, they're covered in filth and the woman's traveling alone. You know what that means."

"No, Perkins, I have no idea," the woman he called Mrs. Garret said in a steely voice. "You tell me. Could it be she's lost her family in the war? We've got a lot of women even around here like that these days."

"But . . . but look how dirty—"

"We're dirty because we found ourselves in the middle of a bank robbery the minute we stepped off the stage," Shanna fired at the clerk, her indignation renewed with the obvious sympathy she sensed in Mrs. Garret. "We were luckier than the man who was killed. All we got was a little mud on us."

"Bank robbery?" Mrs. Garret's voice rose in shock and she reached out to grab Shanna's arm. "My God! When?"

"A few minutes ago. I'm surprised you didn't hear all the shooting. The hotel's right next door to the bank."

"Some . . . sometimes my hearing isn't what it should be," Mrs. Garret admitted. "And I was napping with Melinda until just now. Please. Tell me what happened."

Before Shanna could answer, Toby stepped from behind her cloak. "It was terrible," he said. "There was a whole bunch of men and one of them pointed his gun at us. But he killed the man who came up the street instead. It wasn't nothing like they try to tell you it is in books." Toby hunched his small shoulders and shivered slightly as he concentrated on his words. "Real life's different from books, ain't it, Shanna?"

"Isn't," Shanna corrected. She looked at Mrs. Garret to see the woman's hand at her breast and a white pallor on her face. When Mrs. Garret swayed, Shanna grabbed her waist and assisted her to one of the chairs at the side of the lobby.

"Please rest, ma'am," Shanna said in concern. "Do you want me to have the clerk send for the doctor?"

"No," Mrs. Garret gasped. "The man . . . the man who was killed? Who was it?"

"I don't know."

The clerk scurried over as Shanna spoke. "It was one of the divinity students from the school, Mrs. Garret. George Wymore. They brought him to the morgue out back of the hotel. I let them in, and that's where I was when this woman came in for a room."

"Not Cody, then," Mrs. Garret said, a look of relief coming into her face with the returning color. "Of course, I'm dreadfully sorry about the young student," she added quickly. "But . . . I thought for a moment . . . Cody was due here about now."

"He went with the posse, ma'am." Toby carefully took her gnarled hand in his small one and patted it. "Don't worry. He saved mine and Shanna's life, and then the sheriff asked him to go with him."

"How do you know that, Toby?" Shanna asked.

"That was his name. Don't you remember, Shanna? He was the man who got us into the building when that robber was going to shoot us. I heard the sheriff call him Cody."

"I guess I was too frightened to recall his name. Is Cody rather tall and broad shouldered, with chestnut hair

Bittersweet Promises

and brown eyes?" Shanna questioned. "He was wearing a sheepskin-lined coat and denim trousers."

"That sounds like my Cody," Mrs. Garret replied. "He's a very nice-looking young man."

"I . . . I didn't notice that," Shanna stuttered.

"But you seemed to describe him so well," Mrs. Garret said with a smile. "You must have gotten a pretty close look at him."

"Heck," Toby said. "We should have. He was lyin' under us and on top of us for long enough. That's part of the reason we're so dirty. He had a bunch of mud on him."

"Toby!" Shanna cried. Another blush stole over her cheeks, and her knees threatened to give way at the remembered feel of those hard thighs wrapped around her own. "He was only protecting us from the glass from the windows those robbers shot out. And I'll thank you not to use words so close to profanity! Heck is not a nice word!"

"Sorry, Shanna. I didn't know what that word meant. Eddie pointed it out in one of his books."

Shanna glanced at Mrs. Garret to see her stifling laughter, her brown eyes twinkling merrily.

"I understand what you're going through, my dear," Mrs. Garret said. "Why, Cody's Melinda is a few years younger than this young man, and sometimes I have a time with her. Her mother's dead," she continued in a softer voice as she studied the blond-haired woman in front of her. "And Melinda's quite a handful for someone my age."

"I'm sure she must be," Shanna agreed. "I wish you would thank Cody again for me when you see him. I didn't really do that properly."

"I will, my dear. I guess Melinda and I'll just have to wait here until Cody returns before we can head home."

"That might be a while, Mrs. Garret," the clerk informed her. "There's quite a blizzard blowing up outside."

"Then we'll wait it out snug in the rooms upstairs, won't we, Perkins?" Mrs. Garret said with a stern look at the clerk. "That is, as soon as you give this young woman a key. And while you're at it, I'll take a key for Cody when he returns. We may be another day or so before going back to the plantation."

"Of . . . of course, Mrs. Garret," the clerk said. "Right away, ma'am."

Mrs. Garret watched the clerk hurry over to the desk, then shook her head as she turned back to Shanna. "That man needs to be taken down a peg or two. Now, you know my name. I'm Bessie Garret and Cody's my nephew. Most folks just call me Aunt Bessie, though." She shot a glance at the clerk. "Except for those I insist do otherwise. And you two are. . . ."

"Shanna V . . . Allen," Shanna stuttered, strangely loath to lie to this woman. But it was necessary, she reminded herself as she introduced Toby. "And this is my little brother, Toby."

"Pleased to meet you, Toby." Bessie nodded and received Toby's polite greeting in return. "You've just arrived in Liberty, I presume?"

"Yes, ma'am," Shanna confirmed.

Silence lingered for a moment while Bessie waited for Shanna to continue. As soon as she realized the young woman would volunteer no more information, Bessie led the way back to the desk. After waiting until Shanna signed the register and paid the clerk from the reticule hanging on her arm, Bessie turned to the stairwell.

"I'll show you where your room is," Bessie said. "It's just across the hall from mine. And I'm sure Perkins will have some food and hot bathwater sent up as soon as he

Bittersweet Promises

can arrange it. Won't you, Perkins?" she said over her shoulder. "And the little boy seems to have injured his hand. Don't forget to bring your medicine kit, so his sister can rebandage the wound."

"Yes, Mrs. Garret," the clerk replied.

"What's a barfly, Shanna?" Toby questioned as he followed Shanna toward the stairway.

"Shush, Toby," was Shanna's only reply.

"I suppose that's something else we'll talk about later," Toby muttered not quite loud enough to reach Shanna's ears and draw a censuring look from her.

An hour later, Shanna gazed down at Toby's small form, huddled under the blanket on the double bed. One hand lay on top of the blanket, a clean bandage replacing the handkerchief Shanna had rinsed out in the bathwater and spread to dry on the back of the rocking chair beside the fireplace. Further examination had proven the cut was indeed minor, despite the amount of blood that had flowed from it. Toby would probably sleep for an hour or two now, his stomach full and his little body scrubbed clean, though not without another somewhat grouchy protest about a bath on any other day than Saturday.

Shanna gazed longingly at the other pillow for a second, but a nap right then would leave her sleepless that night. And she'd had enough of tossing and turning at night the last few weeks to last a lifetime—nights filled with unanswered questions and visions of a cold, empty future facing her if her one-and-only plan disintegrated into the dust of failed ventures.

Instead, she reached to loosen the belt on her dressing gown, which she hadn't allowed herself the luxury of wearing until after they had eaten. Then she decided to investigate her carpetbag for the cleanest gown with the fewest wrinkles.

Loud, clumping footsteps sounded in the hallway, halting just outside Shanna's door. Shanna hesitated, waiting for a knock to sound, then decided whoever it was must be going to the room across the hallway. Mrs. Garret's nephew was probably back. Cody. Cody Garret, she guessed his name might be. Shanna unthinkingly hurried to the door, her curiosity as to whether the robbers had been caught making her forget her improper appearance.

Toby, too, would want to know, she thought as she pulled the door open. And maybe if she at least properly thanked the man, she could get him out of her mind once and for all. She would ignore their confrontation over Toby and. . . .

The chiseled face that turned toward her when the door squeaked made Shanna gulp and realize she should have waited to ask Bessie Garret the outcome of the manhunt. It contained eyes darkened to mahogany in fatigue and lips that lost their fullness when Cody tightened his mouth grimly and swept his gaze over her.

"I . . . I just wanted to know if you'd caught the robbers," Shanna said quickly.

"What do you care?" Cody asked in a tired voice. "You didn't have any money in the bank."

"Toby," she hastened to explain. "He'll want to know."

"Tell him they got plumb away. They split up and went ten different directions, and we never even got close enough to follow a trail before the snow covered it."

"I'm sorry. Really. I know I didn't lose anything, but that doesn't mean I don't care about the people who did. Will it mean an awful hardship for them?"

Cody removed his hat and swiped his fingers through the flattened chestnut locks of hair, tousling them into new life. He rested his palm on the back of his head, the heavy coat gaping and the tan shirt beneath it taut with strain across his chest. Deep lines of concern etched his face, both from weariness and worry, making Shanna wish for an instant that she could say something to ease them—or brush them away with her fingertips.

Shanna thrust her arms behind her, clenching her hands into fists to still her wavering fingers.

"Hardship?" Cody said with a shake of his head as he stared at the floor. "Disaster might be more like it. Hell, we've just started rebuilding around here, and now most of us won't have any money for seed to plant this spring. And what's more, the bank won't be able to help us out. Taxes are coming due and...."

Shanna unconsciously took a step forward, the gravelly words stirring her and her heart swelling with compassion at the agony she sensed underlying his voice.

"I'm sorry. What will you do?"

"Do?" Cody said with a shrug, his eyes drawn to the tiny slippered foot peeping out from under the dressing gown, then traveling up the skirt to where the belt hung loosely around a waist he could easily span with his fingers and thumbs.

"Well," he said with a wry twist to his mouth, "we sure won't sit around pitying ourselves."

"No, I don't imagine you will. The people here seem like they're extremely capable of banding together and taking care of their problems. It didn't take the sheriff long to get a posse together. If it hadn't been for the snowstorm, I'm sure they would have caught those bandits and gotten their money back."

Cody kept silent and flickered his gaze on upward. The orchid dressing gown gaped where Shanna's breasts swelled, allowing a glimpse of white lace. The promise of fullness that he had felt when he covered her with his body in the land office was fulfilled now that the woolen cloak didn't impede his discovery.

"I. . . ." Shanna licked full pink lips gone dry with a tongue just as powdery. "I also wanted to tell you something else."

"Ummmm?" The slender neck was graceful beneath the stubborn little chin that had lifted in defiance when she'd tried to interfere in his talk with her little brother. Well, hell, he had been too abrupt with Toby—his patience at an end after dodging flying lead and failing to keep his bank account safe. He ought to apologize. . . .

That golden hair, tied back with a matching orchid ribbon, cascaded down past that enticingly minute waist. . . .

"I wanted to thank you properly for what you did for Toby and me," Shanna said, interrupting his pleasant thoughts. "Not . . . not interfering with Toby," she qualified. "But he seems to have accepted that. However, I realize now just how much danger you put yourself in to get us out of harm's way. The clerk. . . ."

Shanna cleared her throat, confused at how hoarse her voice was getting as Cody silently studied her and waited for her to continue.

"The clerk confirmed that the man out in the street was killed. It could very easily have been me or—thank the Lord, it wasn't Toby. And thank you. I wish I could think of something stronger to say to let you know how much I appreciate what you did, but thank you is all I can think. . . ."

Shanna clamped her mouth shut when she realized she was babbling. What in the world was it about this man that muddled her senses so? Her teeth tugged at her bottom lip as she ordered her legs to take her back into her room and her arms to close the door. She'd told him what she had to say, quite adequately thanked him this time.

She stood rooted in place, though, when he took a step forward.

"Sometimes words fall short," Cody agreed in a musing voice. "I don't guess I'd be adverse to you *showing* me your appreciation." He raised one hand to caress her cheek with the back of his index finger, while his other hand, out of Shanna's line of vision, flipped the sagging belt of the dressing gown free.

Shanna's lips parted slightly and her eyes widened into pools of cobalt. Her indrawn breath caught in her chest, swelling her breasts and crinkling her nipples when they rubbed against the stiff lace of her undergown. His arm snaked around her waist, and his fingers played against the full swell of her hip, kneading it as he lowered his head. A spreading warmth flowed down her legs from her feminine center.

Cody's lips nibbled gently at first, and Shanna fought the lassitude spreading through her, her eyelids slowly descending. The instant the long, feathery lashes met the curve of her cheek, Cody took her mouth fully and pulled her close against the length of his body.

She had been right, Shanna thought as her arms fell into place around his corded neck. There was a haven in his strong arms—a place she could steal away from the maelstrom in her life.

Cody's lips released hers and traced a path down the delectable neck, tasting it and then flickering his tongue up toward the full earlobe.

"Why don't I go get a room key so we can continue this in privacy?" he whispered.

Shanna gasped in horror and wrenched free, her thigh brushing against a strange protuberance below Cody's waist with her movements. The dressing gown slithered off her shoulders, and she grabbed it, pulling it back up, her fingers searching wildly for her belt.

"You . . . you . . . you . . . bastard!"

Cody smiled smugly, then bent down to retrieve her belt and his hat from where he had dropped them on the floor. He plopped the hat on his head and pushed it back, dangling the belt from one long finger.

"My, my, Shanna," he growled low in his throat. "You certainly do have a problem finding words. If you'll remember, you've already called me that once. No wonder you had to show me your appreciation, rather than voicing it."

Shanna swiped the belt from his hand, her blue eyes changing to aquamarine and throwing those familiar daggers at him. He chuckled wryly while she wrapped the belt around her waist and glared at him.

"You are an insufferable, conceited ass," she snarled. "I had thought there might be a measure of decency about you, since you have such a marvelous aunt. However, my heart goes out to Bessie. She definitely has a cross to bear with such an unfeeling clod for a nephew!"

"Now just a damn minute!"

But Cody found himself talking to the unyielding door, the resounding slam echoing in his ears and drowning out his words.

Cody's anger died a hasty death and a snicker of mirth escaped his lips. She'd definitely found some different words to use. And he was right. Fire and ice. Ice and fire. Banked fires, but nevertheless still there.

Rather than the observation placing an effective wet blanket on his ardor, though, Cody found himself more than a little intrigued again.

Ardor, hell! Intrigue! Here he was thinking in the highfalutin, overblown language he had taunted that delightful little package of contradictions into using.

What was it about her that goaded him into implausible actions? he wondered as he stared at the closed door. Granted, there was an air of vulnerability about her that tugged at him—made him want to wrap her in his arms and kiss away any pain she had suffered, cocoon her

Bittersweet Promises

from any danger waiting for her in the wings. And that body fit just so exactly against his, sexy curves snuggling into those sensitive spots he had almost forgotten during these last few years of war, grief and rebuilding the plantation.

That had to be it. He'd been too long without a woman, and the stiffness bulging against his denims was pure, down-to-earth sex—lust. He was going to have to stand there a few minutes until it subsided or risk Bessie's knowing gaze when he removed his coat. His aunt didn't miss much. Besides, he didn't think he could walk just yet.

Unbeknown to Cody, Bessie silently closed the door she had opened at the sound of the ringing slam across the hallway, leaving her nephew alone, chuckling to himself and fixated on the door across the hallway. She'd give her eyeteeth to have been privy to the few minutes preceding that slamming door!

Oh, well, she wasn't about to let the friction evidently boiling between Cody and that sweet little Yankee spoil the plans she had spent the last hour or so finalizing in her mind.

Chapter Four

Shanna glared her rage at the closed door, then whirled to hurry over to the bed. Toby still lay cuddled beneath the blanket, undisturbed by the loud bang of the door; and she studied him silently while one hand, trembling with repressed anger, rose to wipe at her lips. When her fingertips caressed her mouth instead, she gave a quiet snort of disgust and dropped her arm.

How stupid she had been to willingly place herself in a position to contend with that overbearing lout's complete disregard for proper behavior. Evidently the old man at the land office had been right—a completely different set of etiquette governed these Southern men. She was going to have to be very careful that Toby wasn't corrupted.

Toby, whom she loved with a deep, abiding ache that was every bit as strong as the love she had seen on her friends' faces when they gazed at their own children. That Toby was her little brother, rather than her own child, hadn't mattered one whit to her when she had found out about her father's plan to separate them. Toby, the center of her world right now and the reason she had journeyed to this godforsaken place and had to tolerate men like Cody Garret.

Funny how that confident streak she admired in Cody's elderly aunt came through in her nephew as a smug, masculine assumption that she should appreciate his dictatorial browbeating of her little brother—and that he could paw her just because she tried to express her gratitude. Of course. His aunt must be related by marriage, Shanna thought as she heard the door across the hallway close.

"Oh, for pity's sake," Shanna growled, keeping her voice soft as she glanced down at Toby. "Quit thinking about a man you hope you'll never have to see again and get dressed!"

Shanna shook her head and walked over to her carpetbag. How different the men in the South were from what she had heard—not courteous and gentlemanly at all. And she was going to have to be careful they didn't corrupt her, too. Great day in the morning. She had already uttered the first profanities of her life, once where Toby could hear!

And what a dunce she had been to open her door wearing her dressing gown. It was her own fault he pawed her. His superior, masculine arrogance had probably misread her actions as an attempt to entice him. She could almost imagine him quirking those full lips into a leer and pulling a devil's tail from behind him, holding and stroking it in his hands while he eyed her!

Shrugging her shoulders in exasperation at the anger still boiling in her mind, Shanna determinedly started sorting through her clothing until she found enough unsoiled undergarments to wear. Next she pulled out a blue, woolen day gown, the same shade as her eyes. It would definitely be warm, though it wasn't one of her better gowns. Deciding the wrinkles would smooth out by the time she wore it down to supper that evening, she removed her dressing gown and slipped into the clothing.

She dug a dry pair of wool stockings out of the bag. They weren't the most attractive ones she owned either.

"Good grief, why should I care whether the garments I choose are flattering or not?" she murmured in a pique at the frown she found on her face as she eyed the ugly stockings in distaste. "There isn't one person in this town whose opinion of my appearance matters to me. I just want to be warm!"

And recalling how cold her feet had been on the trip to the hotel in the freezing weather, she determinedly pulled the wool stockings on and knotted them above her knees. No one would see them anyway, and just now she couldn't bear the thought of wearing her corset in order to have something to fasten the stockings on.

Her kid shoes were stylish, but definitely not warm. Shanna probed deeper into the bag, searching for her riding boots. She could even pull on another pair of socks over her stockings inside the somewhat larger boots.

Suddenly Shanna's fingers froze in their quest. She stared down in horror at where her thumb protruded from a rip in the carpetbag. Her heart in her throat, she pushed her arm deeper into the bag and swallowed a stab of terror as her entire hand came out through a tear in the bag.

"No. Oh, please, God, no," she breathed in denial.

Frantically Shanna tore the remaining articles from the carpetbag, flinging them around the floor. The riding boots landed with a thump and she heard Toby stir on the bed. How he could sleep through that slamming door and wake up at the lesser noise made by the boots was beyond her. She forced herself to stand when she heard his faint voice.

"Shanna," Toby muttered drowsily. "Shanna, what was that noise?"

Shanna quickly crossed to the bed again. "It . . . it's nothing, Toby," she managed to say. "Go on back to sleep."

Toby blinked his eyes open once, then snuggled back against the pillow. She stood watching him until his even breathing told her he had returned to sleep, then gently tucked the blanket around his neck before she went over to pick up the carpetbag again.

Somewhat hopefully Shanna upturned the bag and shook it. The darned bag was indeed empty. A sob rose in her throat and, with a glance at Toby, she tried to muffle it. It was gone. The entire sack of money she had found in her mother's desk was gone—slipped out through the tear in the carpetbag.

Or—Shanna's brow creased as she examined the tear. Or had someone slit the seam and taken it? Maybe the stagecoach driver. Who else had handled the bag?

Shanna plucked at the seam threads, and they came away loose in her fingers. No, no one had slit the seam. The threads were just rotten. Why had she been so foolish as to entrust the money to the bag, instead of carrying it on her person? When had the money fallen out?

Shanna retraced the last day of their journey in her mind. The money had been there last night at the way station where the stage stopped. She knew it had been, because she had checked. Suddenly a vision of the bag lying against the land office with her clothing strewn across the walkway surfaced. Could the money have fallen out then? Or maybe when the driver dropped the bag from the top of the coach?

Shanna silently crossed to the window and drew the curtains back to peer outside. She couldn't even see through the glass. A howling wind blew sheets of snow against the window and ice crystals covered the pane.

She had to go out there, though. She had to find that drawstring bag. She barely had enough money left in her reticule for meals and another few days at the hotel. And she wouldn't be able to wire her bank in New York for a possible advance on the trust fund her mother had left her without her father finding out where she was.

Toby. She couldn't leave him alone. What if he woke while she was gone and went out in that weather looking for her? Oh, dear God, what was she going to do now?

Shanna moved from the window and dropped into the rocking chair. Burying her head on her knees, she clenched her teeth and tried to hold back the sobs threatening to break loose. She couldn't go to pieces—Toby depended on her.

But just look how she was taking care of him. In an attempt to locate a man she had never met, she had brought Toby with her on a journey that had no promise of ending successfully. Indeed, she barely knew more than the man's name. Now they were hundreds of miles from home and almost penniless.

Resolutely, Shanna sat up in the chair and retrieved her boots, along with a pair of socks. She pulled them both on, then tossed another log onto the fireplace grate. After securing the fireguard, she picked up her cloak from the foot of the bed and stared down at Toby.

Almost as though sensing her eyes on him, Toby stirred and his small mouth opened. "Promise, Shanna?" he whispered in his sleep. "C-cross your...."

"I promise, Toby," Shanna whispered in return, restraining herself before she could move around the bed and caress his forehead. Her actions would probably bring him back to full wakefulness, and it would be better if he stayed asleep. Surely she wouldn't be gone very long. She could leave him a note.

Bittersweet Promises

* * *

A few minutes later, Bessie Garret opened the door to her room, determined to check on the two occupants across the hallway. Probably she was just a nosy old woman, but something about the young woman she had met downstairs told Bessie that Shanna needed a friend. Besides, at her age, she had a right to poke her nose into situations other people would think didn't concern her.

Bessie's eyes widened when she caught sight of Shanna disappearing down the stairway dressed in a cloak. Surely Shanna couldn't be going out into that storm. Bessie quickly crossed the hallway and turned the knob on the door of Shanna's room. It opened smoothly, and Bessie shook her head at Shanna's foolishness in leaving the door unlocked. Peering inside, Bessie saw Toby curled up alone in the big bed and Shanna's clothing still scattered all around the floor.

That confirmed it. Something dreadfully wrong had to be troubling that young woman. Bessie closed the door quietly and hurried back to her own room.

"Cody Garret, put that child down on the bed and come out here into the hallway. Right now!"

Cody raised his head from where he had been nuzzling his nose into the stomach of the golden-haired child in his arms, and immediately the child's giggles stopped. They both stared across the room at Aunt Bessie, and Melinda's small lips rose in a pout when she caught the look on Bessie's face.

"I want to play with Daddy," Melinda said.

"You can play with him later," Bessie said sternly. "Right now, I want to talk to your father."

Cody picked Melinda up and plopped her onto the bed. When the little girl tossed him a tremulous look, he patted her curls and smiled down at her.

"I'll play with you some more in a minute, honey, like Aunt Bessie says. And if you wait for me quietly, I'll see if the hotel kitchen has a big piece of cake for you."

"Chocolate," Melinda insisted.

"All right," Cody said with a chuckle. "Chocolate." He placed the doll lying on the bedspread in Melinda's arms before he joined Aunt Bessie in the hallway.

"You spoil that child rotten, Cody Garret," Bessie said in a firm voice. "You know how picky her appetite is. I won't have her dinner ruined."

Cody sighed resignedly, determined not to get into yet another battle over Melinda with his aunt. "What did you want to talk about, Aunt Bessie?" he asked to forestall Bessie's sharp tongue.

"That young woman over there just left her room," Bessie informed him. "She had her cloak on, and the little boy's alone. She must have a desperate reason to go out in this weather, and I want you to go after her. She might need some help."

"No, you don't, Aunt." Cody emphatically shook his head. "You're not getting me involved in another of your charity cases. I've got enough to worry about myself right now. You know most of the little bit of money we did have was taken in that bank robbery."

"That doesn't mean we can't help other people who need it," Aunt Bessie insisted. Her head rose proudly and she returned his glare with one just as frosty of her own. "We'll get by. We always do. Now, are you going after the poor woman or am I?"

Cody's lips thinned, and he continued to stare down at the small woman in front of him, refusing to answer her. Besides, how could he explain that he would be the last person Shanna would want to come to her aid again?

"Fine," Bessie said as she started to move around him to the door of the room. "You keep an eye on both these children, in case that little boy over there wakes up. His name's Toby."

Bittersweet Promises

Cody caught her arm, and Bessie looked up at him, her challenge plain in the clear brown eyes. Immediately Cody knew he had lost yet another battle of wills with his aunt. He dropped Bessie's arm, giving in grudgingly.

"I know his name," he said in a fatigued voice. "And I'll go. Just let me get my coat." He paused inside the room as he reached for the heavy jacket hanging on a hook in the wall. "Aunt Bessie," he said, keeping his back to the elderly woman. "What did that young woman say her full name was?"

"She said it was Shanna Allen, Cody," Aunt Bessie replied with a strange look on her face that Cody couldn't see. "But if my instincts don't fail me—and they shouldn't, given the seventy years' experience I've had reading people—I think she's hiding something. She stumbled over her name and gave the little boy a funny look when she spoke. Now, that young lady has to be at least twenty, and you'd think she'd know her own name by now, wouldn't you?"

"Yes, Aunt," Cody said with a grim smile on his lips. "You'd think so, wouldn't you?"

Cody set his hat on his head and turned back to his aunt, determined to give one more try at convincing Bessie that any involvement with Shanna Allen wasn't in their best interests.

"Aunt Bessie, why don't we just keep an eye on the boy for her until she returns? That way—"

"That way, we don't even have to let her know we're watching over her, is that what you mean, Cody Garret? What are you hiding from me? And," she continued before Cody could form in his mind the lie he knew he would have to tell his aunt, "do you really think I could rest easy here in my warm room, knowing that young woman was wandering around on the streets of this town just after a bank robbery and in the middle of a snowstorm?"

Trana Mae Simmons

Cody pulled his hat brim down over his eyes and strode out the door, refusing to answer either of his aunt's questions. One answer might lead to another one, and he wasn't really sure what he was hiding from Aunt Bessie just yet. But his every instinct told him that Shanna Allen—or whatever the hell her name was—was going to explode into his life with an even bigger impact than the loss of his money in the bank robbery.

"The hell with the money," Cody muttered to himself as he went down the stairway, his boot heels clumping on the uncarpeted steps in time to the anger pounding in his mind. "How the heck am I ever going to tell Aunt Bessie that her own grandson might have been one of those robbers, along with two of our closest neighbor's sons who helped save Aunt Bessie and Melinda's lives?"

Chapter Five

Head bowed in dejection and gloved hands shoved into her cloak pockets for added warmth, Shanna toed the snow drifted on the walkway outside the boarded-up windows of the land office. Nowhere could she find a large enough crack for the drawstring bag to fall through. Instead, the boards were tightly nailed together and fairly new. They abutted the land office wall, and walking around on them didn't give any indication of a weak spot that might yield under a heavy footstep and open a wide crack for the bag to slip through.

She sighed in defeat. Her plan had been to notify the sheriff and ask him to have someone crawl under the walkway and search out the bag. She could recite the exact amount—$500—and even quote the denominations of the gold coins to prove her ownership. The only place left to look was where the stagecoach had stopped.

Plodding on down the walkway to the general store,

Shanna wished she had paid a little more attention to exactly where the stage had pulled up on arrival. Even on the somewhat sheltered walkway the gusty wind swirled around her, and she snugged her cloak tighter. Catching a whiff of wood smoke carried on the wind, she glanced through the store window to see a potbellied stove glowing red with heat.

Shanna stifled the urge to warm herself inside the store, which seemed to be the only place still open in town. She couldn't imagine how the store owner could expect any customers in this weather.

The only other people she had seen were two riders who passed by in the street while she searched in front of the land office. Bundled up against the frigid winds, the men sat astride horses with lowered heads that obeyed their commands to plow ahead through the six-inch-deep snow covering the street. The figures emerged into sight only a few feet from her, with even the horses' hoofbeats muffled in the adverse weather, and disappeared as silently as ghosts in the swirling snow almost as soon as she glimpsed them.

Determinedly stiffening her shoulders, Shanna stepped into the street and paced off what she thought to be the distance to where the stage had stopped. She stumbled over a rut beneath the snow and almost went sprawling. After catching her balance, she stared around her, knowing it was hopeless to try to find the bag of money. The muddy streets had crusted over in the falling temperatures, and even before that, street traffic had churned furrows and ruts, now covered in a blanket of snow white. Her shoulders slumped, but she glanced behind her to measure the distance to the walkway. She had to try. What else could she do?

The driver had dropped the bags from the top of the coach at hers and Toby's feet before he climbed down and headed for the general store, ignoring Shanna's request to assist her in carrying the bags out of the street.

"Crusty old coot," Shanna muttered to herself, recalling the driver's tobacco-stained beard and lack of manners.

Shanna knelt in the snow, ignoring the icy coldness penetrating to her knees through the cloak and wool dress. She brushed aside snow, continuing her efforts until she had a wide swath around her. The blowing winds quickly covered the area anew, and the snow soaked her knit gloves, numbing her hands.

When the wind died for an instant, Shanna noticed something sticking out of the snow. It looked like the top of a drawstring bag—the one holding her money! Heart quickening with hope, she closed her numb fingers around the object and pulled. It refused to move and Shanna jerked off a now useless glove to work her fingers into the frozen dirt. At last she managed to clear enough of the crust to yank the object free, her excited and hopeful mind ignoring the blue fingers whitening with frostbite.

A man's dirty sock dangled from her fingers, and Shanna dropped it in disgust. There was probably a story behind how the sock got there—a story Shanna didn't remotely give a darn about just now.

"What the hell are you doing? Trying to get yourself killed again?"

Cody swept Shanna into his arms just as a horse and rider emerged from the swirling snow. The startled horse reared over them, and the rider cursed them roundly as Cody carried Shanna back to the walkway. Ignoring the rider's threats to follow them and give them both a sound thrashing, Cody plopped Shanna on her feet in front of the general store and glared at her.

"My God, woman," he said angrily. "Don't you know you're practically invisible in that gray cloak out there in the snow? I had a heck of a time finding you myself.

Why the hell were you out there groveling in the dirt where anyone could ride right over you?"

Shanna shivered violently, trying to clamp her chattering teeth together and searching her mind for a suitable retort to fire into the brown eyes scowling at her.

"I . . . I . . . you . . . d-damn it!" She lifted one hand and pounded on his chest to make her point without words.

"Good Lord," Cody breathed as he caught her hand. "You're going to lose those fingers if we don't get them warmed up quick. Here."

Cody jerked the other sodden glove from Shanna's fingers. He opened his jacket and pulled her into his arms, placing the frozen hands against his chest and wrapping both their bodies in the sheepskin-lined jacket. The shock traveling over him when Shanna gave up her brief resistance and snuggled into the warmth he offered wiped the chill from him, and even his denim-clad legs, protected from the wind by only the thin cloth, radiated with warmth.

Gratefully, Shanna spread her hands on Cody's chest. Just for a minute. She had never been so cold in her life, and the welcoming warmth spread through her—awfully swiftly it seemed to her when she could think rationally. Surely even the warmth from the potbellied stove inside the store couldn't be this soothing.

Something tickled Shanna's nose and her eyes flew open. A mat of sandy hair curled around her face where the top two shirt buttons were open, and the skin beneath the wiry curls warmed her cheek. Though it took every bit of effort she could muster, she recoiled in Cody's grasp, recalling just who it was that held her.

"Let me go!" she demanded. "There's a stove in the store and I can get warm there. I don't need your help!"

"Yeah," Cody muttered as he reluctantly loosened his arms. "You never do."

Bittersweet Promises

Despite Shanna's outraged elbowing against his chest, Cody refused to relinquish his hold entirely. Keeping Shanna firmly within the shelter of his coat, he opened the door on the store and walked her inside. With one hand he pulled a ladder-back chair up to the stove and pushed her onto it. He knelt in front of her and reached for her blue hands, chafing them gently between his own and ignoring her mutinous attempts to free them.

"Gramps!" he yelled over his shoulder. "Do you have anything hot to drink back there?"

"What's going on, Cody?" A little round man emerged from the door to his living quarters behind the store. "Good heavens. That little mite looks half frozen. You want I should go for Doc?"

"No," Cody tossed back. He gently picked up one of Shanna's fingers and rolled it between his own. "We need to get her warm right now."

"Well, I ain't got no coffee ready. Was fixing a pot, but it's just startin' to perk."

"How about some of that brandy you keep behind the counter to nip on?"

"Now, Cody," Gramps replied in a hurt voice. "You know Doc said I have to give up the spirits. My heart, you know."

"Gramps!"

"All right. All right."

A second later, Gramps joined them at the stove and handed a brown bottle to Cody.

"For Pete's sake, Gramps," Cody said in an exasperated voice. "Don't you have a glass?"

" 'Course I do!" Gramps held out his other hand, which held a clean juice glass. "You think I don't have no manners when it comes to knowin' how to treat a lady? I didn't 'spect her to drink from the bottle!"

Cody ignored Gramps's injured comments as he filled the glass over half full of brandy. Turning back to the shivering woman in front of him, he offered her the glass, which Shanna tried to grasp in her shaking hand.

Cody cupped his calloused palms around Shanna's hand and guided the glass to her mouth. When Shanna tried to take a small sip, he tilted the glass, forcing a large swallow down her throat. Cody watched her blue eyes widen as the brandy hit her stomach; then he pulled the glass back quickly.

"Oh . . . oh my!" Shanna said when she could catch her breath.

Cody offered the glass again. "You better finish this. It'll help warm you. But just sip it this time."

"That's what I tried to do before," Shanna grumbled, but already the brandy had abated her shivering somewhat and she accepted the glass.

Cody stood and looked at Gramps. "How about that coffee? Think it's about ready?"

"Probably, Cody. It'll be just a minute."

Cody waited until Gramps disappeared through the door in the back of the store; then he stared down at Shanna, who resolutely averted her face as she took small sips from the juice glass. Her hood had fallen back, and reflected light from the lantern hung on a ceiling hook shot highlights from the silky mass of blond curls. Now that he had a quiet moment to study her, she didn't look as much like the picture his friend had carried through the war.

For one thing, she was definitely years younger, though her features still held a startling similarity to that other face. He shouldn't have such a clear remembrance of that face after all these years, but somehow it hadn't buried itself along with the war memories trapped behind a closed door in his mind. Why, he even recalled dreaming about that other face a time or two, feeling guilty when he woke because it hadn't been his own golden-haired wife in his dreams.

Bittersweet Promises

When Shanna shifted uncomfortably under his gaze and tried to muffle a small hiccup, Cody chuckled and knelt to take the glass away.

"I think you've had enough of that for now. Are you warmer? Let me see your hands again. They looked like they were getting frostbitten, and you could lose a finger or two if that happens."

"Oh, no!" Shanna thrust her hands out. "I hadn't even thought of that. Can you tell anything? They're much warmer now."

Cody examined her hands and caught his breath when Shanna bent her head close to study her fingers, because a golden curl fell over Shanna's shoulder, brushing his cheek. The same perfumed scent he'd caught when he held her on the walkway surrounded him and her breath mingled with his own.

Cody abruptly dropped Shanna's hands and stood. He let his indrawn breath out and forced a measure of irritation into his voice to counteract the tangled emotions crowding his mind.

"Your hands look like they're doing fine, no thanks to your crazy actions. They should be tingling with the blood returning. Are they?"

"Crazy actions?" Shanna shot to her feet, rubbing her hands together and unconsciously confirming Cody's comments on her returning circulation. Blue eyes now darkened to indigo in indignation, she straightened to her full height and tilted her head back.

"I didn't have any choice about what I had to do! And you have no right judging me. You don't even know why I was out in the street!"

"Well, why?" Cody questioned after the silence had lingered a moment. "As far as I'm concerned, I've got a right to know. I've rescued your pretty little bu . . . skin twice already today, Shanna Allen. And Aunt Bessie's watching over your brother, in case he wakes up, while

I chase you all over Liberty and try to save you from your own stupidity!"

Slowly his words penetrated and the anger drained from Shanna's face, replaced with a dejected look that tore at Cody.

Oh, how much she needed a friend right now. Shanna hung her head. But not him. Not this man who had already taken such familiar liberties—even if he did seem concerned now.

But she was so alone. . . .

Shanna's face crumbled, and she covered it with her hands as she sank back into the chair. A suppressed sob shook her body. She couldn't tell *him*. He thought she was crazy—and stupid. And she had to keep her secret— tell no one her true reason for being in Missouri.

What if her father found her—or worse yet, her father found the man she was searching for to plead with for Toby's future? Her father would do anything to thwart her, maybe even kill the man, if he found him first. Her strangled sobs echoed louder in the room.

"Aw, hell. Look, don't cry. Whatever you do, don't cry, darn it. I'm sorry for acting so crass. I can't stand to see a woman cry!" Especially a blond spitfire whom his words had changed into a bruised angel with haunted eyes.

Cody reached out a hand and stroked the golden hair. Tendrils curled around his fingers, and he fought the urge to pull her into his arms as the slight shoulders shook with agony—agony his own foolish words had brought to the surface.

"Shanna, please," he tried again, searching for his handkerchief with his free hand. But she still had the handkerchief, he recalled. Wildly he scanned the room until he saw a pile of handkerchiefs on a nearby shelf. He hurried over and grabbed one, then returned to kneel in front of Shanna and gently pry one hand from her face.

Bittersweet Promises

"Here," he said as he tucked the white cloth into the inch of space he'd managed to open. The back of his knuckles brushed the wetness on her cheek as he withdrew, and Cody unconsciously brought his hand to his mouth to taste the salty liquid.

Shanna concealed her face in the handkerchief and straightened in the chair, shifting away from where she could sense Cody still kneeling in front of her. She wiped at her eyes, then blew noisily into one end of the snowy cloth. A final tear trickled down her cheek, and she swiped it away, dropping her hands to her lap, wringing the handkerchief between them.

"Is there any more of that brandy left?" she choked.

"Yeah. Sure." Cody grabbed the bottle and glass from the floor and quickly poured a couple more inches of brandy into it. He held it out in front of her face, not daring to touch her, lest the silver sheen of tears cover her face again.

"Thank you," Shanna murmured before she took the glass and swallowed a deep draft.

Cody pulled another chair near. Straddling it, he leaned his arms across the back and watched her take another small sip of brandy. The stubborn little chin on her profile rose a degree, and he breathed a sigh of relief, hopeful it was a sign that her tears were under control.

"I . . . look, I'm sorry," he began. "I don't usually say such stupid things or act so dumb."

A tentative lift of the corner of Shanna's mouth was his reward for chastising himself.

"You just said *I* was the stupid one," she reminded him.

"I hoped maybe you'd forget about that," Cody said around a groan of embarrassment. "I apologize. But . . . well, heck. You almost got trampled out there."

"I know. It was very foolish of me. But not stupid. I

loathe being called stupid for taking the only alternative open to me, given what had happened."

"Maybe I can help, if you'll just tell me what in the world you were doing crawling around in the street like a rabbit looking for a burrow."

Shanna stabbed him with an angry glance, and Cody dropped his head onto his arms.

"Oh for Pete's sake," he muttered. He took a deep breath before he risked raising his head again. "I apologize. Again."

"At least you called me a rabbit, rather than a mole," Shanna said with a sniff of laughter. Oh, she was much warmer now. "I much prefer being likened to a cute bunny than a gray mole."

Cody bit his lip, but when Shanna slipped another glance sideways at him, this time with her eyes twinkling with suppressed laughter at his discomfort, he choked on his mirth. A funny little giggle met his ears, and he saw Shanna cover her mouth with the remaining clean edge of the handkerchief.

When her giggles subsided, Shanna stared down ruefully at the handkerchief.

"I'm going to owe you another hanky."

"Forget it. Please. I'll have Gramps put that one on my account. Consider the hankies part of my payment for acting like such a dolt and forgetting I'm supposed to be a gentleman. Why don't you tell me the reason you were burrowing around out there like a cute little bunny and let me see if I can help you out?"

Shanna settled back into the chair. "My . . . my money fell out of my carpetbag," she finally admitted. "I think it happened when the driver tossed the bag off the stage. I found a tear in the bag after Toby and I got into our room, and that's the only thing I can figure out that could have happened."

"You were carrying your money in your bag?" Cody

shook his head, biting back any further comment on her foolishness.

"I know it was the wrong thing to do," Shanna admitted. "At least, now I do. But that's not going to help me get it back. It's probably covered up in the street."

"Or maybe someone took it from your bag."

"I thought of that, too."

"We'll report it to Dan, but I don't have much hope that, even if someone does find it in the street, they'll return it. How much was there?"

"Five-hundred dollars. And it was in a gray drawstring bag."

Five-hundred dollars? Good grief! "Where are you headed? Maybe you can wire ahead and have your family send you enough to get there."

Shanna clamped her lips shut determinedly and refused to answer that query. Instead, she took another sip of brandy and stared at the store wall.

"Look, if Aunt Bessie and I are going to help you...."

"Here's the coffee, Cody," Gramps said as he came into the room. He carried a coffeepot in one hand, its handle wrapped in a towel, and three tin cups dangled from the gnarled fingers of his other hand.

"Sorry it took so long," Gramps said, setting the cups down on the countertop and beginning to pour the steaming brew. "I had to wash out a couple extra cups."

"I . . . thank you, mister . . . Gramps." Shanna rose to her feet and pulled up her hood, swaying a little from the effects of the brandy. "But I really have to get back to the hotel to check on my brother. Thank you, also, for the brandy."

Without a glance at Cody, Shanna tottered to the door. The moment she stepped through it, the icy wind tore at her, chasing away some of the warm glow suffusing her. She gripped one hand to the neck of her cloak and resolutely marched forward.

It was several seconds before Shanna became aware of a set of matching footsteps beside her. She craned her neck and looked up at Cody, gratefully accepting the arm he offered when she missed a step.

"I'll walk you back," Cody said with a laugh. "Aunt Bessie will want to know you're all right, and I shouldn't have let you drink so much brandy. I'm afraid it made you a little tipsy, and I don't want to have to hunt you down again in this storm, if you slip and fall before you get to the hotel."

Shanna nodded agreeably. Tipsy, huh? At least he hadn't said she was drunk. Only men got drunk.

"That's true," Cody replied.

"What?" Shanna asked with a frown.

"That ladies only get tipsy—not drunk."

"Oh. I din't realize I sh . . . said it out loud."

Cody slowed his steps, keeping one hand firmly over the smaller one on his arm. "Let's walk a little slower and let the cold air do its work. Maybe we should have stayed and had a cup of Gramps's coffee."

"Humph," Shanna sniffed. "Firsh you wanted me to get warm. Now you want me to get cold again. Women are s'posed to be the ones who have trouble making up their mindsh."

Cody only shook his head and continued down the walkway. Shanna could go see the sheriff after the storm let up—for all the good it would probably do her. And here he was feeling protective again, though he also had to admit it took an effort not to take advantage of the sheltered nooks along the walkway.

Those lips had tasted awfully sweet, and the brandy had effectively melted some of her antagonism toward him. But the next time he kissed her, he wanted it to be a mutual decision, not the result of his taking her by surprise or of her having too much liquor in her veins.

Bittersweet Promises

Next time? Huh-uh! There would be no more kisses between them, shared mutually or otherwise. He was taking Shanna Allen back to that damned hotel room and getting on with his life. He had a daughter and an aunt to care for, a plantation house to finish rebuilding, fields to plow and crops to plant this spring, if he could come up with a way to get the seed he needed. There wasn't a spare bit of room in his life right now to take on the problem of a curvaceous little bundle who seemed alone and friendless.

No matter how sweet her lips were or how the diamond-dotted sheen in her blue eyes tore at him when he made her cry. No matter. No matter, the rhythm of his footsteps confirmed. Ah, hell.

By the time they reached the door to Shanna's room, her mind was much clearer, though a warm glow still curled in her stomach. It had to be from the brandy, she told herself, not the feel of the solid arm under her fingers and the remembered planes on other parts of Cody's body that she kept recalling as she walked so close to him.

Cody glanced inside as Shanna opened the door. Aunt Bessie sat in front of the fireplace, the rocking chair swaying gently as she held Melinda in her arms. On the bed, Toby still slept peacefully, curled into a small ball as he lay on his side.

"Daddy!" Melinda scrambled from Bessie's lap and ran across the room. "Did you bring my cake?"

Cody chuckled softly and bent to scoop her up. "Mind your manners now, sweetheart. I haven't forgotten, but right now, don't you remember what you're supposed to do when you meet someone new?"

Melinda glanced at Shanna, her brown eyes frowning beneath the tousled golden curls. Instead of greeting Shanna, Melinda turned her head and snuggled against her father's chest. "Cake," she said in a pouting voice. "You promised."

Cody tossed Shanna an embarrassed look. "This is my daughter, Melinda."

"I'm pleased to meet you, Melinda," Shanna said to the child's back. Melinda only snuggled deeper into Cody's embrace as Shanna's words hung in the air.

"Maybe you should take Melinda on down to the dining room, Cody," Bessie said as she rose from her chair and crossed the room. "But you make sure she eats her dinner first. And before you go, I want her to say hello to Miss Allen."

At the sound of Aunt Bessie's voice, Melinda's attitude changed. She straightened in Cody's arms and looked over her shoulder to meet Aunt Bessie's eyes. Though her lower lip protruded, she turned to Shanna.

"Hello, Miss Allen," she said.

"Hello," Shanna replied with a soft smile. "How old are you, Melinda?"

"Four."

"That's much better, Melinda," Aunt Bessie said. "Now, I'll walk you to the top of the stairs, Cody. Then I'd like to come back and visit with Miss Allen."

"It's Shanna, please," Shanna said. "And I want to thank you so much for keeping an eye on Toby."

"It's nothing," Bessie said as she followed Cody out the door. "I'll be right back." She closed the door firmly behind her and walked a few feet away before she pulled Cody to a stop.

"What in the world was that child doing out in the storm, Cody?"

"Cake, Daddy," Melinda said as she pulled on Cody's coat. "I want to go get cake *now!*"

"Melinda Garret," Aunt Bessie said in a stern voice. "If you interrupt your father and me once more while we're talking to each other, you won't be having cake even *after* your dinner. I'll see to that."

Bittersweet Promises

Melinda hung her head and Aunt Bessie turned her face back to Cody. "Well?"

"It seems she lost the money she had with her," Cody said with a sigh. "And she almost got herself trampled to death out in the street while she was digging around looking for it. She thinks it fell out of her bag."

"Her bag? My word, what was she doing carrying money in her carpetbag?"

"I asked her the same thing, but I sure didn't get much information out of her. She's evidently not had much experience traveling alone, and she won't tell me where she's headed."

"Well, she's obviously from quality," Aunt Bessie said in a musing voice. "I gathered up her things while I waited for you, and we could probably live for a year on what she paid for one of those gowns. I'm sure she has a family somewhere that we can help her contact."

"I don't know, Aunt. She got this stubborn look on her face when I suggested exactly that. She's hiding something, and I'd just as soon not get involved with her any further. We'll . . . we'll talk to Dan before we leave town and let him handle things from here on out. We can do that much, I guess."

"You go on and get your dinners now," Bessie said, patting Cody on the arm. "I'll have something a little later."

"Aunt, I really don't think this is any of our business," Cody said in an exasperated voice. But he found himself speaking to Bessie's back as she walked toward Shanna's room.

Chapter Six

How the hell did this happen? Cody asked himself for perhaps the tenth time two days later as Aunt Bessie led Shanna and the two children toward the house. The trip from Liberty to his plantation near Kearney had taken up most of the day in the wagon he'd had to rent from the livery stable in order to accommodate his extra passengers. And now he would have to make a second trip to return the wagon and pick up his buggy, losing yet another day. Shanna Allen was definitely making his life more difficult.

Cody's stallion shifted restlessly where it was tied behind the wagon and pawed at the snow beneath its front hooves.

"All right, old son," Cody muttered. "Let's get you and these other nags in out of the cold."

Inside the house, Aunt Bessie quickly organized her small party. "There's kindling and wood in here to get the fires started, but we'll need some more logs from the woodbox out on the porch. Toby, you fetch those for us, will you, please?"

"Sure, Mrs. Garret," Toby replied.

"Now, I thought we got that straight yesterday, young man," Bessie said as she gazed sternly at Toby. "I'm Aunt Bessie."

"Yes, ma'am, Aunt Bessie," Toby said with a smile.

Bessie's face softened as she returned his smile and watched him scurry out the back door of the kitchen. "Now," she said to Shanna. "If you'll get the fire in the fireplace started, I'll make one in the stove and get the coffee ready. Melinda, fetch the coffee grounds from the pantry, please."

"The shelf's too high," Melinda whined.

"Then get the stool so you can reach," Bessie told her as she turned to the stove.

Shanna stared around her for a moment. The kitchen would be cozy enough as soon as they got the fires going, and it was clean as a pin. She had felt her heart sink when the plantation house came into view as they topped the last rise. The huge house stood out starkly against the white snow, with smoke-blackened boards surrounding broken windows and the front veranda falling down in places. It wasn't until Cody drove the wagon around the side of the house that she could see a portion of the house rebuilt in the back.

Shanna surreptitiously slipped a look at Bessie, now bent over the stove building her fire. That looked easy enough, she guessed. She walked over to the fireplace and picked up a piece of paper to crumple beneath the kindling already lying in the grate.

Satisfied that she had enough paper to start the wood burning, Shanna struck a match and leaned back on her heels. The paper blazed merrily, and a second later sounds from crackling kindling filled the room as the small sticks caught and burned. The back door opened and Shanna turned to see Toby struggling through it, his arms piled precariously high with small logs.

"Here, Toby," she said, rising to her feet. "Let me help you with those."

"Thanks, Shanna," Toby huffed when Shanna picked the top two logs from the stack. "I wanted to be sure to get enough for two fires."

"You did fine, Toby, but you should take smaller loads and make more trips. You're too little to carry this much."

Shanna dropped the logs into the bin and squinted at the fireplace, where wisps of smoke curled out around the top, burning her eyes. She frowned and reached for the poker to shove the kindling farther back in the fireplace just as the smoke billowed out into the room. Coughing furiously, she backed away from the fireplace and heard Aunt Bessie gasp behind her.

"My word, child! Didn't you open the damper?"

Damper? Shanna's mind echoed.

Aunt Bessie threw a towel across her mouth and rushed to the fireplace as Toby and Melinda both began coughing. Shanna scooped Melinda into her arms and opened the back door, pulling Toby outside with her. She breathed deeply of the clear air as Bessie joined them.

"It's all right," Bessie said when she saw Shanna's stricken face. "It'll clear out in a minute. I've forgotten that myself on occasion."

"I . . . I don't know what a damper is," Shanna admitted.

"Heavens, child," Bessie replied. "Haven't you ever built a fire?"

"No, ma'am."

"The servants always did it for the women," Toby said in quick defense of his sister. "But Jenkins showed me how. He said it's somethin' a man should know how to do."

"Toby," Shanna said, her warning clear in her voice. "My God! What's on fire?"

Shanna looked up to see Cody running toward them from the barn. *Oh, no! Now he'll have something else to gripe about and call me stupid over.*

Bessie held up a hand as Cody skidded to a stop beside them, the bucket of water he had drawn for the horses in his hand.

"It's all right, Cody. We just forgot to open the damper in the fireplace. Nothing's damaged, though I'm sure we'll have to wash the curtains."

Shanna shot Bessie a grateful look for not saying just who had forgotten the wayward damper, sparing her yet another lecture from Cody Garret. The uneasy truce between them since the day in the general store was fragile, at best. He had declined to mention anything about her acceptance of Aunt Bessie's offer, though she had sensed the strain between Cody and his aunt at supper in the hotel last night.

Melinda struggled in Shanna's arms, stretching out her hands to Cody. "It hurt my throat and I coughed, Daddy. I don't wanna go back there in the smoke."

Cody set the water bucket down and took his daughter from Shanna's grasp. "'Course it made you cough, sweetheart. You've still got your cloak on. Why don't you come on out to the barn with me while I finish taking care of the horses? I'll let you pet your pony while I work, and the smoke will be cleared out by the time we come back in."

Melinda nodded happily and Shanna heard Bessie let out a sigh. Expecting Bessie to remind Melinda that she was supposed to be helping inside, Shanna's brows rose in surprise when Bessie only turned and reentered the kitchen.

"Want to come along, son?" Cody asked Toby. "I could use some help pitching down the hay."

"I'm supposed to be fetching wood," Toby told him, but Shanna could hear the yearning in his voice.

"Go on, Toby," she said. "There's enough wood for now. You can get us some more after you're done in the barn."

"Well, if he's supposed to be helping you and Bessie...." Cody said uncertainly.

"Your daughter was supposed to be helping, also," Shanna said before she thought. "But that didn't seem to bother you."

Cody shot her an angry glance. He was definitely going to have to order Shanna to confine her discipline of Melinda to times when he wasn't present to administer it. But he looked down at his small daughter and asked, "Is that true, honey?"

"No," Melinda denied. "I did what Aunt Bessie said. I got her coffee grounds, an' 'most fell off the stool, Daddy."

Cody set Melinda down and gave her a shove. "Well, go on in and ask Aunt Bessie if she has anything else for you to do first. Then, if she doesn't, you can join us out in the barn. Come on, Toby."

Melinda's face puckered into a scowl when her father and Toby walked away, Cody's arm draped over Toby's shoulders. She stepped toward Shanna, and her small boot-clad foot shot out before Shanna realized what the child had in mind. Even the cloak and layers of petticoats didn't cushion the blow, and a stab of pain ran up Shanna's lower leg.

"Meanie!" Melinda shouted over her shoulder as she ran through the door.

Shanna stared after the small figure in astonishment before she bent to rub her leg. Then, with a determined slant to her mouth, she followed Melinda inside.

"Bessie," Shanna said when she saw Melinda clutching Bessie's skirt, her thumb in her mouth, "Melinda and I need to have a talk."

Bittersweet Promises

"No!" Melinda cried. She buried her face in Bessie's skirt and continued in a muffled voice, "She's mean. Don't let her hit me, Aunt Bessie."

"What in the world?" Bessie asked.

Melinda pulled her head free. "She lied to Daddy! And now she's gonna hit me!"

"Melinda, Miss Allen's here to be your teacher and help care for you. I'm sure she doesn't have any such thing as hitting you in mind."

"She does. She does!" Melinda cried. Whirling away from Bessie, she ran from the room.

"What's wrong with your leg?" Bessie asked as Shanna limped after Melinda.

"That's what I'm going to talk to Melinda about."

"Wait a minute, child. Let's sit a second."

"I know what you're going to say." Shanna gave a sigh of compliance and sank into one of the chairs beside the table. "The child's spoiled rotten and she's going to take careful handling. Maybe you should reconsider having me as her teacher."

"I will not," Bessie said, sitting down across from Shanna. "We have an agreement, and I'm going to hold you to your promise to stay at least six months and get Melinda's education started. I've worried about that for so long now. I just hope I can find someone else within that six months."

"Bessie, I just don't know. Melinda and I haven't hit it off right from the start. I think she resents me. In fact, I'm sure she resents me. And Toby's being here doesn't help, either. She pouts every time her father even speaks to Toby."

"She does," Bessie agreed. "It's from being an only child and having just me to raise her for so long after her mother got killed. Cody didn't help matters a bit after he came back from the war. He's the one who spoils her rotten, trying to make up for her mother's death, I guess. But listen to me, Shanna. What sort of person is Melinda going to be if she doesn't have some discipline in her life? She can't be allowed to turn into one of those spoiled Southern belles like we had around here before the war. There's no place left for someone like that in our world now."

Bessie sighed and clasped her hands together on the table. "I didn't care for women like that even when they were fashionable, and I'm not going to have my grandniece grow into one."

"I don't think your nephew would agree with that."

"That doesn't make him right. Shanna, I'm old. I deserve a little peace in my life, and I don't like having a spoiled child around causing problems. I need your help to make Cody see what he's doing to Melinda."

"Cody doesn't seem to think I'm the proper person to influence Melinda. His attitude toward me the last two days hasn't been exactly what you'd call accepting."

"That's just another thing he's wrong about," Bessie said as she got to her feet. "Now, why don't you go on in to Melinda's room and have that talk with her? It's the first one on the left down the hallway. She's probably had time enough now to calm down and realize she's in trouble. She's not a bad child, Shanna. We just need to get her straightened out while she's still young enough for the training to take."

Shanna nodded her head reluctantly and rose from her chair. How hard could it be, anyway, to retrain a child as young as Melinda? She gripped the tabletop for a second, her mind comparing the mutinous look in Melinda's eyes to the stubborn cast in her father's at times. How hard—yes, how hard could it be?

Shanna glanced distractedly into the small parlor as she passed, the bareness of the room scarcely registering as she turned over in her mind what she would say to

Bittersweet Promises

Melinda. In the dim hallway leading to the bedrooms, she paused briefly to light a kerosene lamp on the wall before she moved on.

Outside the half-open door to Melinda's room, Shanna stopped and listened quietly for a moment. A murmur from inside told her Melinda was talking to someone. She peeked around the door to see Melinda curled up on the bed, one of her dolls in her arms.

"Showed her, didn't I, Pansy?" Melinda said to the doll. "Don't want her here. Don't need to learn to read and write. Daddy will always take care of me. He told me so."

Shanna pushed the door open and stepped into the room. Melinda's eyes widened, and she scooted up on the bed, back against her pillows.

"It's rather cold in here, Melinda," Shanna said as she walked over to the bed. "Don't you think you'd be warmer in the kitchen until the house gets heated up some?"

"I can get under my covers if I'm too cold," Melinda muttered, eyeing Shanna warily.

"Guess you could at that," Shanna said agreeably. She sat down on the bed and picked up the doll Melinda had left lying on the spread. "What's your doll's name? Did I hear you call her Pansy?"

Melinda nodded briefly, and Shanna could almost feel the child wondering how much else Shanna had heard outside the door.

"This isn't the same doll you had at the hotel," Shanna said. "Do you have more than one?"

Again Melinda nodded as Shanna smoothed her hand over the doll's golden curls.

"She has hair the color of yours," Shanna pointed out. "Bet she would look cute in pigtails."

"I d-don't know how to do pigtails," Melinda finally said. "Aunt Bessie makes them for me sometimes. Then my hair don't get in my eyes when I play."

"I'll show you how one of these days. By the way, where's your other doll?"

"In the wagon."

"She's probably getting awfully cold out there. Maybe we should go out and get her after you apologize to me."

Melinda glanced down at Shanna's leg, a guilty look crawling over her face. "I s'pose you want me to say I'm sorry."

"No," Shanna said and Melinda darted a surprised look at her. "Not if you're not really sorry. It wouldn't mean anything if you said you were and didn't feel that way. It would be almost the same as telling a lie. You do know what a lie is, don't you, Melinda?"

Melinda's eyes went to the door, as though judging whether she could escape before Shanna caught her, but then she ducked her head and nodded. "I know. I'll tell Aunt Bessie you didn't lie to my Daddy."

"And what about the apology I asked for?"

"What's a . . . 'pology?"

"It's admitting to someone you hurt that you were wrong for doing it. There are certain rules that we go by, both children and grown-ups. One of the rules is that we treat each other with respect and don't take our anger out by hitting or kicking each other. And that's one rule that usually brings on some sort of punishment for the person who breaks it."

Melinda glanced up at her. "I saw two men fightin' one day when we went to town. But Daddy picked me up and took me away. Did they get p-punished?"

"Probably," Shanna told her. "Sometimes the sheriff takes grown-ups who fight to jail. How did you feel when you saw those men?" Shanna asked. "Did it make you feel good?"

"No," Melinda admitted. "It scared me."

Bittersweet Promises

Shanna sat quietly for a while, letting Melinda turn her thoughts over in her mind.

Suddenly Melinda looked up at Shanna fearfully. "Will I go to jail for kicking you?"

With an effort, Shanna stifled the laughter that threatened her and kept a calm look on her face. "No, Melinda. The sheriff does that to control grown-ups, not children. It's expected that the grown-ups will teach their children the rules and see that they follow them. The sheriff's got enough to do without worrying about controlling people's children."

"Are you going to punish me?"

"Not this time, *if* I get my apology from you. But if it happens again, yes, I will see that you're punished. I believe in giving children a chance to correct themselves first. Then, if I have to, I'll give the child a punishment, so she'll remember the rule better if she's tempted to break it a third time."

Melinda slid off the bed and stood before Shanna. "I 'pologize," she said as she scuffed at the floor with her shoe. "And . . . and I think I'm sorry, too. I hope I didn't scare you when I hurt you."

"I accept your apology," Shanna said. "And, no, you didn't scare me, but you hurt me and made me very angry."

"Did you want to kick me back?"

"For a minute, I guess," Shanna admitted, finding herself astonished at how much of their talk Melinda had evidently taken in. The child was definitely very bright and would be a joy to teach if Shanna could ever get some sort of relationship going between herself and Melinda. Away from her father, Melinda was a much more reasonable child.

"But I don't believe in hitting children," Shanna told Melinda. "Or kicking them, for that matter. However, there are other ways to punish someone."

"How?" Melinda asked.

"Oh, maybe by not letting the child have any dessert for a week or so."

"You mean, no chocolate cake?"

"No, I mean no cake at all, chocolate or otherwise. And no pie or pudding or anything else sweet."

"I gotta go tell Aunt Bessie I 'pologize," Melinda said as she raced toward the door.

Shanna stood and shook her head as she smiled after Melinda's disappearing back. When she entered the kitchen, she found Bessie sitting in a chair and listening attentively to Melinda.

"And I 'pologize," Melinda was saying. "I didn't mean to tell a lie." Her brow puckered in concentration. "Well, I mean I didn't mean to say Miss Allen told a lie. But that was a lie, too, wasn't it? I mean...."

"I understand what you're trying to say, Melinda," Bessie said with a pat on Melinda's head. "Now why don't you run along out to the barn? I think Shanna and I can manage here in the kitchen. It's nice to have another woman around to help out."

"Thanks, Aunt Bessie!" Melinda quickly tossed Shanna a shy smile and ran to the door before her aunt could change her mind.

"That was certainly a change," Bessie said to Shanna.

"It's a start. But it won't last unless it's reinforced. I think Melinda and I have a few more battles ahead of us yet."

"Not just with Melinda."

"No," Shanna agreed. A pair of brown eyes flashed in her mind, and she found herself thinking she wouldn't enjoy the other battles at all.

The kitchen door opened again and Melinda stuck her head around it. "Aunt Bessie!" she cried. "Daddy says the baby horse is coming. Don't wait supper for him."

Melinda pulled the door shut again, and Shanna just

as quickly jerked it open to see Melinda running back across the snow-covered yard toward the barn. When Bessie stepped out beside her, Shanna threw a horrified glance at the older woman.

"What did she mean?"

"The mare's foaling. It's a little early, or Cody never would have taken us into town and left her. It's her first and he's been worried about her."

"He's not going to let those children stay out there and watch a mare give birth!"

"I very much doubt he'll let Melinda stay. In fact, here she comes now."

Melinda flew back across the yard and they could both hear her sobbing. She ran up the steps and flung herself into Bessie's arms when Bessie knelt down.

"D-Daddy yelled at me!" she sobbed. "He told me to go away! I didn't even get to pet my pony!"

"My word," Bessie said as she glanced up at Shanna. "There must be something terribly wrong with the mare. I better get some hot water started in case Cody needs it."

"I'll go get Toby," Shanna said.

"First fetch me some water from the well, child." Bessie rose to her feet and took Melinda's hand to lead her inside. "Toby will be all right out there for a while and Cody may need his help."

"Toby's never seen anything like that before in his life," Shanna gasped.

Bessie gave her a stern look and Shanna reluctantly stepped off the porch and started for the well.

Chapter Seven

Shanna pushed the barn door open and marched inside. Toby *would* return to the house. Surely there was a nearby neighbor Cody could send for if he needed help with the birthing. They had passed scattered houses on the trip from Liberty. They hadn't been what she considered prosperous-looking farms, but the people in the yards had waved and called friendly greetings. She could even offer to carry the message herself, if Cody would saddle her a horse.

Eyes adjusting to the dim light after the bright snow outside, Shanna tried to decide where to look for Cody and Toby. The inane thought that she had never been in a barn before passed through her mind. In New York, a stable boy always delivered her little mare to the front steps. She sniffed tentatively, finding the unfamiliar odors strangely pleasant and the interior of the barn far cleaner than she had expected.

A snort beside her made Shanna jump and swivel

toward the first stall in the barn, where a paint pony peeked over a half door. She walked over to pat the soft muzzle, and the pony nudged her hand, then stretched its neck out in an attempt to reach her cloak pocket.

"Oh, no, you don't!" Shanna chuckled and dodged the inquisitive muzzle. "I don't have anything in my pocket for you. I used to carry sugar for my mare, though, and I know what you're looking for. I'll bring you something next time." She caught herself laughing at what she imagined was a look of reproach in the pony's eyes.

Suddenly a loud neigh, heavy with pain and agony, split the air inside the barn. Shanna clasped her throat and whirled around. After the echoes of the sound died in the barn, she heard voices murmuring, the sounds coming from a stall farther in the shadowed recesses of the barn.

"Son," Shanna heard Cody saying when she finally gathered enough courage to approach the open door of the other stall. "If you want to go on up to the house, it's all right. This isn't going to be pleasant."

"No," Toby replied. "She's quieter when I hold her and talk to her."

Shanna stared at the brown mare lying on the straw-littered floor, its sides heaving and its head resting in Toby's small lap. She stifled a gasp when the mare's eyes rolled back and its legs thrashed, sending Cody scrambling away from the iron-shod hooves. Toby bent his head over the mare's ear and spoke soothingly to her, and she quieted again.

Cody caught sight of Shanna standing in the stall door and walked over to her, his face grim in the dim light. "Look, you better get back up to the house."

"I came out here to get Toby."

"That's up to him," Cody said with a shrug. "He's doing a good job keeping that mare quiet. And I'm afraid I really am going to need some help."

Toby raised his head and his eyes implored his sister. "Shanna, I'll come if you say I have to. But she's hurtin', Shanna, and I'm helping her bear it."

"Toby, do you have any idea what's going on here?"

"She's gonna have a baby colt or filly, Shanna. Sometimes it hurts them, but she'll be happy and proud of her new baby after she gets it pushed out."

"Pushed ou . . . my Lord." Her blue eyes flashed at Cody. "What have you told him?"

"Just what to expect. He won't be much help to me if he doesn't know what's going to happen."

The mare gave a moan and her sides heaved again. Shanna's face whitened, and she watched Toby bend down again to murmur to the mare, his hands stroking the sides of her muzzle.

"Make up your mind," Cody barked at Shanna. "I think that colt's turned the wrong way, and I've got to try to turn it around. If you want to be useful, too, go back to the house and fetch the water I'm sure Bessie's got on the stove for me."

Ignoring Shanna, Cody again knelt in the straw by the mare's hindquarters. When he reached for the mare's tail, Shanna gasped and ran for the barn door.

Outside the barn, Shanna pulled in a steadying breath of the cold air. Somewhat calmer, she glanced over her shoulder, her mind filled with the scene inside and her heart aching with pity for the mare. She hadn't reached the age of 20 without knowing something of childbirth, and just last year one of her friends had died giving birth to her first child. Shanna recalled the whispers of breach birth at her friend's funeral.

She hesitated uncertainly. She didn't want Toby to be sitting there with the mare's head in his arms when she died. But Cody had said something about turning the colt. Could that be possible?

Bittersweet Promises

Another shrill neigh from inside the barn helped Shanna decide. She raced down the now well-traveled path through the snow and up the steps into the kitchen.

Bessie barely acknowledged Shanna as she emerged from the pantry, a stack of clean linen towels and a bar of soap in her arms.

"Get the bucket of water from the stove," Bessie ordered as she started for the door. "I heard the mare scream. I reckon it's a breach birth, and Cody's going to have to try to turn the colt."

"Aunt Bessie," Melinda said from her seat at the table. "I don't want to stay here by myself."

"Then come on, child," Bessie said. "But you wait at the barn door. Your father won't want you coming inside."

Melinda slid from her chair and went after Bessie as Shanna grabbed another towel from the rack by the stove. She wrapped it around the hot handle of the water bucket and carried it with her back out the door.

Hours later, Shanna sat on the bale of hay she had dragged up to the stall door, her hands clenched in her lap and her lips moving in prayer. It didn't even dawn on her to look away from where Cody had his arm deep inside the mare. She gave a cry of joy when Cody pulled a tiny muzzle out. A second later, the mare gave a final, mighty heave and the colt slipped onto the straw.

"How wonderful," she breathed. She rose to her feet and quickly glanced at Toby. He was still curled up asleep at the mare's head, his arm around her nose.

"Let him sleep a few more minutes," Cody said as he worked over the colt. "He's done a good job."

"Yes, he did," Shanna agreed. "I never thought . . . he's only nine."

Cody grunted a reply she didn't catch and continued

working. He had long ago removed his coat and shirt, and his broad back glistened with sweat, even in the chilly barn. Shanna watched the muscles play across his back as he wiped the colt with handfuls of straw.

The mare gave another moan and Shanna cried out, "What's wrong?"

"Afterbirth," Cody muttered.

Shanna's stomach heaved. This time she turned away for a few seconds. When she looked back, Cody was replacing a pitchfork against the wall of the stall. Then he knelt by one of the fresh buckets of water Shanna had brought out an hour earlier to wash his hands and arms.

"Now," he said after he dried himself on the remaining clean towel, "let's see if we can get this little fellow on his feet."

Before he could reach for the colt, the mare pulled her legs under her and scrambled to her feet. Her movements woke Toby, and he rubbed at his eyes for an instant before he gave a gasp and jumped up.

"Is it here, Cody?" he asked. "The baby?"

"Right here, son," Cody said with a chuckle as he moved around the mare. "Let's let the mother get acquainted with it first, though. All right? You come on over here with your sister and me."

Toby cautiously walked around the mare, his eyes wide with wonder as he stared down at the colt in the straw. He joined Shanna and Cody outside the stall and watched with rapt attention as the mare nudged the colt to its feet. The colt stood rocking precariously on its outrageously long legs for a second before it collapsed back to the stall floor.

"Oh, the poor thing," Shanna said.

Shanna instinctively started forward, but Cody caught her hand. "Don't," he said quietly. "Just watch a minute."

Bittersweet Promises

Shanna stared down at their clasped hands for a second, then quickly forgot about them when the colt gave a faint nicker.

The second time the colt heaved itself to its feet, it managed to maintain its balance. After a nudge from its mother, it wobbled toward the mare's hindquarters and stuck its head underneath.

"What's it doing, Cody?" Toby asked, his voice barely a whisper as he watched the colt's little broomtail begin twitching from side to side.

"Eatin', Toby," Cody told him. "That bag has the mare's milk in it. He gets it by sucking on those teats hanging down there. All newborn babies that drink milk get it that way, even human ones."

"Oh!" Shanna gasped as a blush of embarrassment stole over her face. She felt a squeeze on her hand and glanced at Cody to meet his smiling brown eyes.

"Sorry," Cody said. "I keep forgetting you two are city folks."

Shanna pulled her hand free and moved a step away from him. Suddenly she whirled toward Toby.

"What did you just say, Toby?" she asked in a voice laced with astonishment as her small brother's last remark penetrated her jumbled thoughts.

"I asked you if you'll feed your babies like that when you have them, Shanna," Toby repeated, his eyes centered somewhere near Shanna's stomach. "Cody said. . . ."

Cody's loud guffaw threatened to drown out Shanna's voice, and she stepped around him to reach for Toby's arm.

"I think you better get on up to the house and eat something, Toby." Shanna gave him a shove toward the barn door. "Aunt Bessie left some sandwiches on the table for us. I'll be there in a minute to show you where we're sleeping."

Toby gave a sigh and looked up at Cody. "I guess that's something Shanna will talk to me about later," he said. "She's always telling me that I'm too young to know about some things and that she'll tell me about them later."

"Go on, son," Cody said around his laughter. "The colt will be here in the morning, and you have to pick out a name for him."

"Me? You mean, I get to name him? And how do you know it's a boy colt? You said it could be either a boy colt or a girl filly."

"Of course you're going to name him," Cody said. "After all, I don't think he—or the mare—would have lived if you hadn't helped me." He glanced at Shanna, again trying to smother laughter. "But let's wait until tomorrow for me to show you how I know it's a colt and not a filly."

"Get on up to the house, Toby," Shanna said through gritted teeth.

"Yes, ma'am," Toby said as he obeyed.

Cody waited until Toby disappeared out the barn door before he turned back to Shanna. "Sometimes that boy acts more like your son than your brother."

"He should," Shanna said without thinking. "I've practically raised him since he was born."

"His mother died in childbirth? Then, I guess I understand why you were afraid to leave him here with the mare being in trouble."

"N-no," Shanna admitted. "Mother died a couple months ago. But she hardly ever left her bed after Toby was born. I took care of him, along with the nu. . . ."

"Nurse?" Cody prodded when Shanna fell silent. "If you're used to a houseful of servants, what in the world are you doing out here all alone? You're certainly of an age that you could have taken over the house after your mother died."

"The only thing that should concern you is that I've had experience with children," Shanna fired back at him, quickly regretting that she had allowed him even a glimpse into her background. "You don't have to worry that you can't trust your daughter to my care."

"That's not what I'm worried about," Cody muttered. "But since you brought it up," he continued before Shanna could speak again, "you've had experience with a child, one child, not children. And that child was a boy, not a girl. My daughter has been through a traumatic experience, and she needs time to heal from it."

"You can allow her to heal without spoiling her rotten. Children grow from bad experiences sometimes, if they're handled right."

"Melinda spoiled?" Cody shot back. "This is probably the first time in his life that Toby ever got a speck of dirt on him. I'm surprised you weren't over there washing his face while he held the mare."

"Well, I wasn't, was I? And I heard you tell Toby what a good job he did. You even rewarded him by telling him he could name the colt."

"Children learn from rewards."

"Not rewards like chocolate cake." Shanna tilted her head up at him, her lips pursed in disapproval. "Rewards like that are meaningless. They only give physical gratification to a child. Emotional gratifications like letting Toby name the colt mean much more. That's something he'll remember long after the taste of a piece of cake has disappeared. Why is it you can see that with a child who isn't your own, yet not with Melinda? Aunt Bessie's afraid Melinda's going to grow into a spoiled Southern belle."

"I know exactly what my aunt thinks about how I treat Melinda!" Cody almost yelled at her, the prissy, self-righteous look on Shanna's face and his weariness making him less guarded than usual with his words. "She and I disagree on just what the difference is between my protecting Melinda and babying her. But just what the hell is wrong with her being spoiled a bit? There's not a damned thing wrong with a woman who depends on a man to take care of her and pamper her! If I'd taken better care of my wife, Melinda wouldn't be growing up without a mother to care for her!"

"My God, Cody," Shanna said, her indignation leaving her as she watched him turn angrily away and reach for his shirt. "You were off fighting a war. Bessie told me what happened when the Jayhawkers came. There were millions of women left behind during the war, and you can't possibly blame yourself for what happened."

"Yeah, I was off fighting a war"—Cody shrugged into his shirt, keeping his back to Shanna—"against Yankees."

Shanna unthinkingly reached out and grabbed his arm. With a force that surprised Cody, she spun him around until he faced her.

"And I guess that's just another thing you resent about me and another reason why you don't want me to care for your daughter. I'm one of those damned Yankees!"

"I'll thank you not to use language like that around my daughter!"

"Oh, and what about you telling Toby about bags and t-teats!"

"That's different. He's a boy."

"A nine-year-old boy," Shanna said with a stamp of her foot. "He's got plenty of time to learn about those things. I bet you wouldn't bring Melinda out here to witness a colt being born, if she was Toby's age!"

"Of course not. She's a—"

"I know, I know," Shanna broke in. "She's a girl. And she's supposed to be pampered and spoiled and protected from the hard things in life."

"That's right," Cody said, a smug look on his face.

"Maybe your wife would have been a little better protected if she'd known some of the hard facts of life," Shanna spat at him before she could stop herself.

Shanna took a step back, horrified as she realized what she had said and wishing she could take it back. The thunder clouding Cody's face told her he would never forget the words.

"What was between my wife and me is none of your damned business!" Cody took a threatening step toward her. "Just like you seem to feel your background is none of mine. And if I ever hear you say something like that in front of my daughter, I'll send your fanny packing so fast you won't know what hit you!"

"I . . . I'm sorry. I had no right to say that, and I'm really dreadfully sorry about it."

When Cody continued to glare at her, his anger not abating one iota, Shanna dropped her eyes. "Look, this is obviously not going to work. If you'll take Toby and me back to town in the morning, we'll get out of your life."

"And go where?" Cody demanded. "I sure as hell don't have any money to lend you in order to get you off my hands. What little I had was in the bank."

"I . . . I'll get work in town," Shanna quickly decided. "I heard the desk clerk asking someone if he knew anyone who was looking for a waitress job. The one they have now is going to have a ba . . . is in the family way and wants to quit."

"Perkins needs someone who knows how to wait on other people instead of just ordering them to do the things that need to be done," Cody informed her. "And his waitress also washes dishes. Those lily-white hands of yours would be cracked and bleeding after the first panful."

Shanna unconsciously rubbed her hand against the side of her cloak, recalling just how Cody knew about the softness of her hands. "I . . . I'll find something," she assured him. "I have to take care of Toby."

The mare whickered softly, and both Cody and Shanna watched quietly as the mare lay down in the straw and began licking the colt curled at her side. Cody glanced at Shanna, remembering how many times she had trudged to the house and back in the cold night air, bringing more hot water for him, and how she had stood resolutely by in case he needed more help than Toby could give him. He found himself surprised, now that he thought about it, at how much her quiet presence had meant during the ordeal. Her face was softened into quiet wonder as she gazed at the mare and colt, and his anger evaporated.

"Look," he said at last. "You and the boy both earned your keep tonight, at least for a few days. We're adults, and we should be able to work this out. Besides, even though I own this place, Aunt Bessie's the one who runs the house and she's decided she needs help with Melinda. I'll admit I hadn't thought about it until she began nagging me a few weeks ago and demanded we send out wires looking for someone willing to come out here. Now that you're here, why don't we give it a try?"

Shanna looked up hopefully at him and saw Cody's hand extended toward her.

"Truce?"

"Truce," Shanna agreed. She gave his hand a short shake, then quickly pulled her own back. "You're right. We're adults and we should be able to set some ground rules without sniping at each other constantly."

"Yeah, well, let's wait until morning to discuss the rules," Cody said with a weary sigh. He arched his back, his hands reaching around to massage the small of it beneath the tail of his unbuttoned shirt. "I don't think I'm up to it right now."

"M-me, either." Shanna licked her lips around a suddenly dry mouth and tore her eyes from his open shirt.

Bittersweet Promises

When Cody dropped his hands back to his sides, she feigned a yawn and lifted a hand to stifle it. "I'll go see if Bessie left any coffee on," she said, willing her legs to move to the barn door. Instead, the trembling muscles telegraphed a message to her brain that they needed a moment to recover, or she would find herself tottering like the unsteady colt.

"Don't bother making any if she didn't," Cody told her, and Shanna breathed a silent sigh of thankfulness when he casually reached for his shirt buttons. "I forgot all about milking the cow this evening. I'll do it now and bring the milk up so we can have some hot chocolate. It's after midnight, and coffee would just keep us awake."

"Chocolate, huh?" Shanna managed a smile as he buttoned the bottom button over his flat stomach. "Is that one of your weaknesses, too?"

"Yeah," Cody admitted. "Guess Melinda gets it from me."

"Who cares for your animals when you're gone?" Shanna asked. Her legs were steady now—almost. "As you pointed out, I'm city folks, but I do know that cows need to be milked every day."

"Our nearest neighbors are the Samuels, Zerelda and Pappy. I grew up with Frank and Jesse James, and now I get one of their little brothers to take care of the stock when I have to be away."

"James? I thought you said their name was Samuel."

"The two oldest boys and Susie are named James," Cody replied. "Zerelda was married to a minister, Robert James, but he died out in California, where he'd gone to spread the word. At least, that's what he told his wife. Folks say he caught the gold fever instead. Zerelda married Doc Reuben Samuel after that, and they've got a brood of their own."

"A doctor? You called him. . . ."

"I know, it's kind of confusing," Cody said with a

laugh. "Folks who know Reuben call him Pappy. He's not a practicing doctor any longer. I heard Zerelda tell Bessie once that she married Pappy so she would have a doctor around to help her with her kids. She lost her second son to fever, and I think she lost her mind for a little while."

"People do marry for strange reasons sometimes," Shanna mused, thinking of her own reason for being in Missouri.

"Oh, Zerelda's just kidding when she says that," Cody told her. "They're quite a pair. She must be six feet and Pappy's just a little man. You can tell when you see them together just how much they really do care for each other, but Zerelda's main love in life is her children. Everyone who knows her sees that. I sure hope the rumors in town aren't true. I think that would just about kill Zerelda."

"Rumors?" Shanna prodded when Cody fell silent.

The cow lowed from its stall at the far end of the barn, and Cody quickly glanced that way.

"I better get Miss Moo taken care of. That's Melinda's name for her, you know. I told her a bedtime story once that had a cow named Miss Moo in it, and she decided our cow should have a name, too. I think she's got names for almost everything on the farm, but I can't keep them straight. We have a time when one of the animals disappears and she can't find it. Luckily, she hasn't made the connection yet with what we have to eat sometimes."

"Oh," Shanna said with a grimace. "I hope she doesn't figure that out too soon."

"Yeah, me, too," Cody said. He looked down at Shanna. "I guess that's at least one thing we can agree Melinda should be sheltered from for a while yet."

"Yes, and Toby, too," Shanna replied, her eyes challenging him.

"Point taken," Cody said with a tired sigh.

Bittersweet Promises

Shanna gave a decisive nod of her head and turned away.

Cody watched her until she disappeared into the blackness outside the barn door, his brow furrowed in concentration. Despite her attempts to keep her background a mystery, he was slowly picking up details here and there. He was pretty sure Bessie hadn't forgotten to open the chimney damper earlier, but Shanna's first thought had evidently been to get the children out of the smoke, since Melinda had been in her arms when he ran to the house.

Shanna wasn't used to being on her own or having to watch out for danger. Look at how she had lost her money and ended up in the middle of the bank robbery, let alone almost getting trampled by a horse.

"In her own way," Cody muttered to himself, "she was probably just as pampered as Nancy."

But, his mind continued, she sure wasn't afraid to try new things, and she was determined to make the best of her situation.

What in heaven's name was she doing here, though? Why didn't she hightail it back to her safe and sound world up north, where she would have a houseful of servants to help take care of her little brother?

Toby—now, there was some boy. If he and Nancy had had a son, Cody would have wished him to be much like Toby. The boy was obedient most of the time, and obviously respected his sister. But he didn't hesitate to speak his mind and reason with Shanna when he wanted her to rethink her orders.

It crossed Cody's thoughts that this was a much better manner for a child to get his way than whining, and a flicker of admiration for the way Shanna had raised Toby came through. Shanna must have only been about 11 when Toby was born, and the only thing she would have had on which to base her concepts of how to teach Toby would have been the principles she was taught herself. Maybe having her pass a few of them on to Melinda wouldn't be such a bad idea.

If he could only keep remembering that Shanna was Melinda's teacher, instead of recalling the soft curves beneath the wool cloak, the cute way she stamped her foot when she got in a pique, the silky blond hair just made for a man's hands to tousle, the eyes as blue as the acres of Texas bluebonnets he had seen one spring during the war. . . .

The cow lowed loudly. Cody sighed and started toward the stall. It wasn't going to be easy keeping his hands to himself with Shanna living in the same house, but by damn, he would do it. The lady had depths and secrets not at all to his liking in a woman. He preferred his women open and guileless—women who appreciated having a man around to lean on. He would keep a wary eye on the way she handled his daughter, but that would be the extent of his dealings with Shanna Allen.

Taking offense at the less-than-gentle hands on her swollen sack, Miss Moo sent the bucket flying, spilling the scant inch of milk in the bottom. The cow turned its head and lowed warningly at Cody when he shot her a disgruntled look and rose to fetch a clean bucket.

"Females," Cody muttered under his breath when he returned to the three-legged stool. This time, though, he patted Miss Moo on the side and laid his head against her warm flank, his fingers coaxing for instead of demanding the milk. Miss Moo gave a contented burp and retrieved her cud from her front stomach, chewing complacently while the milk gushed into the bucket, foam rising from the force of the heavy streams.

Chapter Eight

Sounds of children's laughter outside the bedroom window woke Shanna the next morning. Turning on her side in the unfamiliar bed, she opened her eyes to sunlight streaming through the sparkling panes of the uncurtained window. Drowsiness fled when she realized one of the voices outside the window belonged to Toby, and the events of the previous night chased the fog from her mind.

"Good grief, I've overslept! That's a fine way to start my first day as a teacher. I can just hear Cody now!"

Shanna threw back the comforter and rolled to the side of the bed. When she tried to stand, her leg muscles protested and her arm ached as she stretched to rub one calf. Carrying all that water from the kitchen to the barn last night had taken its toll on her soft muscles, but she forced herself to her feet, determinedly ignoring the soreness, then knelt to pull the chamber pot from beneath the bed. She wasn't quite up to making the trek out back before she dressed.

After replacing the lid on the chamber pot, Shanna sighed and set it by the door. There wouldn't be a maid around to perform that chore for her any longer—she would have to carry the pot to the outhouse herself. She found a pan of heated water on the stand by the window, sitting in the sun to keep its contents warm, and quickly washed. Searching for her carpetbag, she opened the small closet door to see her dresses already hanging among Toby's clothing. Beyond them hung other garments, and she stepped inside for a closer look.

Why, they were men's clothing. She hadn't realized Bessie had put her and Toby in Cody's room. Where had Cody slept? And she would definitely have to remember to thank Bessie for bringing the water and caring for her clothes, but she'd have to assure Bessie that she didn't expect such treatment in the future. How in the world did Bessie manage to keep everything so clean and in place by herself? she wondered, recalling the shining windowpanes.

Shanna removed her yellow day gown from its hanger and returned to the room. No matter how she twisted her arms, though, she couldn't reach all the hooks on the back of the dress. She hated to call Bessie—she certainly didn't want the older woman to think she thought of her as a maid. Continuing to work her hands behind her back, Shanna moved over to the window, drawn by the renewed sounds of laughter.

Melinda crouched behind a large ball of snow, her small figure entirely hidden from Toby. Melinda clutched a snowball, and when Toby walked near, she rose and threw it with unerring aim. The snowball splattered against Toby's back and Melinda's giggles rang out in the still air.

Bittersweet Promises

"I'll get you for that!" Toby yelled. But when Melinda took off down the well-trodden path toward the barn, Toby lobbed his own snowball well to the side of her. He only shook his head when Melinda turned around and stuck her small tongue out at him.

"You missed! You missed!" Melinda laughed gaily.

Turning from the window, Shanna gave up struggling with the dress hooks and crossed to the door. She stared down at the chamber pot for a second, fighting the urge to stick her tongue out at it as Melinda had at Toby. With a sigh, she picked it up and opened the door.

"Good morning," Shanna said to Bessie as she entered the kitchen. "I'm awfully sorry for oversleeping. It won't happen again."

"Forget it, Shanna. Why, I heard you and Cody in the kitchen last night long after I put Toby to bed. We all slept in a little this morning, even Cody, and he's always up before the crack of dawn."

"I didn't realize Toby and I had taken Cody's room, Bessie." Shanna set the chamber pot by the back door. "Where did he sleep?"

"Oh, he threw his bedroll on the floor in Melinda's room. She was happy as a kitten with a fresh saucer of milk when she found him there this morning."

"But he can't sleep on the floor while we take his bed!"

"Don't worry. He's working on the room on the other side of his old one. It's almost finished, and we'll figure out something for a mattress after he builds a bed. Now, sit down and have your breakfast. I've kept it warm for you."

"Bessie, please. I don't expect you to wait on me. You've done so much already. I appreciate your hanging up our clothing and bringing the hot water this morning. Why don't you sit, and I'll pour you a cup of coffee to have with me while I eat?"

"All right, child," Bessie agreed. "But only for a moment. There's always so much to do, and I don't like it to get ahead of me."

Shanna glanced at the chamber pot and washed her hands in a pan of water in the sink before she reached for two cups in the dish drainer. She poured them full and set them on the table, returning to the stove for a plate she had noticed covered with a linen towel to keep it warm.

"Heavens, Bessie," Shanna said after she sat at the table and uncovered the plate. "I can't eat all this." She stared at the crisp pieces of ham lying beside two eggs and three fluffy biscuits.

"'Course you can. You'd be surprised how big an appetite we get out here in the country. All the clean air and that exercise you got yesterday will have it whetted."

Shanna picked up her knife and fork, cutting off a large bite of ham. "Ummmm, delicious. Oh my!" Shanna quickly swallowed the ham. "Don't you dare tell Melinda and Toby that I talked with my mouth full. Toby will never let me forget it."

"I won't," Bessie replied with a laugh. "Here." She pushed the butter plate and a jar of jam across the table. "Fill your mouth with one of those biscuits and my homemade jam. It's strawberry. Cody managed to find a few of the plants left in our trampled garden and saved them for me. I do love my strawberries in the summer."

"Wonderful," Shanna proclaimed a moment later. "Will you show me how you make it?"

"Certainly," Bessie replied, then cocked her head at a noise outside the house. "My word. That sounds like a wagon and horses. Who could be visiting this time of day?" She rose to her feet and started to the door just as it opened.

Bittersweet Promises

"Zerelda and Pappy are here, Aunt," Cody said as he stood in the doorway, stamping his feet to remove the snow from his boots. "Good God! Do you always sit around half naked at the breakfast table?"

Shanna jumped from her chair, almost toppling it over as she swung around to face Cody. The cold air from the open doorway cascaded goose bumps over her upper back, and the chill warred with her flush of embarrassment.

"I . . . my dress. I couldn't reach. . . ."

"For pity's sake, Cody." Bessie set her hands on her hips and pursed her lips. "Get on back out there and greet our neighbors. I'll help Shanna with her dress."

Cody wrenched his eyes away from the front of Shanna's dress this time, where her breasts heaved beneath her crossed arms. His gaze fell on her face, which had turned a delightful shade of pink from the warm kitchen and her discomfort. He caught himself wondering if the skin on the smooth back he glimpsed was as soft as her hands and as warm and silky as her cheeks appeared.

"Cody," Bessie said, suppressing a smile after she allowed the moment to stretch out somewhat. "Our guests?"

Cody slammed his hat back on his head and shut the door.

"Here, child," Bessie said. "Let me hook those for you."

Shanna pulled aside an errant curl that had slipped from the untidy bun she'd managed that morning as she turned her back. "I . . . oh, why do I always seem to let that man catch me in awkward situations?" she fumed.

"It's not as if Cody doesn't know a woman sometimes needs help with things like that," Bessie replied as she began hooking the dress. "Heavens, he helped Nancy enough times. Seemed like every dress she owned had about a thousand buttons or hooks."

Shanna felt a stab of some emotion she couldn't quite identify when she heard Cody's dead wife's name. She quickly stifled it and raised her arms to try to tidy her hair, while Bessie fastened the last hook.

"There." Bessie gave the back of Shanna's dress a pat. "Sit down and let me fix your hair."

"Oh, Bessie, I. . . ."

"Sit, child." A second later, Bessie had Shanna's hair in a tidy knot on her head. "There," she said with another pat. "Listen, here come our neighbors onto the back porch. You finish your breakfast. Zerelda won't care. I'll pour her a cup of coffee and she and I can chat while you eat."

"Maybe I should take my plate to my room."

When the kitchen door opened again before Shanna could stand, she swung her head around. An extremely tall woman entered the room, her black cloak failing to hide her obviously swollen figure. Shanna's eyes widened as she recalled Cody telling her that Zerelda Samuel had children as old as him—and Mrs. Samuel was definitely going to have yet another child.

"Good morning, Zerelda." Bessie helped Zerelda off with her cloak and hung it on the wall. "Sit down and I'll fetch you some coffee. How's your newest bun in the oven?"

"He's just fine, Bessie," Zerelda said with a smile as she caressed her stomach. "Long about July, I 'spect we'll know for certain." She crossed the room and sat down across from Shanna.

"I guess you must be Melinda's teacher." Zerelda stuck her hand across the table. "I'm Zerelda Samuel."

"Shanna Allen," Shanna replied, accepting Zerelda's work-worn hand. "I'm very glad to meet you. Please excuse my still eating. I'm afraid I was a slugabed this morning."

Bittersweet Promises

"Go right ahead." Zerelda took the cup of coffee Bessie held out and set it in front of her. "We don't stand on ceremony around here."

Realizing she was still awfully hungry, Shanna took a bite of her biscuit as Zerelda and Bessie settled down to talk. Most of the people they spoke of were strangers to Shanna and her attention wandered. She finally glanced down in surprise at her empty plate and rose to take it to the sink.

"Well, I guess that would be up to Shanna," she heard Bessie say as she rinsed off her plate, then put it to soak in the pan of hot water.

"What's that, Bessie?" Shanna asked.

"Zerelda was wondering if you had a place for a couple more children in your class for Toby and Melinda."

"Can't pay you anything, Mrs. Allen," Zerelda added. "But I brought over an extra bed we had, knowin' Cody ain't got much furniture here. And we've got a pony your little boy might like to ride while you're here. We'll be glad to furnish the hay for it."

"Heavens. Word does get around quickly, doesn't it? Yes, I'd be pleased to teach your children, Mrs. Samuel. But Toby's not my son—he's my little brother. He does love to ride, though. He had his own pony back in . . . back home. And it's Miss Allen, but Shanna to my friends. I wish you'd call me Shanna."

"Only if you call me Zerelda. And I'm glad that's settled. Oh, and one more thing. My oldest daughter is real handy with a needle. She'll make you some dresses that won't get ruined while you work, though that gown's awfully pretty."

The door opened again and a chubby little man walked in, Toby holding his hand and Melinda swinging from his arm. Toby dropped his hold and ran over to Shanna.

"Shanna! Shanna, Mr. Samuel says he's got a pony I can ride if you'll agree to teach his kids. Will ya,

Shanna? Will ya? I'll take care of it and feed it and curry it and everything. I promise, Shanna!"

"Mr. Samuel's wife and I have already discussed it, Toby. And the answer is yes, as long as Cody doesn't mind and has room for another animal in the barn."

"He does. He said so, Shanna. Oh, goody. Now Melinda and I can ride together."

Shanna watched Mr. Samuel walk over to his wife. He surreptitiously reached out and patted her stomach, his love for her clear on his face. "How's the little gal? She and you aren't too tired from the ride?" Shanna heard him say.

"The child's fine and so am I," Zerelda replied. "But *she's* going to feel awful funny with a name like Archie." Zerelda glanced at Shanna and read the question on her face. "He insists it's going to be another girl," she explained. "And I'm just as sure it's a boy. After all, I've carried both more times than I care to count, and I guess I know as much as any doctor."

"I see," Shanna said. She glanced down at Toby to see him staring at Zerelda Samuel's extended stomach.

"Mrs. Samuel. . . ." Toby began.

"What did you name the new colt, Toby?" Shanna quickly asked.

"I'm still thinking," Toby told her. "Oh, Cody wants to see you in the barn, Shanna. He's building some school seats and needs to know how many."

"Of course." Shanna moved over to the kitchen door and reached for her cloak. "Excuse me," she said to the room at large. Trying for a measure of nonchalance, she bent down and picked up the chamber pot to carry with her.

The sound of a hammer ringing on nails drew Shanna on through the barn when she entered. She glanced at the mare and colt, then moved deeper into the huge barn. At the far end, she found an open door and looked into a room Cody had obviously set up for a workshop.

Seeming to sense her silent presence, Cody laid his hammer down and turned. "Glad to see you're finally dressed," he said, hoping to bring that pretty blush back to her cheeks.

"I . . . oh, you!" Shanna said, glaring at him. "Why do you always have to start a fight the moment we get near each other?"

"A fight? Why, Miss Allen, can't you tell the difference between teasing and fighting? I tease the children all the time, and they don't take offense."

Shanna stared at his twinkling brown eyes and her indignation left her, along with her breath when her chest tightened. She dropped her eyes from his face, and they fell on the top of his shirt, where a few golden hairs peeked through the open neck. Her nose twitched of its own accord when she recalled having it buried in those hairs a few days ago, and she reached up a hand to swipe at it.

"You'll get used to the hay tickling your nose in the barn," Cody said.

"What?"

"Your nose," Cody said with a nod. "There're always particles of hay floating around in a barn, and sometimes they tickle a person's nose."

"It's not. . . ." Shanna clamped her mouth shut, biting back the words she had meant to say, then opened it when her mind would allow her to say something more appropriate. "Yes, the hay. I'm not used to it. Ah . . . Toby said you wanted to know about the school desks."

"Uh-huh. There are a couple stored up in the loft you can probably use for Toby and Melinda. I thought maybe just a bench and long table for anyone else. Does that sound all right?"

"Of course. I don't suppose you have a blackboard up there, too?"

"Yep. And there're some boxes of old schoolbooks. We were lucky the raiders didn't burn the barn, along with the house. Guess it might have gone up, though, if not for the thunderstorm. That saved some of the house, too."

"It must have been terrible," Shanna said with a shiver.

"Well, nothing we can do now will change what's already happened," Cody said, realizing that maybe he was finally starting to heal somewhat himself. "Melinda and Bessie are still alive, thanks to Frank and Jesse. I imagine Bessie told you it was the James boys who ran the raiders off. They're both damned fine shots, and they were able to get into good enough cover that the raiders couldn't drive them out."

"She just said it was neighbors."

"Good neighbors. They buried the rest of my family and settled Melinda and Bessie in town until I got word and came back. Jesse and Pappy paid for it, though. They would have got Frank, too, if he hadn't already left for the war."

"What happened?" Shanna asked, not really sure she wanted to know.

"There's always people who play both sides in any conflict," Cody told her with a sigh. "Someone informed the Jayhawkers who'd been shooting at them. The next raid they made was at the Samuel's place, and they caught Jesse out in the field and whipped him half to death. They strung Pappy up, but somehow Zerelda managed to get him down before he was dead, even though she was with child that time, too. Didn't you notice the rope-burn scars on Pappy's neck and how he's a little addlepated?"

Shanna pictured the little man inside the house. She had noticed his neck, and now she realized his clear blue eyes had held a childlike gaze.

"But . . . but Zerelda's . . . she's. . . ."

"Pregnant again?" Cody said with a laugh. "Pappy may have retreated into childhood a little after losing some of the oxygen to his brain while he hung on that rope, but he's still got a man's body and needs."

"Oh!" Shanna gasped. "Oh, I'll never get used to you people here talking about things like that so easily!"

"Comes from living so closely with our animals, I reckon," Cody said with a casual shrug as he watched Shanna's cheeks turn that delightful shade he enjoyed. It made her blue eyes stand out, and when she bit her lips, their darker shade complemented her rosy complexion.

Darn, she was pretty. No, not just pretty, beautiful. A silky curl had escaped from the bun in her blond hair, falling over the front of her dress and almost to her waist. God, he bet her whole body would have that delightful rosy-pink blush after lovemaking, and he would give a lot to see that hair tangled and tousled after. . . .

Quickly turning his back, Cody groaned and tried to call to mind his vow to deal with Shanna only as Melinda's teacher. Damn, he woke up this morning completely confident that he could keep that vow—until he walked into the kitchen and saw her naked back. Hell, he was going to have to get some larger denims in town if this kept happening. From a hook on the wall, he grabbed a carpenter's apron he almost never wore and pulled it over his head, tying the strings behind him.

"Uh. . . ." he said when he turned back to see Shanna staring at him with a puzzled expression on her face. "Uh . . . would you like to see the colt? I'm about ready for a break here."

"I thought you wanted to talk about the school furniture."

"You've already told me benches will be fine," he reminded her.

"Oh. Yes, I would like to see the colt then. I glanced in, but I didn't want to disturb the mare in case she isn't happy about strangers around her baby."

"Melinda and Toby have been in and out of that stall a half-dozen times already this morning." Cody laughed tolerantly as he walked out of the workshop. "Brownie's the most gentle horse we own, and she just looked at them. I'd almost swear, though, that I heard her give a big sigh at one point."

"Brownie?"

"The mare. Melinda named her. She's not very imaginative when it comes to names. Maybe she'll be able to think of something more creative after you get her to reading."

"What's the apron for?" Shanna asked when they stopped in front of the mare's stall. "You already had sawdust all over your trousers in the workshop."

Cody's half hardness surged full again at the thought of her eyes on his denims, and he silently cursed his lack of control. His mind searching for an explanation to her innocent question, he settled on the pitchfork leaning beside the stall door and picked it up.

"Uh . . . I'm going to muck out the mare's stall."

"Don't you think you ought to tie the mare out first?" Shanna asked reasonably. "There's not much room in there if you don't."

"Hell, yes, I'll tie her out! Damn it, I guess I know how to muck out a stall! I've been doing it for twenty-five years!"

Shanna glanced up in astonishment at the angry tone in Cody's voice. Now what had she done to make him mad at her again?

"I didn't mean to sound bossy," she said in a hurt voice, remembering why Cody had insisted she would never make a waitress. "If you want, I'll hold the colt while you bring the mare out."

"I can handle the blasted colt. And the mare, too, for that matter."

"Then you go right ahead and handle them!" Shanna yelled at him, her temper at last flaring. "I'll see the colt later. You'd probably think I didn't know how to pet him!" She whirled away and ran for the barn door.

"Shanna, wait!" Cody called. He wasn't surprised when she ignored him and continued toward the house. He let his breath out in an exasperated sigh and opened the stall door.

"I think I'm going in after that buggy tomorrow," he muttered to the small colt. "And I better stop off to see one of Ruby's girls on the way home. There's entirely too much birthing and questions about it for a man to keep his mind on business around here."

For some reason, though, the thought of one of his infrequent trips to the whorehouse Ruby ran discreetly on the edge of Liberty didn't appease the ache in his groin at all.

Chapter Nine

Cody didn't make it in for the buggy the next day, nor the following day for that matter. A steady stream of neighbors came by the Garret plantation over the next few days as word of Shanna's presence spread. The bare parlor filled with school benches and one man even returned home to pick up a desk and chair for Shanna to use.

"Can't have a teacher without a desk," he growled in embarrassment when Shanna ohed and awed over the fine piece of furniture he returned with. "My gramma, she taught, and reckon she'd be pleased to know someone's usin' that desk again."

When Mrs. Toggins learned that the Garrets were short a bedroom, she insisted her husband and oldest son help Cody finish the room Cody had started repairing. The women measured the parlor and bedroom windows and soon had them covered with billowy curtains. Then they started on Shanna, insisting she allow them to wrap her in the tape measure and sew up some everyday gowns. Cody's clothes disappeared from the small closet to make room for her dresses, and the first time Shanna looked in to see them gone, a surprising pang stabbed through her.

Shanna couldn't believe how eager these people were to have a teacher for their children. The sideboards in the kitchen groaned with food the women brought so Bessie wouldn't have to cook for all of them. The house rang with sounds of chatter and laughter, mixed with the sawing and hammering noises from the new bedroom under construction. Each evening, the quietness was a jolt when the neighbors left after a discussion of what would be done the next day.

Shanna soon knew all the closest neighbors and had met the children she would teach. They numbered an even dozen and ranged in age from Melinda's four to Zerelda Samuel's daughter of twelve. From some of the remarks she overheard the women saying, Shanna thought she might even have a couple of the older boys in her class as soon as the wives let the husbands know they weren't kidding about wanting their sons in school.

More and more Shanna found herself caring for the children, keeping them occupied while the women worked. She wasn't really that good with a needle, and when she tried to help with the dishes, the women would have none of it, horrified at the thought that Shanna's beautiful hands would get cracked and worn like theirs. Determined to earn her keep, Shanna settled into what she knew she could do best.

On the fourth day, Shanna rose from the rocking chair in Bessie's bedroom and tucked the small baby she had been rocking under the covers. She propped a pillow beside it so it couldn't roll off and glanced out the window. All the finished rooms in the house now had curtains at the windows. Though Bessie had insisted their work should be geared to making Shanna comfortable in the house, a few other touches had appeared.

"Shanna," Bessie said from the doorway, "I hate to bother you, but Toby and Melinda are begging to ride their ponies. Cody's putting the bed together in his bedroom and...."

"Sure, Bessie. They can ride in the corral, like they did yesterday. I'll get my cloak."

Two whoops of delight met Shanna's ears when she went out the kitchen door, and Toby and Melinda raced ahead of her to the barn. Toby already had his bridle on the small chestnut pony Pappy had brought over, and he led him from the stall to tie him at a ring in the wall.

"I'll saddle Melinda's pony next, Shanna," he said. "I know how. Cody taught me yesterday."

"I want to ride Toby's pony today," Melinda said with a pout. "It's prettier than mine."

Shanna sighed in resignation at the familiar whine in Melinda's voice. She had played with the other children fairly nicely over the last few days, but today the women had only brought small babies with them, leaving their other children at home in the care of the eldest child while they finished up a few odd chores. Without the distraction of several playmates, Melinda again assumed she should be the center of attention.

"If you ask Toby, rather than demanding it," Shanna said, "he might be willing to switch ponies with you after you each have a ride on your own."

Shanna motioned Toby to silence when he looked over at them, prepared, she knew, to offer his pony to Melinda. She waited several seconds, then heard Melinda speak beside her.

"Could I please have a ride on your pony, Toby?" she said sweetly. "And use your saddle? I don't like that old sidesaddle I have to use. I think it would be more fun to ride like you do."

Bittersweet Promises

"You can ride Chessy next," Toby agreed. "But you have to use your own saddle. Cody said girls don't ride a-astride. It's not ladylike. He told you that yesterday."

Melinda quickly wiped the pout off her face when she glanced up to see Shanna watching her. "All right," she said meekly. "But can I ride Chessy first?"

"Melinda, Toby already has his saddle on. There's no sense in him changing the saddles now. You can wait your turn and ride your own pony while you wait."

"I don't want to ride Spot today," Melinda insisted.

"Fine, then," Shanna told her. "After Toby gets his ride out, you can ride Chessy."

Shanna walked back outside and opened the corral gate, closing it behind Chessy after Toby rode in. When Melinda tried to climb on the top rail beside her, Shanna helped her settle herself, then turned back to watch Toby.

"Why, Toby," she called after a few minutes. "You're riding better than ever."

"Cody showed me a few things yesterday," Toby called back. "He said Western riding's different. Us Western riders don't do none of that postin' when we trot. He said it looks silly, popping our behinds up out of the saddle like that."

"Any of that posting." Shanna laughed back at him. "And I guess it does look funny, now that you mention it. The way you're riding does look more comfortable."

Toby smiled over at them, then reined his pony into a figure eight. Chessy worked smoothly for the small boy and willingly stepped up into a gallop once around the corral when Toby urged him.

Toby pulled Chessy to a stop in front of Shanna and Melinda, sliding from the saddle and looping the reins over the fence post.

"Soon as he rests a minute, Melinda," he said, "you can ride. Pappy says we have to exercise him a little at a time until he gets used to being ridden again. Chessy's been penned up all winter and got sort of fat."

"Toby, who said you could call Mr. Samuel Pappy? You know, I've told you to not call your elders by their first names."

"Pappy said to, Shanna," Toby insisted. "All the kids call him Pappy. You also said I have to obey my elders and I'm just calling him what he asked me to."

Unable to find a thing wrong with Toby's logic, Shanna shook her head and watched him scramble to the top railing on the other side of her. "You win that one, Toby," she said with a smile.

The pony shifted and Toby gasped as he stared over Shanna's shoulder. "Don't, Melinda!" he yelled.

Shanna whirled and made a grab for Melinda, but her arms fell short when Melinda slipped into Chessy's saddle. Melinda had the reins in her hand, but her short legs couldn't quite reach the stirrups set for Toby's length. Nevertheless, Melinda kicked the pony in its sides and let out a small cry of triumph as she galloped for the far side of the corral.

"Melinda, stop!" Shanna called. Frozen in horror, she watched Melinda start sliding sideways in the saddle, her legs unable to grip the saddle leather through her full skirts.

Melinda dropped the reins and grabbed the saddle horn. A scream left her lips. The pony galloped full tilt at the far fence, then made an abrupt turn when he reached it. Melinda flew through the air and over the top rail, landing with a sickening thump in a snowbank on the other side.

"Oh my God!" Shanna scrambled through the fence and raced toward the other side of the corral, her eyes never leaving the small, unmoving figure, even when she stumbled on the rutted ground.

"Go get help, Toby!" she yelled over her shoulder.

Bittersweet Promises

Melinda stirred and rolled over in the snow as Shanna climbed through the far side of the fence. Her small chest heaved as she tried to breathe. Shanna gathered her into her arms and stroked her face.

"Easy, baby. You've got your breath knocked out. Calm down and it will come back."

A shudder ran over Melinda and she managed to pull in a deep breath. When she let it out, a scream laced more with indignation than pain accompanied it.

"Thank God," Shanna breathed. "The snowbank cushioned your fall." She ran her hands over Melinda anyway, ignoring the unchecked shrieks now coming from Melinda's mouth. Satisfied that there were no broken bones, Shanna picked Melinda up to carry her to the house and check for bruises in a warmer place.

"Hush now, Melinda," Shanna soothed. "You aren't hurt badly, just scared. You'll be fine in a few minutes."

Melinda snuffled once more and gulped back a sob, but at least the shrieks stopped. "H-hate that pony," she gasped.

"Oh, for heaven's sake, Melinda," Shanna said as she awkwardly climbed back through the corral fence, the child in her arms. "It wasn't Chessy's fault. You were told to wait until Toby changed the saddles."

Shanna heard the kitchen door slam and glanced at the house to see Cody racing toward them, followed closely by Bessie and Toby. They reached her just after she crawled through the corral fence again, and Cody grabbed Melinda from Shanna's arms.

"Are you hurt, sweetheart?" Cody said as he smoothed Melinda's hair back from her face.

Another shriek from Melinda was his answer. She threw her arms around Cody's neck and buried her face on his shoulder, thankfully muffling her further screams.

"Is she hurt?" Cody demanded of Shanna.

"No, just maybe a bruise or two. Nothing's broken."

"What the hell happened? You were supposed to be watching her!"

"We can discuss that inside," Bessie said firmly. "Carry Melinda up to the house and put her in her bed, Cody."

Cody shot Shanna another angry glare before he turned and strode away.

"You better put Chessy up, Toby," Shanna said. "Do you need any help?"

"No, I can do it, Shanna. Gee, he was awful mad. Is Melinda in a bunch of trouble?"

"I'm afraid it's not Melinda who's in trouble, Toby," Shanna sighed.

"That's what you think," Bessie said with a grim tilt to her lips. "What was she doing on that pony anyway? I don't imagine you or Toby let her ride with a saddle not set for her."

"We didn't," Shanna admitted. "She slipped onto Chessy when I wasn't looking. But Cody's right—I should have been watching her closer. Thank goodness she landed in that snowbank."

"Wouldn't have been a need for a snowbank if she'd obeyed," Bessie said. "Wouldn't even have been a fall, for that matter. Good heavens, Shanna, a body can't keep her eyes on a child every second. That's one of the reasons we insist children obey us, so they won't get hurt. And a spoiled child, who thinks she can break the rules and have her own way all the time, is a lot more apt to get hurt than one who listens to her elders."

"Try telling that to your nephew."

"Oh, I will. Don't think I won't." Bessie marched toward the house.

"I better go with her, Toby," Shanna said. "Sure you can handle the pony? He's liable to be a little skittish."

Bittersweet Promises

Toby pulled a sugar lump from his coat pocket. "I'll feed him this and let him calm down a little before I take him into the barn, Shanna."

"Good. And you won't try to ride him anymore, will you?"

"No. I'll just rub him down and put him in the stall."

Confident that Toby, at least, would keep his word, Shanna nodded at him and followed Bessie, her steps a lot more hesitant than the older woman's. At the kitchen door, she kicked the snow from her boots and removed her cloak to shake off the snow still clinging to it from where she had knelt beside Melinda. Straightening her shoulders in preparation for her coming confrontation, she opened the door and stepped inside to hang up her cloak.

Shanna stared around her in astonishment. Melinda was curled up in a rocking chair by the kitchen fireplace instead of in her bed. Cody stood at the stove, stirring something in a pan, and Bessie stood ramrod straight in the center of the kitchen, glaring at him. Tension fairly crackled in the room.

"I'm not going to discuss this in front of Melinda, Cody," Bessie said in a controlled voice. "She needs to be resting in her bed for a while after that fall."

"Soon as I get this chocolate ready, Aunt," Cody replied in the same restrained manner. "She's cold, and this will warm her up."

"Uh . . . I'll go run the warming pan over Melinda's bed," Shanna said quickly, glad of an excuse to escape the kitchen. She crossed to the fireplace to pick up a warming pan hanging beside it and scooped in a few embers.

"Are you feeling all right?" Shanna asked Melinda when she caught the child staring at her.

"I guess so," Melinda said with a shrug of her small shoulders. "And Daddy's gonna get rid of that mean pony. He told me so." A satisfied smile quirked her lips, replacing the pout.

"We'll see about that," Shanna heard Bessie say beside her. "I'll go with you and help turn down the bed, Shanna."

Not daring to tell Bessie that she could manage by herself, Shanna followed the older woman down the hallway and slipped the warming pan beneath the bed covers while Bessie held them up slightly. Silence lingered in the room as Shanna ran the pan around. When she pulled it out, Bessie took the pan from her and set it in the fireplace grate in Melinda's room.

"We'll just leave the door open, so the heat from the rest of the house can get in here for now," Bessie said. "No sense lighting a fire this early."

Shanna gasped and grabbed Bessie's arm when the other woman swayed. "Bessie! Are you all right?"

Bessie shook her head slightly, then placed a hand in the small of her back. "Oh, just a little twinge in my back," she said unconvincingly.

"But you seemed dizzy for a moment."

"Just old age creeping up on me." Bessie patted Shanna's hand. "I'm fine. Don't you worry about me none."

"If you're sure. . . ."

Cody came into the room, Melinda in one arm and a steaming cup in the other. Shanna left Bessie to pull down the covers and stood aside as Cody laid the little girl down. He set the chocolate on the bedside table and began unhooking Melinda's shoes.

"There, sweetheart," he said a moment later as he pulled the covers up. "Now, let's drink your chocolate and I'll tell you a story until you get sleepy."

Bessie and Shanna left the room as Cody spoke. They sat down across from each other at the kitchen table, both suppressing a sigh of resignation.

"He's . . . he's so good with her at times," Shanna said hesitantly. "He loves her very much."

"Spoiling is not love, Shanna. Love includes discipline and teaching, shaping a child into a decent human being."

"I know, but how are you going to convince Cody of that? He's obviously carrying a huge load of guilt because he wasn't here when his wife and parents were killed. Lord, Bessie, his grief must have been terrible—even worse than what I felt at my mother's death. He's trying to assuage some of that guilt with Melinda."

Suddenly it dawned on Shanna that they were alone in the kitchen. "Bessie, where did everyone go?"

"They left while you were with Toby and Melinda. We were all done. They all said to tell you good-bye and that they'll see you in a day or so, soon as you're ready for students."

"Oh. I could probably be ready by tomorrow. All I need now are the books from the barn. I'll probably spend the first day or so finding out how much each child already knows and setting up some loose classes."

"Let's say day after tomorrow, then. You'll want to sort out the books and get a lesson plan ready."

"You sound like you've taught yourself, Bessie."

"Years and years ago," Bessie admitted. "And I know you haven't had any formal training, so maybe I can show you a few shortcuts in planning your lessons."

"I'd appreciate that."

Shanna felt Cody enter the room even before she saw Bessie look over her shoulder. The new carpet that had somehow found its way onto the hall floor must have muffled his booted feet. Her muscles tensed as the atmosphere in the room charged again.

Chapter Ten

"Melinda's asleep." Cody stomped across the floor and set the dirty cup in the sink. "And I want to talk to you, Shanna."

"I'm sure you do," Shanna replied. "Let me get us some coffee first."

Cody stood by the back door and crossed his arms over his chest while he watched her. His grim face foreshadowed the tone of the discussion to come.

Shanna set two cups of coffee on the table and murmured quietly to Bessie, "I can handle this. You should take a nap yourself. I don't like the look of your white face."

"Are you sure?" Bessie asked just as quietly. "I am tired, but...."

"I can't keep hiding behind your skirts, Bessie. Go on."

Bessie gave a weary sigh and rose to her feet. She cast a dark look at Cody. "I'm going to take a nap. But before I go, I want to tell you that Toby's pony better be right there in its stall in the morning. It'll break his little heart if you send it back to the Samuels, and it wasn't his fault Melinda got thrown."

Cody passed a hand over his face and dropped it back to his side. "She could have broken her neck, Aunt," he said in a weary voice.

"She didn't have any business on that pony without her own saddle. She was told that, and she disobeyed Shanna. Instead of hot chocolate, a willow switch might have been more appropriate."

"Is that true, Shanna?" Cody asked, some of the grimness leaving his face.

"It's true," Shanna agreed. "But I should have been watching her closer. I knew in the barn she wasn't happy about not being allowed to ride astride."

"I told her yesterday she couldn't do that!"

"Toby said the same thing."

"I'm going in to bed now, Cody," Bessie said. "Remember what I said about Toby's pony."

"Yes, Aunt." Cody crossed the room and dropped down into a chair. He reached for the coffee cup and blew on it, keeping his eyes centered on the steaming brew and away from Shanna's face.

"I suppose you agree with Aunt Bessie about the willow switch," he said when Shanna kept her silence.

"No," Shanna denied. "I don't believe in hitting children. And I think you know Bessie didn't mean it, either. She was just using that as a way to get her point across."

Cody sipped his coffee, then set the cup down. "Melinda will have to be punished. My God, she *could* have broken her neck and it would have been because she disobeyed. And to top that off, she lied about what really happened. She said you had allowed her to ride Chessy."

"I did tell her she could ride him, but only after we changed the saddles."

He glanced at Shanna. "Since you don't believe in willow switches, how do you discipline Toby?"

"I take something that he really cares about away from him for a while. I've tried all the other ways I've heard of or read about. Sitting him in a corner doesn't bother him. He's got a lively imagination, and he only makes up stories in his mind when he's supposed to be thinking of why he's being punished. The same thing if I send him to his room. He usually sneaks a book as soon as my back's turned, and he's perfectly happy trying to reason out the words he doesn't know while he waits for me to tell him his punishment's over."

"What about extra chores? Or . . . or maybe not allowing Melinda to ride her own pony for a while?"

"There aren't a lot of chores a four year old can do, and Melinda's not real attached to riding, like Toby is. She just wanted to ride Chessy because he was Toby's. That's how I ended up punishing Toby, you know. I wouldn't let him ride for a day or so, however long I felt his disobedience warranted. I think it hurt me as much as it did Toby, though."

"Didn't he drive you crazy, whining to go riding?"

"The first couple times. But I gritted my teeth and added a day to the time he couldn't ride each time he whined. Toby loves horses. I started taking him riding with me when he was barely walking. If he was a little crotchety from teething, I'd just bundle him up and take him for a ride. It always soothed him."

"He's a big help out in the barn for only being nine. He's not afraid to tackle any job I give him, and I never have to show him more than once how to do something."

"I'm glad." Thoughts of how hard Toby had tried to please Christian Van Alstyne crowded Shanna's mind and she frowned. But how wonderful it was now for Toby to have a man like Cody around—someone who praised him and took the time to show him the things a boy needed to know, instead of just shoving him away in irritation.

"I'm a tiny bit jealous," Shanna said with a smile that went straight to Cody's heart. "Toby and I have always been so close, and it's a little hard to let go of him and allow someone else to influence him. You are good with him, though."

"He's an easy boy to like," Cody admitted. "Oh, not that he doesn't get into mischief sometimes. Did I tell you about the time he greased my stirrup loop with saddle soap? I started to step into the saddle and my boot slipped right out and I fell on my a... my rear. Toby was laughing so hard I couldn't stay mad at him. When he could talk, he reminded me that I'd told him to be sure to get the soap on every part of the saddle."

Shanna stifled her own laughter with a gasp as she pictured Cody on his rear end in the barn. "Toby did that? I... I hope you weren't hurt."

"Nah," Cody denied. "And I guess he was just getting back at me for teaching him to be sure to tighten his saddle cinch a second time. Sometimes a horse or pony will blow its stomach up the first time you tighten the cinch and when you step into the saddle, it lets its breath out. 'Course the saddle slides sideways and you end up on your rear end. Chessy did that the first time Toby saddled him."

"Oh dear," Shanna managed to say around her laughter. "And I'll bet you laughed at Toby that time, too."

"Yeah, I sure did. And so did Chessy. That pony wrinkled his lip back and gave a pure horse laugh when he looked down at Toby under his belly. Toby took it like a good sport, though. And he always checks his cinch twice now."

"Toby's having so much fun here. He was always a little too serious before."

"He's been good for Melinda," Cody admitted. "She needed another child around to play with. It's awfully far between farms around here, and don't be surprised if all your students don't show up each day. A lot depends on the weather."

"As hard as everyone worked to get things set up, I'll bet they get here fairly often."

"They will. But, look, we still haven't settled on Melinda's punishment. And here I was, giving her hot chocolate when I should have . . . dessert! That's it. Melinda loves her sweets."

"Yes, she does," Shanna agreed, glad the thought had come to Cody without her prodding.

"She won't have any sweets for a month. That should get it through her mind that she has to obey."

"A . . . a month?" Shanna asked hesitantly. "Maybe a week might be more appropriate."

"A month," Cody said with a decisive nod. "She could have broken—"

"I know," Shanna interrupted. "She could have broken her neck. But do you really have it in you to sit across the table from her for an entire month and watch her face while we eat our desserts and she does without? A week's a very long time to a child her age."

Cody frowned, picturing his small daughter's face in his mind. "You're right," he said with a shiver. "Hell, I don't know if I can stand even a week of that. Maybe a willow switch *would* be faster and get it over with sooner."

"That's not the point. . . ."

"Teasing again, Miss Allen," Cody said with a laugh. "It would kill me if I ever had to lay a hand on Melinda. And now, I've got to get back out to the barn to see about bringing down those books for you. Want to come along?"

"What if Melinda wakes up?"

"She'll sleep for at least an hour or so. She always does. Aunt Bessie insists she take a nap almost every day, but she's been spacing them out lately. She said Melinda's getting old enough to do without her afternoon nap and she'll sleep better at night."

"That's true. Toby stopped napping at three."

Cody got to his feet and handed Shanna her cloak at the kitchen door. "Shanna," he said as he wrapped the cloak around her. "Is Aunt Bessie all right? She didn't look very well, but I thought it was just because we were fighting about Melinda again."

"I think we should keep an eye on her. She had a dizzy spell in Melinda's bedroom."

"Next time Pappy comes over, we'll have him take a look at her."

"I thought he didn't practice anymore."

"He still remembers all his doctor training. That's another thing the hanging didn't force out of his brain."

"Hummm. That and his manly urges, huh?" Shanna turned blue eyes sparkling with mischief up to his face.

Cody stifled a groan as the heat rushed into his groin, and he barely managed to echo the teasing lilt in Shanna's voice. "You're learning, Miss City Girl. Why, we might make a country girl out of you yet."

"You've got a little less than six months to do it," Shanna told him as they walked through the snow. "I promised Bessie I'd stay at least that long. I have to admit, though, it's very beautiful here, and I have to keep reminding myself that I'm here to do a job. Bessie's so wonderful to me and the rest of the people around here are so friendly and helpful, not snobbish at all. The city's so dirty sometimes, and there's a lot of sad things there. Did you know they even use children in some of their factories?"

"I've heard that," Cody murmured, tucking away in his growing list of clues this latest information Shanna let slip. City, huh? Didn't some people call that town up north in New York just the city? And wasn't that where JT said. . . .

Toby came to an abrupt halt as Shanna and Cody entered the barn, his hesitant gaze on Cody's face. "Is . . . is Melinda all right?"

"She's fine, Toby," Cody told him as he knelt before the boy. "And I know what happened wasn't yours or Shanna's fault, so I don't want you to worry about it. Do you have Chessy all settled in his stall?"

"Uh-huh. I rubbed him down and gave him a little grain."

"Good boy. You're a fine horseman, son. Not only do you ride like you were born to the saddle, you take care of your mount."

Cody returned Toby's smile when he beamed with pleasure, then rose to his feet. "Now," he said as he clasped a hand on Toby's shoulder. "I'll bet you're getting cold. I made Melinda some hot chocolate and left some in the pan to stay warm on the stove for you. Shanna and I are going up in the hayloft to get some books for her classes. Why don't you go on in and get your chocolate?"

"How soon is school going to start, Shanna?" Toby questioned.

"Day after tomorrow, Toby."

"Oh."

"Is something wrong, Toby?" Shanna asked. "I thought you enjoyed learning."

"Yeah, I do," Toby replied. "But back home there wasn't much else to do. Everybody did it all for us. Now I've got my own chores and lots of other things to learn."

"Well, young man, your schoolwork comes first."

"I know. Thanks for the chocolate, Cody." Flashing Cody another smile, Toby ran from the barn.

Bittersweet Promises

Shanna shook her head after the retreating figure. "I think I'm going to have a different set of problems with Toby now."

"Maybe so," Cody laughed. "But he's given me an idea about Melinda."

"What's that?"

"I think Melinda's bored. Oh, she helps Bessie out sometimes in the kitchen, but my aunt has such a tussle with her each time that a lot of times Bessie just does things herself. I think Melinda needs her own chores—things she can handle and have a good feeling about doing well. I told you how she loves the animals. She's not too small to feed the chickens or gather the eggs. And one thing she did enjoy last summer was helping me plant garden seeds. It helped her learn to count when she had to know how many seeds to put in each hill."

"Why, that's a wonderful idea."

"And I thought of it all by myself, huh?" Cody teased.

"Yep." Shanna smirked back at him. "We might make a daddy out of you yet."

Shanna turned away from him and started for the ladder leading to the loft. She gasped and whirled back around when she felt a slight sting on her rump.

"Cody Garret, you keep your hands to yourself!"

Cody gave her an innocent smile and shoved his hands behind his back. "I have no earthly idea what you mean."

"Oh, yes, you do!" The giggle that erupted from Shanna's pursed lips belied the sternness of her words and she clasped a hand to her mouth. She really ought to give him a tongue-lashing, but it would shatter the easiness between them and she couldn't bear to do that. Instead, she tried to work her brow into a frown and glare at him.

Cody let out a loud guffaw when her efforts failed. The twinkling blue eyes gave Shanna away and a deep laugh rumbled in his chest. When Shanna dropped her hand and joined his laughter, the feeling that stole over him had nothing to do with the sexual urges he had felt before. This woman was insinuating herself in his life, making him laugh, giving him a companion to talk with about his feelings for his daughter, sharing the minutes of each day.

He was right back in Liberty, he thought as his laughter died. She had exploded into his life, but with a different result from what he had anticipated. The loneliness that had been so much a part of him since he returned from the war had receded to a tiny corner in his mind.

"We better get those books," he told Shanna when she fell silent. "You go first."

"Uh-uh." Shanna shook her head at him, her golden curls shifting around her face. "You go first."

"Gee whiz," Cody said, sounding so much like a disappointed Toby that Shanna smiled again. "You don't trust me."

Shanna giggled and pointed at the ladder. "Up."

"All right. But give me your cloak to carry. You can put it back on at the top. I don't want you to trip on it while you climb."

Shanna walked over to the ladder and removed her cloak. Taking a step back, she handed it to Cody and waited until he had climbed a few steps before she started up. Curious as to what Cody might have seen had he been the second one on the ladder, she glanced up. The denim material tightened around Cody's rump with each step and outlined a bulge on the front of the trousers.

Shanna's foot slipped from the next rung she tried to negotiate and she grabbed the ladder.

"Hey, you aren't afraid of heights, are you?"

Shanna looked up to see Cody peering down at her.

"N-no. Of course not." She determinedly grabbed another rung and resumed her climb.

Bittersweet Promises

At the top, Cody helped her into the loft and started to wrap the cloak around her shoulders. He frowned at her when she quickly pulled the cloak from his hands and shrugged into it herself.

"What's wrong? Oh, I see," he said before Shanna could answer. "I guess you know what happens in haylofts."

"I've never been in a hayloft in my life," Shanna denied, gazing around the shadowy confines.

"But you've read books, huh?" He took a step toward her and lowered his voice. "I'm sure someone at one time or another wrote about the privacy men and women can find in a dark hayloft."

"Speaking of dark," Shanna said with a gasp as she stumbled back and sat down on a hay bale. "Don't you have a lantern up here?"

Cody gave a resigned sigh and walked over to a lantern hung on a peg. He dug in his denim pocket and pulled out a wooden match, striking it on an overhead beam.

"We have to be careful with this up here," he said over his shoulder. "Dry hay goes up in a flash if any spark gets near."

"I understand."

"The books are over here on these shelves my father built. Come on."

Feet sinking into soft hay, Shanna followed him to the far wall of the barn. The next few minutes passed with them opening wooden crates and perusing the books in the lantern light. Shanna found plenty of books for the children to use and stacked them in an empty crate Cody gave her so they could get them down the ladder. She leafed through one book, surprised at not finding it musty from being stored in the barn.

"The loft's built tight," Cody told her, reading the expression on her face. "It has to be, to keep the hay dry, and it's a good place to store other things."

Shanna glanced over at him. "What about the blackboard? And we'll need slates for the children to write on."

Cody pried the nails from another crate and stood up. "I think the slates are in that one. You go ahead and look, while I lower this box to the floor with the rope over there. I'm not about to try to carry this heavy crate down that ladder."

"All right."

While Cody picked up the books, Shanna removed the lid from the newly opened crate. Instead of slates, she found more books and pulled one out to hold it in the lantern light to read the title.

"Law books?" she said to herself. "What in the world is he doing with law books?"

Cody reached over her shoulder and grabbed the book. "That's the wrong crate." He shoved the book back and slammed the lid. "I'll open the other one."

"Whose books are those?" Shanna asked as she watched him work.

"Mine," Cody said shortly.

"Do you plan on reading for the law someday?"

"I already did. Your slates are in here. We'll just take the whole crate down after I get the other one on the floor."

Shanna clamped her mouth shut on her next question. He obviously didn't want to discuss the law books, and she wasn't about to destroy the easy camaraderie between them and start another argument.

Surprising her, Cody sat down on a hay bale and began answering her unspoken questions.

"I read for the law before the war," he said, realizing he wanted her to know about this part of his life. "It was what my father wanted, but I was never really that interested in it. All I wanted to do was farm. When the war finally ended and the plantation was in such a mess,

I decided to settle in here and bring it back to what it should be."

"Did you ever practice at all?"

"For a year or two. I had an office in Liberty with Ned Peters, the man who taught me law. It didn't work out, though. Ned used to yell at me every time a client paid me with a pig or some chickens instead of money. And a lot of times, I didn't even tell him I was helping someone I knew couldn't afford to pay me at all. He found out about a couple of those times, and we almost came to blows."

"That sounds like a wonderful thing to do," Shanna exclaimed. "So many people can't afford to get legal help when they need it."

"Yeah, but it doesn't pay the bills or put money in the bank. I still help people who come by and ask me, though, and nowadays when they give me a pig or chicken, it helps me rebuild the farm."

"Toby would make a good attorney," Shanna mused. "He thinks so logically and he wins more arguments with me than I do with him. But I want him to do whatever he's happy with in his life."

"He's a smart enough little boy to figure that out for himself."

"Well, he's got to get his schooling in first. We better get these things down so I can organize them. And Melinda might be waking up soon."

"Right." Cody grabbed the box with the slates and carried it over to the edge of the loft.

Recalling Cody's cautioning about the lantern, Shanna blew it out before she followed him. She waited while he lowered first one crate, then the other down to the barn floor. Then she walked over to the ladder and stepped for the first rung.

Shanna's foot tangled in her long cloak and she screamed as she teetered on the edge of the loft. A second later, she was on the floor, wrapped in Cody's arms, their fall cushioned by the soft hay beneath them.

"I . . . thank you," Shanna breathed as she stared up at his face, so near to her own that their breath mingled. "I . . . I forgot to take my cloak off."

"Are you all right?" He brushed his index finger against her cheek to remove a piece of clinging hay. "You didn't bruise yourself when we fell?"

"No. Did you?"

"No. Well, maybe one place."

"Where?"

"My lip," he murmured. "I think I caught it on my tooth. Will you kiss it and make it feel better?"

"Q-quit teasing," Shanna gulped. "We. . . ."

"You definitely have a problem knowing when I'm teasing and when I'm serious, Miss Allen," Cody murmured. He lowered his head a fraction of an inch and brushed Shanna's lips with his own.

"Ummm. That feels better."

The feel of the feathery light caress lingered on Shanna's lips, and her breath caught in her throat as she raised a hand to touch her mouth. Her trembling fingers were stilled when Cody caught her hand and held it against his cheek.

"It still hurts a little," he whispered. His kiss lingered a little longer the second time, and the third kiss went on and on as Shanna willingly kissed his pain away.

Shanna buried her hands in Cody's chestnut hair. His lips were so soft, then demanding, then soft again as kiss followed kiss and waves of wonderful feelings swept over her. She didn't protest when Cody shoved her cloak aside and snuggled her against him inside his own sheepskin jacket. His hold on her crushed her breasts against his chest, flattening the pebbled nipples, sending a new wave of heat over her.

Bittersweet Promises

And the bulge Shanna had noticed earlier on the front of his trousers was much larger now, nestling against the juncture of her thighs. A moan of pleasure erupted from Shanna's throat, startling her with its intensity as it echoed in the quiet loft and penetrated her drugged senses.

Shanna wrenched her lips free. "Stop!" she demanded. She pushed against his chest and rolled free when Cody loosened his grip.

"I tried to tell you what could happen to a man and woman alone in a hayloft," Cody said when Shanna scrambled to her knees. "And my lip feels much better now."

"If it starts hurting again, you'll have to find someone else to k-kiss it."

"Why, Shanna? Didn't you enjoy it? You seemed to."

"It doesn't matter what I felt."

"Why?" Cody repeated.

"Because I came down here to find the man I'm going to marry. And you aren't that man."

Chapter Eleven

Shanna recoiled from Cody, horrified that she'd let such vital information slip. Diedre's solicitor had warned her what could happen if Christian Van Alstyne found his wife's lover before Shanna did.

More alarming, though, was the stab of pain coursing through her as she stared at Cody's face, where the teasing glint quickly disintegrated into a stone mask.

"I see," Cody said in a cold voice. "And just why haven't you contacted your fiance to tell him you're here?"

"You *don't* see. He's not ... he's ... I can't discuss it with you. I can assure you that it won't interfere with my caring for Melinda."

"Oh? And just how the hell can I be sure of that? What else have you lied to me about?" Cody fired another staccato question, ignoring her outraged attempt to interrupt. "Damn it, was I right when I brought up how Toby acts more like your son than your brother? Is Toby really your son—the child of your fiance?"

Bittersweet Promises

Shanna scrambled to her feet, prepared to defend herself against Cody's despicable allegations, only to see him climbing down the ladder.

"I haven't lied to you, damn it!" she called after him, fighting tears and choking on her words. "I have good reason not to tell anyone why I'm in Missouri. And you can *assume* any damned thing you want, Cody Garret, but you'll be assuming wrong! You better not say something like that to Toby or I'll . . . somehow I'll make sure you regret it!"

Cody jumped from the last rung of the ladder and glared back up.

"I wouldn't dream of shattering a blameless child's illusions. However, having someone of questionable moral character teaching my daughter is another matter. I'll give you a couple days to think about it, but I want a full explanation by then. Otherwise, I'll have a talk with Aunt Bessie!"

With Shanna standing in the shadowy loft as she was, Cody couldn't see the tears on her face, but he couldn't ignore the agonized panic in her voice. When she whirled from the edge of the loft, he reached out a hand to climb up the ladder, his anger turning to torment as he thought of her crying alone in the darkness.

And, hell, in a corner of his mind he had known even as he hurled the words at her that they couldn't be true. Shanna hadn't kissed him like a woman experienced in love, though, if he'd held on to that dastardly temper of his a moment longer, he might have changed that. Why had her words goaded him into such stupid retaliation?

Now wasn't the time to talk to her—not with both their tempers so hot—not when he had climbed down the ladder to stifle the urge to shake her silly. He damned sure couldn't trust himself up there in the dark alone with her right now, especially with the green pangs of jealousy so close to the surface of his emotions. Especially with the taste of her lips and the feel of her pliant body still lingering. And, most especially, not with the words of love he came so close to uttering still ringing persistently in his mind.

Love? Like hell!

Cody shook his head vehemently. Hell, he'd only known her a little over a week. Admiration, yes, and respect. He wasn't sure just when his prickly defense at her interference in his life had changed to reluctant admiration and respect as he watched her tackle any task set before her. His eyes were always drawn unerringly to her whenever he encountered her, surrounded by either a bunch of children or a group of women, chattering easily while they sewed curtains or dished up a meal for the men.

He had come to look forward to her presence at supper, a meal now an enjoyable experience of shared conversations of the day just past, rather than a dogged fight between Bessie and Melinda as to how much Melinda would eat before she got dessert. How easy that had been—allowing Melinda to choose her own portions from the bowls and platters on the table. Last night, she had even asked for a second helping of mashed potatoes.

And sexual desire—definitely he felt a desire to possess Shanna's delectable body. That was all it was when he reached down to brush that piece of hay from her flushed and rounded cheek in the dim light, drawn by her eyes misty with unleashed passion and lips pouting for his kisses. Hell, he'd fought that urge before when necking with a woman—his thrusting manhood yearning for the secret pocket of moist pleasure that could send both him and his partner into such a frenzy.

He'd never given in to the empty promises of love other men used to gain access to sexual coupling without ending up bound by a marriage band. And he wouldn't do it now—especially since Shanna was obviously saving that lush body for some other man! Hardening his heart, Cody strode out of the barn, the echoes of Shanna's muffled sobs following him.

That evening, Bessie passed around pieces of the pie she had made from the last of the dried apples, carefully perusing each face as she set the dessert down. She made a matter-of-fact effort to ignore Melinda's mutinous pout when she bypassed the little girl's plate, but the other figures at the table each cast a surreptitious look at the little girl. Instead of digging into their pie, they each took a small, polite bite and began pushing the pie around on the plates.

Except for Toby, Bessie realized with a smile. After his first bite, he glanced somewhat guiltily at Melinda and dug in with unrestrained ardor.

"May I be excused, Daddy?" Melinda asked after a moment.

"Go ahead, child," Bessie finally answered when she realized Cody wasn't even going to acknowledge Melinda's good manners. "But take your plate to the sink first and rinse it off."

"Yes, ma'am." After one last, longing glance at the pie still on the table, Melinda slid from her chair and picked up her plate.

Bessie scraped her own untouched pie back and pushed the pan toward Shanna and Cody.

"If you two don't want your pie, put it back and we'll save it for tomorrow night. I just don't know what's going on around here. I baked that pie as a celebration for the school getting started, but the atmosphere around this table tonight sure doesn't do justice to my efforts!"

"Excuse me," Cody said, shoving his chair back. "I'm going out to finish the evening chores."

"I'll be there in a minute, Cody," Toby called after Cody's retreating back.

"Take your time, son," Cody replied distractedly. He jerked his coat from the hook on the wall and let the door slam behind him.

Toby shoveled his last bite of pie into his mouth, then glanced apprehensively at Shanna while he chewed the morsel of pastry. When Shanna didn't notice his too-full mouth, instead continuing to toy with a chunk of apple on her plate, he swallowed and slipped from his chair.

"Excuse me?" Toby directed his request to Bessie, while Shanna cut the chunk of apple into ever smaller fragments.

Bessie nodded, and Toby gathered his dirty plate and utensils to carry to the sink, where Melinda still stood on a chair she had pulled up in order to reach the pan of water left for the dishes.

Surprising Toby, Melinda reached for his plate. "I'll rinse it, Toby," she said in a small voice. "Was . . . was the pie good?"

"Best I ever ate," Toby said honestly. "Maybe Aunt Bessie will make another one when you can have some."

"I hope so," Melinda said, scraping his plate into a bowl of scraps for the chickens. "Toby, I . . . I'm sorry I rode your pony without per-permish. . . ."

"It's all right. I'm just glad you didn't get hurt too bad."

"I . . . I was scared when Chessy ran and I couldn't stop him."

"Bet you were," Toby said sympathetically. "Next time, we'll put your own saddle on and make sure you've got a good seat first."

"Thanks, Toby."

A few minutes later, Shanna gave a start, eyeing the empty table before looking around the room. She found

Bittersweet Promises

Bessie at the sink, dipping plates into a pan of hot water to rinse them.

"I'm sorry, Bessie. Where on earth is everyone?"

"Melinda asked if she could go out and help Toby and Cody with the chores."

"Then at least let me finish those dishes," Shanna said as she crossed to the sink.

"I'm just about done. You better get busy on your lessons. I'll be in to help you, soon as I dry these."

The stern set of Bessie's mouth told Shanna any further attempt to assist would be met with a cold shoulder. Reluctantly, she turned and walked into the parlor.

She couldn't really blame Bessie, she thought as she settled into the chair behind the desk, now polished to a high sheen. Her distraction that afternoon while she helped prepare the evening meal had exasperated Bessie. At one point, Bessie had grabbed the salt container from Shanna's hand when Shanna started to shake it over the apples instead of the cinnamon Bessie had told her to use.

Shanna didn't have much more luck now in focusing her thoughts. After scribbling a couple lines, she pushed the lesson book aside and leaned back in the chair. Staring at the dark window beyond the lantern light, she noticed streaks of moisture running down the pane. It must be thawing out—at least the children would have no trouble getting to school the day after tomorrow.

Instead of the thought cheering her, as it would have earlier today, Shanna blinked her eyes in an attempt to keep her face from tracking like the window. How on earth was she going to be able to concentrate on teaching a classroom full of children with her own life in such a turmoil? Would she even be here the day school started—or would Cody insist she leave? If he did, how would he explain it to all the parents, who were depending upon her to teach their children?

And, why, oh why, did the remembrance of those soft, then demanding, stirring kisses in the barn overshadow all her worries about everything else?

It would have been so easy to yield to that heady desire. In fact, she admitted, she had for a time, drinking in that exhilarating pleasure, straining for more, realizing she had been longing for more of his kisses ever since the first one at the hotel.

Why had she found the one man who could satisfy her craving to experience complete womanhood now? Why did he have to be a man so good with Toby? With such tempting kisses—hands callused by his work, but gentle, yet strong, whether he was soothing a hurt child or caring for a new colt—or tracing circles on her back, spreading sensual ecstasy through her veins and a gluttonous desire for more pounding through her mind.

How could only being with him for one short week change her absolute certainty that he was an overbearing, arrogant oaf to the knowledge that only Cody Garret could fill the dim image in her mind of a man to share her life completely—a father for the children she yearned for—a man with whom she could grow old and gray, until they retired to twin rocking chairs and watched their grandchildren grow?

Somehow even the hostility she sensed for years between her mother and father hadn't quelled Shanna's dreams. Somewhere out there waited her own knight in shining armor, whom she could love wholeheartedly.

Even before Toby's birth, Shanna and her girlhood friends discussed the men they would eventually marry. Tall and handsome, of course. Some favored dark, but the description varied depending upon which of the young swains caught their eyes at the most recent soiree. Smuggled love stories made the rounds, read under covers and hidden beneath mattresses. The stories told just what to expect when they finally experienced that wonderful passion called love.

Bells ringing, shortness of breath, actual swooning. Shanna silently shook her head at the childish, girlhood fantasies. But one by one her friends succumbed to what they insisted was love. As young as 16 they married, and surely by 18, each casting pitying looks at Shanna as they asked her again and again to be an attendant. And almost all changed their pity to a begrudging envy within a year or two after their marriage.

"That's why I know love doesn't work. Why my dreams were false," Shanna murmured quietly. "That's why I can do this for Toby. It's better this way. It will be an arrangement, and no one will ever be able to take Toby away from me. I don't need love—lots of people live without it."

Cody's fist froze before it could make contact with the parlor door and announce his presence. He waited silently, knowing he was unabashedly eavesdropping, but unable to tear himself away. She looked so small and fragile sitting behind that large desk, lantern light casting shadows around her face and shoulders. As he watched, her shoulders slumped and Shanna laid her head on her arms.

"Do you want to talk about it?"

Shanna jerked upright. Battling the threatening tears, she stared at Cody standing in the doorway, outlined in a misty aura of light. Though she knew the aura was an illusion, caused by the unshed tears, she couldn't stop the fleeting impression of her knight finally appearing from dancing across her mind.

But . . . how much had he heard? Did she really speak aloud, or were the thoughts only in her mind?

"What do you want?"

"I was passing by. You looked upset."

"I didn't hear you come in."

"Stepped in some muck in the barn and left my boots on the porch until I could clean them. Aunt Bessie would have run me back outside with a broom, if I'd come in smelling like I was."

Cody started to step into the parlor and Shanna held up a hand. "Don't. You gave me two days to make up my mind, and you have no right to push me. And if I'm upset, maybe you ought to look in the mirror and see who upset me."

"Then at least be honest with yourself that it's not the possibility of love that's bothering you, Shanna," Cody said quietly before he turned and walked down the hallway to his room.

Shanna gripped the edge of the desk until her knuckles whitened. "You're so wrong, Cody Garret," she whispered. "That's exactly what's bothering me."

"Well." Bessie bustled into the parlor. "Are we ready to get started on those lessons?"

"Let's leave them until morning, Bessie," Shanna said in a tight voice. "I'm not really in the mood to make the effort just now."

"You're probably right. It's been a long day, and we'll be more productive when our minds are fresh. Or... Shanna, do you want to talk?"

"No! I mean... I'm sorry. I didn't mean to shout. But please, Bessie, not just now."

"All right. Good night, Shanna."

"Good night. I'll go to bed as soon as I straighten this desk."

She lingered, though, long after each article on the desk lay in pinpoint precision to the one beside it. She finally blew out the lone lantern left glowing and settled again into the chair behind the desk. She would only toss and turn, disturbing Toby, if she tried to fall asleep now, and she didn't want Bessie to glance into the hallway and see the parlor still lit. She needed some privacy for a while to sort through her thoughts and come up with some sort of solution to her dilemma.

But no matter how she twisted and wrestled with the matter, there was just one answer. Her mother's letter had only begged Shanna to find the man Diedre was sure would love Toby. Accept him, offer him a life far removed from the coldness and neglect—sometimes even cruelty—Toby suffered from Shanna's father. The marriage was her own plan—necessitated by what she considered a totally heartless statute of law.

She could never let Toby go. She loved him more than she ever thought possible to love anyone, more even than she had loved her mother—as much as she could imagine she would love the shadowy children she might one day have herself.

The only solution—granted, a tentative one offered by her mother's trusted solicitor during Shanna's surreptitious visit—was for Shanna to share Toby with his true father. To marry, so Shanna would have her own legal claim to Toby as the man's wife, if he did indeed gain custody of his son. No one could ever take Toby away from her then.

She had to find that man. Toby was depending upon her to thwart Christian Van Alstyne's attempt to banish his wife's love child from his life. She had to show Toby's father the other letter her mother had left, addressed to him.

She hadn't dared pry into that letter, leaving it sealed over what were assuredly her mother's most private feelings. She had to have faith that Deidre wouldn't place Toby's entire future in the hands of a man who would turn his son away—that the man her mother's letter assured Shanna was a kind, loving and considerate man, the one man Deidre had truly loved, would be the answer to Toby's future.

So many unanswered questions remained, though. Why hadn't the man contacted Diedre in all these years? Or had he and her mother remained somehow in secret contact? If they had, why hadn't her mother's letter given Shanna more information than just the man's name and where he had lived when Diedre had her affair with him?

And what would this man be like, ten years later? Would he be the same kind, considerate person? Or would he have changed, the way most of her friends' husbands seemed to change as they aged?

Shanna's one last hole card was her trust fund, set up by her mother before Toby's birth—probably when Diedre first suspected she was with child, Shanna realized now. Her grandmother's will had left her entire estate to Diedre, and Shanna well remembered the conversation her mother and father had had after the reading of the will.

Christian Van Alstyne, in the presence of the solicitor, had assured Diedre she could do as she wished with the inheritance, that he had no need of his wife's money to keep up their affluent life-style. Probably, Shanna comprehended with her added years of experience, it was a pompous gesture on her father's part in front of the solicitor, but Diedre took him at his word and hired her own attorney to draw up the trust.

She had sat Shanna down afterward and explained the document to her, pointing out the parts that even Shanna's young mind could tell were written in irrevocable terms. Showing Shanna, too, her father's signature on the document, agreeing to the terms.

Shanna could hear her mother's soft voice echoing down through the years, telling her that Diedre was sure Shanna would share if she ever had a little brother or sister. Saying that she wasn't going to put that part in the document, that she would trust Shanna to do what

Bittersweet Promises

was right, if that ever came into being.

Despite all the other unanswered questions in Shanna's mind, one thing she was sure of. Her mother had meant that money to take care of her second child. How could her mother ever have known that the money would always be secondary to Shanna? Shanna's love for Toby would always be the most important thing in her life—the money only a means to keep her small brother at her side. But she couldn't touch that money until she was 21, almost six months from now.

Her mother's own, handwritten will would also help somewhat, Diedre's trusted solicitor had assured Shanna at the private meeting he had requested with her shortly after Diedre's death. The will admitted that Toby was not her husband's child, and in it Diedre gave guardianship of the boy to her lover. That and Toby's birth certificate were enough to base a custody fight on—though it could turn into a nasty, scandalous battle, he warned Shanna.

He went on to explain that there were no guarantees—that the judge would have to interpret the law, along with deciding what was in Toby's best interest. But Shanna had no choice, since she had no legal claim to Toby herself.

She remembered the solicitor's grim face as he told her that he knew how Shanna must have felt when she realized her father intended to banish Toby to a permanent boarding school and totally abandon him, allowing not even Shanna to contact him. Diedre had obviously confided everything to this man, more than even Shanna knew herself. He told her that he was fully aware of the type of man her father was, and that his heart bled for Toby. Only Diedre had stood between her husband and Toby while she lived, but now that Diedre was dead, Van Alstyne had a clear field to do whatever he wanted with the boy.

Shanna had felt the man's pain and wondered for a moment if the solicitor's feelings for her mother had perhaps gone beyond the bounds of their business relationship. But the thought quickly passed as she realized how powerless she was against her father under the law.

She had leaned forward and pounded on the man's desk, telling him how much she loved Toby and how much Toby loved her. It wasn't right for a stupid law to take precedence over people's feelings for each other.

He was so sorry, he had told her, but her mother, knowing the state of her health, had done everything she could possibly do to assure Toby's future. She had left the will and the birth certificate—and her trust in the man who had fathered Toby. Her little brother's real father was the only one who could ask for custody of his son.

After a moment's silence, Shanna had found the courage to voice the question in her mind. She watched the solicitor's face cloud over as he shook his head and told her that her mother had absolutely no intention for something like Shanna proposed to ever take place. But when pressed, he admitted that there were no legal statutes against Mr. Randolph—her mother's lover—marrying Shanna, since there was no blood relationship between them. And, yes, Mr. Randolph would have a better chance at custody if he had a wife, and Shanna would be able to remain close to her brother.

As she rose to leave, refusing to even consider the thought that Mr. Randolph might already have another after ten years, the solicitor had stopped her to tell her one last thing. Shanna was to have Mr. Randolph contact the solicitor if and when she found him. There was something else he needed to discuss with Randolph—something he wasn't at liberty to divulge to Shanna, under orders from her mother. He refused to even answer

Shanna's question as to whether this information would assist in the custody fight.

She didn't pressure him further—she had already started formulating her plans to do everything in her power to thwart her father.

What she hadn't counted on was finding her own love during her search for Toby's father, and the heartbreaking choice she faced now.

Shanna frowned as a noise broke her concentration. A horse approached the house, though the hoofbeats were muffled by the noise from the rain now pounding on the roof. She rose and crossed silently to the window to draw back the curtain. Just as the rider passed the corner of the house, a flash of lightning split the sky, illuminating the crouched figure in a streaming poncho.

Shanna glanced at the huge clock a neighbor had hung on the wall by the window. Good heavens, it was after midnight. She'd been sitting lost in thought for hours. Who could be arriving so late?

A shadow slipped by the parlor door and Shanna froze beside the window. No mistaking that shape—Cody had heard the rider, too, and was hurrying to the kitchen door. And weren't his movements sort of furtive? He had glanced into the parlor, but her dark gown blended with the curtain and Cody missed seeing her standing there.

Hearing the kitchen door open, Shanna silently glided across the room and stood just inside the parlor door, waiting for Cody to light a lantern. Instead, she heard a grunt of recognition from Cody, then a murmur of low voices and a log being tossed into the kitchen fireplace. Shrugging, Shanna started down the hallway toward her room. It probably wasn't anything to concern her.

Cody's raised voice halted Shanna in her tracks. Bank robbery? Did he say something about the robbery?

Shanna turned back and stopped in the shadows beside the kitchen doorway.

Chapter Twelve

The two men stood in front of the fireplace, their silhouettes outlined by flames licking around the new log. The stranger was shorter than Cody, but much the same in build. He shook his slicker over the hearth, drops of rain sputtering into steam when they hit the flames.

"Well, I don't much give a damn whether you want the money or not, Cody. What do you expect me to do? Turn myself in?"

"That would be a start."

"Believe me," the shorter man said with a tired sigh, "I've thought about it. I was an ass to get mixed up in something like this and I knew it as soon as it was over with. It sounded like a good idea at the time. We'd take the money and give it back to the farmers, who need it to get their places back into shape. Only thing is the money got divided up, and there wasn't that much when it was cut all those ways."

"Come on, Johnny. There were thousands in that bank."

Bittersweet Promises

"Like hell. Or, if there was, it never all got put on the sharing block!"

"Did it ever occur to you that the money already belonged to those very people you were trying to steal it from and give it back to? I had my own money in the Liberty bank, since we don't have one in Kearney."

"I told you, that's why I'm here. All I'm keeping is enough to get me to Texas. I know you recognized me in Liberty when we rode in and, God, Cody, you've got to believe me. I didn't know anyone would get killed."

"I suppose you thought they'd just hand the money over and thank you for taking it off their hands!"

"Keep your voice down," Johnny muttered. "I don't want Grandma to know I've been here."

"Yeah. It sure wouldn't do her health any good to know her favorite grandson was a bank robber with the band of men who killed George Wymore. Damn it, Johnny, George was a divinity student!"

"It wasn't me who killed him! It was. . . ." Johnny quickly shut his mouth. "Has Grandma been sick?"

"She's old, Johnny. She does as much around here as she can—more than anyone has a right to expect her to at her age. We finally hired someone to help with Melinda."

"I heard that. Hear she's mighty pretty."

"You must be in pretty close contact to still hear the news. Who else was in that gang?"

"You don't want to know that, Cody. And you won't find out from me. Too many families will get hurt like Grandma if it gets out."

Cody studied Johnny for a moment in the dim light. He had a pretty good idea who the rest of the robbers were, anyway. He knew who Johnny's friends were—a few of them the same as his own used to be. He had to know about one certain man, though, because he meant to find him and ask him some questions. Not about the bank robbery, however.

"Just tell me one thing, Johnny, and I give you my word I'll let you leave here, as long as you give me your word in return that you'll go to Texas and go straight from now on!"

"That's a promise I'll make on my mother's grave, Cody. I never want anything to do with the outlaw life again. Most of the other guys feel the same way, but I'm afraid there's gonna be a few who keep on."

"They'll get caught, Johnny. And if I ever get word that you've changed your mind, I'll find you myself and turn you in, no matter what the consequences. There's only one reason I'm even considering letting you leave, instead of hauling your ass in to Dan. That's Aunt Bessie."

"I understand."

"Then take this chance and make good with it," Cody said in a cold voice. "Get your ass out of Missouri and don't look back. But first, tell me if JT was with you."

"JT? Naw, you can't get him to leave that place he set up for himself. Hell, he's almost a hermit. He did let us stay there for a while, but I'll bet we didn't see him more than twice the whole time."

"Did you talk to JT at all?"

"A little. He's still bitter—nothing like the man he was before the war. Guess that damned war did things like that to some men."

"Some of us faced up to the changes in our lives and went on," Cody said in an acrid voice. "Even after we lost almost everything."

"Guess JT figured when he lost his leg it was too much, on top of everything else," Johnny mused. "And hell, there wouldn't have been a woman who would even look at him after what that fire did to his face."

"He's still got his mind. There's a lot of good he could do with it. He was always the smartest one of the whole bunch of us, and there wasn't a better officer on the battlefield. Or a braver one."

"Yeah, Cody. And that bravery's what got him into the shape he's in now. Your own hide was one he saved that day. I think we owe it to JT to leave him in peace and let him live his life out the way he wants."

"I may not be able to do that, Johnny. But you better get out of here now. Aunt Bessie sometimes wakes up in the night and wanders around, when her arthritis kicks up."

Johnny shrugged into his slicker and walked over to the door. "Cody," he said as he paused. "If things work out right, I want to start writing Grandma to let her know I'm getting my life together. I don't want her to think I just disappeared—that I don't love her."

"If things work out the right way, I won't stand in the way of that, Johnny."

Cody stared at the closed door a long while before he walked over to the kitchen table and picked up a small sack. The contents jingled as he tossed the sack from one hand to the other. When Shanna stepped into the room, the sack fell to the floor with a muffled clank.

"I guess you've got money to send Toby and me away now, don't you?" Shanna asked in a quiet voice. "That is, if you aren't afraid I'll tell everyone where you got that money."

"How long have you been standing there?"

"Since Johnny first came in the door. I heard everything said between you two."

A lightness filled Cody's heart, but he resolutely kept his face muscles from giving in to the smile tugging at them. It was the perfect opportunity for him to back down from his careless threat to send her away and still save face. As long as Shanna thought she had him over a barrel about knowing one of the bank robbers, she would stay, and he had little doubt that she would actually tell Aunt

Bessie what she knew. Shanna cared for Bessie—almost as much as he did—and Cody couldn't bring himself to believe that Shanna would deliberately break Bessie's heart. It wasn't in his best interests to let Shanna know his thoughts just now, though.

"I suppose it's a standoff then," Cody said instead. "You can stay and teach the children, Melinda included. I'll quit pushing you to tell me what you're hiding, as long as you keep my secret."

"Agreed," Shanna said with a nod.

Cody retrieved the sack of money from the floor. With a glance at Shanna, he walked over to the fireplace and pried out one of the stones near the top. He shoved the money inside and replaced the stone before he turned back to her.

"If you change your mind on your own about leaving, you know where the money is."

Shanna returned his gaze for a long moment. He had given in too easily. This wasn't the Cody Garret she had come to know and lo . . . know and argue with, her mind quickly corrected. Any agreement between them had always only come after a prolonged sniping and jabbing session, which finally settled into a mature discussion. There hadn't been any sniping and jabbing this time, only a strangely abrupt capitulation from Cody.

She was too tired to worry about it tonight. She turned down the hallway. "Yes," she called back. "I know where it is."

The money was the last thing on Shanna's mind over the next month, and even her own problems had to take a backseat as she found her days filled to overflowing. Each morning she rose before dawn to help Bessie with breakfast. Long after Bessie and the children went to bed, she worked on her school plans, paying special attention to each child's needs.

Bittersweet Promises

Never had she been around a group of children so eager to learn. She didn't give a thought to the fact that maybe her own enthusiasm and consideration stirred them. There was so much she wanted them to know and more than one child lingered inside to take his or her lunch with Shanna at the noontime recess.

The days outside slowly changed from stark black and white to green and gold, lit by the springtime sun thawing the ground and renewing the soil for planting. Shanna glanced out the kitchen window one morning before classes to see Cody leading a pair of huge horses from the barn.

"Better get ready to start losing some of your older boys, Shanna," Bessie said beside her. "It's going to be plowing time in a couple weeks, and they'll be needed at home."

"But we just got started!"

"Can't be helped. The fields have to be planted if we expect to have foodstuff to last through the winter. The seasons don't wait for school to let out."

"I suppose. I have had a little trouble with the children staring out the windows the last couple days."

"Spring fever," Bessie said with a nod. "Felt a little bit of it myself lately, though I think it's just time for my spring tonic."

"Bessie, I wish you wouldn't work so hard."

"Pshaw, Shanna. You barely let me do anything around here anymore. Why, you start cleaning as soon as the children leave in the afternoon and do your lessons after I go to bed. Don't think I don't appreciate how much help you've been."

Shanna studied Bessie as the elderly woman walked over to the table and began setting out plates. Bessie hadn't protested when Shanna took over more and more of the household chores, merely letting each of them foster the illusion that Shanna wanted to learn to do them. Shanna now built the kitchen fires and the one in the potbellied stove in the parlor, though she hadn't needed that one the last several days. Shanna and Melinda churned the cream skimmed from the milk into butter and rolled out a pie crust or mixed up a cake each afternoon, while Bessie gave advice from the rocking chair.

Toby disappeared to the barn after classes were over and spent a quiet hour with Melinda evenings after their meal, doing the assigned lessons for the next day. She wasn't exactly sure what kept Cody and Toby so busy outside, but at least it kept her and Cody from running into each other constantly.

"You know, Bessie," Shanna mused, "I wonder if the children realize how much their lives depend on the planting and growing seasons. I think today might be a good time to start explaining it to them."

"Why don't you go out and see what Cody has planned for today? Maybe there might be a lesson in that, especially for the younger children."

"Maybe for the older boys, too. Why, they're so close to the land, they probably take it for granted sometimes. Or they just look on it as more work for them. I don't think they realize what an integral part of our lives nature is. I didn't, before I came out here."

"And an outside lesson will keep you from having to rap their fingers with a ruler when you see them staring out the window."

"Oh, I don't. . . ."

"I'm only funning, Shanna. Why, I've never seen a teacher have so few problems with a roomful of children. Sometimes I sit in the kitchen and listen to you. It makes me almost wish I could be back in school. Now, go on out there and see what you can cook up for a surprise lesson today."

Glowing with the praise from Bessie, Shanna picked up the light shawl she had taken to wearing instead of her cloak and went out the door. A brilliant sunrise was just now fading in the eastern sky and she paused a moment to drink in the beauty.

"Mighty pretty, isn't it?"

Shanna started at Cody's soft voice. He'd been so very polite this last month when they did happen to find themselves alone together—overly so.

"Yes, it's beautiful," she acknowledged. "I'm usually so busy in the mornings that I don't have time to enjoy the sunrise."

"You're doing a fine job. All the parents have said so. But you need to take a few minutes to yourself now and then. All work and no play. . . ."

"Oh, but there's so much I want the children to know," Shanna interrupted. "Bessie just told me some of my students may have to drop out to help at home, and we've only scratched the surface. Anyway, that's one reason I wanted to talk to you. I was wondering how you'd feel about the children following you around today."

"Following me? What for?"

"To teach them about spring and renewal," Shanna said as she glanced up at him, her blue eyes mirroring her excitement. "I don't think they realize what a wonderful thing the changing of the seasons is. I'd like them to get a new perspective on their lives and see them not as just a boring repetition of chores and lessons. Why, if not for the farmers planting the land each spring, the people in the towns and cities wouldn't have anything to eat."

"Sounds like a good idea. And I'm sure the parents will bless you for giving the children a little enthusiasm for their chores. Tell you what, let's make a day of it. You can have the children bring their lunches with them, and we'll ride over the plantation while I explain to them what we'll be doing around here in a week or so. There's a pretty spot out by one of the creeks where the spring beauties are already up, and we can eat lunch there."

"Ride? Well, I guess so. Some of the children ride to school and we can double them up. But I don't have a mount."

"Sure you do. Brownie needs to start getting out for some exercise."

"But the colt?"

"Starlight? He can tag along, since we won't be going very fast. Do you have some riding clothes?"

Shanna thought of the fine habit hanging in her closet. It was awfully fancy for a ride at a country plantation, but it was the only one she had brought with her.

"Yes," she said. "I'll go change before breakfast."

"I'm glad you asked me to do this today," Cody told her. "Tomorrow I have to go into Liberty to arrange for the seed I need for planting. I'll probably be gone overnight."

"Oh, but when you took the wagon back, you made the trip in one day."

"Will you miss me, Shanna?" Cody asked in a teasing voice. "Would you like to go along? You could use a break, and the children wouldn't mind a day off school."

"Of . . . of course not," Shanna denied stoutly. "I'll help Toby with the chores tomorrow evening, if you'll have him tell me what needs to be done."

"That won't be necessary. I've asked one of the older boys in your class to stay over for a while after school that day. And he'll come early the next morning to help out."

"Then it's all arranged," Shanna said as she turned toward the house. "I'll go change."

Cody watched her walk away, a contemplative look on his face. Which one of his questions had sent her hand fluttering to her throat in agitation—his asking if she would miss him or if she wanted to go into town? As far as he knew, she hadn't made any attempt to contact her supposed fiance, unless he could count the questions some of the parents had told him she asked now and then when they lingered after picking up the younger children.

So far, though, she hadn't mentioned any specific names and had explained away her interest in the families living in the area by saying there was room in her class for more children. It seemed the natural curiosity of a person new in an area, especially a teacher who would want to pass the land's history on to her students.

Maybe he should extend his trip an extra couple days to have time to make the side trip he'd been planning. In another week or so, after the land dried out a little more, he wouldn't be able to leave the plantation even overnight. His days and evenings would be filled with plowing and planting, if he expected to have a decent crop this year.

Chapter Thirteen

Shanna pushed aside the riding habit she had brushed out and hung in her closet the night before, trying without much success to stifle the memory of Cody's admiring look when he helped her onto Brownie's back yesterday morning. The close-fitting garment would really need to be altered before she wore it again. She hadn't realized how much her active life had changed her body. The sleeves fit tighter over the new muscles she had developed in her arms from kneading bread and helping Melinda churn. Her corset would have been superfluous on her slender waist, since she'd had to fold the skirt band over a good inch and pin it. At least the long jacket had hidden her alteration.

"Shanna, are you going to wear your riding habit again today?"

"Come on in, Melinda. No, I'm not. Would you like to help me pick out my dress for today?"

"Yes. Wear the blue one," Melinda said as she came

over to the closet. "Daddy thinks you look so pretty in that color."

"Why, Melinda," Shanna said in a flustered voice, "what makes you say that?"

"I asked him yesterday. He kept looking at you, and I asked him if it was because of how pretty you looked."

"Oh," Shanna said in a small voice.

"I hope I'm as pretty as you when I grow up. I want my eyes to look just like yours. Daddy says they're cornflower blue."

"Your brown eyes are beautiful, Melinda." Shanna drew the blue dress from the hanger. "They're like brown velvet, except when you get excited about something. Then they have sprinkles in them, like stars."

"Oh, that sounds pretty, too. Maybe I do like my brown eyes."

Hearing a noise outside, Melinda glanced through the window in Shanna's room. "Oh, Daddy's going. You don't have to get dressed up now."

Shanna hurriedly hung the blue gown up, then jerked it back down when Melinda ran from the room. She didn't dare let Melinda think there was anything between Cody and her. Where on earth did the child get such ideas?

And Cody was leaving without even breakfast! She had built the fires and made coffee before looking in on Bessie on her way back to her room to dress, finding the elderly woman still fast asleep. She hurriedly donned the blue gown and swept up her hair. Entering the kitchen a moment later, she found both Toby and Melinda breaking eggs into a bowl.

"We're helping fix breakfast, Shanna," Toby told her. "Cody took some of last night's leftovers with him. He said to tell you that he'd be at the hotel in Liberty tonight, but he might not be back tomorrow. It might be a couple more days."

"I appreciate your help this morning, Toby, but don't you have some chores to do?"

"Huh-uh. Cody and I've been up for hours. They're all done."

"Hours, huh?" Shanna rescued the egg bowl just before it tipped onto the floor. "Well, what did you have in mind for breakfast?"

"Johnnycakes!" Melinda and Toby echoed together.

"All right," Shanna said with a laugh. "But I'll take over now. Would you and Melinda like to set the table? I guess Aunt Bessie's tired this morning."

"I am," Bessie said with a grumble as she entered the kitchen. "Looks like everything's in hand here. Maybe someone would fetch me a cup of coffee."

Bessie lowered herself into a chair at the table as Shanna frowned in concern. This wasn't like her at all. Even the mornings Shanna could see Bessie wince in pain from her hands as she stirred johnnycake batter or sliced bacon, Bessie still insisted on not sitting down until breakfast was on the table. Shanna turned to the stove and poured a cup of coffee, handing it to Toby when he reached for it.

"When will Toby and I be old enough to drink coffee, Shanna?" Melinda asked. The little girl stretched her arms out when she saw Shanna reach for the flour canister, almost sliding from her chair as she struggled to shove the container closer.

"Careful, Melinda," Shanna said instinctively. "Tell you what. I'll let you have a spoonful of coffee this morning to see if you like it. Now, would you run into the pantry and get me the baking soda, please?"

After breakfast was over, the day flew by again as usual. If Shanna found herself joining her students as they stared out the window from time to time, she quickly took hold of herself. It was only the spring fever Bessie spoke of, even if her eyes did stray to the road to Liberty

Bittersweet Promises

now and then. Distracted as she was, she barely noticed Bessie only picking at her supper and willingly agreed when Toby suggested he and Melinda do the dishes while Bessie gave instructions from the rocking chair.

Shanna smiled at the two children by the sink and decided to take this opportunity to work on her lessons a little earlier than usual. Barely five minutes later, she heard Melinda scream in the kitchen.

"Shanna! Oh, Shanna, help!"

Visions of blood streaming from a cut hand or arm filled Shanna's mind as she scrambled from her chair. Why, oh why, had she thought the children old enough to handle the sharp knives and wash them? She raced into the kitchen, her eyes flying to the sink to find it empty.

"Over here, Shanna!" Toby cried.

Shanna ran to the rocking chair, where Bessie sat with her head slumped on her chest. Heart pounding in fear, she knelt before Bessie and heard a moan issue from Bessie's throat.

"Bessie. Dear God, Bessie, what's wrong?"

"R-Reuben," Bessie managed to gasp. "Get Pappy."

Cody! Oh, God, Cody, why aren't you here? Shanna's mind cried. Quickly she stifled the silent plea.

"Can you make it to your bed, Bessie?" she asked as calmly as she could manage.

"D-don't th-think s. . . ."

Shanna scrambled to her feet. "Toby, go saddle Brownie with one of the saddles that has two stirrups, not a sidesaddle. Can you handle it?"

"Yes, Shanna." The small boy ran for the door and Shanna turned to Melinda.

"Melinda, fetch the comforter from Bessie's bed. Don't mind if it drags on the floor. And bring a pillow."

Melinda raced away and Shanna knelt again to take

169

Bessie's gnarled hand in hers. "What is it, Bessie? Your heart?"

Bessie managed to nod her head and it fell against the rocking chair back. Shanna chafed her hand gently and was grateful when she heard Melinda returning.

"I couldn't carry both, Shanna. But I'll go back and get the pillow." Melinda threw the comforter down beside Shanna and raced off again.

Shanna spread the comforter and gently managed to move Bessie from the rocking chair to the floor, surprised at how easy it was. Bessie felt no heavier than a newborn kitten in her arms. Shanna loosened the top buttons on Bessie's dress and shot a thankful look at Melinda when she returned with the pillow.

"Now, please get another comforter to put over her, Melinda."

Shanna lifted Bessie's head onto the pillow, noting her blue lips and gasping breath. When she took Bessie's hand again, she found it cold and glanced down to see her fingernails edged with the same blueness.

"Bessie, I don't know if I should leave you!"

Bessie's brown eyes flew open, imploring Shanna. "H-have to. Pappy. Get Pappy."

"Shhhh, Bessie. Don't upset yourself any more. I'll go get Dr. Samuel."

Shanna heard a sob and looked up to see Melinda clutching another comforter, tears streaming down her face.

"Is Aunt Bessie gonna die?"

"Oh, darling, I don't know. We have to get Dr. Samuel for her. Will you and Toby be able to stay here and make Bessie comfortable while I go for him?"

Toby threw open the back door as Shanna spoke. "Brownie's tied at the porch, Shanna. I shut Starlight in the stall."

"Good. Do you know where Cody keeps his spirits?"

"I do," Melinda said in a muffled voice.

"Go get them while I change, Melinda."

Shanna raced to the newly furnished room down the hall and grabbed the first pair of Cody's pants she found in the closet, along with one of his belts. She didn't really want to take time to change, but having ridden astride a few times in her life, she knew she could make much better time that way. She threw her dress on the bed and pulled the pants on, along with a shirt she found hanging on the footboard. Deciding her kid shoes could do as well as boots, she flew back into the kitchen.

Melinda held the brandy bottle out and Shanna knelt by Bessie's head. "Please, Bessie," she said. "Just take a swallow of this. It should help you relax until I get back."

Bessie nodded compliance and swallowed the brandy when Shanna raised her head up. Almost at once, her eyes rolled back and she lost consciousness.

"Keep the fire going and keep her covered," Shanna ordered in a stern voice. "Toby, you've been over to the Samuels' place with Cody. How do I get there?"

"Go left at the gate, instead of the way we came from Liberty. That way goes right to Pappy's place."

"How far?" Shanna asked over her shoulder as she grabbed her shawl.

"Not far. I . . . I think five minutes, if you ride fast."

Shanna paused to take in the two frightened faces on the children kneeling beside Aunt Bessie. "Oh, Lord, Toby and Melinda. Will you be all right?"

"We'll do what you said," Toby replied in a stout voice, and Melinda nodded her head as she ran her hands across her eyes.

"Just get Aunt Bessie some help, Shanna," Melinda said with a sob.

Shanna grimly pulled the door shut behind her. They had to be all right. She didn't dare send Toby out by himself, since the sun had already set. She grabbed Brownie's reins and stepped into the saddle from the porch.

Please, God, don't let Bessie die before I get back.

The mare tried to turn toward the stable and her colt when Shanna urged her forward and briefly fought the reins again at the gate. Shanna firmly pulled Brownie's head around and kicked her into a canter. The stirrups were slightly long, but she wrapped her legs tightly around the saddle and settled into the rhythm of the mare's stride.

There wasn't much of a moon, though at least the night was clear and starlit. She could barely make out the road in front of her, but she didn't slow Brownie's speed. The night breeze whipped past her, making Shanna wish she had grabbed a jacket instead of her shawl, and her hair immediately came loose from the bun on her head. The farther they got from the barn, the more the mare settled into compliance with Shanna's commands. The countryside flew past them when Brownie stretched from her canter into a gallop, Shanna's toes just able to reach the stirrup loops when she lay on Brownie's back and spoke to her.

"Come on, girl. It can't be much farther."

Another mile down the road, Shanna caught sight of a light up ahead. She felt the mare falter beneath her and a fleck of foam from Brownie's muzzle hit her in the face. Shanna sawed on the reins, reluctantly pulling Brownie down into a trot, recalling that the mare wasn't used to such an extended run. She had to pull her in or risk hurting the mare.

At the log cabin where the lantern light glowed, Shanna slid from the saddle, her hand leaving a streak on Brownie's wet neck.

"Oh, God, Brownie, I'm sorry," she breathed.

A vision of Bessie's white face and blue lips swam in her mind, and Shanna left the mare to run across the porch. Not even pausing to knock, she burst into the room.

"Zerelda. Zerelda, you and Pappy have to help!"

Shanna slid to a halt, assisted by the arm around her waist. She gasped in horror when she felt something cold beside her ear and swiveled her head to stare into the barrel of a six-gun.

Despite the bulk of her stomach, Zerelda Samuel shot to her feet. "Put it away, Jesse! Now!"

The gun dropped and Shanna stepped away from the man holding her when his arm released her. She turned to see a dark-haired man slipping the gun back into his holster. When he looked at her, a pair of pale-blue eyes met her own, a sheepish look in them.

"Sorry, ma'am," the man said. "Guess I jist get kind of jumpy when folks bust in on us."

Zerelda's voice quickly drew Shanna's attention back to the table. "What's wrong, Shanna? What's happened?"

"I . . . it's Bessie!" Shanna gasped. "I think she's dying. She wants Pappy to come!"

"Where are Cody and the children?"

"Cody's in Liberty. He went in to get seeds for planting. And the children are at the house."

"Jesse," Zerelda said in a calm voice. "Go hitch up the buggy and send Frank in from the barn. Then get yourself cross-country and stay with those children and Bessie until we can get there." Zerelda placed a hand on a young woman sitting at the table, staring wide-eyed around her. "Susie, saddle up and go get Cody. You know the way to town. I'll go wake Pappy."

"Shouldn't one of the men go to town after Cody?" Shanna asked as the door closed on the front of the cabin.

"No," Zerelda replied in a flat voice. "Susie can do it." She quickly turned away and hurried toward the back of the cabin.

Shanna followed Susie out the door after the young woman grabbed a cloak from a hook on the wall. Seeing Brownie standing with head down, Shanna raced to the mare's side, a worried frown on her face.

"What am I going to do with Brownie?" she asked Susie. "She's got a colt, and she's still nursing."

"I'll tend her, ma'am. Send Jesse back when you get home. By then the mare will be rested, and Jesse can bring her over to the colt."

Shanna looked up to see a different man from the one who had pulled his gun on her reaching for Brownie's reins. She couldn't quite make out his features under his low-pulled hat, but his soft voice calmed her somewhat. As Susie left them to go to the barn, she handed Brownie's reins to the man.

"Thank you. I'll ride in the buggy."

"Yes, ma'am. You do that."

Hoofbeats sounded in the direction of the barn, and Shanna turned to see Jesse mounted on a dancing stallion, leading the buggy team toward them. He tossed the lead rope to the man beside Shanna.

"Here, Frank. Mamaw and Pappy will be out in a minute." Tipping his hat to Shanna, he rode off, reining his stallion toward a fence and urging it over the top rail.

"He'll be there in no time," Frank said. "Don't worry. We've both ridden to the Garret place that way lots of times."

"Frank and Jesse." Shanna glanced up at him. "You must be Cody's friends—Zerelda's sons. Cody told me how you saved Bessie and Melinda."

Instead of confirming her words, Frank looped the team's lead rope over the hitching rail and led Brownie away. Shanna watched until he disappeared into the barn, then turned to see Zerelda and Pappy come out the door.

Chapter Fourteen

Shanna jerked her head up and squinted at the stove. She'd only sat down for a moment to wait for the coffee to perk, but sizzling sounds told her the liquid was boiling over onto the hot surface. With a groan, she rose from the rocking chair and hurried over to slide the coffeepot to the edge.

The boiling liquid subsided to a gentle perk and Shanna tossed the towel aside. How soon would Cody return? Though Pappy assured her that Bessie was out of danger, at least for the time being, she longed for Cody's steady presence. Zerelda and Pappy would probably be leaving soon, even if Zerelda had offered to stay over a day or so. Shanna couldn't bring herself to impose on the pregnant woman any longer. Zerelda had admitted to being just over 41 as she carried her eighth child, and she should be taking care of herself, not her neighbors.

Outside, a horse neighed and Shanna ran to the kitchen door. Flinging it open, she saw Cody riding into the yard, his dun stallion as flecked with foam as Brownie had been last night. She waited until he pulled the horse up to the hitching rail and slid down before she lost control and ran into his arms.

"Cody! Oh, Cody, what took you so long?"

Cody held her tight for a minute, stroking the blond tresses tumbling down her back. "Shhhh, honey. I'm here now. Everything will be all right now, Shanna."

Cody gently pushed her away and cupped her chin. "Aunt Bessie?" he questioned quietly.

"She's all. . . ." Shanna gulped back a sob and tried to nod reassuringly when Cody's hand fell from her face. "She's all right for now. Pappy said it's her heart. She's going to have to take it very easy from now on."

"And you? And the children?" Cody stroked his index finger down a tear streak on Shanna's face.

"We're fine. At least, we are now that you're back. I . . . oh, I've never been so scared in my entire life!"

Cody pulled her back into his arms and buried his face in her hair. Why had he left them alone—even considered extending his time away to ride out to the outlaw hideout? What if Susie hadn't found him at the saloon, where he was playing poker? Closing his eyes against the guilt in his mind, Cody breathed in Shanna's special scent for a moment. Then, reluctantly, he released her.

"We better go in, so I can see Bessie."

"She's probably asleep. Zerelda and Pappy are still with her."

Cody kept one arm around Shanna as they climbed the steps. Shanna gave a soft sigh and wrapped her arm around his waist as they crossed the porch. In the kitchen, he allowed her to pull free and walk over to the stove.

"I'll get us some coffee. It's fresh," Shanna said.

Cody dropped into a kitchen chair. With an effort, he kept from burying his head on his arms.

Catching the distorted pain in Cody's eyes when she

set his coffee cup in front of him, Shanna murmured a quiet word of solace.

"God, Shanna," Cody replied, his voice laced with agony. "I'm sorry you had to go through last night alone. I should have been here for you and the kids."

Shanna sat beside him and took Cody's large hand in her own, stroking it tenderly. "Cody Garret, you listen to me. Bessie's attack would have happened whether you'd been here or not. You had to go in for your seed. How else could you get your crops planted? We managed. I'll admit it wasn't easy without you, but heavens, Cody, you can't be everywhere at once."

"I know. It's just. . . ."

Cody fell silent and Shanna rose to her feet. She took his hat off and laid it on the table, then pushed his coffee cup nearer. The chestnut hair under the hat was tousled and tangled, and Shanna reached out a hand to smooth it.

Cody gave a groan and pulled Shanna into his arms. Burying his face in her breasts, he clung tightly to her while Shanna stroked his hair.

"What would I do without you, Shanna?" Cody murmured. "I just can't handle everything alone."

"Don't worry. Please don't worry. I'll stay as long as you need me."

"Will you?" Cody raised his head and cupped Shanna's cheek. "Will you stay as long as I . . . as long as Melinda and I need you?" He tangled his long fingers in her hair and gently tugged her face toward his. "I need you so much, Shanna."

The room tilted around Shanna and she clung to Cody's firm shoulders as their lips met. When Cody pulled her onto his knee, she wrapped her arms around his neck and willingly gave in to the increased pressure of his lips. Opening her mouth under his insistence, she sighed in surrender and gave herself up to the thrills coursing through her, chasing away her worry and exhaustion.

She loved this man. Oh, God, how she loved this man! She would stay with him as long as he wanted her to!

Cody released her lips and kissed Shanna's eyes, then nuzzled her ear. "What if it's forever, Shanna?" he whispered. "What if I want you to stay with me forever?"

His words sent a cold shock through Shanna. *Toby,* her mind cried. *I can't have Cody and Toby, too.*

Shanna pushed on Cody's chest and forced herself away from him. When she would have stood, Cody held her in place.

"Please, Cody," Shanna said with a small whimper. "I . . . I can't stay forever. I just can't."

"Why not, Shanna? Shanna, I lo—"

"Best you come on in now, Cody," Zerelda said from the hall doorway. "Didn't want to interrupt, but Bessie's asking for you, and Pappy says it's best not to let her get upset."

Cody held Shanna for another second before he dropped his hands so she could stand. Rising to his own feet, he gave her a long look, then turned to walk down the hallway.

"You go on in, Cody," Zerelda told him as he passed. "Pappy's still there, keeping her calm."

Shanna hurried over to Zerelda, placing a hand on her arm. "Please, Zerelda, sit down. My word, you must be worn out after being up all night."

"Not the first time," Zerelda said with a shrug. But she followed Shanna to the table and gratefully took the chair Shanna pulled out.

"Here," Shanna said as she picked up Cody's cup and gave it to Zerelda. "Cody didn't touch it."

"No," Zerelda mused with a smile in her eyes. "He had something else on his mind besides drinking coffee. Sorry I came in just then."

Bittersweet Promises

Shanna's eyes filled with tears, and the tiredness she had been holding at bay all night overtook her. She sank down into another chair before her knees could give out.

"Now, honey, don't be embarrassed." Zerelda reached over and patted Shanna's hand. "Guess I know what kissing and petting's all about, what with the brood I've got around me."

"It's . . . I'm not embarrassed. I mean, well, not much."

"Cody's one of the best men I know," Zerelda said as she lifted her coffee cup. "You and he will have a fine life."

"That's just it. We can't have a life together."

Zerelda sipped her coffee and raised her eyebrows. "Care to talk about it?" she asked after she swallowed.

Shanna shook her head. "It's not something I can talk about right now. I'm sorry. You've been such a good friend, and I don't know what I would have done last night without you and Pappy. But this is something I have to handle alone."

"We've all got things in our lives like that," Zerelda told her in a tired voice. "Things we can't talk about. Wish it wasn't so. Lord, how I wish it wasn't so. Guess some things we just have to talk about in our prayers."

"I haven't done much of that lately."

"Maybe you should try it then. We don't always get the answers we want, you know, but a body's got to have someone to listen to her from time to time."

"I will," Shanna promised. "And, Zerelda, I'm sorry I didn't get to meet the rest of your family last night. Please tell Frank and Jesse how much I appreciate their help. And Susie, of course."

A closed look came over Zerelda's face. "Frank and Jesse will be gone when I get back, but I'll let Susie know what you said."

"Oh, then our problems kept you from even saying good-bye to them. Maybe when they come back, I'll come over and tell them myself."

"They won't be back. I told them not to come back again. I don't want them around my other young'uns." Zerelda shot a quick glance at Shanna. "And I'd appreciate it if you didn't tell anyone about seeing them there last night."

"Zerelda, what on earth . . . ?"

"Guess you haven't heard the stories going round. They're sayin' it was my Frank and Jesse leading the band that robbed the bank in Liberty."

"Oh, God, Zerelda. Was . . . were . . . ?"

"Best you not finish that question, honey," Zerelda interrupted. "That way, I won't have to spoil our friendship by lying to you. Like I said a minute ago, we all got things we can't talk about."

Shanna nodded and rose to her feet. "It's breaking dawn out," she said as she glanced out the window. "I'll get some bacon from the smokehouse for breakfast. We used the last of the other slab yesterday."

Shanna turned at the door. "Zerelda, I want you to know how much I value our friendship. If there's ever anything I can do for you, promise you'll let me know."

"I will, Shanna. And the same goes for me. I appreciate all you've done to help my children learn, so they'll get a good start in life and maybe make something of themselves. Ain't many young women who'd put aside their own problems for a while and teach a bunch of kids without pay."

"I'm enjoying it as much as the children, Zerelda. And, in a way, it's helping me keep a perspective on my own problems."

"You ever get to the point where you need to talk, you can rest assured it won't go no farther."

"Thank you, Zerelda," Shanna said before she shut the door.

Shanna looked up from spooning broth into Bessie's mouth that evening to see Susie standing in the bedroom door.

"Do you need any help?" Susie asked in her quiet voice.

"No, I'm almost finished. I've had to coax her to take the last two bites."

"Bites? Huh!" Bessie grumbled. "Nothing to bite on in that stuff except the spoon. Could've at least put some soft dumplings in it."

"Now, Bessie," Shanna said. "Pappy told you that you could have something more substantial tomorrow. We have to do what he says."

"He's not the one lyin' here with a growling stomach. Won't get my strength back on broth."

Shanna sighed and handed Susie the soup bowl and spoon. She smoothed Bessie's hair back and smiled down at the elderly woman.

"You're getting your spunk back. Guess you must be on the mend."

"Spunk's not what I need. It's food."

"I don't think it would hurt her to have a piece of toast and butter," Susie said. "And maybe a cup of tea. She does seem a lot better this evening."

"Bless you, child," Bessie said.

As Susie left the room, Bessie's brown eyes closed. Shanna tucked the comforter around her neck and settled back into her chair to wait silently for Susie to return. Bessie needed every bit of rest she could get, if she ever hoped to leave her bed again.

"Shanna, we have to talk about this." Bessie's brown eyes remained closed, though she reached out a hand to Shanna.

Shanna took the extended hand, surprised at the strength of Bessie's grip. "We can talk any time, Bessie. Right now, you need to conserve your strength."

"This is going to take me some time to get over, isn't it?" Bessie asked as though Shanna hadn't spoken. "It'll be too much for you, teaching and taking care of the housework and meals, along with caring for me."

"Zerelda said Susie can stay as long as we need her," Shanna soothed. "Don't worry about it."

"Reckon that will work for a while," Bessie agreed. "Sally's old enough to help out with John and Fannie, and Zerelda says she's carrying this one well, not like the trouble she had with Fannie. No one thought Zerelda would carry Fannie to term after she got out of that stockade."

"Stockade? You mean, like a jail?"

"Took a bunch of them," Bessie told her. "Summer of '63. They hauled off all the women they could prove had anyone riding with Quantrill, like Frank was. Zerelda had Sally and John with her, just little ones they were—and Zerelda expecting another one."

Bessie's words shocked Shanna into silence. How much Zerelda had suffered already. How could Frank and Jesse put her through any more?

Bessie opened her eyes and Shanna squeezed her hand. "Please, Bessie. You shouldn't try to talk so much."

"Just one more thing, Shanna. Cody's gonna need you beside him real bad right now. You will keep your promise to stay, won't you? I know it's not fair of me to ask it of you, since you only agreed to help with Melinda, not nurse me. But. . . ."

"Bessie, please don't fret about it. I've already promised Cody I'd stay as long as I was needed."

"What if you can't, Shanna? What if whatever you're running from catches up to you?"

Not surprised that Bessie had gleaned something of

her past, Shanna met the elderly woman's worried gaze resolutely. "Then I guess I'll just have to stand and face it, won't I?"

"What about Toby?"

Shanna tore her eyes away and stared at the window. The blackness outside reflected the contents of the room back, along with her own drawn face. Toby. She couldn't answer that. She prayed it wouldn't come down to that choice just yet.

Susie bustled into the room with a small tray in her hands, a glass holding wildflowers perched between the slice of toast and cup of tea.

"Melinda and Toby insisted I bring the flowers in, Bessie," Susie said as she sat down on the edge of Bessie's bed. "They picked them this afternoon for you."

"Tell them thank you for me," Bessie said in a tired voice. "And ask them to stop in to say good night before they go to bed."

"I will. It will ease their minds if they at least get to do that. They've been such little worrywarts all afternoon."

"Maybe I should go talk to them," Shanna said as she rose to her feet.

"They went out to say good night to the colt," Susie informed her. "But you go ahead and take a break for a while, Shanna. I'll sit with Bessie. I left the kettle on the stove, if you want a cup of tea."

"Thanks, Susie."

Shanna entered the kitchen to find it spotless, as usual. Susie was just as conscientious as Bessie about keeping things clean, and Shanna had to admit she needed the young woman's help. As she reached for the teakettle, Shanna stifled the guilty thought that she wished Zerelda had sent eight-year-old Sally, instead of 17-year-old Susie, to help out.

Heavens, Shanna told herself, she had no right to feel pangs of jealousy at the easy banter between Susie and

Cody that afternoon. After all, they were neighbors and had known one another for years and years. It was only natural they would feel at ease with each other and have loads to talk about.

Shanna sat down at the table, barely managing to right her teacup when it rattled in her tired hand. Over 36 hours with no sleep had taken its toll on her body. Even the quick sponge bath she allowed herself after Susie arrived had only refreshed her for a little while. Eyes drooping, she stretched her arm out on the table and laid her head down. Just a minute, she assured herself.

Cody opened the back door and turned quickly to shush the children behind him. Finger on his lips, he cautioned them to slip quietly across the kitchen floor to the hallway leading to their bedrooms.

"Why don't you bed down in my room for a while, Toby?" Cody whispered in the hallway. "I'll move you in with Shanna after I take Susie home."

"I'll take care of them, Cody," Susie said from Bessie's bedroom door. "Your aunt wants to say good night to them."

Cody nodded and crept back into the kitchen. He stood watching Shanna for a minute, his eyes caressing the tumbled golden curls and the violet shadows under her eyes from worry and lack of sleep. How had he ever thought her spoiled and used to ordering her own servants around, instead of doing the work herself?

His gaze traveled down the slender arm lying on the table to the hand cupped in relaxation at the end of it. Somehow she managed to keep her nails clean and perfect, but the slightly darker shadows of beginning calluses marred her soft palm. Recalling the gifts tucked in his saddlebags, which he had completely forgotten to pass out today, he made a mental note to bring them out first thing in the morning. The bottle of lotion he had picked out for Shanna would, the salesclerk had assured him, render her hands as soft as butterflies.

Just like the butterflies fluttering in his stomach at that moment as his eyes touched her barely parted lips. When had the sexual urge he felt around her turned into this all-encompassing feeling that he would die without her in his life? Yes, most definitely he still wanted her body. What man wouldn't want to make those perfect womanly curves his own? But he would kill any other man who tried!

Cody's shoulders slumped. There would be one man he couldn't kill—the man Shanna had already picked out as her own to marry. Why couldn't he bring himself to wish her happiness—wasn't love supposed to mean that he wanted the other person's life to be all velvet and roses, even at the expense of losing that person from his own life?

Was it because he couldn't bring himself to believe that Shanna really loved this mysterious other man—the shadows he saw in her eyes the one time she talked about him? Or was it his own selfishness?

Cody sighed and quietly walked over to Shanna's chair. She barely stirred as he gently lifted her into his arms, only snuggling contentedly against his chest. He carried her into her bedroom and placed her on the bed she normally shared with Toby. Susie had already turned the comforter down, and Cody searched the room until he found her shoe-button hook on the dresser. He deftly unbuttoned the kid shoes and massaged her feet for a few minutes, enjoying the quiet sigh of pleasure that escaped Shanna's lips, though her eyes never opened.

Cody unbuttoned a few of the buttons on the front of Shanna's dress, leaving off as soon as he glimpsed the lace-covered edge of her chemise. He had better leave any further undressing to Susie, he determinedly told himself when his denims tightened on his groin. Before he took Susie home, he would ask her to make Shanna more comfortable.

He couldn't seem to stop himself, though, from gently running his finger along the swell of Shanna's breasts under the lace. He caught his breath in wonder when he heard her breathe his name at his touch. Glancing at Shanna's face, he saw that she was still asleep.

Cody pulled the comforter over Shanna, then bent and kissed her lips.

"Night, darlin'," he said as he stood.

"Night, my love," Shanna murmured in a barely audible voice before she turned on her side and snuggled down under the comforter.

Chapter Fifteen

Cody hoisted the last bag of seed from the wagon bed to his shoulder. "I appreciate this, Fred. I didn't expect you to deliver this load out here."

"Shucks, Cody, you'd have done it for me. Reckon I ain't forgot how you helped me when I had that little problem."

"I'll pay you as soon as my first crop comes in."

"I know you will. I'm just glad to be able to help out some of the people around here, 'specially the ones who lost money in that bank robbery. Sure hope we have a good growing season this year, or there's gonna be a lot of folks wiped out."

"Yeah, I'm afraid you're right. Look, it's way too late to start back to town tonight. Stay and leave in the morning. I've got a bottle of good brandy in the house, and we can sit around after supper and catch up on things."

"Well, now, I was hopin' you'd ask." Fred scratched his graying beard and his eyes lit up. "I don't want to be no trouble, though. My boy's taking care of the feed store, but you probably got your hands full around here, with your aunt sick and all."

"Susie James is helping out for a while. She goes home at night, since we're kind of short on bed space, but you're welcome to stay in my room. It's getting nice weather now, and I'll throw my bedroll in the barn."

"Wouldn't hear of it, Cody. Y'all just show me the softest stack of hay in your barn, and I'll be fine."

"We'll talk about that later. Right now, let's wash up and see what the women have planned for supper. Susie mentioned a little earlier that she'd found some of last year's canned peaches out in the root cellar. I think she had it in mind to mix up a cobbler."

Fred smacked his lips as he followed Cody toward the outside pump.

Cody found Fred waiting on the back porch when he returned from escorting Susie home later that evening. After turning his stallion into the corral and giving him a brief rubdown, he joined Fred and sat on the bottom step. Pushing his hat back so he could gaze at the star-strewn sky, Cody gave a satisfied sigh and leaned against a post.

"Sure is a pretty night."

"Yeah," Fred agreed. "Thought we might sit out here and talk. The kids are in bed, but Miss Allen's working on her lessons in the parlor. She gave me this before I came out."

Fred held out the brandy bottle, along with the extra glass Shanna had given him. He waited until Cody poured a measure from the bottle and set it down before he spoke again.

"Everyone's talking about how much they appreciate having Miss Allen round here. There's even some talk about putting up a permanent school this fall."

"I don't think they better get their sights set on Shanna being here to teach in the fall, Fred." Cody stifled a stab of pain. "She only agreed to stay for a few months."

"Be a shame to lose her. There oughta be somethin' we can do to help her out, so's she can stay."

"What do you mean?"

Fred reached into his shirt pocket and pulled out a piece of paper. "Dan asked me to bring this with me when he heard I was coming out here with the seed," he said in a cautious voice. "I wanted to wait till we was alone before I showed it to you."

Something in Fred's voice made Cody hesitate, but he reluctantly took the paper. He squinted at it, unable to read the print in the dim light. Glancing at Fred, he heard the old man give a resigned sigh.

"It's from the Pinkertons, Cody. Seems some feller in New York named Christian Van Alstyne hired them to look for his daughter and son, who ran off. The descriptions fit Miss Allen and the little boy to a tee, and that telegram says they traced them to Liberty. They want Dan to be on the lookout for them, and this Van Alstyne's on his way here."

Cody's heart pounded in his chest and he took a long swallow of the brandy. Were the pieces of Shanna's past finally going to fall into place? But good God—Pinkertons! They usually only went after criminals. What kind of father would send Pinkertons after his children?

"How many people know about this, Fred?"

"Just me and Dan. And, 'course, the telegraph operator. But Dan said he told the operator he'd run him out of town if word got out."

"That won't do much good when Van Alstyne gets here. He'll turn the whole town upside down looking for Shanna and Toby. We can't expect people to keep their mouths shut."

"You got any idea why she and the boy ran away from him, Cody?"

"No. She's been real tight-lipped about why she came here. She's not going to have any choice now, though. I've got a bad feeling about this, Fred, especially with the Pinkertons involved."

"Hell, Cody, folks around here ain't gonna let nothin' happen to her and Toby. Why, I never even met that little gal until this evening, but she's made a stir all around the county. She took those kids in to teach and actually made them want to go to school every day. Word's got around, and everybody kind of thinks of her as one of our own now, even though she's only been here a couple months."

"She might need all that support, Fred," Cody said as he rose. "I better talk to her. Why don't you ask her to step out here when you go in? My room's at the end of the hall. I saw an old cot in the hayloft the other day, and I'll fetch it into the house when I get ready to bed down."

"Well, now, if you're sure, Cody."

"I'm sure. Here, take the brandy with you and leave what you don't want on the table. I might need a drink later."

Cody finished his brandy before Shanna appeared at the kitchen door. He stared at her, standing framed in the light still burning in the kitchen, a slight frown on her face.

Realizing he didn't even know how to begin, Cody stretched out a hand. "Let's go for a walk, Shanna."

"I really should be working on my lessons. But Fred said you needed to see me for a minute."

"Please, Shanna," Cody urged. "You shouldn't work so hard all hours of the day and night."

Shanna stepped onto the porch and pulled the door shut behind her. Taking Cody's proffered hand, she followed him from the porch and gazed up at the night sky.

"It is beautiful out tonight. I do love spring nights. Melinda said one of the cats had a new litter of kittens a couple days ago. Do you think I could see them?"

"Sure. Toby and I fixed them up a box in the lean-to on the side of the barn. I'll show you."

Cody desperately tried to marshal his thoughts as he led Shanna toward the lean-to. His free hand swung by his side and the telegram brushed his thigh, the paper crackling in the night silence. He quickly shoved it into his pants pocket.

"What's that?" Shanna asked.

"Look," Cody said, ignoring her question. He knelt beside the lean-to and reached inside, pulling out a hay-lined box. The mother cat gazed up at them, her eyes slowly blinking in the starlight.

"Oh," Shanna said as she knelt beside Cody. "Will she let us touch them?"

Cody picked up one of the small bundles and held it out to her. The mother stirred briefly, but didn't protest, though she kept her green gaze fixed on the kitten. Cody watched Shanna raise the kitten to her cheek and rub her face against the soft fur.

"It's so little—so defenseless."

"It'll grow fast. In a week or so, its eyes will start to open, and within a month we'll be tripping over kittens whenever we go to milk."

Deciding her baby had been admired enough, the cat stood and meowed stridently. Laughing down at her, Shanna replaced the kitten and stood, waiting until Cody pushed the box back into the lean-to before she walked over to the corral fence and propped her arms on the top rail.

"Cody," she said when he joined her. "Is there something you wanted to tell me? Fred acted awfully funny when he asked me to come out here."

For a long minute Cody stared down at her, studying her innocent gaze in the shadowy light. At last he pulled his hat from his head and draped it over the fence post beside him, then ran his fingers through his hair. With his free hand, he pulled the telegram from his pocket.

"Do you know someone named Christian Van Alstyne?" he blurted.

Shanna's face crumbled in distress. "No! He can't be here!" She whirled and grabbed Cody by the shirtfront. "Please. You have to help Toby and me get away! Please, Cody. Don't let him find us. He'll take Toby away from me!"

Cody gripped her arms tightly as Shanna's shrill voice rang in the night. "Listen to me, Shanna," he pleaded. "I can't help you unless I know what's going on. You're going to have to trust me now."

"There isn't time. Too many people know I'm here!" Shanna tugged on Cody's shirt and threw her head back to fix heartrending eyes on his face as her words tumbled out.

"You don't understand, Cody. If Father takes Toby away, I'll die! He doesn't want him—he just wants to ship him off to a boarding school to get him out of his life. Please, Cody. Lend me some of the money Johnny left you, so Toby and I can get away. I'll pay you back in four months. I promise!"

Cody shook her roughly, trying to still her near hysterics. "I can't, Shanna. I mailed that money back to the bank anonymously while I was in town one day. It wasn't mine to keep. And I'm not going to let you and Toby run off half-cocked on your own again!"

"You have to! Cody, please!"

Cody swept Shanna up and carried her to the barn, with her beating her fists ineffectively on his chest. Once inside, he sat down on a hand-tied hay bale and captured her fists to pull her onto his lap. When she collapsed in sobs, he held her close, her tears wetting his shirtfront and her agony echoing in the nearly silent barn.

"Shanna. For God's sake, talk to me. Tell me what I can do to help."

"There's *nothing* you can do," Shanna sobbed. "He's got the law on his side. He can take Toby away from me, and there's not a damned thing I can do!"

Cody held her, stroking her hair and murmuring quietly, trying to reason out her ravaged pleas. When her sobs subsided into small hiccups, he pulled a handkerchief from his back pocket. Shifting Shanna in his arms, he gently wiped under her eyes.

"Where . . . where is Father?" Shanna gulped. "How near?"

"I'm not sure. Dan got that telegram from the Pinkertons. It described you and Toby and just said that Van Alstyne was on his way to Liberty. The telegram's right then—he is your father?"

"Y-yes. And Toby's *legal* father, at least that's what my mother's lawyer told me. I can't stop Father, if he wants to take Toby back to New York."

"Legal father?"

Shanna blew her nose into the handkerchief and straightened her shoulders. "I . . . I guess I might as well tell you the rest of it. But if I do, you have to promise that you'll help me keep Toby away from him. Cody, don't you see how happy Toby is here? What do you think will happen to him if he's shut away somewhere in a boarding school, far away from everyone who loves him? How could a man even think of doing something like that to a little boy?"

"I'll do everything I can to help, Shanna, but don't you think it's time you quit running and faced up to this? What kind of life will Toby have if you drag him around with you, never having a permanent home? What kind of man do you think he'd grow into?"

"It won't be for long. Just until. . . ."

Shanna fell silent, biting her lower lip between her teeth as she turned her head away from Cody and stared out into the dark barn. She had to tell him. She had to trust someone. Taking a deep breath, she wiped a stray tear from her check and began.

She told him all of it, all except the name of the man Diedre fell in love with. What if somehow her father learned the man's name and had him killed before Shanna could find him? Shanna alone knew how deep the hatred her father felt for his wife's lover went—it even extended to the child born of the affair. She couldn't take a chance that her father would put forth an all-out search for the man. He had found her and Toby, hadn't he? Christian Van Alstyne was a man with considerable power and resources—power and resources he wouldn't hesitate to use to get what he wanted.

When her words trailed off, Cody studied her tear-streaked face. "And just how do you expect to keep your father from claiming Toby?" he asked at last.

"There's only one way." Shanna rose to her feet and turned her back, unable to face Cody while she delivered her sole alternative.

"I have to find Toby's real father and convince him to fight my father for custody of Toby. I . . . I have a copy of Toby's birth certificate. I don't know how she managed it, but my mother listed her . . . her lover as Toby's father on the document. The lawyer I talked to in New York—the one who handled my mother's affairs, not my father's—he told me this man could do that. He could fight for custody of Toby."

Shanna glanced at Cody, trying to surmise his reaction, but his face was set in a stone mask. She took another step away from him and focused on the nearest stall.

"He . . . the lawyer told me that it alone, the birth certificate, probably wouldn't be enough—that it wasn't as strong a document as a marriage certificate. He has Mother's handwritten will, too, but he said there was something else this man—Toby's real father—would know. Something the lawyer wasn't at liberty to discuss with me."

"Is that all of it?" Cody demanded into the silence while Shanna searched for words to continue—words that would shatter her own soul, but words that had to be spoken.

"No," she said in a soft voice.

"I didn't think so."

"I . . . when I find this man, I'm going to beg him to marry me. The lawyer said the man would have a better chance at custody if he had a wife. And it's the only way I can remain a part of Toby's life."

"Marry you!" Cody shouted. He clenched his fists, fighting the urge to jump up and shake her until her scrambled brain righted itself and began thinking clearly again. "You don't have to *marry* him to keep on being a part of Toby's life, damn it!"

Shanna whirled on him. "You're out of your mind if you think I can just live with this man and not be married to him!"

"That's not what I meant. You can live nearby—share Toby. Still be a part of Toby's upbringing!"

"Oh, Cody, how can you say such a thing?" Shanna held up a hand when Cody started to speak again.

"Let me ask you something hypothetical, Cody. Suppose . . . just suppose now, that some young couple came to you and tried to convince you that Melinda would be better off with two parents. Said that Bessie was too old to be raising a child and that Melinda should have a mother."

"It's nobody else's damned business!"

"It's not, is it? But even if they convinced you that they would be good parents and give Melinda a more balanced life, could you give her up and agree to just *visit* her? Just see her now and then?"

"I'd see them in hell first! But, damn it, Shanna. Toby's not your son. He's your brother!"

"And my half brother, at that, is that what you're trying to say? Tell me this, Cody. Do you think you would love Melinda any less if your wife had already had her when you married her? I've seen you with her for weeks now. Do you think you love her just because you're her father, or is it for Melinda as a person?"

"It's for both reasons. Hell, I sat up with her when she had colic to give my wife a break. I put her up in front of me for her first ride. I stayed out of that damned war as long as my conscience would allow me, just to be with her and my wife. I . . ."

"Exactly, Cody. *I* raised Toby, not my mother, though she loved him with every fiber of her being. Toby means as much to me as any child of my own that I might have in the future. I intend to be there whenever he needs me—watch him grow and develop—be a part of that development. And it's because I love him."

Cody sat thunderstruck on the bale of hay. It was true, then. He would lose her to another man—a man she didn't even love—a marriage of convenience, where he wouldn't even have the consolation of knowing she was happy in the life she chose. For the sake of a little boy Cody had come to love as deeply as though he were his own son.

"C-Cody? Will you help us?"

Cody sprang from the bale and rushed to the barn door. He breathed in a deep gulp of the clear air, his back rigid and his eyes staring unseeingly before him. Help her? God, how could she ask that of him? How? She might just as well ask him to tear his heart out and offer it to her father instead.

"What. . . ." Cody cleared his throat when his words stuck. "What makes you think this man will marry you?"

"I'll pay him, when. . . ."

"Pay him?" Cody shouted as he spun around. "With what? Your body? What if that's not enough for him?"

Shanna flinched back at the palpable anger in Cody's face. She clenched her hands in front of her and resolutely held her ground, telling herself it was all for Toby.

"I'll have money in four months. That's what I meant a minute ago. There's a trust fund my mother left me, which my father can't touch. I'll give this man every penny of it, if he'll agree to help me keep Toby."

"You'll buy him, huh?" Cody sneered. "What if he can't be bought? Hell, what if he's already married to someone else? You don't sound like you know one damned thing about this man. How do you know he won't beat you and Toby? What the hell *do* you know about him? Do you even know his name?"

"Shut up! Shut up!" Shanna clapped her hands over her ears, trying to drown out Cody's shouts. He was only screaming questions at her that she'd tried to bury in her own mind. But how could he be so cruel?

"If you won't help me, I'll do it alone somehow! Can't you see? I don't have any choice!"

Shanna dropped her hands and took a steadying breath. "And it's not true that I don't know anything about the man, Cody. My mother left a letter for me. The man she describes in her letter isn't the sort of man who would turn away from his own son."

Maybe at one time he wouldn't have, Cody thought. But Shanna didn't have any idea what the war had done to some men. He couldn't let her sacrifice her entire life to live with a man like his old friend had turned into, if indeed his suspicions about the identity of the man Shanna searched for were true. There had to be another way.

Shanna couldn't have found out yet where JT was hiding. Could she?

"Who is he—this man you're looking for and determined to marry?"

"I . . . I won't tell you his name yet. You don't know my father. He's a very bitter, angry man. Even though my mother's dead, he's using Toby to get his revenge on her for"—Shanna forced herself to say the distasteful word—"cuckolding him. Father's insane about the matter."

"Insane enough to have you arrested for kidnapping Toby?" Cody asked in a calmer voice as he studied her ravaged face. "That's what you did, you know. Remember, I've had some legal training, and I can't see the Pinkertons helping your father, unless he'd brought some criminal charge against you. Otherwise, he'd have had to hire some other private agency to find you."

"Kidnapping? Toby's my brother! How can Father say I kidnapped him? My God, he could send me to jail if a judge found me guilty of that, and then do whatever he wanted with Toby! I have to get Toby away from here!"

Cody grabbed Shanna as she ran past him, capturing her hands when she struggled in his hold. She screamed incoherently at him and fought against him until he wrapped one arm around her waist and clapped his palm over her mouth. She was going to wake up the entire household if she kept this up.

"Calm down and let's think this thing out!" he ordered.

Shanna bit down hard on his finger, and Cody yelped in pain. His hold on her loosened and she twisted in his grasp, nearly making her escape. He lunged for her and grabbed the back of her dress, the fabric ripping under his hand, but holding long enough for him to jerk Shanna back against him.

Shanna fought like a wild thing when he picked her up to carry her back into the barn, so hysterical that she could barely make a sound. Only gasping chokes emerged from her throat and she twisted and writhed in his grasp. Caught between not wanting to hurt her and somehow having to calm her enough to talk some sense into her, Cody dropped her on a pile of loose hay and covered her body with his own.

Why in God's name had he mentioned kidnapping? All he wanted to do was care for her and Toby for the rest of his life—never let anyone hurt her or take away what she loved.

His scathing words, jealously thrown at her from the depths of his own hurt, were torturing her. God, what an ass he was. But how, dear Lord, could she ask him to help her find her way into another man's arms?

Cody buried his face against her neck and pressed his body down on hers. The hay gave under them at first, but finally Shanna was immobile in his grasp, her tangled hair spread out against the hay.

"Please, Shanna," Cody mumbled. "I'll let you go if you promise not to run. You've got my word. I'll do whatever it takes to see that you don't lose Toby!"

Shanna's muscles slackened. After an instant, she nodded her head slightly against his hair.

Cody rolled to the side. He reached out a hand and brushed a lock of hair from her face, unsure of exactly what to say, but knowing his next words could either send her back into hysterics or make her hate him forever.

"Shanna, I. . . ." Cody gulped and the words tore from his throat, with him unable to stop them. "Oh, God, Shanna. Do you know how much I wish I could just kiss you and make it all go away? Do you know how much I've come to love you?"

Shanna stared at him, eyes wide in her tear-streaked face. Hesitantly, tenderly, she touched his cheek. "I love you, too, Cody Garret. I think I've known it since that night we talked about Melinda. Oh, God!" Shanna pulled away and tucked her legs under her, sitting up in the hay. "What am I saying? I shouldn't have said that."

Cody sat up and faced her, reaching across to tip her face up from where she had buried it on the arms wrapped around her knees.

"Is it true, Shanna? Do you love me?"

"I . . . it's . . . I shouldn't have said it. I wouldn't have, if I hadn't been so upset."

"Is it true?" Cody demanded again.

"All right." Shanna lifted her chin proudly and met his eyes. "All right. It's true. I love you, but nothing can ever come of it. I can't have you and Toby both."

"Right now, that's enough for me. Maybe it will have to be enough for the rest of my life. If it turns out that your way is the only way for you to keep Toby, Shanna, I'll stand behind you. And I'll always be there for you after that, if you need me."

"Thank you, Cody," Shanna whispered.

Cody gently took her arm and pulled her back down beside him. He had to tell her what he knew about JT, and he might just as well get it over with. Maybe there was some other alternative they could come up with. She had a right to know, though. He had put it off as long as he could, wanting only one more day close to her—telling himself Bessie and Melinda needed her, when all along it was his own heart crying out for her nearness.

"Shanna, I . . . oh, God, Shanna, I love you."

When Cody kissed her, Shanna felt herself opening to him as surely and completely as the spring flowers had welcomed the sunlight into their sheltered nests after the snow finally fled. This was what life was all about—this feeling of rebirth and renewal after a long waiting period. His lips drank from her own, taking even her breath as his own, yet offering a nourishment her soul craved even more than the life-giving breath.

Shanna returned his kiss hungrily, her arms twining around his neck and her body pressing to the length of his. The need to be close to him crowded out everything else from her mind. Desire so strong it shook her to the very core swept over her, and when Cody tried to draw back, she refused to loosen her arms.

"Kiss me just once more, Cody," she murmured. "Let me at least have this much to remember the rest of my life."

Cody groaned and complied, his tongue tasting her, sweeping around her mouth to memorize the feel and taste of her. His arms swept up her back and he buried one in her hair, the other finding its way around to her breast when he pushed her back against the hay, his lips never leaving hers. One long leg curled around her thigh and snugged her close to him, rocking her against his growing need.

Cody's palm cupped her breast and his thumb flicked her nipple into a hard point. Twin flames of need raced from Shanna's breasts and womanhood to meet in her stomach, then pulsed through every vein in her body. She ached with wanting him and offered no resistance when Cody's lips traced a path down her neck and his fingers worked to loosen the buttons on her dress.

As soon as the ribbons on her chemise fell away, Shanna arched up to meet Cody's seeking mouth. She felt the rigidness between his legs surge against her, then ran her hands down his back, tugging on his shirt to pull it free. His bare skin was hot against her palms, even sweaty, though the night was cool. A small whimper came from her throat as she moved her hands around to his ribs and clasped a handful of his shirt to pull it upward.

Cody reluctantly left the delectable breast he suckled and straightened his arms to stare down at her. "I can stop now, Shanna," he said in a tortured voice. "At least,

I think I can. But I want to show you how much I love you. I want us to share this, even if it's only this one time. I need you, Shanna. I love you and need you so damned much."

The cool air whispered over her damp nipples and Shanna pulled him back. "Please, Cody. Cody, I need you, too. And I want to show my love to you."

"Are you sure?"

She was sure—so sure, but the words were clogged with the passion in her throat. She showed him how sure with her body, and their remaining clothing whispered away in tune with the sighs and moans that accompanied the delight they found in trying to give each other more pleasure than they each got in return.

Even the flash of pain Shanna felt at one point was brief and seemed part of her joy—her burning desire to be one with the only man in the world she would ever love. Her rapture, when their joined bodies made the journey into complete fulfillment, had her whispering the words of love she would never be able to say to another man. Whispering them over and over, trying to say them all in one night.

She had more than one chance to tell Cody how much she loved him that night and drank in every word he returned to her. Finally their bodies gave up in satiation, and she had to be content to speak the words to him in her dreams as she curled her exhausted body against the one that had shown her why she was born a woman.

Sometime during her dreams, she forgave her mother. Diedre's face swept briefly into her unconscious thoughts and Shanna smiled in her sleep.

I forgive you, Mother, she sighed in her mind. *I only hope you found as much love with your lover as I found with mine.*

Chapter Sixteen

Wanting to savor every possible moment, Cody let Shanna sleep until an hour before dawn. Occasionally a sound broke the night silence in the barn—a faint nicker from Cody's restless dun stallion, the brush of a huge plow horse's hindquarter against its stall, once the slurp of Starlight's lips on his mother's bag as he foraged a nighttime meal.

None of the familiar sounds penetrated Cody's muddled thoughts. He cradled Shanna close, memorizing the feel of her, mentally tracing every inch of her body.

Once before he had known love—or thought he had. His life with Nancy had been perfect—everything he had always told himself a marriage should be. Never once had his wife raised her voice to him or defied him. Never once had she denied his lovemaking and, if Nancy had been somewhat apprehensive about relaxing enough under him to accept her own fulfillment, he had at least managed a few times to coax her into a climax.

But never had his wife responded like Shanna. Never had she taken fire at his touch—acknowledged her pleasure with touches of her own, which sought Cody's rapture, also—transported him to a plane of ecstasy and sharing he had never dreamed existed.

It was more than physical gratification. His love for Shanna, though inching into recognition at first on the sly feet of sexual desire, now controlled his entire being. Her quiet wonder at the birth of the colt, her steadfast, scrappy opposition to his spoiling Melinda, loving his daughter despite Melinda's whiny demands for indulgence, correcting her with equal measures of discipline and tenderness.

The way Shanna gave of herself emotionally when the ghosts and guilt crept forth from his past. The way her eyes twinkled when she returned his teasing banter. The way the sunlight caught her hair, transforming it into spun strands of liquid gold.

The way her body blended into his, the sensuous utopia they found together. . . .

Cody groaned softly under his breath, then gently kissed Shanna's shoulders and lips until she responded.

"Ummmm," Shanna said in a languid voice. "Tell me I'm not dreaming. Tell me this is real."

"It's real, darling. As real as the feelings we've shared. But. . . ." Cody sat up and reached for Shanna's dress. "I'm afraid there are some other realities our loving each other won't keep away. You better go on in to bed."

"What are you going to do? Did you get any sleep?"

"I'm fine. I want to dig out some of my old law books. There's got to be something there we can use. We need to be prepared, when your father shows up."

"Cody, I'm not going to let him take Toby away from me."

"I know. And I promise I'll do everything I can to see that doesn't happen. Everything will be all right."

Shanna reached for the chemise lying beside her and pulled it on, then silently slipped her arms through the dress Cody held out.

"I'm sorry I tore your dress, sweetheart."

"I can sew it," Shanna said with a shrug as she buttoned the dress.

When Cody stood and helped her to her feet, she leaned against his chest while he brushed pieces of hay from her hair. Beneath her cheek, Shanna heard his heart beating and the rise and fall of his breathing.

"Cody," she said, clinging to him tightly. "Cody, what if it's not enough?"

"What, darling?"

Shanna tilted her head back to study the haggard face above her. "What if everything you can do for Toby and me isn't enough? What if the judge says I have to give Toby back to my father?"

Straining to see his worried expression in the dim light, Shanna felt Cody's muscles tense under her hands. When he didn't answer her, she took a deep breath.

"I'm not going to ask you to do anything that will get you in trouble, Cody. You have to care for Bessie and Melinda. But I will ask you to draw up some sort of paper giving you authority to handle my affairs if I can't. Will you do that for me?"

"I'm sure we won't need—"

"Sure? Sure as in positive, Cody?"

"No, but . . . look, if worse comes to worst, I know a place I can take you and Toby where you'll be safe for a while until we figure out what to do."

"Then you'll be in trouble for helping us. Besides, Cody, you don't know my father. He'll hunt Toby and me down to the ends of the earth."

"Then we better eliminate all our legal alternatives first."

"What are they?"

"Is there anything at all you could use against your father to prove he's unfit to raise Toby? Any secret in his background that you know of that he wouldn't want brought out?"

"Only the affair my mother had, but he doesn't seem to care that people will know about that now. And what about him having me thrown in jail?"

"That's not going to happen," Cody said in a flat voice. "That's one thing I am positive about."

"No, you're not," Shanna said sadly, gently touching his cheek. "You can't put yourself on the line for me. You have other people depending on you."

Shanna kissed Cody lightly on the lips and pushed away when he would have held her close.

"Just do the best you can, Cody. I know you will."

Shanna studied Cody's bent head for an instant, then walked out of the barn. Though she had just shared the most glorious closeness there was for a man and woman, she had never felt so alone in her life. The forthcoming decisions were going to be hers alone, and she had to make them carefully.

Cody waited until the kitchen door closed behind Shanna, then slammed his fist into the post on the barn door. Ribbons of pain sliced up his arm, but he drew his fist back again and slammed it even harder. His shoulders slumped and he cradled his battered hand against his chest while he sank back down into the hay.

Sure, he had promised her everything would be all right, but how in hell could he keep his promise? He had searched his mind all night, in between reflections of how deeply he loved this woman, for any possible way to get her out of this mess.

Granted, he wasn't the most knowledgeable lawyer in the country, but he could read the law as well as any of the old circuit-riding solicitors. The scant amount of written law there was would probably favor JT, if he did intend to fight for the child of his loins.

The handwritten will Shanna's mother left—Shanna hadn't really explained the document, but he could imagine what it contained, if that city-slicker lawyer had told Shanna it would be part of the proof JT needed. That and the birth certificate—both explosive documents, sure to cause a scandal if ever brought to public light. Coupled with Van Alstyne's desire for revenge on a small child in no way to blame for his existence and added to JT's honorable reputation on the battlefield and his wounds suffered for the glory of the South....

Hell, any Southern judge would give the boy to JT, even if he had to interpret the law on a fine line. And the lawyer had even hinted at something else that would disfavor Van Alstyne.

What a hell of a choice Shanna must have had to make—leaving her luxurious life in New York to search for a man who could legally claim Toby and possibly take him from her. He could only imagine what hell Toby's life would have been to force Shanna to that choice.

Any way he turned, the end result would be the same. JT could probably get Toby, and hell, why wouldn't he marry Shanna—the picture of the woman JT had loved? Shanna could never be his. That big-city lawyer was right. Her only hope to have any kind of claim on Toby was to marry the boy's real father—if he could convince a judge Shanna hadn't kidnapped her brother.

Cody slowly rose to his feet and headed for the ladder to the loft, the air around him already echoing with his coming loss. What sort of twisted fate had made him the instrument to show the woman he desired with every fiber of his being the way to another man's arms?

Cody laid his forehead against the ladder and gripped the side. Wincing in pain when his injured fingers curled around the wood, he drew his hand back and gazed into the empty recesses above him.

And did he have it in him? Shanna trusted him to do what was right. He had given her his solemn promise. There wasn't any option other than to do his utmost to see that Shanna kept Toby with her, while still fulfilling his obligations to Aunt Bessie and Melinda.

Good God! What was he thinking of? How could he even let the thought of allowing Toby to go back to New York with his monster of a father so he could have Shanna cross his mind?

Shanna hesitantly pushed open the parlor door later that morning to see hard-bound books littering her desk and Cody with his legs stretched out in her chair, a contemplative frown on his face.

"Morning, love," Cody murmured, rising to his feet when he caught sight of her. "Come here."

Shanna walked into his arms and returned his kiss, trying to be satisfied by the necessary briefness of it, with the house sure to be wakening around them.

"I didn't think you'd mind me using your desk today," Cody said when he released her. "You don't have classes the next couple days."

"Of course not. But have you even been to bed?"

"No. And from the looks of those shadows under your eyes, you didn't get much sleep either."

"Have you found anything?"

"Not much," Cody admitted.

"Well, I'm going to make fresh coffee if you want some."

"I think I've had enough coffee for a while. I'm just going to keep at this for a little longer; then I've got to get out there to do the chores. And sometime today, we have to tell Aunt Bessie and the children what's going on."

"I know." Shanna pulled away from him and walked back to the door. "I know," she whispered to herself as she went into the kitchen.

Bittersweet Promises

"Morning, ma'am," Fred said a few minutes later as he came into the kitchen. "That coffee sure smells good."

"Good morning, Fred. Sit down and I'll get you a cup. Breakfast will be ready in a short while."

When Shanna set the coffee cup in front of Fred, he reached out and placed a hand on her arm. "I want you to know that folks around here think a lot of you, Miss Allen. We're all behind you."

"Thank you, Fred."

"Behind us in what, Shanna?"

Shanna glanced up to see Toby standing in the doorway, rubbing sleepily at his eyes. Her voice caught in her throat as she tried to remember the words she had written in her mind the night before to explain their new predicament, without totally scaring Toby to death.

Suddenly Toby dropped his hands and his eyes widened in fright. "Shanna. Shanna, is something wrong? Has he f-found. . . ."

Shanna hurried across the room to kneel in front of Toby. When she gathered his small body into her arms, he buried his face on her neck. "Toby," she said, stroking his hair when he tried to muffle a sob. "Toby, I'm not going to let anything happen to you." She gripped his shoulders and pushed him far enough away to see into his face. "I've promised you, remember? Cross my heart?"

Toby sniffed loudly and nodded his head. "I . . . I remember, Shanna."

The parlor door opened as Shanna rose to her feet and took Toby's hand. She tossed a grateful look at Cody, then led Toby to the table.

"We're going to talk about it all after breakfast, Toby. We'll think better then."

"All right," Toby agreed as he climbed into his chair.

"Maybe I should go on, so y'all can talk," Fred said, shoving his chair back.

"I wish you'd wait, Fred." Cody sat down across the table. "I might want you to tell Dan a couple things when you go back into town."

"Sure, Cody."

"And were you going to leave us completely out of this discussion?"

Bessie stood in the doorway with Melinda at her side, and Cody quickly jumped to his feet again and hurried over to take her arm.

"Aunt. You shouldn't be up."

"Pshaw. Pappy said I should start trying out my legs as soon as I felt like it. Otherwise, they'd wither and never be any use to me again." But she leaned on Cody's arm until he settled her into a chair.

"Now, we're all here," Bessie said in her usual take-charge manner. "Let's hear what's going on."

Shanna shot Cody a helpless look. "I need to start breakfast."

"Go ahead, Shanna," he replied. "I'll explain while you cook."

"I'll help Shanna," Melinda said, surprising everyone. She scurried over and slipped a small hand into Shanna's, giving a tiny squeeze.

Shanna blinked back a sudden mist of tears at the attempt of comfort. Obviously the child had sensed the atmosphere of tension in the room and was trying in her own way to help—something Melinda never would have thought of doing weeks ago, given her self-centered attitude then.

Shanna listened to every word while she cooked, and from time to time, she caught Melinda turning from the counter to pay close attention to the flow of conversation. When Cody spoke about the possibility of Shanna being sent to jail for bringing Toby with her, Shanna almost dropped an entire bowl of eggs at Melinda's small gasp beside her. She found herself wondering just how much

Bittersweet Promises

Melinda understood in her four-year-old mind, before remembering that both Melinda and Toby would each have a birthday this month. The two children had been delighted to find they were born on the same day and plans for the double celebration had already begun.

But would she even be here for the party? Shanna set the platter of eggs next to the bacon on the table while Melinda passed around a tray of sliced bread, then took her seat beside Cody. Though he reached over and filled her plate, urging her silently to eat, Shanna pushed the food around with her fork, mounding it this way and that in an attempt to make it look as though some had disappeared. When she realized the table had fallen silent, except for Toby and Melinda whispering together with bent heads on the far end, she glanced up to see the three adults' eyes centered on her.

"I . . . I'm just not hungry this morning," she said with a tight smile.

Bessie gave an exasperated sigh. "You're not going to be much help to us if you get sick from not eating, Shanna. We're all going to need to pull together, and I've got a feeling we'll need all our strength to weather this."

"Daddy," Melinda piped up. "Toby and I don't see why everyone's so worried. Maybe you just didn't 'splain it right."

"Explain, Melinda, not 'splain," Shanna corrected.

"That's what I meant," Melinda replied. "Ex-explain. And why can't Toby do that to the judge? He can 'spl . . . explain to the judge that he wanted to come with Shanna."

"Out of the mouths of babes," Cody said with a smile at his daughter.

"We are not babies, Daddy. I'm almost five and Toby's almost ten. We're almost grown-up."

"Yes, sweetheart, you're growing up fast. Faster than I want you to," Cody admitted. "But I don't know if a judge will think Toby's old enough to decide who he wants to be with."

"Sure he will. All Toby's gotta do is show the judge how smart he is, like he does in our lessons. Then the judge will just have to listen."

Satisfied that she had solved the problem, Melinda slid from her chair. "Excuse me and Toby," she said politely. "We're gonna do our chores now, Daddy. I'll come back and help Shanna when you're done drinkin' your coffee. Toby and me don't like coffee."

Shanna blinked back another sheen of tears as she watched Toby follow Melinda across to the door, a satisfied smile on her little brother's face. Oh, if it were only that easy. Where along the way had she lost the faith that children have in rightness? She couldn't bring herself to call Toby back and shatter his illusion that fair play would be done.

"Well, now," Fred said as he scraped his chair back. "I guess I know what to tell Dan, and I think I'll get right on the road so I can make sure he knows it before someone shows up and tries to put our Miss Allen in jail. Seems to me, it's two against one—Miss Allen and Toby's word against this here big-city feller who thinks he can come down here and take our teacher away from us."

Cody followed Fred to the door, but Fred waved him back. "Reckon I can hitch up my wagon by myself, Cody. You finish your coffee. And don't forget to stop by the next time you're in town. Got a bottle of my own we can share."

"Thanks for everything, Fred."

"Glad to help. Glad to help."

Bessie waited until the door closed behind Fred, then spoke to Shanna. "There's a little more to it than just your running away with Toby so he wouldn't be sent to boarding school, isn't there, Shanna?"

Shanna balled the napkin in her fists and stared helplessly at her congealing plate of food. Memories of last night with Cody crowded her mind. More? Yes, there was so much more to explain. Yet how could she tell Bessie that she had fallen in love with Cody—loved him so much that the thought of another man even touching her made her stomach heave. Loved him, yet was going to commit herself and her body to another man.

Forcing her fingers to relax, Shanna tossed the napkin on the table. "Would you mind if Cody explained the rest of it to you, Bessie? I want to ride over to see Zerelda this morning. There's . . . there's something I want to talk to her about."

"If that's what you want, Shanna," Bessie said after a brief moment of hesitation.

"Cody, may I borrow Brownie?" Shanna asked.

"Of course. But don't you want me to go with you?"

"No. I'd really like to have a little time alone just now. Please, Cody."

A few minutes later, after receiving Bessie's promise that she would let the dishes wait until Shanna returned, Shanna mounted Brownie and rode out of the barn. As Brownie trotted down the dirt drive toward the lane that would take her to the Samuels' cabin, Shanna thought of the letters she had hidden beneath her mattress. Maybe she should have brought them with her. But did she even have the right to ask for Zerelda's help? What else could she do? Zerelda was the only person who might understand Shanna's desperate need to keep Cody from doing something outside the bounds of the law and risking his own freedom by helping her.

It was her own fault. She **had** pleaded with Cody to help her but, tossing in her bed while she waited for dawn, she realized just what it could cost him. There could be no assurance that the judge would listen to Toby, as young as he was, and Cody would never allow

Shanna to be sent to jail. No, he would do something foolish, like spiriting her and Toby away somewhere and being charged with helping a prisoner escape.

Who would care for Melinda and Bessie then? No, there was only one choice open to her. Her subtle queries had gotten her nowhere.

Shanna glanced over her shoulder as she became aware of pounding hoofbeats behind her. Lost in thought, she hadn't heard the riders approach, and now saw them almost upon her. Fright surged through her when she caught sight of the grimness of their faces and, their hands cocked on the guns at their hips.

"Stop right there, Miss Van Alstyne!" one rider shouted.

Shanna turned and bent low over the mare, her heels frantically kicking against Brownie's side as she screamed for the mare to run.

Chapter Seventeen

Startled at the desperate scream in her ear and the frantic drumming against her ribs, Brownie shied sideways. Shanna grabbed the saddle horn, cursing her foolishness at using the sidesaddle. She should have known the men her father sent could be close, watching her.

As soon as she regained her balance, Shanna pulled Brownie to a halt. There wasn't really any place to run, and she didn't want to upset Zerelda by leading Pinkertons to her place. Good God, Zerelda might think Shanna had betrayed her—brought the Pinkertons to arrest Frank and Jesse!

Shanna turned Brownie and faced the two men defiantly when they pulled their horses up in front of her.

"What do you want? I suppose my father sent you!"

The men glanced at each other, surprised at Shanna's challenging demeanor and outright admittance of who she was.

"Well, yes, he did, Miss Van Alstyne," the larger one

conceded. "And I'm afraid you're going to have to come with us."

"Where are you taking me?"

"Uh . . . first we're going back to get the boy. Then into Liberty to see the sheriff."

"No!" Shanna said flatly. "I'll agree to come with you quietly, but you're not going to involve Toby in this until the sheriff says you have a right to. I'll fight you every inch of the way if you try to take Toby with us now, and you're going to look like a couple asses dragging a woman into town tied and bound."

"Miss Van Alstyne, we have a warrant for you and a right to take you in any way we can. Isn't that right, Sid?" the smaller man said with a satisfied smirk.

"Yeah, Bobby, but she's right. Hell, we'll have the whole town against us if we bring her in tied up. You know what a time we had even getting any information about where she was holed up."

"Who *did* tell you where I was?" Shanna demanded.

"Some clerk at the hotel named Perkins," Bobby sneered. "Seems like not everyone in town thinks you're such a holier-than-thou angel."

"Shut up, Bobby," Sid said. "Look, Miss Van Alstyne, you'll give us your word that you won't cause a ruckus if we wait and send for the boy later. Is that right?"

"Yes," Shanna said with a defeated sigh. "I will."

"Where were you headed just now?" Sid asked as they turned their horses around, reining one on each side of Shanna.

"That's none of your business."

"Maybe not right now," Sid replied with a tight look on his face. "Come on. We've got a long ride ahead of us."

Worriedly, Shanna glanced ahead of them. The road would take them right past the Garret plantation. "We can probably save some time if we cut across country here," she pleaded.

Bittersweet Promises

"Don't you at least want to let the people you've been staying with know where you are?" Sid asked.

"No. Dan... the sheriff will send someone out."

"Whatever you say." Sid urged his horse off the road and into a trot, mouthing another 'shut up' at Bobby when Bobby shot him a disgusted look.

Zerelda waited until the horses disappeared over a rise in the countryside before she clucked to the horse pulling her buggy. Luckily she had guided the horse to the side of the road around the bend when she heard the pounding hoofbeats ahead of her. She hadn't always been so careful, but the war and two sons who were breaking her heart had changed a lot of things in life.

She fought the urge to send her buggy careening down the road to Cody's place, holding the horse to a steady trot as she glanced down at her swollen stomach. As fearful as she was of Shanna's safety in the clutches of those dreaded Pinkertons, she couldn't take a chance on disturbing her child's rest until he was ready to make his entrance into the world.

Nevertheless, Zerelda's face was covered with sweat when she trotted the horse into Cody's barnyard and called loudly for him. When he emerged from the barn, with Toby at his side, Zerelda glanced at the little boy and jerked her head toward the house, her grim face freezing Cody's query about Shanna in his throat.

"Toby, go on in and tell Aunt Bessie we have company, why don't you?" Cody said, forcing a calmness he didn't feel into his voice.

"Sure, Cody."

As soon as Toby was out of earshot, Cody reached up and grabbed Zerelda's hand. "What is it? Shanna was on her way over to see you. Where is she?"

Zerelda squeezed his hand in return and took a deep breath. "The Pinkertons came on her and took her to

Liberty. I was around the bend in the road, and they didn't see me, but I heard what they said."

"Jesus!" Cody dropped her hand and started for the barn.

"Stop right there, Cody!" Zerelda called, halting Cody a step away from the buggy. "I'm going into Liberty with you, and you need to make some arrangements around here before we go."

"Zerelda, that's a long trip for you to make in your condition."

"You admitted Shanna was coming to see me. She's my friend, too, and I'm going with you to see what she wanted. She's in bad trouble, isn't she, Cody? Pinkertons only come after someone accused of a crime."

"I guess you're sure they were Pinkertons."

"Everyone knows what they look like—wearing those black coats and bowler hats. Yes, I'm sure. And from what I heard, maybe you better send Toby over to my place to stay for a while."

"That won't do any good, Zerelda, and it might cause even more harm. You're right on one thing, though. I need to make sure things will be all right here while I'm gone. Can Susie come over?"

"Help me down, Cody."

Zerelda climbed from the buggy and faced Cody. "Now, you get on that horse of yours and go for Susie. Pappy may want to come with her, and maybe that won't be such a bad idea. Bessie's gonna be awfully worried until we get Shanna back here safe. They can bring the wagon, since I'll need the buggy to go with you.

"Go on," she said when Cody hesitated. "I know you want to go galloping off after Shanna, but you've got responsibilities here to see to first. I'll go in and tell Bessie what's going on. I assume Bessie won't be surprised that this has happened?"

"No," Cody admitted. "And she can tell you the rest.

Bittersweet Promises

The children know some of it, too, and between the two of you, you'll have to explain why Shanna's gone."

"I'll pack us a lunch to eat on the way. I'm not going to be able to travel as fast as you want, but I'm *not* going to be left behind."

Cody nodded curtly and headed for the barn.

Shanna kept her word and rode quietly between the Pinkertons, raising her head proudly as they escorted her down the main street of Liberty. People on the board walkways froze in midstride as they caught sight of her, and at one point a man she recognized as the father of one of her pupils stepped into the street in front of the horses.

"You all right, Miss Allen?" he asked.

"Yes, Mr. Evans," Shanna said in as firm a voice as she could manage when she saw Bobby reach for his gun. "Everything will be all right. There's just something we have to discuss with the sheriff."

"You'll let us know if there's anything we can do for you?"

"Yes. But, please, I don't want you to get into any trouble."

Mr. Evans glared at the two men beside her, then stepped out of their way. He followed behind until they pulled their horses up in front of Dan's office, and Shanna gave him a tremulous smile as she slid from Brownie. When she looked past him, she saw several more men and even a few women in the crowd gathered around.

"Please," Shanna said as she held up an imploring hand. "I'll explain everything to you, or I'm sure the sheriff will. I don't want any of you to get into trouble on my account."

Mrs. Toggins stepped forward. "We already know what it's about, Miss Allen. Them nosy Pinkertons have been going around town the last couple days saying they was gonna arrest you for kidnapping that little boy. And ain't a one of us here won't testify that little Toby's here with you of his own free will."

"Thank you," Shanna said. "Thank you so much."

"If they don't treat you right, you let us know, Miss Allen," another woman called. "And they better not try to have you locked up in that jail. That's no place for our teacher."

Dan stepped through the door of the jail and over to the edge of the walkway. "No one's going to put Miss Allen in jail," he informed the crowd of people. "I've already sent for Judge Howard, and he'll get this mess straightened out tomorrow when he arrives. In the meantime, she can stay with my wife and me."

"Like hell she will," Bobby said as he moved over beside Shanna. "This woman's got criminal charges against her, and Sid and I aim to be right outside her jail cell guarding her tonight."

An angry mutter grew in the crowd and a few of the men surged forward.

"Hold it right there!" Dan drew his gun, as did the two Pinkertons. Instead of aiming his gun at the crowd, Dan trained it on Bobby and Sid.

"Holster those firearms right now!" Dan demanded. "You're in my jurisdiction, and you'll do what I say. In fact, why don't you just turn those pistols over to me? You'll get them back when you're on the stage leaving town."

"We ain't leaving until Mr. Van Alstyne gets here!" Bobby said angrily. "And you don't have no authority to take our guns!"

"He's already here, over at the hotel," Dan said, ignoring Shanna's gasp of horror. "And I've got two deputies at the window behind me with rifles that say I have all the authority I need to relieve you of your weapons."

Sid and Bobby turned toward the jail and found a rifle

Bittersweet Promises

barrel centered on each of their chests. "Do as he says, Bobby," Sid told his companion, and both men shifted their hold to the barrels of their pistols and held them out to the sheriff.

"Put them on the walkway step," Dan ordered, "then get out of here."

The two Pinkertons laid their pistols down and started toward the hotel. "We'll see what Mr. Van Alstyne's got to say about this," Bobby said over his shoulder.

"You do that," Mrs. Toggins said as he passed her. She cleared her throat and a gob of spittle landed on Bobby's boot.

Bobby whirled toward her, fists clenched, and three simultaneous clicks from Dan's six-gun and the two rifles being cocked sounded in the silence. Sid reached over and gave Bobby a shove, starting him on the way again. Several throats cleared as they passed, but Dan's muttered warning kept the crowd in check until the men had crossed the street.

"Wish I could have let y'all do what you wanted," Dan said with a smile. "But the law's the law. Council passed that law 'bout spitting so the ladies wouldn't get their skirts dirty."

"Got a law about keepin' our town free from eyesores, too, don't we, Dan?" Mr. Evans called. "So's it'll be pleasant for people to visit? Those two are the biggest eyesores I've seen around here in a long time."

Several chuckles broke the tension in the crowd, and Dan shoved his pistol back into his holster. "You might be right about that, Evans," he said. "They spend too much time out on the street, I just might have to enforce that law. 'Specially if I get some complaints from the citizens."

"Consider us complaining," Evans called back.

"I'll do that," Dan agreed. "Now, why don't y'all go on about your business, so I can take Miss Allen over to my house and get her settled. You're all invited to stop by later if you want to visit her. The wife has been cooking up a storm ever since I told her she might have some company."

The crowd began breaking up as Dan took Shanna's arm and helped her up out of the street.

"I guess you better start calling me Van Alstyne instead of Allen, Sheriff," Shanna said when they started down the walkway.

"How about Shanna and Dan? And the wife's name is Patty."

"Are you sure you want me at your house? I mean, it could cause problems when the judge finds out."

"Not Judge Howard," Dan denied. "Say, I better send someone out to tell Cody and Bessie where you are. I don't reckon they know what happened, or you wouldn't be here alone."

"No, they don't. I . . . I told those men I'd come quietly, if they'd leave Toby out of it for now. I was on my way to visit . . . visit a friend when they found me. Sheriff. . . ."

"Dan," he reminded her.

"Dan, what's going to happen when the judge comes? Have you met my father?"

"I've met him," Dan said in a voice that told her just what he thought of her father. "He's going to learn to abide by the law, same as everyone else, while he's in my town. And far as your little brother goes, I'm afraid that will be up to Judge Howard. You have told Cody about this, haven't you? After all, he's a lawyer."

"Yes. He knows. Dan, will we have to have a court hearing in front of the entire town?"

"Is there some reason you don't want that?"

Shanna hung her head. The people had been so good to her, and she knew they deserved to hear the whole story. There was still the matter of whom Toby would

Bittersweet Promises

be forced to live with, though. She knew her father would bring that up. Even if she were cleared of the kidnapping charge, he would demand that Toby be returned to his custody.

She had to talk to the judge to see where she stood without revealing Toby's real father's name and giving Christian Van Alstyne a chance to find him before Shanna could.

"Shanna?" Dan prodded when they stopped at the gate to a small white house on the edge of town. "You never answered me."

"I . . . I want some time alone with the judge," Shanna said.

"Well, you and Cody have the right to ask that."

"No. Not Cody, just me."

"But he's going to be your lawyer, isn't he? He needs to know everything you tell the judge."

"He's going to be my lawyer on the kidnapping charge. There's another matter I need to discuss with Judge Howard, without Cody present."

Dan shrugged his shoulders and held the gate for her. "I'll see what I can do."

Chapter Eighteen

Cody shouldered his way through the crowd in Dan's parlor and, heedless of the eyes on him, took Shanna in his arms.

"Are you holding up? Those bastards didn't mistreat you, did they?"

"No." Shanna blushed and tried to extricate herself from his grasp. "Cody, everyone's watching us."

"Tough," Cody replied.

"Hey, Cody," Mr. Evans called. "Remind me not to let my wife use you for a lawyer, if you treat all your female clients like that."

Reluctantly, Cody dropped his arms as Shanna's blush heightened and a titter of laugher ran through the room. "We need to talk," he said, ignoring the laughter.

"Fa-Father's over at the hotel already."

"Yeah. Someone told me when we pulled up outside."

"We? Cody, you didn't bring Toby!"

Bittersweet Promises

"No, only Zerelda came with me this time. But Toby's going to have to come in tomorrow."

The haunted look in Shanna's eyes deepened. "I know. What are we going to do, Cody?"

"We're going to fight like hell to keep Toby where he belongs. With you."

The mutter of agreement that ran through the gathering told Shanna that everyone was listening closely to their words. She smiled bravely at a few faces as Zerelda Samuel approached.

"Cody says you were on your way to see me when those Pinkertons nabbed you," Zerelda said. "Did you want to talk about something?"

"Yes, but...." Shanna shrugged helplessly. She couldn't talk to Zerelda where everyone could overhear their discussion.

"The wife has some mighty pretty flowers blooming out back," Dan offered. "Maybe you two ladies would like to go out to see them. I reckon me and Cody ought to go on over to the hotel to see just what your father has in mind, Shanna."

"I . . . I won't have to see him, will I, Dan?" Shanna asked.

"Not today, not if you don't want to. But you'll have to face him tomorrow. Come on, Cody. Let's get this over with."

"Shanna," Cody said. "We're going to have to talk before tomorrow, too."

"All right. We'll do that when you get back. Cody, how's Toby taking all this?"

"Like a little trouper," Cody said with an attempt at a smile. "He and Melinda had their heads together when I left, planning what Toby would say when he talked to the judge. We had to tell them what was going on, Shanna. They knew you'd gone to see Zerelda, and when she showed up without you, they realized something had happened."

Shanna glanced questioningly at Zerelda, and the taller woman put her arm around Shanna's waist to lead her out of the parlor. "I'll explain outside, Shanna."

As they passed through the kitchen, Dan's wife, Patty, looked up from slicing cake at the countertop. "Oh, is everyone leaving? I was just going to take in some cake."

"Most of them are still there," Zerelda replied. "But Dan's going with Cody, over to the hotel."

"Is everyone treating you all right, Zerelda?" Patty asked.

"One or two gave me a funny look," Zerelda admitted. "But I didn't pay them no mind. We're going out to your garden, if that's all right with you."

"Of course. I'll save you each a piece of cake."

"Thank you." Zerelda opened the back door and walked out onto the porch, with Shanna a step behind.

Shanna followed Zerelda down the two steps and over to a bed of early blooming daffodils. She breathed in their lovely scent for a second before she looked up at Zerelda.

"The townspeople are acting the way they are toward you because of Frank and Jesse, aren't they, Zerelda? I'm sorry you have to put up with that, just because you came in to make sure I'm all right."

Zerelda shrugged resignedly. "I can't stay out at the house all the time and hide. We've all got our crosses to bear. Guess Frank and Jesse are mine."

"I hope Toby never breaks my heart like that." Shanna laid a comforting hand on Zerelda's arm. "It must be terrible for you."

Zerelda shook her head slowly. "You can't even imagine. You try your best to raise them right and then you wonder what you did wrong. Oh, I guess I could blame it on that darned war, but that seems like a poor excuse.

Bittersweet Promises

Other boys went off and came back still decent. Look at Cody, after all he lost."

Shanna patted Zerelda's arm, at a loss as to what to say to ease her agony. A robin called a gay chirrup from a nearby tree branch, and honeybees murmured contented buzzes as they flew from one bright yellow bud to another. The beautiful spring day was entirely out of sync with the morose thoughts shared by the two women. Shanna, especially, caught herself wondering what right she had to burden Zerelda with her own request for help, when Zerelda carried such a load herself.

Who else could she ask, though? Cody? It wasn't fair to ask Cody to trace the man Shanna had informed him that she would marry—not after Cody had told Shanna he loved her. Not after they had sealed their love for each other with the rapture of their shared bodies last night.

How, oh how, would she ever make herself go through with this marriage, even if she did find Toby's father? It had seemed so logical when she started out—loveless marriages were part of life. A woman had only to give her husband an heir or two, then could retire to her own bedroom at night. That logic, though, fled in the face of a chestnut-haired man whose touch had shown her the true depths of what she would be losing.

Toby's father already had an heir. Wouldn't he be satisfied with the money Shanna offered him, or would she, as Cody had angrily accused her, have to buy him also with her body?

She loved Toby, more than anything—had to place that love before her love for Cody. She had given Toby her solemn promise to do everything within her power to keep her little brother with her. How could she have foreseen that her resolve to keep that promise would be tested to the utmost by falling in love with Cody? Cody. Cody, who would be a perfect father for Toby.

She had even come to love Melinda as her own. The little girl had blossomed with Shanna's mixture of discipline and love. What would happen to Melinda if Toby had to leave?

"Well," Zerelda said finally. "We didn't come out here to discuss my problems. I was round the bend from where those Pinkertons took you, and I headed for Cody's soon as you were out of sight. Bessie told me a little before we left the plantation, and Cody explained the rest on our way into town. I reckon there must be something more, though. You weren't just coming over to see me to visit, were you, Shanna?"

"No," Shanna admitted. "I wanted to ask your help in finding someone. Look, there's a bench under that tree. You must be exhausted after that trip, being with child and all. Let's sit down."

Shanna led the way down the flagstone path Dan had laid through the garden to the iron bench under a huge elm tree. The late afternoon sun was still high enough off the horizon to warm the earth, and the shade under the newly leafed tree welcomed them. Shanna waited until Zerelda settled her larger body on the bench before she sat down.

"I have to ask you to keep the name of the man I'm looking for confidential for now, Zerelda. No one knows yet, not even Toby."

"I'm sure you have your reasons, Shanna. And like I told you before, anything you tell me won't go no farther than you want it to."

"Thank you. As for my reasons, you'd know if you'd ever met my father. The man I'm looking for is Toby's real father, and he's the only chance I have to keep Toby with me. Even Cody agrees that it might the only way. I have to convince this man to marry me."

"Marry you? But I thought you and Cody . . . I mean, well, we've all seen you two together."

Shanna shook her head sadly. "I love Cody," she said. "I'll admit that to you. But I have to find Joshua Randolph and talk him into fighting for custody of Toby, so I can keep Toby away from my father's revenge. Father knows Toby isn't his son, but I don't think he knows Mr. Randolph's name. He wants to banish Toby—send him off to a boarding school—never allow me to see my brother again! And I have to marry Mr. Randolph, so I can still help raise Toby."

"Joshua Randolph? JT? Oh, Shanna, honey, you don't want to marry JT! Besides, you've got about as much of a chance of convincing JT to marry you as I do of turning back time and making like the last few months never happened."

"JT?" Shanna said with a frown, puzzling over some half-remembered memory. "Then, you do know him?"

"Yes, I know him," Zerelda admitted. "And I know where he's at. Joshua Tobias Randolph. Guess that's where Toby must have got his name from, but we always just called Joshua JT when he was a little boy. His daddy was Joshua."

"The outlaw hideout. Zerelda, he's at the place the bank robbers hid out after the robbery, isn't he?"

"How do you know about that, Shanna?"

"I . . . I overheard Cody talking to someone late one night. I guess I should have confided in Cody from the start. He could have taken me to Mr. Randolph, and maybe this would all be settled by now."

And maybe I could have found him before I fell in love with Cody, her mind continued.

"Don't bet on it, Shanna. Like I said, JT's not the marrying kind, not now. But you're right about one thing. If you'd told Cody right off, he could have taken you to JT. I'm surprised he didn't make the connection right away, anyway. I know I did, but then, you didn't seem to want to talk about it."

"What do you mean?"

Zerelda studied Shanna silently for a moment before she spoke. "Do you have any idea how much you look like your mother?"

"Why . . . why, yes, I do. I've seen pictures of her at different ages, and they could almost be pictures of me. But what's that got to do with Mr. Randolph?"

"JT was in love with your mama, Shanna. Weren't too many people around here knew 'bout it, but JT, he was pretty close friends with Cody and my boys. 'Course the Randolphs and Garrets had a lot more money than we did, but neither JT nor Cody ever let that make a difference when they were home. Fact is, JT spent a lot of time either at Cody's or my place. Came to think of JT and Cody almost as two of my own boys, and JT confided in me one night when he showed up and Frank and Jesse were off somewhere."

"What . . . what did he tell you about my mother?"

"He showed me a picture of her. Said he'd met her when he was off up north taking care of some of his father's business interests. Joshua used to have a lot of dealings with the Yankees before the war, and guess that more than anything lost Joshua his fortune. He never did believe a real war could break out. Always thought the states were too tied together and dependent on each other to split up."

"Did he tell you my mother was married?"

"Yes," Zerelda admitted. "Not that first night, but after the war broke out, JT and Cody managed to get a few days leave to come home to check on things. Those two rode in the same regiment, but Frank and Jesse, they went a different way, with that damned Bloody Bill Anderson and Quantrill. Anyway, Joshua was dead by then, and JT's mother left to go live with her sister in Carolina after the bank took the house. Some say Joshua took his own life, and it's probably true. There wasn't nothing back here for JT, and he broke down one night and told me what he had planned before the war took it all away. Your mama was going to leave—bring you with her."

Shanna sat quietly for a few minutes, trying to imagine her mother in love with a man so much that she was willing to give up her life in New York and bear the scandal of a divorce. Diedre had always seemed so reserved—so much the proper society wife. There had never been any screaming fights between her mother and father, not like those that some of her friends told her their parents had. Instead, there was always a fastidious politeness, even to the point of her mother addressing her father as Mr. Van Alstyne. Even after last night with Cody and her own understanding of what true love meant between a man and woman, she had a hard time imagining the other side her mother must have had.

"Do you think JT knew about Toby?" Shanna finally asked.

"I guess you'd have to ask Cody that," Zerelda replied. "There's some things a man won't say to a woman, though thank goodness Pappy's not like that."

A stab of pain sliced Shanna's heart at the mention of Cody's name. Cody. He had to have known about JT and her mother, since, according to Zerelda, he and JT were close friends. He had probably seen the picture of Diedre that her mother's letter had told her that JT carried.

Shanna recalled Cody's conversation with the man called Johnny that night soon after she arrived at the plantation. Cody had known—or at least had suspicions about—who she and Toby were almost from the first. He had asked Johnny about a man called JT. Why hadn't Cody discussed it with her during all these weeks, especially if he had known JT had left her mother pregnant?

"All this time," Shanna mused aloud. "All this time I've been so close to finding the man I came here looking for and...."

"Well, not that close, Shanna. The hideout's quite a ride from here—a couple days. And you've got no guarantee JT would even see you. Jesse said JT don't want anyone to see his face now, don't want nobody pitying him. After Pappy had to take his leg off, JT wouldn't even stay around long enough to make sure it had healed properly before he left."

"His leg? My word, Zerelda. What in the world happened to that poor man?"

"Reckon Cody can tell you more about what happened in that battle where JT's face got scarred," Zerelda said, inadvertently sending another twist of misery through Shanna's mind. Cody could have told her a lot of things, if he only had.

"But," Zerelda continued, "I was home when Frank brought JT to the house after he got snake bit out there where he was living like a hermit. Wasn't anything else Pappy could do. Gangrene had already set in, and it was either take the leg off below the knee or give JT a gun like he wanted us to and let him end it. Couldn't none of us bring ourselves to do that."

"He's still out there, though, isn't he?" Shanna asked. "I mean, if he wanted to k-kill himself at one time...."

"He was out of his head with delirium when he asked that, Shanna. JT's not really a quitter when he's in his right mind. But can't you see, Shanna, that he's not a man for you to get hooked up with? He's...."

"He's Toby's father," Shanna broke in. "And I have to find him and talk to him. You're the only one who can help me, Zerelda. Please."

"Cody could...."

"You promised, Zerelda! You can't tell Cody about our talk, because you promised me you wouldn't let what

Bittersweet Promises

I told you go any farther." Shanna took both Zerelda's hands in her own, her frantic gaze on the older woman's face. "Please! You don't know my father, Zerelda. He'll have JT killed, if he finds out what I have planned. I know as sure as I'm sitting here that he will. Then what will happen to Toby? JT's the only chance I have to keep Toby away from my father and with me, where he belongs!"

Reluctantly, Zerelda nodded. Hearing the back door open, she and Shanna glanced up to see Cody striding toward them.

"All right, Shanna," Zerelda said softly. "I'll do what I can to help you. I'll get word to Frank or Jesse somehow and ask one of them to take you out there, if the judge lets you go free."

"Thank you," Shanna breathed as she dropped Zerelda's hands and stood. "Did you see Father?" she asked Cody when he stopped beside the two women.

"No," Cody told her. "The bastard wouldn't talk to us. He slammed the door in our faces and told us he'd see us in court tomorrow morning."

"Then I guess we'd better make some plans," Shanna said. But when Cody reached a comforting hand toward her, she shot him a look filled with distrust and moved a step away.

Chapter Nineteen

"Damn it, Shanna! You've got to trust me with all of it. How the hell can I help you, if you don't?"

Shanna swept her forearms up to knock Cody's hands off and whirled away. Dodging the bench, she leaned against the old elm and wrapped her arms across her stomach.

Trust him? How could she trust Cody when he was obstructing her attempts to locate the man she'd come to Missouri to find? After Zerelda had left them alone, they had sparred verbally for over half an hour, with Shanna adamantly refusing to discuss anything beyond the kidnapping charge. She couldn't take much more.

"Please leave me alone now and ask Zerelda to see me before she leaves," Shanna said in a ravaged voice. "You know all you need to for court in the morning. I don't want to talk about it any more."

"Court in the morning is only half of it, Shanna. What happens after that?"

Bittersweet Promises

Shanna set her lips stubbornly and refused to answer. What happened after court would be her responsibility. Shocked to find out Cody had probably suspected the identity of Toby's father all along—the man Shanna must marry—she still couldn't bring herself to confront him.

Why had Cody thwarted her search? Would he continue to do so, even if Shanna told him that she now knew where his friend, JT, was hiding? Could he possibly be putting their love for each other above a little boy's happiness?

Her heart told Shanna that Cody couldn't possibly risk Toby's future so they could be together—not the Cody who cherished the love of his own daughter so much that he was filled with guilt over being gone when Melinda needed him.

But Toby wasn't Cody's child. Shanna's head throbbed with the suspicion that Cody might be contemplating allowing Toby to be returned to her father's custody. What other reason could Cody have for obstructing Shanna's search for the past two months? How could she trust him, after he had lied to her, even if his lie was by omission?

Cody let out a frustrated breath, and Shanna jerked away when he laid a hand on her shoulder.

"Shanna. . . ."

"I'll see you in the morning," Shanna said firmly. "Please leave now."

She held herself rigid until he strode away, his boot heels echoing his frustration against the flagstone path. Then, as surely as though drawn by a magic, silken thread, Shanna turned to watch his receding back. The broad shoulders were hunched and his hands jammed deep in the pockets of his denims. At the back door he hesitated for a second, and Shanna quickly tore her gaze away and turned around.

Even across this distance he would be able to see the love shining from her eyes—the love even her suspicion couldn't dampen. The love even Shanna had to fight to keep from overshadowing her commitment and love for Toby.

The knowledge gleaned from Zerelda hadn't dimmed her love for Cody, but her suspicion made her realize she had to have enough strength for both of them—made her more determined than ever to keep Cody from getting embroiled any deeper in her and Toby's problems.

There wasn't any way to keep him from defending her in court tomorrow. There wasn't time to get another lawyer and fill him in on her troubles, and she couldn't pay him if one could be found. And she might as well make sure Cody knew their relationship was now ended—that the one night would be all they ever had, as she had breathed to him even in the throes of their passion. It was going to be hard enough to offer herself to JT Randolph, without having Cody around to remind her what she was giving up in return.

The back door opened and Shanna recognized Zerelda's voice when Zerelda said something to Cody, though she couldn't make out the words. A few seconds later, the door closed, and Shanna glanced over her shoulder to see Zerelda walking toward her.

It only took her a few sentences to get Zerelda's assurance that she would somehow retrieve the letters under Shanna's mattress and send them in with Toby. Shanna had to have some proof to offer the judge, if any hope at all remained of gaining the necessary time for her to contact JT and plead her cause with him.

And if the judge didn't give her that time? Shanna didn't have an answer to the question Zerelda asked her—at least not one she wanted to risk telling her friend. Shanna would have to work that out by herself. When they disappeared again, there couldn't be any doubt in anyone's mind that she had run away on her own.

While she waited until she was sure Cody had left, Shanna called to mind the history lessons she had been teaching the children. Thankfully, she had decided to teach them about their own state first. Of course, the area Zerelda mentioned didn't have a name on the map, but if her friend came through on her promise, Shanna would have a guide to the outlaw hideout.

Later that night, curled up in Dan's extra bedroom and wearing her own nightgown, thanks to Zerelda's foresight in bringing her in some clothes from the plantation, Shanna fought vainly to still her thoughts and sleep. What kind of man would JT Randolph be? Physically marred, definitely. Both Johnny and Zerelda had mentioned his scarred face, the result of rescuing his men in one of the battles during the war.

The damage must be severe if JT hid himself away from the world, rather than face averted eyes and behind-the-hand whisperings of either revulsion or sympathy. Had that been why he never returned for her mother? To lose his leg, also, had probably seemed like an unnecessary slap in his face by fate. Rather than being totally revolted, though, Shanna felt a stirring of compassion for the man.

Only when her thoughts wandered inevitably toward the bedroom side of the marriage she must make did the doubts crowd out the compassion in her mind. After what she and Cody had shared, how could she willingly lie with another man?

Toby sat frowning in concentration on Shanna's bed shortly before noon the next morning. The letters he had smuggled to her lay between them, while Shanna clasped both her brother's small hands in her own.

"It's not right, Shanna," Toby said. "How can the judge make me go back with Pop, when all he wants to do is send me away again? I'm away from him now, and he doesn't have to see me. Why isn't that enough for him?"

"I agree with you, Toby. I agree with my whole heart. But judges have to enforce the law."

"Even when it's wrong?"

"When it's wrong, we have to work to change it, Toby."

"Like you told us they do in Washington, DC?"

"Uh-huh. But remember what else I told you, Toby. There's a chance I can talk the judge into giving us some more time, so I can find the man I'm looking for."

Shanna studied Toby's face as he bowed his head. How many inner scars would this experience leave on him? Already he knew things no child of his age should have to contend with. His inquisitive mind had refused to be satisfied until she explained the entire situation to him.

Her face reddened slightly as she recalled having to tell Toby that children were conceived sometimes outside the bonds of marriage. At least he hadn't demanded to know the how of the act. But he had to have started thinking of the concept after seeing the birth of the colt and the other animals multiplying on the Garret plantation as spring developed.

For just an instant Shanna felt a surge of the anger she had carried for so many months after her mother's death. It was replaced by a desire to see her father in a coffin. She even felt a burning desire to have been the one who killed him and pushed the vision from her mind in horror.

"Shanna, let go. That hurts."

Shanna relaxed her grip on Toby's hands with an effort. "I'm sorry. I guess we should get going now."

A knock sounded on the bedroom door, and it opened to reveal Dan, the silver star on his chest gleaming as though he had just polished it.

Bittersweet Promises

"I've set everything up, Shanna," he told her in a cautious voice that had her looking over his shoulder to see Cody listening to his words. "It's time to go now. Judge Howard's waiting for us."

"He still wants to go through with this today, even though it's Sunday?" Shanna responded.

"Judge Howard has to be up in St. Joe next week for a murder trial that may last a while. We have all our witnesses here now. And the townsfolk agree the Lord's day is an appropriate day to deal with keeping a little boy with the sister who loves him."

"We're ready then, I guess."

"Dan, can you take Toby on with you?" Cody asked quietly. "I'd like to talk to Shanna for a second. We've still got a few minutes before Judge Howard calls court to order."

Shanna surreptitiously slipped the letters into the pocket of her dress as Toby stood. She nodded at Toby to go on when her brother glanced questioningly at her, then waited willingly enough until Dan and Toby left the room. If she could have, she would have put off her walk down the courthouse aisle beneath her father's eyes forever. The time had come to face him, though, and no amount of wishful thinking on her part would push time ahead to the conclusion of her trial, without her living through it first.

"I've never been on tr-trial before, Cody," she said to break the lingering silence. "I've never even watched one, though I've read about them. I'm not sure what to expect."

Cody crossed the room and sat on the bed beside her. "It's a simple enough procedure," he explained. "We get to present our side of the story, after your father tells his. I plan to have several of the people you've gotten to know since you came here testify on your behalf—inform Judge Howard that Toby is here with you willingly."

"Will Toby have to testify?"

"He wants to, you know that, Shanna. But that will depend on Judge Howard's opinion of Toby's maturity. He'll want to be sure Toby knows right from wrong, truth from lies. Anyone who testifies in a trial has to take an oath before God to tell the truth. If it's proven later that someone lied to a judge or jury, there are severe penalties."

"Penalties?"

"You don't have to worry about that where Toby's concerned, Shanna. You and I know he'll tell the truth. The problem's going to come in when your father's lawyer tries to convince the judge that Toby isn't old enough to make a choice about how he should live."

"He brought a lawyer with him?"

"No. There's one other lawyer here in Liberty since old man Peters retired. He's Ed Curley, and your father hired him. Look, Shanna, it's different out here from in the big cities, and sometimes a hell of a far cry from those somber proceedings you read about in books. Granted, we've taken a lot of our laws and procedures from our English background, but at times it's a rough-and-tumble justice, where there aren't even lawyers to present the cases for either side. Then Judge Howard just listens to the sheriff's evidence, along with any alibi or defense the prisoner has, and makes his decision. But be assured, Judge Howard knows how to conduct a proper court when he wants to, and today's court will probably be as close to the statutory process as he can make it."

"Are you trying to warn me about something, Cody?" Shanna asked when Cody avoided her questioning look.

"Yes," Cody admitted. "There's one other thing you should know."

"Tell me," Shanna prodded in a battered voice. "What is it?"

Bittersweet Promises

"I talked to Ed a little while this morning. He's really a pretty honest man—a lot older than me—and while he's not real pleased with representing your father, he believes everyone's entitled to representation under the law. But he told me your father's raising Cain because he thinks you should be tried back in New York, where the supposed crime was committed."

"You mean, I might go through this today and be found innocent, then still have to face another trial in New York!?"

"I'm sorry, Shanna. It will take your father time, though, to go through the court system and prove that Judge Howard made a mistake in hearing the charges here, instead of sending you back to New York. It'll buy you an interim period to plan a new defense, if that does happen."

Shanna covered her face with her hands. "It just gets worse and worse," she moaned. "It's not fair! How can we have laws that give a monster like my father the right to tear a small child away from the person who loves him the most?"

Shanna raised her head and tossed her head angrily as she brushed at a silken curl that had fallen from the careful coiffure she had rolled her hair into that morning in an attempt to present an adult face to the judge.

"Damn it, Cody!" she screamed. "We just fought a war that ended slavery for the Negroes! Don't children have the same rights?"

Cody pulled Shanna into his arms. Though she resisted initially, she quickly surrendered and burrowed into the consolation he offered. Her arms crept around him, and she clung to him as though she would never let go. Cody dropped a kiss on her head and stroked her hair, only to feel her jaw clench against his chest.

Shanna pushed herself away and faced him grimly. "Let's get it over with. Just let me fix my hair again."

Cody sat on the bed watching her, while Shanna walked over to the dresser and picked up her brush. With a few sure strokes, she coiled her hair again around her head. He tried without success to catch her eyes in the mirror, but this time it was Shanna who resolutely avoided his gaze.

Though Cody endeavored to come up with something comforting to say to her, his mind remained empty, except for platitudes that sounded inane to him. He couldn't promise her it would be all right, the one desperate assurance he wanted to make—the one he had promised her last night, knowing all along he could be lying.

"I'm ready," Shanna finally said.

Silently Cody rose and took her arm. They left Dan's house and walked down the street without further conversation.

At the door to the courthouse, Cody felt Shanna stiffen and raise her head. He had never been as proud of her as he was then, when Shanna strode regally beside him through the door and down the aisle. But her grip on his arm, which tightened until her nails dug through the thin shirtsleeve, told Cody the agony she suffered. Otherwise, her features remained calm. Only when she glanced at the table where her father sat did her composure threaten to break, but she quickly set her lips and turned her head.

Judge Howard entered the room almost immediately, giving Shanna only a second to turn around to squeeze hands with Toby, where he sat on the bench behind her beside Dan's wife, Patty. She rose when Cody urged her and trained her attention on the judge.

Judge Howard was a tall man, the black robe he wore seeming to accentuate his lankiness. Shanna was reminded of the pictures of President Lincoln she had seen in the newspapers. Dark hair topped a craggy face with hollowed cheeks, and his full mouth was set in stern, no-nonsense lines. The brown eyes that briefly met Shanna's measured and scrutinized her, as they did the other combatants in his arena of justice, before he took his seat.

"The sheriff has explained the charges that are pending before this court today," he said without preamble. "Are both sides ready to present their cases?"

Cody had remained standing, keeping Shanna with him, though the rest of the people in the courtroom had reseated themselves when the judge sat. Cody glanced over at Ed Curley, allowing him to speak first.

"Your Honor," Ed began. "In the interest of not misleading you, I want to state that, though I am at the prosecution table, I am not the prosecutor in this case. I am merely here to represent Mr. Van Alstyne's interests. To that end, I am prepared to proceed."

"Point taken, Mr. Curley. Mr. Garret?"

"I'm ready, too, Your Honor. My client pleads not guilty to the charge of kidnapping levied against her."

"For the record," Judge Howard said, "I want Miss Van Alstyne to state her plea herself."

Hands clenched at her sides, Shanna cleared her throat and spoke decisively, "I plead **not guilty**, Your Honor."

"Thank you, Miss Van Alstyne. Gentlemen, present your cases." Judge Howard leaned back in his chair, his eyes hooded, but alert, beneath shaggy, black brows.

"Judge Howard," Ed Curley said. "For the record, also, Mr. Van Alstyne wishes to protest this trial being held here in Liberty. As I am sure you are aware, the crime took place in New York. Mr. Van Alstyne requests that these proceedings be deemed null and void, and Miss Van Alstyne be returned to the jurisdiction where the crime was committed."

"Alleged crime," Cody reminded him.

Though Cody had forewarned her, Shanna couldn't keep her eyes from blazing with anger. She swung around in her chair to glare at her father.

Christian Van Alstyne sat in his place beside Ed Curley and returned her glare. Anyone studying the two of them couldn't help but note a certain resemblance in their expressions, if not their physical features. Two sets of blue eyes clashed, and one or two of the spectators even rubbed at their ears, as though they had heard the sound.

There the resemblance stopped. Shanna sat trim and straight, her blond hair neatly coiffed above her slender neck. Her father's corpulent body slouched in his chair, his nearly bald head gleaming and his lips sneering his contempt at the small-town proceeding he was forced to tolerate.

"Point taken and request denied, Mr. Curley," Judge Howard said shortly. "Do you have anything further to say at this time?"

"Just a couple things, Your Honor. As I said, I am not prosecuting this case, so it wouldn't be appropriate for me to make a prosecutor's opening remarks. However, I do wish to be allowed to question the witnesses called and even to call my own witnesses to the stand, if I feel Mr. Van Alstyne's side of this is not being presented fully."

"I will grant that request, Mr. Curley. Mr. Garret?"

"I have no remarks for the bench at this time, Judge Howard. However, I do have a question. Will Liberty's sheriff be presenting the prosecution side of the case?"

"That's how we usually work these things in the absence of a valid prosecutor, Mr. Garret. I see no reason to change this. Do you have some objection to that?"

"No, Your Honor. In fact, quite the contrary. However, I want to forewarn the court that I plan to call Dan as a character witness for Miss Van Alstyne, for the defense."

Bittersweet Promises

"That's somewhat unusual, but not entirely outside the bounds of procedure, if the sheriff agrees," Judge Howard said with a nod. "Sheriff?"

"I'm agreeable, Judge," Dan replied as he stood up from his seat on the first bench behind Shanna's father.

Van Alstyne turned and glared at the sheriff, but yielded to the pressure of Ed Curley's hand on his shoulder and closed his mouth over whatever comment he had intended to make.

"Shouldn't you be sitting up at the table in front of you, Sheriff?" Judge Howard inquired.

"If you say I have to, Judge," Dan said with a grimace. "But I'm perfectly content with the smell of the air back here a ways."

Christian Van Alstyne surged to his feet with a roar. "I object to this farce of a proceeding! It's been made perfectly clear to me ever since I set foot in this town that I won't be given a fair hearing in this backwater burg! Even the sheriff's on my daughter's side!"

Judge Howard leaned forward and picked up his gavel. He pounded it twice to quiet the angry mutters running through the spectators at Van Alstyne's denigrating remarks, keeping his furious brown eyes centered on Van Alstyne's angry red face.

"You have a lawyer here to make your objections, Mr. Van Alstyne," Judge Howard said in a steely voice. "And might I remind you that *you* are not the one having a hearing at this time. It's your daughter, and I alone will be the judge of whether all the evidence in this matter is given a fair hearing!"

"I know my rights!"

The gavel silenced Van Alstyne's protests as Judge Howard continued, "And I alone also have the right to decide who remains in this courtroom, or who is removed for unseemly conduct. I also have the authority to jail anyone interrupting these proceedings and causing discord in my courtroom. Do I make myself clear, Mr. Van Alstyne?"

Van Alstyne collapsed in his chair and clamped his lips shut. Judge Howard refused to allow him his silence.

"I asked you a question, sir!" Though quiet, Judge Howard's voice clearly bespoke his warning.

"Yes, sir," Van Alstyne forced out through grim lips.

Judge Howard looked over at Dan. "Now, Sheriff, I guess we only have one other thing to decide. Have you planned on a jury trial, or do you wish me to decide this case?"

"Well, sir," Dan said, scratching his head. "I guess I forgot to ask Miss Allen . . . Van Alstyne's lawyer that question. Seeing as how I think most of the people here in town planned on being witnesses for Shanna, I don't see how we'd come up with a jury, let alone an impartial one."

Judge Howard glanced over at Cody.

"We'd probably settle for a partial jury, Your Honor," Cody said with a chuckle. "However, in the interest of truth and justice, I believe we should leave the weighing of facts in this case in your hands."

"Do you agree, Miss Van Alstyne?"

"Yes, Your Honor."

"Proceed, Sheriff," Judge Howard said with a nod.

"Guess I'm my first witness, Your Honor," Dan said as he moved into the aisle. "If it's all right with you, I'll not ask myself questions. I'll just step up on the stand and tell you what I know."

"Seems reasonable, Sheriff. I see you've appointed one of your deputies as bailiff. He will administer the oaths to the witnesses."

Chapter Twenty

"Well, sir," Dan said after he swore to the oath and took his seat in the witness chair beside the judge's stand, "guess I should start with the first time I saw Miss Allen . . . I mean. . . . Judge, do you think it would be all right for us to call the defendant Shanna? Seems a little awkward, trying to get used to her new name."

Judge Howard looked over at Ed Curley to see him listening to a whispered comment from Christian Van Alstyne. Curley glanced at the bench and nodded his agreement, but Cody frowned as he caught the gleam in Van Alstyne's eyes before he hooded them.

"You may refer to the defendant by her given name," Judge Howard said, though he cast a warning glance at Cody.

While Dan recounted his first meeting with Shanna and his subsequent notification by telegram that she was wanted for charges brought against her in New York, Cody mulled over Van Alstyne's actions in his mind. He hadn't come to any conclusion by the time Dan informed the judge that he had nothing further to say at this time.

"Mr. Garret?" Judge Howard prodded after Dan fell quiet. "Do you have any questions for the sheriff?"

Cody rose to his feet. "Not at this time, Your Honor. However, as I mentioned before, I intend to call the sheriff at a later time."

"Mr. Curley?"

"I do have a few questions for the sheriff," Curley said in a mild voice, rising to his feet.

"Go ahead."

"Sheriff," Curley said. "You brought up something in your very first remarks that I feel needs clarification. Why did you ask that you be allowed to refer to the defendant as Shanna, instead of Miss Van Alstyne?"

"Well, like I said, it's hard to change when you're used to referring to someone by a different name," Dan said with a puzzled look.

Cody immediately grasped the thrust of Curley's questions and jumped to his feet. "I object, Your Honor."

"On what grounds?" Judge Howard questioned.

"I . . . on the grounds. . . ." Cody's shoulders slumped and he sat down. "I guess I don't have any grounds for that objection," he said in a disheartened voice.

Shanna glanced at Cody in confusion. He shook his head and motioned for her not to interrupt as he turned his attention back to the front of the courtroom.

"May I proceed, Your Honor?"

"Yes, Mr. Curley."

Curley placed his hands behind his back and strode toward Dan. "If I'm reading you right then, Sheriff, when you first met Miss Van Alstyne you knew her by a different name. What was that name?"

"Miss Allen. But—"

"Thank you, Sheriff. Now, do people you meet sometimes lie to you and give you a false name, even knowing you are an officer of the law?"

"Yeah, sometimes."

"Why do they do this, Sheriff?"

"Well," Dan said reluctantly, "they don't want me to know their real name, of course."

"I repeat, Sheriff. Why? Could it be they have something to hide? Something you would find out, if you knew their real name?"

"Yeah," Dan said grumpily. "But Shanna—"

"When did Miss Van Alstyne first tell you that her name was Allen, Sheriff?"

"When she came to my office to report that she had lost the money she had with her, the day after she arrived in Liberty. She seemed to think it might have fallen out of her carpetbag when the stage driver tossed it in the street, and she wanted to describe it, in case someone turned it in."

"At that time, she told you her name was Shanna Allen?"

"Yes."

"Did anyone ever turn in this money Miss Van Alstyne supposedly lost?"

"No."

"And what were your thoughts when you received the telegram from the Pinkerton Detective Agency describing Miss Van Alstyne and her brother and informing you that she had kidnapped her brother from New York? Were you, as we would think an officer of the law would be, shocked and dismayed that she had given you a false name? Or did you somehow qualify her deceit in your mind?"

"Objection," Cody said from his seat. "Does Mr. Curley want answers to his questions as he asks them, or does he wish to take this opportunity to pontificate and insinuate things for which he doesn't have evidence?"

"Sustained," Judge Howard said.

"Then," Curley continued, "let me go back to another question you *were* allowed to answer and ask you to repeat that answer. Was Miss Van Alstyne's money ever turned in to you?"

"No. I already told you that."

"Yes, I remember," Curley said. "And what did Miss Van Alstyne do when she found herself out of funds and with no means of support for her and her small brother?"

"Why, she took a job, like we all do when we need to earn money to live on," Dan said stoutly. "She earned her way."

"Who did she find employment with, Sheriff?"

"The Garrets," Dan responded instantly. "Aunt Bessie needed a teacher for Melinda. She'd been looking for someone for quite a while."

"Aunt Bessie? Melinda? Will you please explain who they are?"

"Why, you know who they are, Mr. Curley. Everyone in town does."

"For the record. Please, Sheriff?"

"Aunt Bessie's Cody's aunt. And Melinda's his daughter."

"You're referring to Mr. Garret, the defense attorney?"

"Yes, I am."

"And what happened after Miss Van Alstyne took up her duties for Mr. Garret's daughter?"

"Well, it was something, I can tell you. First thing we knew, Shanna agreed to teach a lot of the other kids who needed schooling around here. Didn't even ask for any pay. Folks were mighty grateful, I can tell you."

Shanna glanced at Cody as he bowed his head and shook it sadly. "What is it?" she whispered, grasping his arm to get his attention. "He's only telling the truth."

Bittersweet Promises

"Just listen," Cody said in an irritated voice.

Curley let the silence linger in the courtroom as he paced back and forth in front of Dan's seat. He paused once and glanced at the sheriff, then shook his head and resumed his pacing.

"Mr. Curley," Judge Howard said finally. "Are you finished?"

"No, Your Honor. I'm just trying to sort this out in my mind."

"Well, sort it out during recess instead of holding up my proceedings," Judge Howard warned.

"All right, Your Honor. But I just want to make sure I've got my facts straight. Sheriff, please confirm what I'm saying. You met Miss Van Alstyne here in Liberty shortly after she arrived. She gave you a false name and told you that she had lost the money she had brought with her to survive on. Then, she quickly associated herself with one of the prominent families in the county, the head of which happens to be a lawyer. After that, she proceeded to insinuate herself into the good graces of as many others as she could by offering to teach any child of school age without charge. Is that what happened?"

The courtroom erupted in discord as Shanna gasped and sprang to her feet. She tried to shake off Cody's restraining arm and gain Judge Howard's attention, but Cody pulled her firmly back into her seat. As Judge Howard pounded his gavel in an attempt to restore order, Cody frantically whispered to Shanna, "For God's sake, he's playing you! Don't lose control, or you'll do just what he wants you to."

"He's lying!" Shanna gasped. "That's not how it was!"

"He's not lying, Shanna. He's twisting and misrepresenting the facts. There's a difference."

Shanna shot him a disgruntled look, then glanced over her shoulder at the faces behind her. The spectators were still muttering furiously, despite Judge Howard's banging gavel. Here and there she caught a look of support from several women, but she quickly realized a few of the men were staring at her with a contemplative frown on their faces. When Toby scrambled under the railing separating them, she caught him to her and held him close.

"Don't worry, Shanna," Toby said firmly. "The judge can see that he's just trying to make something look like it's not. Cody will fix him, won't you, Cody?"

"I'm going to try, son," Cody said as the spectators yielded at last to Judge Howard's shouted orders. "Now, you go sit down again."

After a final hug from Shanna, Toby ducked under the railing and resumed his seat.

"No further questions of this witness at this time," Curley said, taking his seat as soon as the room settled into silence.

"Mr. Garret?"

"Your Honor, I would like a short recess to consult with a few of my witnesses."

"You should have had your witnesses prepared before the trial, Mr. Garret. However, I will grant you ten minutes. Don't try to prolong it."

Judge Howard swept out of the courtroom, his robe trailing behind as he hastened his steps.

"Father's trying to wreck everything before we even get a chance to tell our side, isn't he, Cody?" Shanna said as soon as the door closed behind Judge Howard. "He's trying to make it look as if I planned all of this ahead of time, knowing that I'd finally get caught with Toby and need people to support my side of the story."

"I should have foreseen it," Cody admitted. "That's what a defense attorney is supposed to do. I should have anticipated how he would twist the facts and turn them to his own advantage. I'm too rusty. I haven't been in court for too many years."

Bittersweet Promises

"You're doing the best you can, Cody," Shanna comforted. "We're just going to have to come up with a way to counteract what he's done. Anyone you put on the stand now to attest to my character is going to be suspect. How can we deal with that?"

Neither one of them saw Toby slip away, and when Shanna glanced up to see Patty's seat vacant, she assumed Toby had gone with her. They were quickly embroiled in a host of outraged witnesses, who demanded Cody still put them on the stand to refute Ed Curley's insinuations.

"We can't let that man suggest we're hicks who can't see through an obvious attempt to defraud us," Mrs. Toggins told Cody with an apologetic glance at Shanna.

Shanna clasped the other woman's arm in a gesture of understanding and turned her attention to the hastily called conference around Cody.

Toby glanced behind him, then turned the knob on the door before him without knocking. It opened easily, and he slipped inside, holding his breath as he gazed around until his eyes fell on the black-robed figure standing in the corner of the room.

"Can I help you, son?" Judge Howard asked.

"I think you're the only person who *can* help me, sir," Toby said. "I'm Toby Van Alstyne and my sister is accused of taking me from New York without me agreeing to it."

"Son, I'm not really supposed to be talking to you outside the courtroom."

"Not really, sir? You mean there might be a way around that rule, so I can say something to you?"

"Pretty smart, aren't you, son? How old are you?"

"Ten. Well, ten in a few days."

"Sit down, Toby," Judge Howard said. "I think I'll stick my head out and tell the lawyers I've decided to make that a fifteen-minute recess."

A second later, Judge Howard settled himself into the desk chair and poured a glass of water from the pitcher someone had left on his desk. "Would you like a drink, Toby?"

"No, sir. I'm fine."

"All right, then. What did you want to talk to me about?"

"About tes...." Toby frowned in concentration. "About testifying in Shanna's trial. Cody ... Mr. Garret explained to me that you would be the one who decided if I could, and that I would have to show you how matu ... grown-up I am. And that I'm smart enough to know what's going on. I am, sir. Why, Melinda and I talked about it a lot, and I even practiced."

"Melinda Garret?" Judge Howard asked.

"Uh-huh. She's my best friend. Cody's her father and he's been real nice to me, too. Melinda and me, well, we didn't like each other much at first, but we're real good friends now."

"How old is Melinda?"

"She'll be five the same day I'm ten."

"And how did you do this practicing for what you would say if I let you testify?"

"Well, sir, I asked Cody how it worked at a trial, and he told me that you don't just get up in the chair and tell what happened. That people ask you questions and you have to answer them with the truth. I didn't think that was right, but I practiced the way Cody told me it would have to be."

Judge Howard studied Toby behind a hand raised to hide the slight smile on his lips. "Just what did you think was wrong about how we do things at a trial, Toby?" he asked after a moment.

"Why, the judge might not get to hear the whole story," Toby said logically, his intense gaze fixed on the judge.

"Like it happened out there a little while ago, when Mr. Curley asked the sheriff questions and then didn't let the sheriff explain what he had said. You might just get asked questions that show someone else's side of the story—the side that makes them look right."

"That was only the beginning of the trial, son. We'll get to hear both sides before it's over. Believe me, your sister will have a fair hearing."

Toby swung his legs back and forth and looked around the room. His small hands gripped the armrests in the huge chair, and he bit his bottom lip as he tried to decide what to say next.

"Son, I think I know what's going through your mind," Judge Howard said. "What they're saying out there is making your sister look bad, and you don't like people hearing that."

"Yes, sir. But that's not all of it. I mean, I know it could look to some people like maybe Shanna did take me with her without me wanting to go, her being older than me and all. And I'm used to people thinking Shanna is my mom instead of my sister at first, 'cause it's always just been Shanna and me for the most part. But. . . ."

"Go on, son," Judge Howard prodded.

"Well, it don't seem fair that these people get to ask their questions first and make it look like that. When kids get in trouble, it's usually the kid who gets to tell his side first that has the best chance to be believed. The other kid, 'less he's got someone to back him up, has to do some tall talking to make the grown-ups believe he's right instead of the other kid."

Judge Howard shifted in his chair and took a drink of water.

"Oh, not Shanna, sir," Toby quickly said before the judge could speak. "She's not like that. But some of my friends back in New York, well, I've seen that happen to them."

"So you think your sister should get to tell her story first so she would be believed first?"

"No, sir. Not exactly. What I really mean is that Shanna's going to have a harder time making you believe her after Pop makes her look bad. And Shanna and I are the only other two people here who know what really happened. That's why I have to be able to tell about it, too, so she will have someone to back her up. That's why I have to show you that I'm smart enough to tes-testify."

Judge Howard leaned back in his chair and clasped his hands in front of him, his shaggy brows drawing together as he studied the small figure in front of him. Toby sat quietly, returning his gaze, not shifting nervously as though he were trying to escape the scrutiny.

"Toby, you do realize that, if I let you testify, you'll also have to answer questions from Mr. Curley? That might not be pleasant."

"Yes, sir. But that's something that will be over with when he gets done. If I lose Shanna, it might be for the rest of my life."

A long moment later, Judge Howard straightened in his chair. "Go on back out to your sister, Toby," he said quietly. "I promise you I'll think hard on what you've told me. If I feel letting you testify is the right thing to do, that's the way it will be."

"Thank you, sir." Toby slid from his chair. At the door, he turned around. "Sir," he said. "Are your mom and pop still alive?"

"My mother is, son," Judge Howard admitted. "My dad died years ago, when I was about your age. My mother married again and I had a stepfather after that."

"Did you like him, sir?"

Judge Howard was silent for a moment. "Yes, I even came to love him. He was a fair man who taught me right from wrong and what it means to be a man."

Bittersweet Promises

Toby nodded his head thoughtfully and opened the door. Glancing around the courtroom before he walked out of the office, he saw his father facing away from him and deep in conversation with Mr. Curley. He breathed a sigh of relief and scurried across the room to stand behind Shanna's skirts.

"Toby," Shanna said immediately. "Where have you been? I thought you were with Patty."

"No, I...."

Judge Howard opened his door again and stuck his head out. "Five more minutes," he called, then shut the door again.

Chapter Twenty-one

"Sheriff," Judge Howard said when he reconvened court, "do you have anyone else to call?"

"Well, sir, guess we should call the two Pinkerton men to tell their side, then Mr. Van Alstyne."

Dan called Sid first, and Sid explained how he and Bobby had received the assignment of tracing Shanna and Toby from their commanding officer. They had been given a picture of both Shanna and Toby, he informed the sheriff, and it had been easy enough to trace their trail by train out of the city and finally on the stagecoach to Liberty.

"We had a little trouble finding where they had gone once they hit town here," Sid admitted. "But eventually the hotel clerk told us what we needed to know."

Dan shrugged his shoulders and glanced at Cody.

"One thing I'm not clear on," Cody said as he stood. "I thought the Pinkertons' office was in Chicago. How did you get an assignment in New York?"

Bittersweet Promises

"We worked out of Chicago during the war," Sid explained. "Now Mr. Pinkerton's expanding. Besides, Mr. Van Alstyne is an important man. Probably Mr. Pinkerton would have helped him out even if we hadn't just started our New York office, if Mr. Van Alstyne had contacted him in Chicago."

"I see. Then Mr. Van Alstyne is not a man without influence. He must be used to getting what he wants."

"Objection," Ed Curley called. "Mr. Garret is making assertions about my client's character, not asking questions about facts in the case."

"Mr. Garret," Judge Howard said with a frown. "Please confine yourself to the facts."

"Yes, sir. I only have one more question. Did Shanna come with you willingly when you finally found her?"

"At first I thought she was going to run. But she stopped right away and came back to Liberty with us. She only asked us not to go get the boy just then, and since we didn't really have any authority to take him, just the warrant for her, we had to agree."

Cody sat down after thanking Sid, and Dan called Bobby to the stand. After he confirmed Sid's story, Cody asked Bobby the same question about Shanna's willingness to accompany them.

"Yeah, she did," Bobby said with something of a snarl. "But, boy, when we got back here in town—"

"Thank you," Cody said, cutting him off.

In one of the rows of spectators, a woman cleared her throat. A titter ran through the courtroom, and Bobby's face flamed hotly.

"Y-your Honor," he sputtered to the judge.

"I believe your testimony is finished," Judge Howard said, covering up his smile as he recalled the story Dan had told him. "Step down, please."

Christian Van Alstyne walked resolutely to the stand when called next. Shanna felt her hands tremble as she watched her father take the oath, and she gripped them together in her lap. As soon as her father started telling his story in curt tones, she leaned closer to Cody.

"What are you going to ask him, Cody?" she whispered. "Are you going to let people know what he wants to do with Toby?"

"Judge Howard wouldn't allow that, Shanna," Cody replied in a hushed voice. "This trial isn't about that. It's not related."

"But, Cody...."

"Shhh. Judge Howard will have you taken out of the courtroom if he notices us talking and not listening to what's going on. Besides, you're the one who insisted the matter of the kidnapping charge and the custody issue be kept separate. You haven't given me enough information to even try to bring that into this hearing."

Shanna shot him a sorrowful look and leaned back in place. Lips trembling, she twisted her hands and tried to pay attention to her father. Her mind had other ideas, though, and she felt her heart break yet again as she contemplated Cody's words.

So you're still playing it that way, she thought. *Why can't you see that trust is a two-way thing?*

When Cody rose to question Shanna's father, a hush fell over the courtroom, broken only by the sounds of clothing rustling as people shifted in their seats to get a better view. Cody approached to within a few feet of Van Alstyne.

"We've heard you say what *you* did, Mr. Van Alstyne," he said in a mild voice. "You found your son and daughter missing and filed kidnapping charges on your daughter for taking your son away, after Shanna didn't voluntarily return on her own. Might I ask why?"

"Why?" Van Alstyne blustered. "A man doesn't have to have a reason to enforce discipline on his children."

"Oh, it was a matter of discipline, then," Cody mused. "You didn't feel your son was in any danger? You just wanted to discipline your daughter for taking him with her when she left? Tell me," he continued before Van Alstyne could answer. "If Shanna had left without taking Toby with her, how would you have disciplined her?"

"That's none of your business!"

"You made it the business of the court when you filed these charges against your daughter! But let me get back to my other questions. Isn't it true that your wife is dead and that she hardly left her bed after Toby was born?"

"Yes, but—"

"Isn't it true that Toby was more or less raised by Shanna, that she was more like a mother to him than an older sister?"

"I can't say that I ever noticed that. There were nurses and governesses to take care of both of them from the time they were born."

Ed Curley rose to his feet. "Your Honor, can we stick to the facts that are before the court, or are we going to have to sit through a biographical history of the Van Alstyne family?"

"Mr. Garret?"

"Right, Your Honor. The facts . . . or fact is that Miss Van Alstyne is charged with kidnapping. Now, according to our laws, kidnapping is abducting someone by force. And, as I was explaining to my client before this trial today, the supposed facts behind the charge against her must be backed up by proof. What proof, Mr. Van Alstyne, do you have that your daughter took your son with her by force?"

"Why, I . . . I. . . ."

"Were you present when Shanna and Toby left your house, Mr. Van Alstyne? Or did someone come to you and tell you that Toby was struggling against Shanna when they left—that Toby was kicking and screaming, crying to be left with you, instead of going with his sister?"

"He could have been asleep!" Van Alstyne insisted. "Maybe he didn't even know they were leaving until they were too far away for him to come home by himself."

"I'm not asking what *could* have happened, Mr. Van Alstyne. Would you like me to repeat my questions?"

"No! And my answer's no, too."

"Thank you," Cody said mildly. "Now, did either of the Pinkertons, then, as they followed the trail and traced Shanna and Toby to Liberty, ever come across anyone who could say Toby was unhappy with his sister? That he wanted to go back to New York and be with you?"

"I guess you'd have to ask them," Van Alstyne grumbled.

"Well, we can do that, too, since they're still in the courtroom. But, as I understand your explanation, you filed the charges against Shanna as a matter of discipline, not because you feared your son was with her against his will or was in any danger. Is that true?"

"No, it's not!" Van Alstyne yelled. "Tobias is legally my son, and I won't be made a fool of by my daughter!"

"I don't think you need your daughter's help for that," Cody said as he shook his head.

Judge Howard pounded his gavel yet again, silencing the laughter erupting in the courtroom and casting a warning glare at Van Alstyne when he leaned forward and gripped the railing in front of him. As soon as silence descended, the judge ordered Cody to the front of his bench.

"Mr. Garret, I will not tolerate your spoken opinions in my court. Whatever they are, I suggest you keep them to yourself and stick to the facts."

"Yes, Your Honor," Cody agreed with a straight face.

"Now," Judge Howard continued with a sigh. "Do you have any more questions of Mr. Van Alstyne?"

"No, sir."

"Mr. Curley?"

"Not right now, Your Honor."

"Then let's get on with it, Mr. Garret."

Cody called several of the townspeople to the stand as he had intended, but Ed Curley met the testimony of each one of them as Shanna had anticipated. They had to admit they had only known Shanna for a short while, though each made the point that Toby and Shanna had a good relationship. The only surprise was when Dan was called to the stand. He testified that he had sent a few telegrams to New York and received answers back attesting to the fact that Shanna was considered a woman of good moral character.

Shanna, herself, took the stand at last, her face white and strained, but her voice calm when Cody began questioning her. Cody carefully led her through the events of her life since Toby's birth in an attempt to refute Van Alstyne's allegation that Toby had been raised by the servants in his house.

"Miss Van Alstyne," he asked, "how old were you when Toby was born?"

"Eleven. Almost twelve."

"And what was your mother's health like after Toby's birth?"

"She remained confined to her bed for several months. Even after she regained some strength, she never left the house. She had a nurse who cared for her, and she spent part of each day in her rose garden when weather permitted. Once in a great while she would come down to have lunch with Toby and me, but otherwise she stayed in her suite of rooms upstairs."

"Was there also a nurse for Toby?"

"Yes," Shanna admitted. "And later a nanny. But they mostly only cared for Toby until I was sixteen."

"Was your father aware that you had taken over the care of your brother?"

"I'm really not sure. We hardly ever saw him. He spent his days at his office, and he never entertained again in our home after Toby was born. He purchased a small town home near his office, and many evenings he never even came home. It is true that we had a complete staff of servants—gardeners, stable help, maids, and a very capable housekeeper. Any slight problems we had that the housekeeper couldn't handle, well, I consulted with Mother and we solved them."

"Weren't you still pursuing your own education at the time, Miss Van Alstyne? How did you manage that, along with everything else?"

"With tutors, of course. Mother agreed when I decided I'd rather have my classes at home. As Toby grew, he even seemed to prefer playing in a corner of our sitting room while I had classes. That may sound as if we were isolated, but afternoons I would visit friends or go riding. Usually Toby went with me. My friends were very understanding. They knew about my mother's ill health, and most of them had small brothers and sisters Toby played with while I visited."

"How was Toby's health as he grew?"

"He had a terrible time teething," Shanna said with a smile of remembrance. "And now and then he would get the sniffles and we'd have to stay home for a few days. The worst time, though, was the day he climbed the apple tree and fell out. I thought he'd broken his arm, but the doctor assured me it was only sprained."

"And you cared for Toby during each of these incidents?"

"Yes. The nurses would sometimes get impatient with him, and Mother and I dismissed a couple of them. I walked the floor with him at night while he was teething and took him for rides during the day—that always seemed to soothe him. When he had the sniffles, I'd let him sleep with me. I never told Mother about the fall from the apple tree. I guess I felt guilty about not watching him closely enough."

"And you decided to leave New York after your mother's death? And take Toby with you?"

"Yes. I'd never have left him there. His place was with me, because I was really more of a mother to him than a sister. And, before you ask, Toby never once expressed a desire to stay behind. He was excited about the trip and maybe seeing some cowboys and Indians, though I explained to him that the Indians were farther west."

"One last question, Miss Van Alstyne. At any time since you left your former home, has Toby once requested he return?"

"No," Shanna said flatly. "Never."

"Thank you." Cody took his seat and Ed Curley rose.

"I only have a couple questions, Miss Van Alstyne. How old are you?"

"I'll be twenty-one in a little less than four months." Shanna faced Curley resolutely, her eyes only once or twice slipping aside to her father.

"But you are now only twenty, and you were twenty when you left New York. Is that true?"

"Yes. If what you're trying to get at is the fact that I'm still legally under my father's rule, the answer is yes."

"That's not what I asked. However, I'll accept that answer. Now, since in your own words you are still legally under Mr. Van Alstyne's rule, did you ask permission to leave your home or take your brother with you?"

"My father hadn't shown any interest in either Toby's life or my own for years. It wouldn't have crossed my mind to ask his permission."

Curley glanced around to see nods of encouragement on some of the townspeople in response to Shanna's answer and shook his head.

"Miss Van Alstyne," he said, at the risk of further antagonizing any slight support that might remain for Van Alstyne. "Could you please just answer my questions yes or no?"

"Yes," Shanna agreed shortly, bringing a titter here and there from the courtroom.

"Did you ask your father's permission to leave?" Curley repeated.

"No."

"No further questions," Curley said as he took his seat again.

Judge Howard turned to Shanna. "Miss Van Alstyne, I have a question for you. Something is puzzling me, and for some reason neither side in this courtroom wants to bring it out into the open. Why did you take your brother and leave New York?"

Shanna glanced frantically at Cody but, surprising everyone in the courtroom, Ed Curley jumped to his feet.

"Your Honor," Curley said loudly. "I don't think Miss Van Alstyne's reason for this has any bearing on the charges before this court. It's a personal matter between her and her father, and nothing will be gained by airing a matter somewhat embarrassing to . . . ah . . . to. . . ."

"To your client, or to whom?" Judge Howard demanded.

"Sir," Shanna spoke from her seat. "It's not just my father who will be discomfited. It could besmirch my mother's memory and embarrass my brother."

"Do you think I can judge this case without knowing all the facts, Miss Van Alstyne? It's to your advantage, you know, for me to have these facts."

"I . . . I will tell you my reason, if we can do it in private first, Your Honor. Then, if you feel it needs to come

Bittersweet Promises

out in open court, I'll leave that to your discretion."

"Is that agreeable to both sides?" Judge Howard asked.

Though Cody spoke up with his agreement, Judge Howard sat and watched Ed Curley and Van Alstyne with their heads together for several long moments. It was clear to all that Van Alstyne was adamantly against Shanna's request. He shook his head time and time again as Ed whispered to him.

Finally Ed Curley raised his head and looked at Judge Howard. "My client would like to be present if he agrees to this, Your Honor."

"I won't allow that, Mr. Curley. As you pointed out in the beginning of this trial, you are not here in the position of prosecutor—you are only here to oversee Mr. Van Alstyne's rights. He does not have the right in my courtroom to sit in on a private consultation that I may have with any witness or the defendant. However, Mr. Garret, as Miss Van Alstyne's attorney, and the sheriff, would be allowed that privilege. And, to that end, though I have given you an opportunity to present any objection you might have, I am not asking your permission to have this consultation with Miss Van Alstyne. I'm only waiting for the sheriff's agreement."

"I agree," Dan said quickly.

"Then I request that Mr. Van Alstyne have that same privilege," Curley said. "He should be allowed to refute anything his daughter might say in private against him."

Judge Howard looked at Shanna and she slowly nodded her consent.

"Before we get into this, however," Judge Howard said, "I want to be sure I have all the other facts in this case. It occurs to me that there is one other witness to what actually happened in New York. Mr. Garret, had you planned to call this witness?"

"Yes, sir, with your permission. I'd like to ask Toby Van Alstyne to tell his side of the story."

For just a second, Ed Curley looked as if he would object; then he waved a dismissing hand at Van Alstyne to still his whispered imprecations.

"If Your Honor feels the boy is of age to tell his story coherently and truthfully," Curley said, "I can't see where we would have any valid objection."

Cody motioned for Toby to duck under the railing so he could talk to him. He placed his hands on Toby's shoulders and looked directly into Toby's eyes.

"Son," he said quietly, "I'm only going to ask you a few things. There may be more you might think you should say to the judge, but you'll have to trust me on this. Only answer what I ask, and don't say anything else. The same when Mr. Curley asks you questions, unless I object to what he asks. Then don't answer that question at all."

"Yes, sir," Toby said quietly.

Cody patted him on the shoulder and stood. "I call Toby Van Alstyne as my last witness."

Toby walked to the stand and, as he had seen the other witnesses do, placed his right hand on the Bible the deputy held out to him, raising his other hand in the air.

"Son," Judge Howard said before the deputy could administer the oath. "You realize that you are swearing on the Holy Bible that you will tell the truth here, don't you?"

"Yes, sir," Toby agreed.

"Proceed."

"Do you swear to tell the truth, the whole truth and nothing but the truth in the matter before this court, so help you God?" the deputy asked.

"I do," Toby said in a clear voice. The deputy nodded and Toby climbed into the chair beside Judge Howard. Clasping his hands on his lap, he looked at Cody when he approached.

Bittersweet Promises

"Will you please tell us your full name?" Cody said.

"Tobias Van Alstyne," Toby answered.

"And will you tell us how you are related to the woman who is sitting at the table I just came from?"

"She's my sister, Shanna Van Alstyne."

"How old are you, Toby?"

"Nine until three weeks from now. Then ten."

"Do you know the difference between the truth and a lie, Toby? And, if you do, will you explain it to us, as you understand it?"

"Yes, sir. The truth is how something really happened. A lie is something you tell to cover up something or when you try to make someone believe something happened different from the way it did."

"What happens to a person who tells a lie, Toby?"

"Well," Toby said with a frown of concentration. "If it's a kid and he gets found out, he gets punished, like not being able to ride his pony for a long time. But even if he doesn't get found out, it usually bothers him something fierce, 'cause he knows he's done wrong."

"Thank you, Toby. Now, you've heard everything that's been said here in court today. You're aware that it's being said that Shanna took you with her from your home without your agreeing to it. Tell me, Toby, how long before you left New York were you aware that Shanna was planning to leave?"

"Oh, a long time," Toby said. "At least two or three weeks."

A couple people laughed, but they were quickly quelled by Judge Howard's glance.

"All right, Toby. Now, tell me. Did Shanna ask you if you wanted to go with her?"

"Well, no. We never talked about that."

"No? Why not?"

"No," Toby agreed. "It really wasn't something we would have had to talk about. Shanna knew that wherever she went, I wanted to be with her."

"Why, Toby? Because she's your sister?"

"Yeah, partly. But mostly because I love her more than anyone else in the world, and she loves me that way, too."

"Then you were totally in agreement with Shanna that you two would leave together?"

"Yes, sir."

"At any time during your journey here to Liberty and even after you got here, Toby, did you ask your sister to send you back to New York?"

"No, sir! I don't ever want to leave Shanna. I made her promise over and over that we would stay together."

"Thank you, Toby. I don't have any more questions for Toby, Your Honor."

"Sheriff? Mr. Curley?"

"No questions," the sheriff replied.

Ed Curley stood. "Toby, will you tell us again how old you are?"

"Almost ten."

"Truly, you are still nine, though, aren't you, son?"

"Yes," Toby admitted.

Curley contemplated Toby for a second, then foolishly blundered ahead.

"What makes you think you are old enough to decide who you should live with, Toby?"

"Because a person should be allowed to live with the person who loves him," Toby answered without hesitation and in a firm voice.

"And your father doesn't. . . ." Curley quickly realized his mistake and sat down. "Nothing further, Your Honor," he said one sentence too late.

Cody glanced curiously at Ed Curley. He'd never heard the older attorney make such an ill-advised remark before in court. Curley kept his head down, though, staring at the floor in apparent abashment. Funny, Cody caught

Bittersweet Promises

himself thinking. There was no flush of embarrassment on Curley's face.

"If everyone is through," Judge Howard said from the bench, "I'll have that consultation with Miss Van Alstyne now."

Chapter Twenty-two

The late-afternoon sun shone through the window of Judge Howard's chambers, bathing his face in warmth as he stared out the window and contemplated Shanna's story. In his mind, he pictured the young woman sitting behind him, still as water on a windless day, her only sign of agitation the supple, white-knuckled hands clasped tightly in her lap. Had she tried to justify her actions and place herself in a meritorious light in front of him, he would have had little sympathy. Instead, Shanna had explained the situation she had found herself and her little brother in after her mother's death in a clear, concise manner.

A couple of times, when she had explained her mother's affair and had to admit that Toby was aware of the situation, she had dropped her eyes, though she never interrupted her story until it was finished.

Judge Howard swiveled around in his chair. "I assume

Bittersweet Promises

you brought the letters you found in your mother's desk with you, Miss Van Alstyne."

Shanna nodded and reluctantly drew the letters from her pocket. Before she handed them across the desk, she made one request of the judge.

"My father has not seen these letters, sir. I don't wish for him to know the name of the man I'm searching for. In fact, my father doesn't even know that I've found out the man's name. He only knows that I'm aware of Toby not being his son, because we had a rather heated discussion one night, and he let that much slip."

"You haven't explained what you intend to do with your knowledge, Miss Van Alstyne."

Shanna took a deep breath. "That's the other thing I wanted to talk to you about privately—the reason I asked Dan to try to arrange a meeting with you. I realize that, even if I'm cleared of the charge against me now, my father will fight me for custody of Toby in order to continue carrying out his vendetta against my mother.

"If you believe there is sufficient proof in my mother's letter to show that Toby is not my father's son, what chance will Toby's real father have of gaining custody of Toby? And I might as well tell you that I intend to ask this man to marry me—so I can continue being a part of Toby's life, if the man does get custody."

"Do you have a copy of Toby's birth certificate?"

"Yes. It's with my mother's letter to me."

"Let me see your mother's letters."

Shanna handed over the letters and waited quietly while Judge Howard read the open one. After a moment, he looked up.

"The other letter is still sealed."

"It's addressed to the man my mother loved. I didn't feel right prying into it."

"We'll leave it for now," Judge Howard agreed. "Then what we have here is basically a dying woman's confession. I will tell you this much, Miss Van Alstyne. A document like that carries a lot of weight in a court, much on the order of a confession of a dying man who has killed or robbed someone. It's felt that the prospect of death brings out the need for truth and forgiveness in a person. However, that confession by itself wouldn't be sufficient for me to deny a legal parent his child."

"But what about the rest of it? The birth certificate? You can see that Mother put Mr. Randolph's name on it. And the lawyer told me Mother also left a handwritten will, admitting Toby's paternity in it, too, and giving custody to this Mr. Randolph. He said he would file it in New York and send me a copy, whenever I contacted him to do that."

"I can see why you wanted to discuss this in private. Are you willing to face the scandal these documents will cause? In a custody hearing, they will have to be brought out."

"I don't have any choice. My father only wants to retain custody of Toby so he can ship him off again immediately to a boarding or military school. He's only doing it for vengeance against my mother."

"A lot of children are sent away to schools at an early age, Miss Van Alstyne. It doesn't necessarily mean they are unwanted and, in fact, most of them turn out to be solid citizens. We only have your word that your father is doing this because of his wife's adultery."

"But my mother herself was afraid of what would happen to Toby after her death! You can read that for yourself!"

"There is that," Judge Howard mused. "Custody is usually only denied a legal parent if the parent is proven unfit, Miss Van Alstyne. I'm sure your attorney in New York told you that, and so far you have no proof that your father is an unfit parent, other than his lack of wanting to keep the boy at home with him.

"However, there are mitigating circumstances here.

Bittersweet Promises

You are facing that fact, aren't you, that all the law is on the side of this Mr. Randolph—that you have absolutely no claim on the boy yourself."

"Yes, sir."

"And you're willing to give up any chance you have to find love yourself? Marry this man, just so you can still stay with your brother?"

"Yes, sir. I promised Toby we'd stay together."

"Miss Van Alstyne, your little brother has no idea just what you're giving up on his behalf, as I'm sure you are aware. Have you really thought this through?"

"Yes, sir. You can't know how much I've thought about it."

"Then, your best legal right, Miss Van Alstyne, is to carry out your plan. If you can find this man—if he will admit to the truth of your mother's allegations—if he will fight for custody of Toby—if you marry him. . . ."

Judge Howard chuckled softly. "That's a lot of ifs, I know, but I'm only telling you this because you already know where you stand as far as the law goes, in my court anyway. I can't promise what will happen if this goes back to New York. However, if Mr. Randolph comes to my court and asks for custody of his son, I feel I have enough evidence to grant him that, if you send for a copy of your mother's will. And you will share that custody, of course, if you are Mr. Randolph's wife."

"Thank you," Shanna said. "But I guess this will all be beside the point, if your decision out there goes against me."

"I am still weighing the facts, Miss Van Alstyne. I can't make a final decision until I know everything." Judge Howard handed the letters back to Shanna. "I'll speak to your father now. Wait in the courtroom for me."

Shanna walked out of the small room and made her way to the table where Cody waited. He didn't speak, only pulled her chair out for her to sit. A second later, though, he reached beneath the table and took her hand in his.

Try as she might, Shanna couldn't bring herself to pull away. She gripped his hand tightly and closed her eyes, whispering one of the small prayers she had promised Zerelda she would say as her father stomped across the floor to enter Judge Howard's chambers.

Not one of the townspeople had left the courtroom during the time Shanna talked with Judge Howard. She wanted to turn around to thank each one who had testified for her, but a strange lethargy swept over her while she waited for the judge to return. She had done all she could—told the judge all she could. Now she could only wait until the judge made his decision.

Feeling a small hand on her left shoulder, Shanna opened her eyes and looked into Toby's face.

"Shanna, I . . . have to use the outhouse," he said.

Shanna dropped her eyes. "I can't take you, Toby. They won't let me leave right now."

"That's all right." Toby picked up her hand to pat it, slipping a piece of paper into her palm at the same time. "Dan will show me where it's at and take me."

Toby stepped away and Shanna glanced behind her to see one new face among the spectators. Susie James sat beside the sheriff's wife, and she dropped one eyelid in a surreptitious wink. Shanna managed a tiny smile and turned back around, adding the message to the pocket containing the letter to JT Randolph.

Ten minutes later, Judge Howard opened his door and ushered a red-faced Christian Van Alstyne into the courtroom. When Van Alstyne attempted to push through the swinging gate to enter the aisle, Judge Howard's whiplash voice stopped him.

"Mr. Van Alstyne! You will remain in this courtroom until I have voiced my verdict!"

"Why?" Van Alstyne turned with a snarl. "You made

yourself clear in there. I don't have to stay here and be humiliated further!"

"Take your seat or I'll have the sheriff give you a seat over at the jail!"

Shanna glanced hopefully at Cody as her father strode to the table beside them. Cody gave her a reassuring hug, then urged Shanna to her feet as Judge Howard climbed onto his dais.

"I'll get right to the point," the judge said, "since I see Miss Van Alstyne is already on her feet and prepared to accept my judgment. I find the charges against her not only unfounded, but ridiculous. I find her not guilty of kidnapping her brother."

Though a murmur of agreement ran through the courtroom, everyone quieted when they realized Shanna was still standing, staring at Judge Howard.

"There is another matter connected to this, however, that must also be decided," Judge Howard said. "Toby Van Alstyne is too young to be on his own, obviously. I regret that my circuit is too busy at this point for me to take time to settle this related matter today. So, a month from now, we will hold court again and decide whom Toby must live with. Until then, he will remain with his sister, Shanna Van Alstyne. That's all. Court dismissed."

Shanna's eyes blurred and tears streamed down her cheeks, but she ignored them as she turned to search for Toby. He sprang into her arms and they clung together, unaware of the tumult erupting in the courtroom around them. Finally Shanna reached out to Cody. A second later, she and Toby both were wrapped in Cody's arms.

"I . . . I don't know how to thank you," she said in a muffled voice as Cody held her against his chest. For this one last time, she told herself, she would allow herself to hold Cody close. Let everyone else think it was the emotion of the moment. Too soon, very soon now, she would never be able to feel his embrace again.

She had Toby, though, at least for a little while longer. Forcing herself with every bit of strength she could muster, Shanna pushed Cody away. Her hand lingered for just another second on Cody's trim waist as she drew it toward her, and she stored up the feeling to savor later, before she bent down again to Toby.

"We won, Shanna," Toby said excitedly. "We won. He didn't take you away from me."

Shanna hugged him close again. "No, he didn't, Toby. Not this time." She pushed him away and stroked the side of his face. "But you heard Judge Howard, Toby. He'll be back in a month, and we'll have to see him again."

"That's a long time, Shanna. You'll take care of that, too, when it happens. I know you will, Shanna."

"I'll try." Suddenly feeling a strange sensation crawl up her spine, Shanna glanced at the other table. Christian Van Alstyne met her gaze with a malevolent glare, sending Shanna's stomach plummeting with fear. He held her gaze for only a second, but it was long enough for Shanna to know her fight wasn't over yet. Nowhere near over.

Cody caught the direction of Shanna's stare and stepped between her and her father. "Let's go home, Shanna. Melinda and Bessie will want to hear the good news."

Home, Shanna's mind echoed. *Would that the plantation could truly be mine and Toby's home, but it can't be.*

Judge Howard's words in his private chamber ran through her mind, also, confirming the uselessness of Shanna's desperate desire.

However, if Mr. Randolph comes to my court and asks for custody of his son, I feel that I have enough evidence to grant him that, if you send for a copy of your mother's will. And you will share that custody, of course, if you are his wife.

Chapter Twenty-three

It took Shanna two full days to make her plans to slip away from the plantation. A strangely rebellious Toby had her almost at wit's end. Over and over he repeated that he would not stay behind while Shanna searched for JT Randolph, though Toby had still not learned the name of the man, lest he let it slip.

"He's my real father," Toby said with a mutinous pout. "I want to meet him and see him for myself."

"You'll see him when I get back," Shanna said in exasperation while they stood at the corral fence watching the ponies frolic. They had managed to leave Melinda in the kitchen helping Susie James bake cookies, but Shanna knew Melinda wouldn't stay away from Toby for long. She had followed him around like a puppy whose long-lost master had reappeared ever since they got back.

"Listen, Toby," she said when Toby continued to glare at the ponies. "Look at Chessy."

"I see him." Toby's lower lip protruded.

"Well, how far do you think Chessy would get trying to keep up with a larger horse, like I'm taking? It's going to be a long ride, and we can't ride double. That would be too hard on my horse."

"You haven't even got a horse yet. And you can't take Brownie. She has to feed Starlight. Melinda said Cody had to have someone from town bring Brownie right home after he got there, so she could feed her colt."

"I've got a horse, Toby. I just don't want to tell you how, in case Cody questions you after I'm gone and you feel you have to lie. If you don't know my plans, you can't let anything slip by mistake."

"Couldn't let anything slip if I was with you, either," Toby said stubbornly. "Besides, you ain't . . . don't have any business going off by yourself. You should have someone with you."

Shanna clenched her fists on the top rail, trying to decide just how much of her plans to trust to Toby. "All right. I'll tell you this much. I'm meeting someone who knows the way to where I'm going. Will you accept that and stay here, as I've asked you to?"

Toby looked at her and Shanna's heart wrenched when a tear trickled down his face.

"I don't want you to leave, Shanna," Toby said with a sob. "How do I know you'll come back?"

Shanna hugged him close. "Oh, Toby, have I broken any of my promises to you yet? I haven't, have I?"

Toby shook his head against her shoulder.

"And I give you my solemn promise that I'll be back just as soon as I talk to this man, Toby. My solemn, cross-my-heart promise."

Toby pulled away and sniffed loudly. He raised his arm to wipe at his nose, but Shanna caught his arm and thrust her handkerchief into his hand. As soon as he blew his nose, she tipped his face up with a hand under his chin.

"Will you wait here for me, Toby? Please? Believe me, I would take you with me if I could, but this is the best way for me to do this. You'll have to trust me."

"All right," Toby finally agreed. "You better hurry back, though."

"I will," Shanna promised.

Later that night, taking care to step over the board in the hallway that creaked, Shanna left the house, carrying her boots in one hand and a small pack she had found in the closet in the other. She pulled the boots on before she stepped off the back porch and made her way down the drive. At the gate, she turned and whispered a good-bye to Toby, but her eyes were trained on the window of the far bedroom, which she had heard Cody enter over an hour ago.

A short walk later, Shanna rounded the first bend in the road past the Garret house. She heard a nicker and hurried forward, her hand going out to soothe the gray mare she found tethered to a large oak tree.

"Shanna."

Shanna screamed and jumped back from the mare.

"I'm sorry," the voice whispered. "It's me, Susie. Mother told me to be sure and not leave until I saw you on your way and made sure you knew where you were going."

Shanna dropped her hand from her throat. "I almost didn't *get* going, Susie. You scared me half to death."

"Sorry," Susie said again. "Do you have everything you need?"

"Yes. And I've studied the map you gave me yesterday. The directions are clear enough to get me to where I'll meet your brother."

"Shanna," Susie said in a hesitant voice. "I wish . . . I wish we'd been able to get word to Frank instead of Jesse to lead you to JT."

"Why, Susie?"

"Jesse's changed. Oh, you'll be safe enough with him, I guess, especially since he knows Mother considers you one of her dearest friends. It's just . . . Shanna, if you don't feel comfortable with Jesse, promise me you'll get word back to us and wait somewhere until we send someone else to help you. Promise me, Shanna."

"I promise," Shanna said distractedly. The string of promises she had made over the past few months ran through her mind. One more on her shoulders would only add to her burden, but she wasn't going to let anything keep her from the end of her quest at this point.

"Now, I have to get on my way, Susie. Tell Zerelda how much I appreciate all her help."

Shanna swung onto the mare, glad to see Zerelda had provided her with a Western-type saddle. The old denims of Cody's she had snitched from the clothesline hung loosely on her, and she hitched them up her hips when they slid down with her movements. With one last wave at Susie, she turned the mare onto the road, already thinking ahead to the first landmark on the map in her pocket.

East, first, Zerelda's directions had said. Then south when she was well past the chance of running into Liberty's perimeters. South, toward the wild Ozark Mountains, where men could hide and become lost in the wilderness, and where men did exactly that.

The small derringer Susie had slipped to her that morning rode securely in her jacket pocket, giving her a little comfort, though she had never fired a gun in her life. She shrugged her shoulders. It couldn't be that hard. Susie had told her all she had to do was cock and aim it, then pull that little piece sticking down beneath the gun.

There was even a rifle in the scabbard of the saddle. In a patch of moonlight, Shanna pulled it a ways out of the scabbard and studied the mechanism. Looked just like the derringer, only larger, she decided. She hoped it, too, was loaded, as Susie had assured her the derringer was. Not that she would need it, she told herself, but one thing Susie had neglected was showing her how to put new bullets in the gun.

Shanna turned the mare to the right at the first fork in the road. For just a second she thought she caught a sound behind her. It must have been Susie on her way back to her own house. She kicked the mare again and headed on down the road.

The surefooted little mare carried Shanna through the dark night and on into the next day. She came to the waterfall on Zerelda's map near dawn and left the faint trail to ride deeper into the ever more towering hills ahead. Several times she drew the mare to a halt to enjoy the beauty of the countryside around her—not farmland, like that which she had left behind.

She crossed brooks filled with clear water bubbling its cheery way over smooth stones, and she rode up hillsides covered with tall jack pine, elm and oak. Huge granite rocks protruded from some of the scarred hillsides, where rain had washed away the covering soil. At the top of each high rise, she rested the mare and gazed over the undulating waves of hilltops both behind and before her. The peace and serenity of the spectacular views lulled her, soothing her troubled emotions and allowing her, for the time being, to push aside her concerns.

Late the next afternoon, Shanna rode up on a small lake in a valley, where a doe and fawn triplets raised their heads to watch her approach. Showing little fear at Shanna's unexpected presence, the doe calmly walked toward the underbrush, the fawns gamboling and frisking behind her.

Shanna dismounted and led the mare to the lake to drink. She dipped her bandanna—another item borrowed from Cody's attire—into the water and wiped her face. Glancing around to assure herself she was still on the proper path, she saw a huge tree split by lightning on the far shore of the lake. That tree was the next to last landmark. She smiled to herself, amazed that she, having never even ventured onto the bridle paths in New York without a groom in attendance, had found her way through this unmapped country, with only the aid of a hand-drawn set of directions.

It took her a few minutes to figure out how the hobbles worked for the mare. She finally tightened them on the horse's front legs, slipped the bridle off and poured out a measure of the corn she had found in the saddlebags. Stomach growling in hunger, she removed the bedroll from the saddle and spread it on the ground, then sat down and opened her pack to take out some bread and cold meat.

Fighting the drowsiness from her all-night and most-of-the-day ride, Shanna gulped down the food and finished off her meal with two of the cookies Susie and Melinda had made. After glancing over at the little mare to assure herself the hobbles were working, she stretched out on the bedroll. Just for a moment, she told herself.

A pain in her side woke Shanna, and she grumbled to herself as she shifted without opening her eyes. How in the world had a rock gotten into her mattress? The ache relieved somewhat, she tried to hang on to the delightful half wakefulness and soothing warmth of the sun on her face.

Sun? Rock? Shanna sat up with a shot, her eyes wide and her brow furrowing as she recalled the sounds in the dream she had experienced just before she woke. She thought a horse had neighed, then been answered by another one.

The pain in her side had been the derringer, she realized, slipping her hand into the jacket pocket as she slowly swiveled her head.

"'Bout time you woke up. Thought I'd ride a little farther on and meet you when you were late. Guess I should have known a city girl wouldn't make as good a time on the trail."

Shanna's grip on the derringer relaxed when she recognized the man kneeling a few feet away. "You're Susie's brother. The one I saw at Zerelda's house that night. Jesse."

The dark-haired man nodded his head, his piercing blue eyes never leaving Shanna's face.

"Jesse. Dingus," he said with a shrug. "I'm called different things—even been called a bank robber lately. You being close to Mamaw, reckon that's no surprise to you."

Shanna shifted on the bedroll in order to see him better. "You're breaking your mother's heart. I hope you know that. You and Frank, both."

Jesse surged to his feet. "Ain't your place to go meddlin' into our affairs. If you want me to take you to where you're going, you'll keep your pretty trap shut while you follow. Elsewise, you can go on back the way you came. I'm only doin' this 'cause Mamaw asked me to."

Shanna stood and shook out the bedroll before she curled it into a roll again to retie it behind the saddle. The icy glare in Jesse's blue eyes warned her to watch her tongue, and she couldn't help remembering Susie's tentative caution about her brother.

Shanna caught her little mare, then tied the bedroll securely in the rawhide thongs behind the saddle. Before she removed the hobbles, though, she was forced to face Jesse again.

"I . . . I have to go over in the brush for a moment before we leave."

Trana Mae Simmons

"Hurry up," Jesse said without acknowledging Shanna's embarrassment. "We spend too much more time here, we might's well stay the night. The rest of the way we're going ain't no country to be riding through after dark."

Shanna stepped around the mare and trudged toward the brush where the deer had disappeared. Concealing herself behind a huge pine, she unknotted the scarf she had used for a belt to hold the oversize denims over her slender hips. After using the handkerchief placed in her pocket in anticipation of stops such as these, she rose and pulled the denims up.

A twig snapped and Shanna glanced around her, expecting to see some small animal. She met the blue eyes and smirking grin of her guide.

"Just wanted to see what was really under them baggy britches," Jesse said with a cold chuckle. "We'll be spendin' a night together, you know."

"You bastard!" Shanna hissed, her cheeks red with mortification at the picture she must have made squatting in the brush. "You'll never lay a hand on me! If that's your idea of payment for guiding me, you can forget it right now!"

Jesse looped his thumbs in the belt holding his twin six-guns and stared at her while Shanna fumbled blindly with the scarf, not daring to take her eyes from him. She managed to pull the scarf tight before he took a step toward her.

"Stay away from me!" she screamed, her hand delving into her pocket.

"If you're lookin' for that little gun, it fell out on the ground there behind you when you set down."

Shanna whirled and dived for the derringer. She rolled over in the leaves and turned around, sitting on her rump and pointing the derringer in Jesse's direction. Her astonished gaze saw him backing away, his hands

Bittersweet Promises

out to the sides, well away from the deadly six-guns on his hips.

Shanna smiled grimly and placed her index finger on the trigger of the derringer. Suddenly it dawned on her that Jesse's eyes weren't on her. Instead, he looked off to the side, toward the clearing they had just left. Following his gaze, though still keeping the gun aimed approximately at Jesse, she saw a rifle resting on a broad shoulder, pointed directly at Jesse's heart.

"Now, Cody," Jesse said as he backed up yet another step. "I wasn't gonna do nothin' she didn't want me to. You know me, Cody. I jist like to look at a pretty woman, as well as you do."

"Yeah, I used to know you, Dingus," Cody snarled. "When your name was still Jesse and when you were a true neighbor. The only reason I didn't drill you without warning was because of what you and Frank did for my family. You aren't that same person anymore, and if I ever catch you within a mile of Shanna again, you won't get a chance to get any closer than that to her."

"All right. All right, Cody. Just drop that rifle a little and I'll go. Reckon you're takin' over now to get the little lady to where she's going."

"You reckon right. It's not my rifle you ought to be worried about, though. Looks to me like Shanna's finger's twitching awfully close to that derringer trigger."

Shanna looked at the little gun and saw her finger wrapped around the trigger, her hand trembling slightly. She gasped and dropped the gun to the ground, then scrambled to her feet.

"Oh, Cody," she said as she ran over to him. "I've never been so glad to see anyone in my life."

Cody ignored her for the moment and waved his rifle barrel in the direction of the clearing. Obeying the unspoken command, Jesse strode toward his horse. A second later, they heard the pounding hoofbeats as

Jesse galloped away, and Cody turned his furious glare on Shanna.

"You stupid fool! If I'd had any idea who you were going to meet, I wouldn't have just followed behind you, waiting until you got lost. Where'd you ever get the fool notion that you could trust Jesse James?"

Shanna set her hands on her hips and stepped closer, blue eyes flashing and her nose a bare inch from Cody's.

"From his mother!" she shouted. "And if you were so worried about me being with him, why did you wait so long to join us? He was probably sitting there watching me sleep for a long time, and I'm sure you saw it if you've been that close to me all the time. Damn you, Cody Garret! You stood back and let that man watch me p—"

Suddenly Shanna clapped a hand over her mouth to still her words. A blush joined the anger red on her face and deepened when she saw Cody's lips twitch. She dropped her hand and stamped her foot.

"All right, that's what I was doing over here. I suppose you think it's funny, knowing how embarrassed I am!"

"Not really," Cody said, though his stifled chuckle gave lie to his words. "Serves you right, though. You should have trusted me, like I asked you to."

"Me trusted you? You've known all along it was JT Randolph I was looking for, haven't you? Why didn't you take me to him when I first got here, instead of waiting until I...." Shanna's voice dropped and she looked away from him. "Before I fell in love with you," she whispered just loud enough for Cody to hear.

Chapter Twenty-four

After unsaddling and hobbling his stallion, Cody built a small fire on the edge of the lake. An evening breeze ruffled the azure surface, lapping small waves onto the sandy beach washed out on the side of the lake where Shanna had stopped to rest.

Small stones littered the area, glistening wetly, and Cody gathered a few to pile around the fire. On the far side of the lake, faint tinges of violet, gold and scarlet reflected on the water as the sun neared the mountaintops. The valley would be in shadow before long, when the sun dropped behind the sheltering vistas, bringing on an early twilight.

Cody leaned back on his heels as he fed a couple dry branches into the leaping flames, then glanced over his shoulder to where Shanna sat again on her bedroll.

They hadn't spoken beyond agreeing to spend the night there, after Shanna's admission that she still loved him. He didn't trust himself to even attempt to reply, not with the urge to turn her over his knee and pull down those baggy britches to give her a sound spanking still burning in his mind. He hadn't even told her that he'd fallen aseep against a tree when he stopped to rest his stallion, allowing her to get a lead on him.

God, her revelation had stunned him. It had almost been better when he thought she had changed her mind—had second thoughts after their lovemaking. Almost.

Yet here she was—riding deeper into the Ozarks to find a man she insisted she was going to marry. Did her love for him mean so little to her, then? After all, it wasn't common, but there was such a thing as divorce.

He gritted his teeth and shook his head at that foolish thought. Shanna wasn't the type to pledge herself to JT only long enough to get his help, then walk out on him. She kept her commitments—and he had to admit he would think less of her if she carried on a relationship with him while married to his longtime friend. And a divorce would still cost her Toby.

"Do you want me to try to catch a couple fish for supper, Shanna?" he asked finally into the quiet stillness.

Shanna shrugged her shoulders. Her stomach was knotted in response to Cody's unexpected presence, and she probably couldn't eat anyway. She had made the break—put him behind her, at least physically, though she would carry the ghost of his memory to her grave.

She watched him walk over to his saddlebags, lying a few feet away. When he squatted to unsnap the clasp on one bag, his denims pulled tight against his muscular thighs and firm rear. A wave of desire swept over her, and she closed her eyes, waiting until she heard his boot heels scrunching in the sandy soil as he approached the lakeshore before she opened them.

The breeze ruffled his hair as he stood on the edge of the lake and tossed out his fishing line, the sun rays turning the chestnut color to molten gold. The fitted blue shirt stretched across his shoulders with his actions, outlining the sinews of his back. She stored these memories, too, in that special corner of her mind marked Cody Garret, unable to find the strength to deny them to herself.

Cody pulled in two bass within five minutes and cleaned them on the edge of the lake, while Shanna readied an iron skillet by the fire. When Cody carried the fillets to the fire, she reached for them, but he pulled them back with a smile.

"I think I better do the cooking. I don't reckon you've had experience fixing a meal on an outside fire, and I'm not much in the mood for burnt fish."

"You're probably right." Cody's light tone ran through Shanna like a caress, and the breeze blew his scent to her. She involuntarily took a deep breath, breathing in the scent of sweatiness and horse, but also the special odor she associated with Cody—a hint of sunlight and strength, the outdoors and tenderness.

His callused hands and long fingers expertly coated the fish with cornmeal spread on one of the tin plates, before dropping the fillets into the hot grease Shanna had melted in the skillet. Those same hands could gentle a frisky horse, soothe a frightened child—or play across her body softly, tenderly, more firmly, until she lost herself to the special feelings he created.

Shanna drew her knees up and clasped them in her arms, determinedly laying her head down and turning her face from the firelight. Though the smell of frying fish replaced the special Cody scent for the moment, she would always be able to dust the other scent off in her memory.

Cody touched her shoulder, holding a plate out.

"That didn't take long," she murmured.

"No? You've been staring off into the woods for over ten minutes. I finally decided the fish was going to get cold if I didn't interrupt you. What were you thinking about?"

"Just things." Shanna picked up a crispy piece of fish and bit into it. Finding her appetite returned, she ate the fillet and the beans Cody had heated in another pan, and even mopped her plate with a cold biscuit. Her hunger satisfied, she reached for Cody's empty plate.

"I'll wash the dishes in the lake. I read somewhere that the Indians used to scrub their plates with sand to clean them."

"The dishes can wait," Cody said with a shake of his head. He pulled Shanna's plate from her hand and laid it beside the fire. "I think we need to talk about which way we're going tomorrow."

Shanna dropped her gaze and sat back on her bedroll. "I suppose you think you're going to talk me into going back to Liberty with you. I can't do that, Cody. I just can't."

"I see. No, damn it, I don't see! Unless you were lying a while ago, when you admitted you still loved me!"

"I wasn't lying, Cody," Shanna said in a quiet voice, contradicting his anger. "I do love you. I'll always love you, until the day I die."

"Then why don't you trust me to help you find another way out of this mess? You can't have love without trust."

"Trust you? Cody, how long have you known that JT Randolph was the man I was looking for? Toby's father? I had a lot of time to think while I rode, and I believe you knew it the first day I came to Liberty. You gave me such a strange look that day, after the bank robbers left town. And Zerelda told me that you and JT were close friends. She said JT still carried a picture of my mother, and that he had even told her the story of their love."

"All right," Cody admitted in a gruff voice. "I had my suspicions. JT and I served together throughout that whole damned war and, yes, he told me about Diedre. But, Shanna, you're living in a dreamworld if you think you can talk a man like JT into marrying you. And even if you could, I can't let you throw your life away like that—throw away what we could have together."

"I don't have any choice, Cody. Remember when I went into Judge Howard's chamber to talk to him alone?"

"Yeah."

"You're an attorney, Cody. Lord, we even talked about this before, in the b-barn that night. Judge Howard confirmed it. He said he would give JT custody of Toby if JT admitted Toby was his son and asked for it. And he agreed that I don't have any valid claim on Toby, unless I get it as JT's wife. Cody, how could we ever find happiness together at the expense of a small child? How can you ask me to choose between you and Toby?"

"You've already made your choice!" Cody snarled.

The firelight illuminated two tears trickling down Shanna's face. Cody scrambled over to sit beside her, wrapping his arms around her and pulling her tightly against him.

"Damn it, Shanna, I'm sorry. I didn't mean it that way. Oh, God, Shanna, I don't know what I'm going to do. I don't know what I'm saying anymore. I just know that I love you, and that I can't stand the pain of thinking about you with another man. Shanna, Shanna, I love you. I love you so damned much. How am I going to live without you?"

Shanna buried her face against his neck and her arms crept around him. The desire she had been fighting all evening raced through her veins, and her nipples crinkled against his chest. She turned her face to his, and Cody took her lips harshly, without preamble. His body covered hers as he pushed her back onto the bedroll and pulled her beneath him. His tongue ravaged her soft inner mouth, laying claim to that part of her while his hands did the same to the rest of her body.

Cody's newly grown whiskers rasped against Shanna's cheeks when he tore his mouth away and kissed her neck, his fingers working on the buttons of her blouse. Her breasts sprang free, one going into his mouth at once. She arched against him, losing herself in the sweet fire his caresses and seeking mouth spread through her.

Suddenly Cody wrenched free and stiffened his arms to raise himself. Shanna moaned in loss and reached for him, her eyelids shadowing the passion in the blue depths. The breeze whispered over her wet breast, spreading chill bumps over the area Cody had suckled.

"No. Damn it, no!" Cody rolled away and hunched before the fire, his broad back stiff and his body rigid.

"C-Cody?" Shanna whispered.

"I won't do it, Shanna," he said in a ravaged voice, without turning. "I won't take the chance of putting my own child in your belly, then having you raise it with another man as its father!"

Cody heard Shanna's sob, then the rustle of her blouse as she sat up and began to close it around her. He clenched his fists and waited until he was sure she had covered her beautiful breasts before he turned.

Her blond hair was tousled from his fingers, lying in wild disarray around her shoulders. His fingers opened of their own accord, yearning to bury themselves in the silky mass again. Drawn by a force he couldn't resist, his eyes traveled down her bodice and lingered on the soft swells he could still taste in his mouth.

"I . . ." Cody gulped back the moisture in his mouth. "Shanna, you have to tell me something. You . . . you did have your monthly flow after we made love, didn't you?"

"I'm not pregnant, Cody," Shanna admitted in a soft voice. "I worried about that myself for a while. I'm well

Bittersweet Promises

aware of what could have happened after that night, but my . . . my flow started that next morning."

Shanna gazed yearningly at him. "I had mixed feelings about it, you know," she conceded. "I knew in one part of my mind how awful it would be if I was carrying your child. But another part of me wanted it—wanted a part of you with me, instead of just my memories of our love."

Cody groaned and sprang to his feet. "I'm going for a swim," he said over his shoulder as he strode toward the water, unbuttoning his shirt as he went. He threw the shirt aside and sat down long enough to remove his boots. Still wearing his denims, he plunged into the cold water, hoping it would soften the turgid rigidity between his legs. If it didn't, he was in for a mighty uncomfortable night from the ache he felt.

Shanna watched Cody swim in the dark water, his arms windmilling and splashing a white froth. He finally halted and dove beneath the surface, and she rose to her feet, her hand on her breast as she waited for him to come back up. She let her breath out in a soft whoosh when his head broke the surface a little farther down the shoreline, and her hand smoothed down over her breast, resting on her stomach.

She thought of her friend Zerelda, and the growing life in Zerelda's stomach. In only three short months now, Zerelda would have another babe suckling her. By then, Shanna might have a life growing in her, too, but not a life given to her by the man she loved.

How would she feel, giving birth to a baby fathered by her mother's ex-lover? It almost seemed like incest. Sometimes she wished she wasn't so well-read—hadn't run across that word one day and searched out the meaning of it.

Toby's face wavered before her, and Shanna latched onto the vision. Toby. Whatever children she had with

JT would be Toby's half brothers or half sisters. She would love them because they were a part of her, she resolutely told herself. It wouldn't matter that they were conceived in a bed with a man she didn't love.

Wondering if making love with one man while closing her eyes and pretending it was someone else was considered adultery, Shanna sank to the ground and added some more wood to the fire. Cody would be cold when he returned. Whatever had made him decide to take a swim after the sun had set, taking the warmth in the valley with it?

She welcomed the cold air on her own body, not deigning to draw the bedroll over her shoulders while she waited for Cody to return. It dimmed the warmth in her that was completely unrelated to the renewed flames of the fire.

Chapter Twenty-five

"Cody, how do you know where we're going?" Shanna asked the next afternoon, unable to bear the silent ride any longer. "The map Zerelda gave me only showed me how to get to where Jesse would be waiting. He was supposed to lead me to where he and the rest of his gang hid out—where JT's staying."

"I traveled this whole state and all the area around it during the war, Shanna. Our entire regiment camped and spent the nights in the caves in these mountains one week. Besides, they'll probably find us first. The kind of men we're going to run into won't feel safe without a lookout posted, even this far away from civilization."

"Do you think we'll be in any danger from them, knowing where they're hiding out?"

"You should have thought of that before you started out, Shanna." At the look of fear on her face, Cody relented and softened his voice. "No, Shanna, we won't be in any danger. I know most of these men, and they're handy enough with their guns not to be afraid of the law coming after them. The law probably already knows where they are, anyway, but it would take an entire army to capture them. Men like these choose their stronghold well—make sure it's a place they can defend, or at least run from without getting trapped."

"I don't understand why Toby's father would be living with men like these," Shanna said, unwilling to let the silence return after Cody had started talking again. "From what I've learned, he's not one of them. He's not an outlaw."

"No," Cody agreed. "JT's an honest man. He's probably just glad of the company, no matter what kind it is. He came out here at first to get away from people, but I imagine it got pretty lonesome after a while."

"I'm glad he's not one of the outlaws."

"There won't be anything keeping him from returning to live in polite society with you, Shanna," Cody snapped. "If you do talk him into marrying you."

"That's not what I meant," Shanna fumed. "I wouldn't want Toby to have an outlaw for a father."

"What if he was, Shanna? An outlaw. Would you be willing to live out here with him? Give up any hope of having Toby grow up and make something of himself?"

"I'm thankful that's one decision I won't have to make," Shanna shot back at him. "Toby will be able to have all the advantages I can give him in a few months."

"Yeah, you'll have your money and even a husband and a father for Toby. Tell me, Shanna, will you melt in JT's arms like you do mine? Will you be as eager to make love to him as you were to me last night?"

The walnut pools of Cody's eyes threw daggers at Shanna, but rather than firing her anger further, she fought back the pain his words gave her. She slowly shook her head.

"No, Cody. I can't lie to you and say I haven't thought about that part of what I'm doing, and I'll probably never make love to him without having your ghost between us. But make love to him I will, if he insists on it in our marriage. I'll do what I have to, in order to keep Toby by my side."

"You'll have to keep your eyes shut pretty tight or the lights off and shades drawn down," Cody warned her in a bitter voice. "His face isn't pretty."

"And he lost part of one of his legs, also. I'm aware of that. Zerelda told me."

Cody pulled his stallion to a halt and turned it across the trail.

"Shanna, you can't... *I can't*...."

"Go on back if you want to, Cody. As you said, the men probably have a lookout posted. I'm sure one of them will find me sooner or later. Just tell me how much farther I have to go."

"It's not too much farther, little lady," a voice drawled beside the trail. "I'll see you safely there, if Cody wants to head back."

A roan stallion stepped onto the trail, the man on its back nodding slightly to Cody as he rode up beside Shanna's mare. Cody's stallion laid its ears back at the scent of another stud, and Cody took a firm grip on his reins to hold the dun in place.

"Hello, Frank," Cody said. "Thanks for the offer, but I don't reckon I'll take you up on it. 'Course I wouldn't be as apprehensive about Shanna with you as I was when I found her with Dingus."

Frank snorted softly and pushed his hat up from his eyes. "Well now, Cody, Mamaw did send the message to me. Problem was I was out hunting, and Jesse got it first. I wouldn't have let him go in my stead, if I'd've known."

"I believe you, Frank. What I don't understand is why you're still riding with Dingus. Hell, man, don't you know he's going to get all of you killed sooner or later?"

"Maybe so. But he's my little brother. We've always been together, 'cept when we rode with different outfits at times durin' the war. Mamaw expects me to take care of him."

"Yeah, he always was her favorite. Best thing you could do for him, though, would be to talk him into giving himself up and taking his medicine."

"He'll never do that, Cody. Somethin' snapped in him during the war—even before that, when he took that whipping. I can't talk any sense into him."

"If he ever even looks at Shanna again, I'll kill him, Frank."

"Well, reckon that will be JT's responsibility from now on," Frank mused.

"How . . . he knows I'm coming?" Shanna broke in. "And why?"

"He knows," Frank told her, his blue eyes, a paler shade than Jesse's, studying her closely. "Mamaw wouldn't have let you come out here without tellin' us why she was sendin' you."

"Has . . . has JT said how he feels about my arrival?" Shanna asked, her heart in her throat.

"Nope. Just said it was all right to bring you on in," Frank said. "You'll have to talk to him about his feelings on going back with you. JT's not one to open up easy these days, even to his friends."

"Yet he told Zerelda and Cody about being in love with my mother," Shanna replied.

"Yep," Frank said. "But they're the only two knowed about it until here in the last few days. And I'm not real sure how JT's takin' it, 'specially since Mamaw had to tell him in her letter that your mother was dead. And that he had a little boy."

Shanna's hand went to her jacket pocket, feeling for the letters. They had become almost a part of her the last few months. Giving a deep sigh, she lifted her reins.

"Then I guess I better go on and talk to him. Are you going back, Cody?"

"No," Cody denied, though his fingers whitened on his reins as he turned his stallion out of the way. "I'll see it on through now."

The three horses made their way on down the faint trail through the mountains for another two hours. Shanna paid no attention now to the beautiful scenery around her, her mind filled with questions about her long-delayed meeting with JT Randolph. Her eyes kept focusing again and again, though, on the broad back ahead of her. Cody kept his stallion a good length in front of Shanna's mare while they rode, leaving Frank to lead the way. The trail was wide enough for two horses to ride side by side, but when Shanna urged her mare to walk a little faster, Cody moved his stallion to the center of the trail.

Shanna gave up trying to talk to Cody and followed behind the other two horses, left alone with her thoughts. Frank finally slowed his horse to a snail's pace and lifted the hat on his head. He waved it once toward the top of a high hill, then settled it back and rode forward again.

Frank's actions again brought to Shanna's mind where she was headed, and she gazed around her, even turning in her saddle to look behind her. The timber-covered mountains around them were smaller than the mountains in New York, but their thick cover would surely hide anyone approaching. On the other hand, they would give good cover to anyone leaving the area. She hadn't seen the man Frank waved to, but he would have had a good view for a long ways from his position.

When Shanna looked ahead again, she saw they were coming into another valley. A crude log building sat in the valley, a corral filled with horses beside it. A man opened the corral gate and let the horses out, while another man on horseback herded them down the valley.

"Kept our horses near until we knew who all was coming," Shanna heard Frank say to Cody. "Not that we really didn't trust the little lady, but it pays to be prepared."

Shanna gazed at the hillsides surrounding the valley. The dark mouths of several caves dotted the steep slopes, huge trees growing right to the entrances on some, bare granite rock outlining others. Their horses splashed across a small creek, and a door slammed. Glancing back at the log house, Shanna saw two men walking away from it.

Frank pulled his horse up and nodded at the men. "They'll be going to tell JT you've got here," he said as Shanna rode up beside him. "He'll probably want to see you alone. You'll have to climb a little ways up to that cave there."

"You mean he lives in a cave instead of that cabin?" Shanna asked in astonishment.

"His choice," Frank said with a shrug. "Hell, it's warmer up there than it is in that cabin in the winter. Wind just whistles in the cracks between the logs, and I can't seem to get anyone interested in helping plug 'em."

"What *do* you men do here all the time? I think I'd go crazy, just sitting around all day, or playing cards, or . . . well, I'd just go crazy after a while."

"Some do," Frank acknowledged. "Some do. Look, there come Jesse and Ben back now. They're waving you to go on up to JT's cave."

"You're not going up there alone, Shanna," Cody cut in grimly. "I'm going with you."

"No, Cody," Shanna said, shaking her head. "I *am* going alone. This is something I have to do without your help."

"You've done plenty without my help the last few days," Cody growled. "I'm going with you."

"Not unless JT says it's all right, Cody," Frank said mildly. But his hand rested on the gun at his hip. "I know you can outdraw me, Cody," he said, glancing at the six-gun strapped to Cody's thigh, "but the rest of these men here all kind of take to JT, too. They're grateful to him for sharing this place with them and sort of protective of the privacy JT wants."

Cody glared at Frank for a second, then swung down from his horse, making no move toward his pistol when he stood on the ground. He walked over and lifted his hands to Shanna, pulling her from the mare and gripping her waist for a moment.

"I don't want you to go up there alone, Shanna."

"I have to, Cody. Besides, I'll probably be spending a lot of time alone with JT pretty soon."

Cody dropped his hands as though her words had scorched his palms, and Shanna immediately regretted them. She could feel his pain, along with her own, yet she had only spoken the truth. When Shanna lifted a hand toward his shoulder, Cody turned away without a word, leaving her clutching at thin air.

Shanna lowered her arm and looked at Frank. "I'm going up there now."

Frank nodded agreement and walked beside her toward the hillside. "Cody—he's in love with you, huh? Wonder how JT's gonna react to that?"

"He won't have any reason to react." Shanna's voice wavered and she blinked against the mist in her eyes. "If he agrees to marry me, I'll never see Cody again."

"Love," Frank said with a shake of his head. "Funny thing, love. So many different kinds of it—love a man and woman have—love for your maw and paw. Wonder if love can be learned?"

"I don't know," Shanna replied evasively. "Look, I can go on from here by myself." She stopped at the foot of the hill, a few dozen feet below the cave.

"Suit yourself."

Frank strode away, leaving Shanna to stare above her alone. She stood for several long moments, waiting for the apprehensive pounding in her chest to still. Suddenly she saw a movement at the mouth of the cave and a shadow that could belong to a man standing there. The shadow stepped into the sunlight, taking on form and substance.

JT. Joshua Tobias Randolph. Curious, Shanna watched him closely as he made his way down the hillside, leaning on a wooden crutch under the arm on the side of his body with the pant leg folded up. Everything she had heard about this man ran through her mind, and she peered closely at his face, but his hat was pulled down almost to his nose, leaving barely enough room for his eyes to look out beneath the brim.

"Thought we might as well get this over with out here in the daylight," JT said as he stopped in front of her. His gravelly voice held a pronounced drawl, deeper than any Shanna had heard since she arrived in Missouri. "Don't reckon you want to buy a pig in a poke, though I never had any doubt about how you would look, you being Diedre's daughter. Me, now, that's another matter."

Without warning, JT leaned on his crutch and removed his hat, while staring directly into Shanna's face. She gave a soft gasp as he revealed the scar that ran from his hairline down to his left eye and the wrinkled tissue on his forehead. Then she made a puzzled moue with her mouth.

"Is that all that's the matter with your face?" she said without thinking.

"All? Ain't that enough?"

Shanna ran her eyes over the rest of his face. His hair was still dark brown, though gray had begun invading it at his temples. His eyes were blue, the same color as Toby's, and she immediately saw the resemblance to her small brother. The straight nose, the high cheekbones—and a dimple in only one cheek. The lips were a little fuller than Toby's, but her mother had had a small mouth, too, thinner than Shanna's own.

The shoulders, encased in a spotless white shirt, were wide, and the shirt followed the contours of his body to a trim waist, which was surrounded by a leather belt. He wore no gun. The denims hugged his thighs until they met his knees, one leg of them, as she had already noticed, ending about a foot above the ground. The other leg stood firmly, holding him in an upright stance, and a run-down leather boot encased his right foot.

"Well?" JT prodded, drawing Shanna's eyes back to his face.

"Well, what?" she returned. "I understand you got that wound on your face rescuing your men on the battlefield. Seems to me you'd be proud of it, rather than using it as an excuse to drop out of life."

JT threw his head back and laughed. "You even sound like Diedre," he said as he moved over and sat down on a nearby rock. "I hoped maybe she might say something like that to me, but I never had the guts to go back to find out." He shook his head sadly. "She always ... always liked to touch my face, though. Sometimes I still dream about her fingers on it. Her hands were as soft as powdered sugar."

JT placed his hat back on his head and motioned for Shanna to sit beside him. "Now," he said. "Tell me about my son. I ... I'll want to talk to you about Diedre after a while, but it's still pretty fresh in my mind, and I'm having a little trouble with it. She ... well, she was still alive to me, until a few days ago."

"Why didn't you come back for her?" Shanna couldn't stop herself from asking. "She might have truly still been alive, if you had."

JT clapped a hand over his stomach as though Shanna had punched him, and his crutch fell to the ground. He curled his shoulders forward and dropped his head, a deep moan issuing from his throat.

Without thinking, Shanna placed a hand on his arm. "I'm sorry," she said quietly. "Really. I shouldn't judge you. After all, I can't know what you've been through."

JT raised his head and stared ahead of him. "I . . . I didn't know she'd been sick. Honest to God, I didn't. I was so damned young back then—barely twenty—and she was six years older, not that we ever let that bother us. But I didn't have nothin' to offer her, compared to the life she had. I promised her and myself, too, that I'd go back soon as I could give her a decent life—kidnap her, if I had to.

"Maybe . . . maybe she just gave up on me, or maybe she tried to write to tell me what was going on. But then that damned war came up and there wasn't much mail gettin' through to anyone. After I saw what my face looked like, I thought she'd be better off back there. Then, when they cut my leg off . . . little lady, I swear. . . ."

JT bit off his words and seemed to be gathering his emotions for a moment before he turned his head to look at her. "It's Shanna, isn't it? I saw you once. You were walking in the park with some of your friends, and Diedre pointed you out. She was awfully proud of you. We . . . we were looking out a hotel window at the time," he admitted.

A faint blush stole over Shanna's cheeks at his admission. At least, he was being open with her—she had to give him credit for that. And Toby had come into the world from this man's union with her mother. They had to have found a bed—or at least some place—to share their passion.

"I loved my mother deeply," she said, deciding to address the fact of her mother's pride in her, instead

Bittersweet Promises

of where Diedre had spoken of it. "It's only since she's been dead that I've realized just how much—and how much she must have gone through before she died."

"Your father was a bastard... *is* a bastard," JT growled. "I'll see him dead before I let him raise my son—mine and Diedre's son. I'll see him in hell before he touches that kid."

"I can empathize with your feelings about that," Shanna agreed. "His name is Tobias, but everyone calls him Toby. Zerelda told me your name is Joshua Tobias. I guess my mother named Toby as close to your name as she dared."

JT breathed out the name with a sigh, "Toby. I have a son named Toby after me and still have a part of Diedre alive in him. What's he like, Shanna?"

For the next few minutes, Shanna told JT about her life with Toby and described the boy to him. At one point, she touched the dimple on JT's cheek, telling him of the identical one in Toby's. JT smiled finally, his face taking on a look of wonder, and the tenseness leaving his shoulders.

Down below, Cody stood at the cabin window watching Shanna raise her hand and touch JT's face. The fading sunlight outlined the two figures on the rock, and though he couldn't see their features from that distance, he could see how close they sat. How their heads bent close together. How they talked to each other effortlessly, their relaxed bodies telling him they shared an easy camaraderie.

"Dingus!" Cody turned abruptly from the window. "You got any liquor around here?"

"Sure, Cody." Jesse nodded to a shelf behind him, which was lined with a row of bottles. "Only thing is we got a rule around here that we lock our guns up in that closet over there when we start drinkin'. Frank's the only one's got a key to the door. Frank, he holds his booze better than the rest of us do."

Cody unbuckled his gun belt and handed it to Frank. While Frank placed it in the closet, Cody grabbed the first bottle on the shelf.

"Wait a sec', Frank," Jesse said when Frank started to close the closet door. "Here." He removed his double gun belt and handed it over. "Reckon I'll join Cody. Ain't been drunk with my ol' friend in a long time. Can't see him drinkin' alone."

"Just so you remember we aren't exactly friends anymore, Dingus," Cody replied.

"Whatever you say, Cody. Might change your mind, after a few drinks of that stuff."

"Not likely. I won't forget how I found you with Shanna."

"She'll have someone else to watch out for her now, old pard," Jesse said with a laugh. "You won't have to worry about keeping an eye on her while we get drunk together."

Cody lifted the liquor bottle and took a long swig without answering Jesse. He withheld the bottle and nodded at the shelf when Jesse reached for it.

"Get your own. This one's mine." Cody pulled a coin from his pocket and laid it on the shelf. "I'll pay as I go. It's probably hard to get booze out here."

"Not as hard as you'd think." Jesse picked up the coin and tossed it to Frank, then reached for the next bottle on the shelf.

Chapter Twenty-six

"How in the world do you live out here like this, Mr. Randolph?" Shanna asked.

JT smiled at her. "It's JT, Shanna. If we're gonna be friends, let's do it on a first-name basis." A shadow crossed his face as he continued, "I . . . I've been living on money of my own that I saved up before the war—what I was gonna use to go back for Diedre," he admitted, then gave a deep sigh. "I guess I might as well be honest with you and tell you the whole damned bit about how stupid I was after I woke up in that field hospital."

JT picked up a handful of small pebbles from the ground. Opening his palm, he chose one and tossed it onto the rocky hillside. He frowned in concentration as he tried to decide which pebble to choose next, then dropped the entire handful and brushed his hand against his leg.

"I don't remember much about the actual battle," he said. "Hell, after a while they all run together. Men and horses screaming in pain. Guns roaring and the powder smell mixed with the smell of blood. It gets so damned smoky you can't tell sometimes if you're shooting at the enemy or your own men, especially near the end of the war. Weren't hardly any of us who still had a complete uniform. We'd picked up pieces of clothing where we could, when our own got too ragged to cover us any longer."

He glanced at Shanna to see her watching him closely, a look of sympathy, rather than horror, on her face.

"The last battle I was in wasn't even much of a fight. The Union troops had all the firepower, and they had us pinned down. We hadn't had any horses for so long that we joked about having to learn to ride again. Fact is, we'd eaten the last one a couple months before. But the Yankees still had plenty of horses, and they had several small cannons, too. I looked around and realized I'd gotten separated from my men, and about that time I saw a cannon being circled behind us, aimed at where some of my men were firing from behind a pile of dead wood.

"I ran screaming like hell toward my men. 'Course the noise was too loud for them to hear me. A Union officer rode out of the woods and tried to cut me off. I got my hands on his saber and pulled him out of the saddle, but he managed to give me this scar first." JT touched his face, then dropped his arm.

"I used his own saber to kill him. The horse must have been pretty well trained, 'cause it stood by its master while I climbed into the saddle. I was wiping blood off my face, but I still had one good eye. My men saw me as I rode hell-bent for leather at the deadfall, waving my arms at them to scatter. They did, just as the cannon hit the deadfall and caught it afire."

JT gave a sardonic chuckle. "That horse wasn't trained to stand up to fire, and it tossed me right into the middle of the mess. Cody tried to tell me later that I'd saved their lives, but one of the other men said it was Cody who came back to get me. I don't remember. The first memory I have after that is of one of the women at the hospital helping the doctor change my bandages. She screamed and fainted beside my cot. They told me later she was new and hadn't seen many wounded yet, but I'll never forget how she looked when she saw my face."

"So you got it into your mind that your face was too ugly for a woman to look at," Shanna stated. "Don't you know a woman doesn't love just how a man looks? There's so much more to the feelings between a man and woman than the physical side. There's companionship, shared laughter, caring about the same things in life. Especially, there's the feeling of being loved in return by someone you care deeply about."

"Sounds like you've had a little experience in love yourself, Shanna. Who's the lucky man in your life?"

Realizing she had been staring downhill at the log cabin, Shanna tore her eyes away and shook her head. "No one," she denied. "At . . . at least, not anymore." She glanced at JT from the corner of her eye, then back at the ground. "Didn't Zerelda tell you in her letter why I was coming out here?"

"She said you had some crazy idea about us gettin' married. Hell, Shanna, I can't let you throw your life away like that. You're young and beautiful, and you still have your whole life ahead of you. Diedre wouldn't want you to do this. And if I'm not mistaken, there's someone else you'd much rather be married to—someone who's probably got two good legs and can make a living well enough to support you. I don't even know what I'm going to do when my money runs out."

Shanna frantically marshaled her arguments in her mind. She had to convince him. She had promised Toby.

"Toby needs me, JT," she pleaded. "Please, don't make up your mind until you hear everything. I can help you get to know Toby and raise him."

While JT waited for further explanation, Shanna drew the letters from her pocket and held them as she verbally sketched the events of the last few months. She included the fact of her trust fund and assured JT there would be adequate money for him to start a business, instead of having to depend upon physical labor to make a living.

JT let her ramble on. The only sign that he was paying close attention to her was the dark look that crossed his face now and then—especially when Shanna told him of the kidnapping charge she had faced.

"That friggin' bastard," she heard JT murmur at that point.

At last Shanna held the two letters out. "You're the only hope I have. You have to marry me, so I can stay with Toby, as I've promised him I would. Even the judge said it's my only chance."

JT accepted the letters, making no move to read them in front of her. "There's another way to keep Toby away from Van Alstyne, Shanna—one you're trying not to face, because you don't want to think about it."

"I . . . I know, but. . . ."

"You admitted the judge would give me custody of my son, with the documents Diedre left. You'd have your own children someday, Shanna. Toby's probably all I'll ever have."

"Oh, God," Shanna moaned. "Please. I've fought so hard to keep Toby with me. You can't turn against me, too. I've promised Toby that I'd always be with him, and I'm really the only mother he's ever known. Please, JT. Don't do this to me—to Toby! I'll. . . ."

Shanna took a deep breath and forced herself to continue. "I'm not asking you to marry me as strictly a business deal, JT. It will be a complete relationship, including the physical side, if that's what you want. I'll bear your children and honor all my wedding vows. I'll be the best wife I know how to be, and I give you my word that it will be a lifetime commitment on my part."

JT studied Shanna's resolute face and had no doubt she meant every word. He skimmed his eyes down her lush, young body, feeling stirrings he had thought long dead in his groin. Could it be possible he was being given another chance at life—another bridge to cross with the promise of a decent, fulfilling life on the other side? Or would this bridge blow up in his face, too—or, more likely, collapse behind him after he crossed, leaving him with only an empty shell of mocking what-could-have-beens?

He hadn't expected her offer of lovemaking in a loveless marriage. He could satisfy his lust on her body—hell, there wouldn't be any profit in whorehouses if men didn't have the ability to separate the physical release they craved from a woman's desire for a wedding ring before she opened her legs.

This was Diedre's daughter, though, not a whore who had plenty of practice at feigning passion for her customers. Shanna had no idea what she was promising him. Oh, he could probably bring her to physical fulfillment—he had never had any complaints from women about his prowess in lovemaking, especially since he cared as much about the lady's pleasure as his own.

That was before, though. Now, would Shanna cringe from his scarred body? Or, just possibly, could he again find the complete melding of bodies and spirits that he had so thoughtlessly thrown away once before?

No, not thoughtlessly, JT admitted to himself. The decision had come after days, weeks, even months of agonized indecision. It was far too late, though, to realize he had made the wrong choice. Perhaps he owed it to his dead love to atone for their missed chance at happiness by doing whatever was within his power to give her daughter the one request she made of him.

Realizing Shanna was staring at him, waiting for a decision he wasn't prepared to vocalize just yet, JT avoided Shanna's eyes by reaching down for his crutch. He propped his hands and chin on it, hoping his hat shadowed his face enough that Shanna couldn't read his expression.

"You say this judge told you he'd give you and me joint custody, if we were married?"

"Yes, but... he also said it might only be binding in his court," Shanna had to admit. She might as well tell him all of it, she decided and continued, "And Cody told me I might have to go back to New York to stand trial again, if my father fights Judge Howard's decision in the trial I just went through."

"Jesus, if there wasn't a lady sitting here, I'd call your father something a lot worse than a bastard!" JT spit, then muttered an even viler curse under his breath. He rose to his feet. "All right, Shanna, I'll think about it. Was that Cody I saw ride in with you?"

Shanna nodded.

"Go on down there now. Cody will see that no one here bothers you. I'll talk to you in the morning."

"Morning?" When JT frowned, Shanna quickly nodded her agreement and started walking away. "I'll see you then."

JT glanced at the letters in his hand. "Diedre, darlin'," he murmured. "What a damned mess we made of our lives. How can I let your daughter sacrifice any chance she might have for a decent life because I was stupid enough not to come back for you?"

JT sat down on the rock and bowed his head as he propped his crutch beside him. His fingers clenched around the letters, the paper rustling as it wrinkled in his grip. With an effort, he opened his hand and smoothed the letters against his thigh, the familiar writing leaping out at him on the top envelope. Though that envelope was addressed to Shanna, how many times had he seen those same feminine letters outlining his own name, agreeing to meet him just one more time? How many times had they said good-bye?

"Evidently, one time too many," JT said aloud with a mirthless chuckle.

JT pulled out the pages of the letter addressed to Shanna, fighting the pain tearing at him while he scanned the familiar hand. Nothing new there—it only confirmed what Shanna had told him.

One page fluttered to the ground, and JT bent to retrieve it. He opened the folded paper and stared at a birth certificate—Tobias Randolph. How in hell had Diedre managed that? His eyes centered on the line listing the boy's father—Joshua Tobias Randolph. Diedre had even used her maiden name, Forsythe, on the line marked mother.

JT slowly shook his head. He didn't know how legal the document was; he'd have to ask Cody about that. It was mighty convenient for Shanna to have brought a lawyer with her.

JT looked at the log cabin. Or was it just coincidence? He hadn't missed the way Shanna kept glancing at the cabin while they talked, her heart in her eyes. Hell, she was in love with Cody—one more reason for him to turn down her marriage proposal. Cody had saved his life. How could he step between Cody and Shanna, especially if Cody felt the same way about her?

"But I have a son," he murmured. "A son who's part of Diedre. Sorry, Cody, old pard, but that bastard Van Alstyne's not gonna raise my boy. And if it's Shanna that Toby wants as a mother, I'll see that she's the other piece of our little threesome. I'll see that boy gets whatever he wants in life, even if I have to kill Van Alstyne to do it."

JT smiled grimly. No, he didn't have to kill Van Alstyne. He could let him live, live with the knowledge that his daughter was the wife of his wife's lover. That the boy, who was the result of JT and Diedre's love for each other, was also a part of that marriage.

Realizing he had probably made his decision when he first read Zerelda's letter, despite what he had told Shanna, JT stuffed the letters into his pocket. He couldn't face reading Diedre's last missive to him just now. First, he'd dig out that bottle of fine bourbon hidden in the cave, then maybe that suit he'd bought in a weak, drunken moment in Charleston. Man should look good when he got married.

Scowling as he recalled why the suit had remained unworn, JT tried to push from his mind the sight of his own mother's grimace of disgust when she saw his face later the same week he had bought the outfit. Hell, she and his aunt had even canceled a small dinner party they'd planned that evening. He could still recall his aunt's whispered insistence to his mother that she wouldn't be able to eat a bite with JT sitting at the table.

Shanna hadn't turned away from him, though. He had seen sympathy in her eyes—granted, mixed somewhat with pity. Marriages had been made without love since the beginning of time, and they had the boy in common, along with their shared love for Diedre. It had been easy to talk to Shanna, and he'd felt an immediate liking for her. He hadn't realized just how much he missed a woman's companionship, and Shanna looked so much like Diedre. It would almost be like living the life he and Diedre had planned before that damned war intervened.

Chapter Twenty-seven

At the door to the log cabin, Shanna hesitated, then turned away. Voices and bursts of laughter sounded inside the dilapidated structure, and she glanced through the dirty window, seeing several men seated at a rickety table, piles of cards scattered before them and two brown bottles upright on the littered surface.

Cody looked up at that moment, his eyes narrowing when he caught sight of her. He deliberately reached for the bottle in front of him and took a long swallow, holding Shanna's gaze all the while. Thumping the bottle back, he lowered his eyes and picked up his cards.

So much for JT's assurance that Cody would watch over her, Shanna thought as she walked toward the corral. The little gray mare whickered and ran over, and Shanna slipped between the railings to meet her. Those lazy drunks inside hadn't even unsaddled the poor horse, and Shanna removed the mare's bridle and saddle. She didn't see Cody's dun or Frank's roan.

A haphazard barn sat on the far side of the corral and Shanna searched it for feed for the mare. Inside, she found Cody's dun tied near a feed trough, its saddle, too, still in place. She struggled with the larger saddle, but managed to remove it, then headed toward some covered barrels in a far corner. Mixing a measure of the corn and oats she found together, she fed the horses.

Untying the bedroll from behind her saddle, Shanna headed toward the creek they had ridden across at the valley entrance. No way would she sit inside that smoke-filled cabin and watch a bunch of men play cards and get drunk while she waited for morning. She'd much rather be out in the clear mountain air, with the squirrels and birds for company.

She could probably even manage to get a fire going. She had taught herself a lot of new things these last few months—not the least of them being that a person never knew what skills she was capable of until called upon to learn new ones.

Even new emotional skills could be learned—the skill to hide a breaking heart—the fortitude to face a life of endless days stretching before her, perhaps alone, without even Toby beside her. Maybe even in a jail cell, she realized with a shiver of dread. What would JT's decision be?

"Well, what'd he say?" a voice snarled.

Shanna gasped and turned from clearing a spot for the fire. Cody stood swaying beside a tree, a bottle clutched in his hand. Engrossed in the questions crowding her mind, she'd been lax in her vigilance.

"Well?" Cody prodded when Shanna didn't answer.

"You better sit down. How in the world did you get so drunk so fast?"

"Ain't dh-drunk," Cody slurred. "Leashways, not drunk 'nuf." He wavered again and put a hand out to the tree trunk to steady himself, missing the support by several inches. His knees folded and he sat, cradling the bottle against his chest to protect it.

"Th-there. That suit you? Now, answer my queshun. Whensh's the wedding?"

"He's thinking it over. He said he'll let me know in the morning. Cody, let me fix you something to eat. I'm getting a fire going, and there's still some bacon and bread left."

"Nah," Cody said with a wave of his arm. "They're fixin' some stew inside. I'll eat with 'em later."

"If you're able," Shanna murmured, glancing at the nearly empty bottle in his other hand.

"Want a drink?" Cody asked with a cocked eyebrow. "Shellebrate your engagement?"

"I already told you, Cody. JT hasn't given me a definite answer yet." She rose and took the bottle he extended. "But, yes, I think I will have a drink. Thank you."

Shanna tipped the bottle and took a tentative swallow. The liquid burned inside her mouth and her eyes watered, but she forced down a second swallow. A pleasant warmth stole through her stomach as she lowered the bottle.

"Not as good as the brandy we had the first day I met you," she said, blinking back the moisture she told herself came from the whiskey, not her memories. "But I guess it will do."

Cody grabbed the bottle, finishing it off in one long drink. "Guess I'll go get us 'nother one," he said, trying to draw his legs under him and get to his feet.

"I don't want any more, Cody. And you shouldn't have any, either. Don't you think you've had enough?"

"Nope," Cody said shortly as he gained his feet. "Not near 'nuf."

Cody staggered away, and Shanna turned to the pile of kindling behind her, rather than watch him stumble up the bank. Shaking her head and blinking her eyes to clear her blurred vision, she bit her bottom lip.

"Tipsy," she muttered. "I see what the difference is now. He's not tipsy, he's blind drunk."

No, not blind. Shadowed pain lay in those brown eyes, red-rimmed now from the whiskey Cody had gulped during the hour since they arrived. The same aching longing refused to stay shuttered behind the eyelids Shanna closed over her blue eyes; it seemed to crawl through the feathery lashes and invade her body. How could she bear this excruciating anguish the rest of her life? Would it ever lessen? Why hadn't Cody stayed behind at the plantation, rather than put them both through this torment?

A loud crack exploded in the air, and Shanna stared at the piece of kindling broken by her hands. She swiped the back of her hands against her cheeks before she gathered a small bundle of the sticks to start the fire.

Shanna had the fire blazing by the time Cody returned, his steps faltering more than ever and his whiskey-laden breath fanning her face when he sat on the bedroll beside her and held out the bottle.

"Oops!" Cody caught the cork between his teeth and pulled it loose, spitting it aside. Then he pulled a small glass from his shirt pocket and poured it full, sloshing some of the whiskey over the side when he handed it to her.

"Lady drinks out of a glash," he said with a knowing nod of his head that brought a smile to Shanna's lips.

Shanna took a sip of the brown liquid, grimacing at the taste. She started to set the glass down on the ground, but Cody stayed her arm and clinked his bottle against her glass.

"Toast," he said with a smirk. "Heresh to your new life, Shanna."

Shanna took another obligatory sip of whiskey and saw Cody wipe his lips when she looked at him.

"I might be drunk, Sh-Shanna," Cody said in a pain-laced voice. "But I meant that. I want you to have wh-whatever makesh you happy in life. And I don't guess it's wis... within my power to be the one to give that to you, much as I wish like hell it could be."

"I'll never forget you, Cody," Shanna acknowledged. "And I... I wish the same thing for you. Someday you'll find someone else and fall in love. I hope she makes you happy, and is a good mother to Melinda."

"Melinda's gonna miss the two of you sh-something terrible—you an' Toby." Cody tipped the bottle again, then leaned on one unsteady arm. "Aunt Bessie, too. Maybe... maybe you can write to Aunt Besshie from time to time—let her know how you're doin'."

"I don't think that would be a good idea, Cody."

"Probably not."

"Besides." Shanna took another swallow from her glass. "JT hasn't said he'll marry me yet."

"He will," Cody told her with a solemn, drunken nod. "He'd be a fool not to, even wit'out gettin' his own son in... in the bargain. But promise me one thing, Shanna. Promish you'll let me know if it don't work out. Promish you'll come back to me, if that happens."

Shanna shook her head and gazed into the fire. "No, Cody. I won't make that promise."

"Damn it, why not?" The whiskey bottle fell unnoticed when Cody grabbed Shanna's shoulders and pulled her around to face him.

"Why not?" he demanded again, giving her a small shake, his fingers biting into her arms. "Don't you think I'll want to know?"

"It wouldn't be fair to you, Cody. You have to be free to find someone else, and you won't do that if you think I might come back someday. I won't let you waste your life that way."

"But you can waste your life with a man you don't love!"

"I've made my decision and I'll live with it, whatever happens, Cody. Don't you see? It wouldn't be fair to JT either, if I didn't totally commit myself to this marriage. I have to go into it in the frame of mind that it will be a lasting commitment—that I'll build a good life with him for Toby. He has a right to expect that much, knowing I'll never love him."

The expletive Cody uttered in a harsh voice made Shanna gasp. He dropped his hands, his eyes searching for the whiskey bottle until he found it beside him. Picking it up and seeing there was still a good measure that hadn't drained out, Cody took another swallow.

"Yeah," he said in a contemplative voice. "That's what I think of love. Sh . . . screw it and the horse it rode in on. You've got the right idea. Keep love out of a relashionship and you keep out the hurt that goes along with it. I'll 'member that the next time myself. Hell, all a man needs is a warm body once in a while— someone to cook his meals and wash his clothes. Shit, any two-legged, two-armed woman oughta be able to do that."

"Cody, please. Your language. . . ."

"What, Shanna? Screw? Shit? Hell, they're just words for our basic body functionsh. Ain't like some abstract word that can't be p-pinned down—like *love!* A man's body knows just 'sactly what it's doin' when it screws a woman or takes a. . . ."

"I don't have to sit here and listen to this!"

Cody's hand caught her in midrise, spilling the whiskey from Shanna's glass over her bodice when he jerked her down beside him. The fumes stung her eyes, mixed with the odor from Cody's own breath as he pulled her head toward him. She braced her hands against Cody's chest, shaking her head.

Bittersweet Promises

"Don't, Cody. Please don't. It'll only make it worse."

"Probably, darlin'," Cody said in a ravaged voice. "But right now I just don't see how the hell it can be any worse."

Shanna fought him for a brief second, twisting her head as she tried to avoid his lips. When his mouth brushed her cheek, she turned much as a newborn turns instinctively to its mother's nipple. She returned his kiss with her whole soul in the embrace, her arms going around his neck and her body sliding willingly down beside him.

Cody's hands roamed over her, sliding the jacket from her shoulders and tossing it aside. He pulled her against his chest, one arm sliding past her waist to cup her hip and drag her lower body close. His moan of passion joined Shanna's as she snuggled against his hardness, and Cody shifted to bring Shanna onto his stomach.

"No," Shanna moaned again, tearing her lips free. "Cody, don't. We can't!"

"We can, darlin'," Cody insisted, his lips and tongue nuzzling at her ear. "There's ways we can pleasure each other without worrying about you getting a babe from it. Trust me, darlin'. Let me show you."

Cody grasped Shanna's hips and rocked her against him. The delicious feeling spread through her, and her arms grew useless when she tried to push herself away. When Cody's hands left her hips to unbutton her blouse, she continued the rocking motion, the need to join herself to him driving out all thoughts of resistance.

Cody's mouth claimed her breast at the same moment Shanna dug her fingers into his chest and cried out. She heard him groan in his throat and felt him give a final buck against her. But when she regained her senses a few seconds later, a strange, hollow feeling filled her, not the complete fulfillment she had felt when they made love before.

Cody seemed to feel the same lack. "I'm sorry, love." He shifted Shanna from his body and held her at his side. "I couldn't help myself. It wasn't right, just using our bodies like that. Are you all right, darlin'?"

Shanna nodded against his chest, unable to speak around the lump in her throat.

"Forgive me, darlin'," Cody murmured. "I love you."

"There's nothing to forgive, Cody," Shanna managed to say. But Cody's fingers loosened their hold in her hair and a sound rumbled under her ear. She pushed free and looked down at him.

Why, he'd fallen asleep. No, more likely passed out, Shanna realized when she saw his slack mouth and heard a loud snore. She buttoned her blouse, then reached out a hand to stroke his cheek.

"I love you, too, Cody," she whispered. "I'll say it this one last time, for myself, since you can't hear me. Then I'll put it behind me. I love you, Cody Garret, with all my heart."

Chapter Twenty-eight

Shanna made one last trip to the barn and returned with Cody's bedroll and the rifle from her saddle scabbard. Though she watched the cabin door a bit apprehensively, it remained closed. Returning to the creek, she checked her jacket pocket for the derringer, finding it still in place. She pulled the jacket on again and made do with the rest of the bread and cookies in her saddlebag for an evening meal.

Shanna unrolled Cody's bedroll and fed more wood onto the fire. Spying the whiskey bottle Cody had propped against a rock when the fire gleamed on it, Shanna picked it up. Surprisingly, despite Cody's rough handling, it still contained an inch or two of liquid. Maybe it would help her sleep, too. Otherwise, she would probably lie awake all night, dreading the coming morning and JT's decision.

"Person shouldn't drink alone."

Damn it! Didn't these men ever make any noise when

they walked? Shanna immediately recognized Jesse's voice and dropped the bottle from her mouth, her other hand plunging into her jacket pocket.

She swung around, the derringer in her hand.

"I'm not alone. Cody's passed out, but this gun's company enough."

"Whoa, little lady," Jesse said with a laugh. "I ain't packing any iron. I jist brought you and Cody some stew. Thought you might be hungry."

"Set it down there. I'll get it after you leave."

Jesse shrugged and knelt to set two bowls in the grass. "Sure you don't want to share a drink with me?" he asked after he stood.

"She's sure, Jesse," JT said as he limped around Jesse. "I brought my own bottle with me, if Shanna feels like drinkin' company. You can get your ass on back to the cabin now."

Jesse met JT's stare for a moment; then his eyes traveled to JT's waist. "Thought we had a rule around here 'bout not packin' when we drink."

"That's yours and Frank's rule, to keep yourselves from gettin' drunk and killin' each other," JT said tightly. "And don't forget, you never was quick enough to take me, when we used to practice together."

"Maybe I've gotten better over the years. An' maybe you've gotten slower."

"And maybe I haven't. Like Shanna and I were talking about a little earlier, there's not much to do out here. Plenty of time to make sure your gun hand doesn't get rusty."

"Aw hell, it don't matter anyway. Frank won't let me have my guns until I sober up." He turned away, jamming his empty hands in his pockets.

"That boy's gonna get himself killed one of these days," JT said as he made his way down the slight bank of the creek. Using his crutch as a support, he lowered himself onto the bedroll beside her.

"You want some of that stew? I wouldn't recommend it as tasty, but it's filling. Or would you rather take me up on that drink? This is fine Kentucky bourbon—lots better than that rotgut in your hand."

"I've already eaten something." Shanna placed the derringer back in her pocket and set her bottle aside again. When she looked at JT, she saw he had found her glass by the fire and was wiping it on his shirttail.

"I can wash that in the creek," she said. "You'll ruin that shirt. How do you keep it so clean out here anyway?"

JT finished with the glass and held it out to reflect the firelight. "It's clean. And this shirt's not one I've ever worn before. Bought me a couple that were packed away with a suit I got 'bout the same time."

"Your wedding suit?" Shanna asked as she accepted the refilled glass.

"Yeah," JT admitted. "Still fits me, too. I tried it on a while ago."

Shanna took a swallow of whiskey, steeling herself for his decision. At least she wouldn't have to wait out the long night not knowing.

"Like that better than the stuff in that other bottle?" JT asked.

"Why, yes. Yes, I do. It's not as harsh tasting."

"It'll knock you on your as . . . rear end just as fast, though. 'Specially if you aren't used to drinkin'. You don't drink, do you, Shanna, honey? Never did fancy bein' married to a woman who liked whiskey more than I did."

"I never even tasted liquor until a few months ago. Cody . . . Cody gave me some brandy once. That's all I ever had until tonight. And I don't think you'll have to worry about me getting to like it too much. Does . . .

does your coming here tonight, instead of in the morning, mean you've made up your mind?"

"Not hardly," JT denied, sending Shanna's hopes of at last having her future settled plummeting. "Marriage is a big step. Man's gotta weigh all sides of it and get used to the thought. Remember, Shanna, you've had several months to think about this. I'm still not real sure this is what we should do. I sure wish Cody hadn't passed out so early, because I was hoping to talk to him."

"You wouldn't have been able to make much sense out of what he said the way he was. You'll have to wait until he wakes up."

"Guess so," JT agreed. "In the meantime, there's something I want to ask you about."

JT reached into the pocket of his pants and pulled out a single piece of paper, holding it out to Shanna. She finished the drink in her hand, hardly aware of swallowing the liquid, before she accepted it. Setting her empty glass down on the ground again, she unfolded the paper and held it close to the firelight.

"It's Toby's birth certificate," she said with a nod. "I've already seen it. Mother left it in with her letter to me."

JT stuffed the birth certificate back into his pocket. "It's got my name on it as Toby's father. It puzzles me how Diedre got by with that."

"She had her own attorney. That's one thing she stood up to my father about and how she set up the trust fund. She did that before anyone knew she was carrying Toby, and I assume the same man must have helped her out with this."

"Probably. Anyway, Shanna, there's something I want to ask you. Here. Let me fill your glass again."

Shanna picked up her glass and held it out. She probably shouldn't drink any more, but the bourbon didn't seem to be affecting her. She didn't see JT give a nod of satisfaction as she raised the glass to her lips once more.

"What else did you want to know?" she asked after lowering her glass, surprised to find her tongue somewhat thick when she spoke. "I'll discuss anything you want."

"Then tell me what sort of plan you had in case you didn't find me, or if I didn't marry you if you did find me."

"I . . . I tried not to think about that." Shanna toyed with the rim of her glass, her nervous finger tracing a circle.

"You're much too smart not to have thought of a contingency plan, Shanna. I want to know what it was."

"Mother has relatives in England," Shanna said grudgingly. "I thought I might go to them and ask for help. I didn't think Father would follow me there and risk facing them, since, from what I gathered from Mother over the years, they didn't think much of him."

"Why didn't you go there first?"

"Because my mother's letter asked me to try to find you. She wanted you to know Toby. And Toby to know you."

An ember popped in the fire, the only sound in the silence as JT contemplated Shanna's words. Shanna finished her drink while she waited for him to speak again; then she reached for the bourbon in his hand, which he gave her without protest. Watching her refill her glass, JT studied her closely, then retrieved the bottle and took another drink himself.

"Shanna," he said finally. "You've got to have some dreams of your own. Don't you want your own family? Didn't you think about that while you were growing up, want a man to love you—children with him?"

"Not without Toby," Shanna denied. "Not since he was born. He's always been part of any future I envisioned for myself—after my mother wasn't able to care for him."

"Still, though, you could be a part of Toby's life if I had him. I'd never deny you seeing him. You could live near us and—"

"No!" Shanna hissed. "It wouldn't be the same, and I promised Toby we'd always be together! You can't just waltz into his life and take him away from me!"

"I didn't waltz into his life, Shanna," JT reminded her. "You came lookin' for me. And a boy needs his father."

"He needs his mother, too," Shanna said hotly. "Or at least, the only mother he's ever known." She pounded a fist against her chest. "And that's me! I cared for him, not those nurses my father hired. I dried his tears and oversaw his lessons. He called me mama at first, until he was old enough for me to explain that I was his sister and taught him to call me Shanna and my mother Mama!"

"Calm down, Shanna," JT soothed. He glanced at the bedroll when Cody gave a groan and turned over, disturbed by the loud voices. "And what about Cody's stake in this?" he demanded. "At least be honest with me and tell me what your feelings are for him."

"I love him! There. Does that satisfy you? You asked about my dreams in life. Well, if I could only have one dream come true, it would be to marry Cody and have him be Toby's father and me be a mother to Melinda. But that can't happen, can it? You're the only one who can get legal custody of Toby!"

Shanna angrily brushed at a tear trickling down her cheek, the firelight reflecting the anguish in her eyes. She drained the whiskey glass and reached for the bourbon bottle again.

"Huh-uh. No more, Shanna." JT drew the bottle beyond her grasp and steadied her with a hand on her shoulder when Shanna swayed toward him.

"I see," Shanna said as she sat back. "Liquor's only for men to drown their sorrows in."

"Is that why Cody's lying over there passed out?" JT asked in a mild voice. "Because he's in love with you, too, and can't bear the thought of you marrying me?"

Shanna shrugged, refusing to answer. She turned her head sideways, the light outlining her profile.

Damn, she looked so much like Diedre. She wasn't Diedre, though. She had a lot more fire in her than Diedre had. If it had been Shanna he had fallen in love with, JT could almost imagine her following him into the war, instead of waiting complacently for him to return.

Shanna also held the key to gaining his son's love, JT told himself as he watched her brush at another tear. He couldn't imagine Toby ever coming to love him if he stepped between the boy and Shanna.

And he had one other question answered. She had a place to go—England, no less, where he would face an angry mob of relatives if he tried to follow to see his son.

No, two questions answered, JT realized as he looked at Cody. She had another man ready and willing to step in to be a father to Toby. A man who already loved her, and maybe felt the same about Toby. Even if he did use the information he'd found in Diedre's letter, JT had no guarantee that Cody would allow him to be a part of Toby's life.

JT got to his knees, using his crutch for leverage to stand. "Better get your beauty rest," he said. "I don't fancy having a bride with bags under her eyes."

Shanna glanced up. "Then . . . then you'll marry me?"

"Wouldn't be gentlemanly to turn down a woman's marriage proposal," JT said with a ragged laugh, stifling the irritation he felt at the dead sound of Shanna's voice. "Reckon it's just as hard for a woman to screw up her courage and propose as it is for a man. We'll head back to Liberty in the morning, if you and Cody aren't too hung over. I want the whole shebang—you have yourself a white dress made that's fancy enough to match my new suit, hear me, woman? I've got some money left, enough to take care of us for a while. Time it takes to make your dress and for us to decide where to live, I'll use to get to know my son."

"Thank you," Shanna whispered.

JT tried, but he couldn't detect any relief in her voice. Had he seen her head drop when he mentioned the white dress? He frowned in Cody's direction, then settled his crutch under his arm. Diedre hadn't been a virgin, either. In fact, she had been several years older than he. It hadn't dimmed his feelings for her. Fact was, he didn't much care for the thought of breaking in a virgin, not that he'd ever had one. A woman with some experience would be a much better bed partner.

"Good night, Shanna," JT said as he made his way up the slight rise beside the creekbed.

"Good night," she called after him.

As soon as JT was out of sight, Shanna dragged her bedroll over beside Cody. The whiskey in her stomach gave her courage, making her not give a damn if the whole camp saw her lying beside Cody in the morning. Soon enough, she would wake with a different man's head on the next pillow, and she wasn't going to deny herself one final night of closeness to Cody.

Cuddling against her lover, Shanna buried her head on Cody's unresisting shoulder and let her tears flow freely, while her last vestige of hope crawled from her shattered spirit and fled in the night. Had she really thought JT might have a solution that would allow her to stir the embers of her dream of a life with both Cody and Toby to new flames? Had she really thought he might offer a platonic marriage—a short-lived one—realize Toby would be better off with her—give up his claim to his son?

JT's words left no doubt. A ceremony that encompassed the whole *shebang*. A wh-white dress.

How many times over the years had she dreamed of floating down a church aisle in that white dress, drawn irresistibly to a man she loved with her entire being waiting at the altar? Why had the dream refused to stay trapped in the corner of her mind, where she had buried it after her mother's death?

Cody. Cody refired that dream. Cody's teasing banter and twinkling brown eyes. Cody's voice roughened in passion and those eyes pooled into chocolate depths of longing. Cody's hands, work roughened with calluses, spreading delicious sensations over her silken skin.

Cody's arms around her, his head buried on her breasts, seeking solace only she could give from the guilt he carried. Cody's tender concern for Melinda and Toby. His standing with her to confront her father. Following her to make sure she arrived safely, even on her journey to another man's arms.

Cody stirred slightly and wrapped an arm around Shanna, drawing her against his length before he sank back into deep slumber. Shanna pressed her body to his, straining to breach the invisible barriers to their love.

How cruel fate was. She was spending what should have been one of the happiest nights of her life—the night of her marriage proposal—in the arms of the man she desperately wanted to marry, not the man she had agreed to wed. She was filled with anguish, rather than ecstatic joy.

Try as she might to muffle her sobs on Cody's chest, somehow they escaped and joined the cadence of spring peepers in the reeds lining the creekbed. An owl swooped silently onto a nearby limb, blinking its huge round eyes at the scene below. Somewhere on an Ozark mountainside a puma screamed, the piercing shriek echoing an accompaniment to the agony of shattered hopes and dreams raining from Shanna's eyes with her tears.

Chapter Twenty-nine

"Oh, pshaw, Shanna," Bessie said with an exasperated sigh. "There are only three small children coming for half a day now. The older ones are all in the fields helping plant, even the girls. How do you expect me to fill my days, with Cody still insisting we need Susie every day and me not being quite ready for that rocking chair on the porch?"

"I worry about your health, Bessie."

"My body's a little slow, but there's still not a thing wrong with my brain. I've found looking forward to the little ones coming for a time each day gives me something to get out of bed for. And Pappy says it's good for me. What's really bothering you?"

"I feel as if I've gone back on my word. After all, I promised to stay six months."

"For pity's sake, Shanna, I could have taught Melinda all along, if Cody had hired me a housekeeper."

"Bessie, I know Susie's not working for free. At first,

she was just helping out, but now...."

"Cody's promised Zerelda and Pappy a share of the feed we grow for their own stock this winter, and I'm sure he'll also give Susie a little something for herself, after the crops are in. It's all taken care of. Now, tell me what the dickens has got you so jittery. A person would think you'd be glad of the free time to prepare for your wedding, but you didn't come back from that trip yesterday exactly the blushing bride-to-be."

Bessie's shrewd eyes studied Shanna, who wandered around the empty classroom. They hadn't had a private moment to talk the previous evening amid the flurry of Shanna's return, since Shanna spent most of the evening talking to Toby out by the corral, preparing him for today's meeting with JT.

"I'm just worried about how things will go today when I take Toby over to Zerelda's," Shanna finally replied evasively. "And I'm really going to miss you and Melinda when I leave. JT ... JT thinks I should move into the hotel in Liberty until the wedding."

"Wants to keep you and Cody as far apart as he can, does he?" Bessie asked astutely.

"No! I mean...."

"JT's not blind. Cody's been stomping around like a wounded bull since he got back, and you've got shadows under your eyes you never had before. You've lost weight—that dress just hangs on you. Maybe JT has the right idea. I don't fancy living here with you and Cody the next two weeks, while your wedding day gets closer and closer."

At the even more forlorn look on Shanna's face, Bessie steeled her resolve. Though it tore at her to see Cody and this woman she had come to hold dear throwing away their chance at happiness, she had to think of Cody and Melinda first.

"It's better to make it a clean break," she said to

Bittersweet Promises

Shanna. "I'm not kicking you out. Please don't think that, Shanna. I just don't see any other way to do this."

"There isn't any other way." Shanna stared out the window, where Cody was already in his fields, walking behind a pair of sturdy plow horses. Exhausted from her trip, she had missed him at breakfast.

He hadn't been there the next morning by the creek, either. Instead, she found JT waiting for her to wake, the horses already saddled and ready. He told her Cody had asked what their plans were, then informed JT that he would make better time riding back alone, using the excuse that he needed to get started on his planting.

Yesterday evening, when she finally mustered enough courage to ask, Bessie said Cody was in Kearney, waiting for the blacksmith to repair one of his plows. Shanna had heard Cody ride in late, but her nerve failed when she reached for the doorknob as he came down the hallway toward his room. The thin wall that separated them that night might as well have been as thick as a medieval castle wall.

"I'll pack mine and Toby's things," Shanna said as she turned from the window.

"Never mind. I'll have Susie do it after you leave. I imagine JT's expecting you over at Zerelda's."

"Yes, he is."

"Then, best you get going." Bessie rose from the chair behind the desk. At the door to the parlor, she reached out and pulled Shanna into her arms.

"I want you to know, honey," Bessie said when she released her, "that I wish it could have been different. I'll never forget you."

"Nor I, you and.... You will come to the wedding, won't you?"

"Yes, Melinda and I'll be there." Bessie purposely didn't mention Cody.

"Thank you, Bessie."

Shanna walked quickly through the kitchen, giving Susie only a nod when Susie turned from the counter, where she was stirring something in a bowl. But before Shanna could pull the door closed behind her, Susie caught up, wiping her hands on her apron.

"Shanna, we haven't talked about your wedding dress. You are going to let me make it for you, aren't you?"

"Of course I want you to," Shanna replied, mustering a smile. "But I'm going to be moving into the hotel this afternoon. How will you manage the dress, along with working here?" The last thing Shanna wanted was to have the fittings for her dress in Bessie's kitchen, where Cody could walk in at any moment.

Susie understood the dilemma—Shanna saw the knowledge in her eyes. Did everyone in the entire state know she was in love with Cody, but marrying JT Randolph?

"You can spend a night or two with Mother and me," Susie insisted. "I've already got your measurements, from when I helped with your other dresses. Maybe Melinda can even visit with Toby those evenings."

"All right, Susie," Shanna gave in. "I'll get some material in Liberty and bring it out in a couple days."

"I'll see you then," Susie agreed, turning back to her baking.

Shanna found Toby and Melinda, as usual, with their ponies. Melinda willingly headed into the house to wait for the other children to arrive for lessons, skipping along the way, her blond braids bouncing against her back. Still unaware of the impact the coming marriage would have on her young life, Melinda's sunny disposition gave them all a great deal of pleasure now. Shanna knew the responsibility for telling Melinda rested on her own shoulders, and she didn't look forward to it. She wouldn't avoid it, either.

The road to Zerelda's ran several hundred feet along

Bittersweet Promises

the field Cody was plowing. Shanna, mounted on the gray mare still on loan from the Samuels, kept the mare at a slow pace in deference to Chessy's shorter legs. Drawn against her resistance, Shanna watched Cody until they rounded a bend. Never once did Cody glance in their direction—at least, not while Shanna could see him.

As they rode up to Zerelda's log house a while later, Shanna looked apprehensively at Toby. His sandy hair ruffled in the wind, and he sat his small saddle straight, his face calm and accepting. When he caught Shanna's glance, he smiled.

"It's exciting, isn't it, Shanna? Almost like my birthday. I feel like I'm getting a present!"

"I'm proud of you, Toby. You know that, don't you?"

"Uh-huh," Toby responded with a bob of his head, drawing a chuckle from Shanna with his unexpected answer. He pulled Chessy to a halt in front of the hitching post and slid down, his eyes wide with anticipation when Shanna joined him and looped her mare's reins beside the pony's.

"How soon can I see him, Shanna?"

The screen door opened. "Right now, son," JT said, limping onto the porch. "If that's all right with your sister."

Toby threw Shanna a question with his eyes, and she nodded her head. Toby slowly walked up the porch steps and stopped a few feet from JT, studying the tall man closely.

JT hadn't worn his hat. Zerelda had washed his shirt, and Toby wore a matching white one. JT leaned on his crutch, accepting Toby's close scrutiny and seeing Diedre in this small figure, too, though Shanna had spoken of how much Toby resembled him. He shifted his stance nervously, nonplussed to realize just how much this little boy's approval meant and how deep his own emotions ran. Being faced with Toby's physical presence stirred him beyond anything he had ever imagined in his mind the last few days.

Balancing on his crutch, JT held out his right hand. "Hello, son."

Toby stuck out his own small hand and accepted the handshake. "Hello, sir. I'm really glad to finally get to meet you."

JT reluctantly broke the handshake before he could drag the small body into his arms, as he found himself wanting to.

Take it slow, he reminded himself. *He doesn't know you yet.* He nodded at the porch swing. "Want to sit and talk for a while, Toby?"

"Yes, sir. I've got lots of things I want to ask you."

"Ask away." JT lowered himself to the swing seat. "I'll tell you anything you want to know. Do you want to join us, Shanna?"

"No, I think I'll go talk to Zerelda. I'll be going back over to Co . . . to the Garret's after a while to get our things, Toby. We'll be staying at the hotel in Liberty until the wedding."

"But I didn't say good-bye to Melinda," Toby said with a frown. "I didn't know we were leaving this soon. And what about Chessy?"

"Shanna told me the Samuels had agreed to let you use Chessy while you were here, Toby," JT put in. "If it's all right with them, I'll rent a stall for Chessy in Liberty. That way, you'll be able to ride in town, when you and Shanna aren't busy with your lessons."

"Yeah, I'd forgotten about that," Toby said, the frown still in place. "Guess I won't be going to school out here anymore, either."

"It's way too far to ride every day, Toby," Shanna said. "And, if you like, I'll take you back with me to say good-bye to Melinda. You'll be seeing her again in a couple days, though. I'm bringing the material out here for Susie to work on my wedding dress. We'll probably spend the night then."

"Not over at Cody's?" Toby asked in a puzzled voice.

"Son, we've got a lot of plans to make," JT said before Shanna could form an answer for Toby. "I know your head's probably spinning with all the changes you've had in your life these past few months, but I want you to know that Shanna and I will talk everything over with you. Your own feelings will be a part of any decision we make."

"All right," Toby agreed in a hesitant voice, the impact of further changes in his life settling almost visibly on his small shoulders. "Are we still going to have mine and Melinda's birthday party Saturday?"

Shanna's heart went out to him. "Nothing will stand in the way of that party, Toby," she assured him. "Why, Susie's already baking cookies, and you should see the picture Bessie drew of the cake she's going to decorate for you both."

A smile crossed Toby's face again, sending a spasm of relief through Shanna. She opened the screen door as she heard Toby ask for JT's promise that he would be at the party, too.

"That's going to be a little awkward, isn't it, Shanna?" Zerelda asked from where she had been standing inside the door. "Cody and JT both at that party. Would you rather have it over here?"

Shanna shook her head. "Melinda's going to want Cody at her party, wherever we hold it, Zerelda. We're just going to have to be adult about this."

"I suppose," Zerelda said unconvincingly. "Is Cody still going to be your attorney for the final hearing on Toby's custody?"

"I haven't discussed it with him. If Judge Howard returns when he said he would, it will be two days after the wedding. Isn't there another attorney in Liberty besides Mr. Curley?"

"No. He's it, unless you send to Kansas City. Maybe Ed could recommend someone there for you, though I don't know if you could find someone on this short of notice."

"I'll just have to try, I guess."

Toby's voice came through the open window. "Shucks, I'll bet your men were glad to see you comin'. Chessy wouldn't have throwed me off like that."

JT's laughter rumbled, and Shanna glanced out the window to see him ruffle Toby's sandy hair. Toby immediately climbed onto the swing seat and returned the gesture, his giggles joining JT's laughter. The brief tussle set the swing swaying, and Toby lost his balance, tumbling into JT's arms, which closed securely around him.

Chapter Thirty

"I spy Cody!" Toby's gay voice rang out, and he made a beeline for the post that had been designated home base, his short legs pumping faster when Cody erupted from his hiding place behind a wagon wheel. Toby tagged the post first, then whirled, his laughter joining Cody's as he danced around in a circle.

"You're it next, Cody! I beat you to home base!"

"Toby did, he did, Daddy," Melinda confirmed in a gleeful voice. "I saw him, and he beat you!"

"Fair and square," Cody replied. "Just let me sluice some water over my head to get rid of some of this sweat before you kids all take off to hide again."

"I'll work the pump for you, Cody." Toby raced ahead, already pouring the water to prime the pump when Cody joined him. His small arm pumped the handle until a stream of cold water ran onto the ground, and Cody bent to duck his head under it.

"He still thinks an awful lot of Cody," JT mused beside Shanna.

Shanna tore her eyes from Cody, who was flinging hair out of his eyes, throwing sparkling drops of water into the sunlight from the chestnut mass. Water cascaded over his shoulders, soaking into his white shirt.

"Of course," she replied. "They became close while we stayed here."

"Wish I could be out there running around with those kids. Looks like fun."

JT glanced at his rolled-up pant leg with a grimace, and Shanna laid a consoling hand on his arm.

"There'll be a lot of other things you can do with Toby."

"I reckon so. Are you still planning on spending the night at Zerelda's?"

"Why, yes. At least, that's what Susie suggested earlier. She's ready for a fitting on my dress. There isn't much time left to finish it, especially with her working days here."

"Would you mind terribly if I went on back into town now? Cody's letting me borrow his dun and bring it back tomorrow, when I come out to get you and Toby. My horse was limping when we rode in, and I don't know enough about blacksmithing to check its shoes. Cody said he'd look at them after the party."

"That will be fine. You'd better go, if you want to get back before dark."

"I'll see you tomorrow afternoon." JT dropped a kiss on Shanna's forehead. So far, he hadn't made a move to kiss her more familiarly. Shanna could never quite quell a shiver of tenseness whenever he tried, and JT had respected her unspoken wishes.

JT made his way across the yard, spying a child hidden here and there around the area. He pretended not to see them, knowing each thought himself safe from discovery. He approached the dun, already standing saddled and tied to the corral, and picked up his hat from where he had

Bittersweet Promises

dropped it over a fence post when he arrived.

The hat fell down over his forehead and JT pulled it off with a frown. No wonder. That was Cody's hat, the same color as his. He shrugged and returned it to the post, picking up the one beside it. Before he attempted to mount, he removed his jacket. The day was far too hot for a long ride fully clothed.

JT propped his crutch against the fence and grabbed the saddle horn. He'd mastered an alternate way of mounting as soon as his leg healed. He bent his knee and, with the assistance of his hands on the saddle horn, sprang onto the dun's back. Reaching down for his crutch, he turned the dun and lifted the crutch in a wave to Shanna before he slid it into the rifle scabbard for the ride to town.

Shanna watched JT stop for a word with Cody, then ride out of the yard, pulling off his string tie and unbuttoning a couple buttons on his white shirt. She gave JT a final wave when he turned at the gate, then centered her attention on the game of I Spy, until she realized Susie might need her help cleaning up the mess in the kitchen.

Shanna immediately noticed the worried frown on Susie's face as she entered the kitchen.

"Susie, what's wrong? Here, I'll help you with those dishes. My word, those children sure made a mess in here."

"That they did," Susie replied distractedly. "Shanna, I'm worried about Mother. This heat's not good for her in her condition and at her age. I hate to leave you with this mess, but I really think I should take her on home."

"You go on, Susie. I don't want to break up the games just now, although I expect the children's parents to start arriving any minute to pick them up. I'll finish in here while I wait for them, and Toby and I will come on over this evening, after I fix some supper for everyone. I'd rather not leave that for Bessie."

Susie shot her a grateful look and picked up a small towel to dry her hands. "There're plenty of leftovers for supper, Shanna. Fried chicken and bean salad. There's cake, and probably even some ice cream left in the maker, though it might be getting runny. There's still ice in the icehouse, though, if you want some more."

"I'll handle it, Susie. Go on. Zerelda and Bessie are sitting in a couple chairs out under the apple tree. Maybe you should ask Bessie if she wants to come in for a nap after Zerelda leaves."

"I'll do that, Shanna. And I'll tell Bessie that Mother will probably be fine by morning, so I can return."

"Shoo," Shanna said. "Everything will be fine."

Cody tightened the saddle cinch on JT's gelding and called through the corral fence, "Time to go, Toby. I'm riding over to Pappy's with you, and I've still got a couple things to do here when I get back."

Toby gave Starlight a final pat, then climbed through the fence and ran toward the buggy, where Shanna waited. He scrambled into the seat and stifled a huge yawn.

"You can lie down if you want, Toby. There's plenty of room."

"I'm fine, Shanna. I'm still too excited to sleep." Another yawn escaped, and he smiled sheepishly. "Well, maybe just for a second." He curled into a ball as Cody rode up.

"Did you find out why the horse was limping?" Shanna asked Cody.

"Just a loose shoe. It's fine now. Let's go."

Cody rode beside the buggy silently for several minutes, and Shanna relaxed back into the seat, allowing the buggy horse to match its pace to the gelding's slow

Bittersweet Promises

walk. The days were lengthening, yet the sunset had caught her by surprise as she lingered over the dishes in the familiar kitchen. Melinda's arrival in her nightgown prodded Shanna to finish up, when she realized it was long past Toby's bedtime, too.

A slight mist hovered above the cooling ground and a few clouds scuttled overhead, dimming the light from the stars and a half-moon. At least the coming rain would break the heat spell of the last few days.

Toby's snore sounded in the night stillness, and Shanna and Cody both laughed out loud.

"It was a lovely party," Shanna said. "They both had a wonderful time."

"Yeah, they did. Melinda will remember it the rest of her life. She really liked the locket you gave her. She wanted me to ask you if you'd have a picture made for her to put in it."

"I'll . . . I'll see what I can do." She wasn't really sure a reminder left behind in the form of a picture would be the best thing for Melinda. "I wore that locket as a child myself," Shanna said instead. "It was really too small for me now. Besides, it couldn't have made Melinda nearly as happy as Toby was when he found out you'd bought Chessy for him. Cody, that was too much for you to do."

"Boy needs a pony. Besides, the deal had been made long before the party. I set it up with Pappy when I decided to ask Susie to come over on a permanent basis. I was just waiting until the party to tell Toby."

For a few seconds, only the sound of the horses' clopping hooves broke the silence. Shanna felt her own eyes droop in weariness, then sat up straighter when Cody spoke again.

"Shanna, I heard something today I wasn't real happy about."

"What was that?"

Trana Mae Simmons

"I heard you'd asked Ed Curley to find you another attorney out of Kansas City. I hope that doesn't mean you don't think I'm capable of representing you at the custody hearing in front of Judge Howard."

"Oh, Cody, no," Shanna denied with a shake of her head. "I just felt.... I thought maybe you'd rather I get someone else."

"Couldn't you have asked me first? Forget I said that," Cody hurried on before Shanna could answer. "I guess we haven't had much to say to each other lately."

"I don't want it to be like this, Cody."

"I know," Cody said quietly. "And I've tried. I've been as decent as I could to JT. Trouble is, every time I get near you, I want to go off somewhere and get drunk again. Can't do that, though, with all there is to get done in the fields."

"Was that where you were the night I got back?" Shanna couldn't stop herself from asking. "I saw you ride in that night. You were on your stallion, and I didn't see him pulling a plow behind him."

No, he'd been over at Ruby's whorehouse, but he wasn't about to tell Shanna that. At least, he'd been there until it was time to quit dallying around and take the girl he had chosen up the stairs. Then he had slammed out of the house like a horse with a burr up its rear, leaving the black-haired woman staring after him in astonishment.

"No, I was somewhere else," was as far as he would go without lying to Shanna. "But, gettin' back to you needing my help week after next...."

The dark horse sprang out of the mist without warning, the rider on its back dressed in black and a scream issuing from the man's throat. The first shot from the blazing pistol creased the gelding's shoulder when it reared in fright. Another flash of fire lit up the darkness from a second shot a split second afterward.

The buggy horse neighed shrilly and plunged forward.

Bittersweet Promises

Shanna frantically wrapped the reins around her hands and struggled to keep her hold, the straps biting cruelly into her palms. Toby tumbled onto the floorboard, and Shanna screamed at the horse, bracing her feet against the footboard and yanking on the reins.

The horse bugled in pain as the bridle bit dug deep into its tender mouth, then reared, shaking its head. It dropped back to earth and stood trembling in its traces.

Shanna unwrapped the reins and set the buggy brake, ignoring the deep welts on her hands. Grabbing Toby, she lifted him from the floorboard as she heard another horse gallop away. Cody or the attacker? But Cody wouldn't have left them there alone.

"Toby! Are you all right?"

"Yeah. I just bumped my elbow. What happened, Shanna?"

"Shhh. We'll talk in a minute."

Shanna pushed Toby onto the seat beside her and picked up the reins. Releasing the brake, she cautiously turned the horse halfway around in the road, prepared to flee if necessary. JT's gelding was the first thing she saw, head hanging as it stood beside a sprawled body. Cody's white shirt stood out clearly against the ground in the dim light.

"No! No, Cody. No, God. Please, no!"

Shanna scrambled from the buggy and raced to Cody's side. Kneeling in the dirt, her shaking hand went out to touch his face.

"Please, God," she whispered.

His breath feathered over her palm, and she could see his chest heaving. Tearing open his shirt, Shanna stared at the blood gushing from the hole in his shoulder.

"He's not d-dead, is he, Shanna?"

"No, but he's hurt awfully bad." Shanna voice broke and she fought her rising terror. They had to get Pappy.

Trana Mae Simmons

But first, she had to do something about that blood.

Lifting her skirt, she tore off a piece of petticoat, folded it, and pressed it against the gushing blood.

"The horse," Shanna said as she glanced at Toby's pale face. "Where is it? Can you catch it, Toby?"

"The gelding took off when you ran up. It looked like it had blood on its shoulder. I tied the buggy horse after I climbed out, though."

"Good boy, Toby," Shanna breathed. "Do you think you can ride the buggy horse to get Pappy and a wagon—if we can unhitch it?"

Toby took a deep breath. "Sure, Shanna. At least, I think so, even if it is lots bigger than Chessy. But, Shanna, you'll be here alone."

Keeping one hand on the bandage, Shanna pulled from its holster the six-gun Cody had strapped on before he left the plantation.

"I've got to make sure the man who shot Cody doesn't come back, Toby. And we have to get Pappy here in a hurry."

A thunder of hooves sounded from up the road. Shanna whirled and switched hands on the bandage, shifting the pistol to her right hand.

"Get behind me, Toby," she ordered.

Toby scrambled behind her without hesitation. A second later, Shanna heard a shout and lowered the pistol when she recognized Pappy's voice.

"It's Pappy, Toby. They must have heard the shots." Shanna laid the gun down and turned back to Cody's wound.

The wagon pulled up amid a rumble of hooves and shouted whoas from the driver—Susie James. Even as it stopped, Pappy was climbing to the ground, his medical bag in his hand.

"What happened?" he demanded when he knelt by Shanna. "No, never mind, I can see he's been shot. We heard it at the house and knew you'd be headed over 'bout this time."

Pappy set the black bag on the ground and shouted over his shoulder for Susie to bring the lantern from the wagon.

"It's right here, Pappy." Susie held the lantern over them, and its flickering light outlined Cody's chalk-white face and blood-soaked chest.

Shanna caught her lower lip between her teeth, biting down until she tasted blood herself to keep from flinging her body over Cody's and screaming out her fear.

"Are either you or Toby hurt, Shanna?" Susie asked.

Shanna shook her head and glanced at Pappy when he reached for her hand.

"You have to let me examine the wound, Shanna," Pappy said sternly.

Shanna forced her wrist loose and pulled her hand away. The blood continued to seep from the dark hole on Cody's shoulder, a little slower, though, it seemed. She watched Pappy probe around the wound and draw his hands back, the fingers covered in Cody's blood, as were her own.

"How . . . how bad?"

"Bad enough," Pappy said in a grim voice, instead of the childlike tone he usually used. "Missed any main blood arteries, far as I can tell. Bullet's gonna have to come out, though—it's still in there. We'll have to get him back to the house, where there's more light, before I can do that. Jostling in the wagon's gonna make it bleed more, but can't be helped. Give me a couple more pieces of your petticoat, Shanna, to staunch the blood and tie this up."

Shanna pulled up her dress again and ripped another layer of petticoat free, then a third. She and Susie held Cody upright until Pappy had the bandage in place to his satisfaction; then they gently laid him back on the ground.

"We'll never get him in the wagon," Shanna said with a moan.

"We'll do it," Pappy told her. "Have to."

Cody never regained consciousness as they struggled to load his heavy body in the wagon, with Pappy showing an amazing amount of strength for such a little man. Shanna scrambled up beside Cody and pulled his head onto her lap, wrapping her free arm around Toby when he crawled up beside her.

No one spoke as Susie slapped the reins on the horses' backs and turned the wagon. The few hundred yards to the Samuels' cabin passed quickly enough, each second of the journey another instant of life for Cody in Shanna's mind. She stroked his cold cheek, her silent prayers winging skyward in between her attempts to comfort a whimpering Toby.

Susie backed the wagon up to the cabin porch when they arrived, and Zerelda hurried out the door, carrying a litter.

"Who's hurt?" Zerelda demanded.

"Cody," Pappy informed her as he climbed from the wagon seat. "Here. Give me that thing, woman. It's too heavy for you to be carrying."

Pappy took the litter and carried it to the back of the wagon. With Shanna and Susie helping, he scooted the litter under Cody's unresisting body and dragged it to the edge of the wagon bed.

Waving off Zerelda's attempt to help in fear of disturbing her pregnancy, Pappy ordered Shanna and Susie to one end of the litter and picked up the heavier end by Cody's shoulders himself. They struggled up the cabin steps, to where Zerelda held the door open.

"Put him on the table in here," Zerelda said as soon as they got inside the door. "I'll bring in some lanterns from the kitchen and hang them up. I put some water on as soon as Pappy and Susie left, just in case we'd need it."

Bittersweet Promises

Several lanterns soon hung around the room, the greater quantity of light displaying the pallor of Cody's skin and the blood-soaked bandage. Shanna pulled Toby closer as Pappy began unwrapping the bandage, neither of them noticing the stains Shanna's fingers had already left on Toby's shirt.

"You got my things boiling, Zerelda?" Pappy asked, his eyes staying with his task.

"They're boiling, Pappy."

For just a moment, Shanna let the thought of Pappy's childishness after his near hanging cross her mind. The little man before her didn't show a trace of his former simpleminded behavior. His knowing fingers, recalling their training, again probed Cody's wound, then began laying things from his bag on the towel-covered seat of a chair beside the table.

"He's like that with his doctoring," Zerelda said in an aside to Shanna, seeming to read her mind. "Remembers just how to do it." She laid a hand on her stomach. "Those bastards didn't take all his memories when they tried to hang him."

"Cody said something like that one day," Shanna said with a tremulous attempt at a smile. It died on her lips when she glanced at the table as Cody moaned in pain.

"Can't be helped, son," Pappy muttered to his patient. "An' it's gonna be worse before I get done." He looked at Shanna and Susie. "I want everyone out of here, 'cept Zerelda," he demanded. "Git, now."

"Can't I help?" Shanna insisted.

Zerelda took her arm and led Shanna onto the porch. "Susie will put Toby up with the other children in the loft," she said. "Then she'll come and sit with you."

"But Toby will still hear. . . ."

"No, he won't," Zerelda assured her. "He's dead on his feet after his party and all this. Young'uns go out like a light—not like us older folks who have trouble sleeping. Please just do like Pappy says, Shanna. He's got his ways of doing things, and he don't like them disturbed."

Shanna reluctantly nodded and waited obediently until Susie joined her. Inside, she could hear Cody's muffled groans as Pappy probed for the bullet. Susie finally forced Shanna to sit in the swing, and Shanna leaned forward, covering her ears with her hands.

A long while later, Susie rose from the swing and walked to the cabin door. She returned and touched Shanna's shoulder.

"I think we can go in now," she said when Shanna looked up.

Shanna sprang to her feet. "Is he . . . he's all right, isn't he?"

"For now, probably. Otherwise Pappy would have come out to tell us—if he hadn't made it."

Shanna moaned low in her throat.

"You love him an awful lot, don't you?"

"More than my own life," Shanna admitted fervently.

"Someday I want kids of my own. I hope I never have to choose between one of my kids and a man I love. Toby's lucky to have you."

"He's the only thing that keeps me going sometimes, Susie. My mother's dead and, although I know it's against everything I've ever been taught, I despise my father for what he's trying to do to Toby. He's using an innocent child to seek vengeance on a dead woman."

"You've got JT now, Shanna. He's a good man."

"I know. I only wish. . . ."

"That you could love him like you do Cody?" Susie finished for her.

"In a way, I guess. But I just can't make myself regret loving Cody. The only thing I'm truly sorry for is how

Bitterswe et Promises

much his loving me in return has hurt him."

"We can only do what has to be done," Susie said in a voice wise beyond her years. "We can only contend with what the Good Lord puts in our path and trust in Him to make it come out right. I know how you feel about your father. Sometimes I wish I'd been my mother's only child by her first husband. Jesse and Frank are tearing her apart, and I can't say I'd cry too hard if something happened to them, as terrible as that sounds, since they're my full brothers. I've even thought maybe God gave Mother this pregnancy, despite how old she is, to comfort her somehow over Frank and Jesse turning outlaw."

"Perhaps He did," Shanna mused. "We . . . I want to see Cody now."

"Come on." Susie led the way and held the door for Shanna. "You wait by Cody," she said inside the door. "I'll bring you in some warm water to clean up with."

Shanna stared at her stained hands, then quickly hid them in the folds of her skirt as she steeled herself to walk over to the sheet-covered figure lying on the table.

"I'm gonna ride over to get Jed Williams and his boys out of bed to help us move Cody into mine and Zerelda's room," Pappy said in a tired voice as Shanna approached. "I don't have enough strength in me to lift him again, and they're good neighbors. They won't mind."

"I'll go, Pappy," Susie insisted.

"No. You're not going out on those roads with a killer on the loose," Pappy said in a firm voice. "I'll be back in a few minutes."

"Pappy," Shanna asked before he could walk away, her ravaged gaze on Cody's chalky face. "Will he live?"

"I can't promise you that, child. He's young and strong. I've seen men live through this kind of wound before, but there's still a lot could happen. Blood poisoning—gangrene."

At Shanna's whimper of pain, Pappy picked up her hand and patted it. "I'm sorry, child, but I believe in being prepared for the worst. I'll tell you this, though. The bullet came out clear.—wasn't shattered like I've seen sometimes. But now we've got to watch him close for signs of fever. That's where you'll come in. If the fever hits, it helps to have people who love a person around. Talk to the sick person. Give him a will to go on living, something to look forward to when he wakes up."

"I won't leave him until I know he's out of danger," Shanna assured him, her free hand going out to stroke Cody's white cheek.

Chapter Thirty-one

JT pushed open the bedroom door and quietly watched Shanna sitting asleep in a rocking chair pulled up close to the bed. She hadn't removed her bloodstained dress, and her hair tumbled down her back, shining in the sunlight coming through the window. Her devastated face hadn't relaxed even in sleep, and the long lashes lay pillowed on deep hollows beneath her eyes.

Cody gave a moan and Shanna's eyes flew open, centering immediately on the bed.

"I came as soon as I heard, Shanna," JT said when she saw him standing in the doorway. "One of Jed Williams's boys rode in to get Dan. Dan thought I ought to know, and I came out with him. Dan... he's got some questions to ask you, Shanna, if you think you're up to it."

Shanna nodded and rose to her feet. After a glance at Cody to assure herself he was still unconscious, she walked to the door.

JT pulled her close with his free arm. For just a second, he felt the initial stiffening she always had when he touched her intimately; then she sighed and leaned against him, arms clinging to his waist.

"Thank you for coming so soon," she said, her voice emerging in a croak.

"Have you been sitting there crying all night?"

"No. It's just the strain. Bessie came over earlier and insisted on taking Toby back with her and Melinda. Melinda—she wanted to stay here with her daddy. She was awfully upset."

JT stroked her back, soothing her, before he pushed her away. "Has he been awake at all?"

"No. And I'm so afraid the fever will set in, as Pappy warned might happen."

"I'll stay with him. You go on out and talk to Dan. Maybe you ought to ask Pappy to come in. Shanna, do you want me to send to Liberty for another doctor?"

"Please don't. I have complete faith in Pappy, after the way he cared for Cody last night."

"Go on, then." JT gave her a little shove.

As soon as Shanna left the room, JT limped over to the bed. Cody, face flushed, started tossing his head. "Shanna, honey," JT heard Cody mutter in a barely audible voice.

"She's here, Cody." JT sat in the rocking chair and laid a hand on Cody's shoulder. Cody's head stilled, and he breathed out a sigh.

"Old pard," JT said in a soft voice. "We rode some rough trails together, didn't we?"

Cody's eyes flew open, but JT saw that Cody was staring around him without any sign of recognition as to where he was. JT leaned over and poured a glass of water, propping himself on his good leg and crooking Cody's head in one arm. He managed to get Cody to

Bittersweet Promises

take a couple sips of the tepid water, then laid Cody's head on the pillow.

Glancing at the door when it opened again, JT saw Pappy enter, worry clear on his face.

"Will he make it, Pappy?" JT asked, echoing Shanna's words of the previous night.

Pappy felt Cody's face, then carefully unwound the bandage and lifted the dressing before he answered. "Well, hell, JT," he said in satisfaction. "I think he just might. Looks like I did a pretty good job here. Don't hurt none that Cody's strong as an ox and we kept tricklin' water down his throat last night to replace the blood he'd lost."

"Thank God," JT breathed. "Shanna was worried about fever."

"Naw, he's just got too many covers on." Pappy threw back the top comforter and reached for a stack of clean bandages on the bedside table. "I'll just change this again while I'm here. That bullet didn't hit anything major, so he'll have full use of this arm after it heals. I was worried about the blood he'd lost most of all, but look how nice and pink his skin is gettin'."

"Is there anything else you need? Some medicine from town? Anything I can do?"

"He's doin' fine, JT. He's sleepin', and that's the best healin' medicine for him right now."

JT propped himself on his crutch and rose to his feet. "There's gonna be a lot of people glad to hear that, sir. I'll go on over to check on Toby and Cody's family and tell them the good news. Jed said he'd send his boys over there to do the chores as long as they're needed. And I have to tell Shanna before I leave that her father's back in town. Will you watch over her while I'm gone? I'm going back into Liberty this evening to try to find out a little more information about something I heard last night, and her father's staying at the hotel. I want to keep her and Toby away from him for a while yet."

"I'll care for her like one of my own, JT," Pappy promised.

Zerelda looked up from her coffee cup on the table as JT entered the small living room. "Shanna's out on the porch with Dan. Does Pappy need me?"

"I don't think so, Zerelda. He says Cody's doin' lots better. I . . . can I talk to you for a second?"

"Always could, couldn't you, son? Want some coffee?"

"No thanks." JT crossed to the table and held an envelope out to Zerelda. "I'd like you to keep this for me for the time being. Toby's birth certificate's in here, along with my last letter from Diedre."

"What do you have in mind to do, son?" Zerelda asked in a suspicious voice.

"Will you do it? Please?"

Zerelda took the envelope and stuck it in her skirt pocket. "You just remember one thing, JT. You've got a boy now—something to live for. He won't appreciate losing his daddy when he's just found him."

"Toby's happiness is the most important thing in my life right now, Zerelda. I won't do anything to jeopardize that."

JT limped across the room and turned at the door. "You'll give those things to Shanna, should the need arise?"

Zerelda slowly nodded her head.

JT pushed the screen door open to see Shanna standing with Dan, shaking her head.

"I've already told you, Dan," Shanna said. "It was dark and he was dressed in black. He might even have had a mask on his face—I couldn't really tell. The horse . . . well, it was a dark color, too."

"Could that horse have had one white stocking, Shanna?" JT asked.

Bittersweet Promises

Shanna's brow crinkled in concentration. "Maybe. Yes, yes, I think it did. Why? Have you seen it?"

"I'm not sure," JT replied evasively. "Shanna, Pappy says Cody's doin' lots better, and he's sure that Cody's going to make it now."

"Oh! I have to go see for myself!"

JT caught her arm to hold her. "Just a minute. I hate like hell to have to tell you this right now, but your father's back in town."

"No! He shouldn't have come back until next week. JT, you have to get Toby and bring him back over here to me!"

"Shanna," Dan broke in. "I've already sent one of my deputies to the Garret place and told him to stay until the hearing. Jed Williams's boys will take care of the chores, and the deputy won't have a thing to distract him from keeping guard. He's a good man and knows what he's doing."

"I suppose it would be better for Melinda to have Toby's company right now. If you're sure they're safe."

"They are," JT soothed. "And I'm on my way now to check on them myself. I probably won't be back tonight—there's some things I need to do in town. If you need me, send one of Jed's boys in."

"All right. Take care and I'll see you in a day or so." Shanna kissed JT's cheek in a distracted manner, her mind already in the bedroom with Cody. She hurried across the porch and disappeared through the screen door.

"That's some woman," Dan mused.

"Yeah. She deserves a hell of a lot more out of life than she's been gettin' the last year. Dan, can we walk out away from the house? There's something I need to tell you—something I should have told you on the way out this morning."

JT carefully made his way down the porch steps and skirted a puddle left from last night's late rain. He stopped beneath a huge oak on the edge of the yard.

"JT," Dan said before JT could speak. "This is the first time I've seen you packing iron since you came back to town."

"Yeah, well, I still know how to use it."

"You ain't figuring on using it on that Pinkerton man, are you? That one they call Bobby—the one who rides a horse with one white stocking? That's my job, JT, investigating any wrongdoings around here."

"I guess you haven't heard. Bobby's not with the Pinkertons any longer. He was in the saloon late last night, bragging that he'd found a way to make a lot more money than the Pinkertons paid him. Fact is, he let slip that he was fired from the agency—something about a report a man named Sid made. He was talkin' like he might be leavin' town pretty quick to look for this Sid and pay him back. He was drunk already when he stumbled in—must have visited a couple other saloons first. He didn't even notice me sittin' in the corner."

"I'll pick him up for questioning soon as I get back into town. If he was drunk enough to mouth off like that, he's probably still nursin' a hangover this morning. Maybe I can catch him before he gets his senses back."

"Dan, there's something else you ought to know. That man wasn't shootin' at Cody. He thought he was shootin' at me. I had Cody's dun in town, and that was my gelding we found wandering around on our way here, with the blood on its shoulder. Cody and I were both dressed sort of similar yesterday, and Cody was with Shanna and Toby last night, where I might have been expected to be."

"Reckon I already figured that out, JT. But it's not proof enough for me to arrest Van Alstyne, unless Bobby breaks down and fingers him."

Bittersweet Promises

"I want a chance to talk to Van Alstyne first," JT demanded. "Before he knows we're on to him."

"He'll kill you on sight."

"Well, now, since I've told you that I'm going to see him, you'll have the proof you need if he does that, won't you, Sheriff? But don't worry. I'm not about to let him get the drop on me. Man like Van Alstyne usually hires his killin' done anyway, but he'll probably have a hidden gun on him somewhere."

"And what if Bobby's with him, instead of in his own room? The only way I'm going to allow this is for me to go with you, JT."

"Dan, damn it!"

"You want to try to see if you're quicker on the draw than the law?" Dan asked with a raise of his eyebrows.

"Hell, Dan," JT said after a moment, his laugh diffusing the tension between the two men. "You ain't seen the day. But I don't fancy having to ride back into those mountains because I assaulted a peace officer. Come on, let's hit the road."

At Zerelda's urging, Shanna finally left Cody's side long enough to change into the extra dress she had brought with her in anticipation of staying over a night for the dress fitting. She gave Zerelda her petticoat for her ragbag, borrowing one of Susie's, which she had to turn over a few inches at the waist, since Susie almost matched her mother in height. Hurrying back into the bedroom, she found Pappy standing over Cody with a look of satisfaction on his face.

"He's awake," Pappy told Shanna.

Shanna flew across the room, and Pappy stepped back with a chuckle to avoid her.

"Cody. Cody, can you hear me?" Shanna asked, sitting on the bed and picking up one of Cody's hands.

"Are you all right, darlin'?" Cody opened his eyelids with an effort, his brown eyes, shadowed with pain, searching her face.

"Oh for Pete's sake, Cody Garret," Shanna said with a shaky laugh. "You're the one who got shot. Toby and I are fine."

"Good."

Cody's eyes closed, and Shanna glanced frantically at Pappy.

"He's only resting again, child," Pappy said. "A healin' sleep. He keeps goin' like this, we can probably move him over to his own place tomorrow in the wagon. I can show Susie how to change the bandage. Couple weeks, he'll be good as new, 'cept maybe for a twinge or two when a storm's comin'."

"I'll stay here, in case he wakes up again."

"You're going in to Susie's bed and take a nap," Pappy said firmly. "You're dead on your feet, child, and I've got my hands full with Cody. Don't need another patient right now. Zerelda will help me."

"Yes, sir," Shanna said in a meek voice. "I'll send her in."

A while later, Shanna tossed and turned in the strange bed. With Cody out of danger, her mind diverted to other matters.

Why had her father returned so soon? He'd made it obvious on his last trip, the little she saw of him, that he detested the town and the people in it. The wedding was scheduled for next Sunday—the hearing set for the following Tuesday. Her father had returned a full week and a half before he needed to.

The wedding. Cody's getting shot wouldn't delay it— Shanna had to be married to JT before Tuesday. She had tried so hard to build a comfortable relationship with JT over the last week. They talked easily to each other, and shared a joke now and then over Toby or some other silly thing they noticed. Shanna didn't mind being close to him, as long as it was her own choice, and she touched him from time to time without thinking, when she wanted to make a point in their conversations.

The only problem came when JT reached out to her. That she could accept his scarred face and missing leg Shanna had no doubt. She barely noticed them anymore. JT could ride as well as any man with two legs, and he shared Toby's love of the saddle. He couldn't share in the running games with Toby, yet he and Toby had discovered a mutual passion for fishing and reading. Toby's vocabulary was already expanding as JT read to him from books beyond Toby's own capabilities, then discussed the stories with his son.

They hadn't spent all their time in town with Toby. Dan's wife, Patty, assured them she would love to have Toby spend an evening or two with her while JT took Shanna to dinner or for a buggy ride. Shanna would feel herself tense up, though, each time they headed back to the hotel after an outing. She had thought JT might force the issue the second evening they spent alone, insisting it was too late to wake Toby, that he could spend the night with Patty and they would fetch him in the morning.

Shanna made herself hold his arm and smile as they neared the door of her room, not realizing her fingers were digging into JT's arm more deeply with each step. He gazed at her sadly in the light from the wall lamp as he removed her hand, then took her key and opened the door. He only dropped a kiss on her cheek, before he gave her a push and said good night.

"It's not fair to him," Shanna murmured aloud. "But what can I do? Every time he touches me, I wish it was Cody instead. JT can feel it—I know he can. What in the world am I going to do on our wedding night?"

The door opened and Zerelda stuck her head inside. "I thought you were talking in your sleep. Why aren't you asleep?"

Shanna flung the comforter back and sat on the side of the bed. "I can't sleep. Maybe I'm too tired right now, though I did sleep for a while in the chair last night."

"There's a difference between sleep and rest. But if you're sure, I've got some fresh coffee on."

"How's Cody?" Shanna asked a moment later as she came out of Susie's room. "I'll just go look for a second."

Zerelda smiled and waved her hand toward the bedroom door. "Reckon I know better than to try to tell you not to. He's still sleeping himself, though."

Shanna found Cody alone, but Zerelda had left the door ajar so she could hear him. She walked to the bed and caressed Cody's cheek, noting with relief the returned color. Unable to resist his slightly parted lips, she bent to kiss him tenderly.

Cody's hand caught her behind the head before Shanna could end the kiss. He deepened it, with Shanna complying fully to his desire, and twined his fingers in her hair to hold her close when he released her lips.

"I love you," he said. "I . . . I promise I won't say it again, but I had to say it one more time, with you able to hear me. I love you. Be happy, darlin'." He dropped his hand and allowed her to stand.

Shanna didn't dare try to speak. Even if her throat hadn't been clogged, keeping the words of love she wanted to scream to the whole world safely locked inside, she couldn't find the courage to reply to Cody's avowal. One tiny chink in the wall she kept intact around her emotions would bring the entire structure tumbling down.

Tearing her eyes away from Cody's, Shanna sat in the rocking chair. "How are you feeling?"

Bittersweet Promises

"Like hell," Cody said with a grimace. "Pappy wanted to give me some more of that laudanum a while ago, but I told him I'd rather sleep on my own, when my body felt it needed it. Do Melinda and Aunt Bessie know what happened?"

"They were here earlier. They'll be back this evening. I'm sure Dan's deputy will escort them."

"Deputy? What the hell's a deputy doing guarding my family?"

"Please, Cody!" Shanna jumped from the chair and pushed him back against the pillows just as Zerelda came through the door.

"You lie down in that bed, Cody Garret," Zerelda said, placing her hands on her hips, which were almost overshadowed by her protruding stomach. "If you don't, I'll hold you down myself while Pappy gives you that laudanum. I want Bessie to come back and find you better, not raving out of your head with a fever because you won't rest!"

Cody collapsed on the pillow, more in weakness than in obedience to Zerelda's stern warning. "I have to know what's going on. Can't you both understand that?"

"We understand," Zerelda said, walking over to the bed. "And we'll tell you the whole story, just so long as you agree to lie there like a good patient and listen, without trying to haul your wounded butt out of that bed!"

"Zerelda...."

"Cody, listen, please," Shanna broke in. "Everything is taken care of. The deputy's only there because my father came back to town early, and Dan's making sure he doesn't try to take Toby away before the hearing. My father would do something like that, you know. And I'd have brought them all over here, if I hadn't believed Dan's assurance that the deputy is fully capable of watching over them."

"Where's JT?" Cody asked quickly. "He was here earlier, wasn't he?"

"Yes," Shanna admitted. "So was Dan. They left together."

"To go where?" Cody demanded.

Shanna glanced at Zerelda in bewilderment, unable to make any sense of Cody's questions. "Why, back to Liberty, I think, after they stopped at your house to check on things. JT said he'd be back out tomorrow."

"Jesus," Cody said with a groan. He struggled once again to rise, then fell back on the bed with a gasp of agony.

"I warned you, Cody," Zerelda said, taking a step closer. "Don't try to get up."

"I have to! Damn it, the two of you can't be that stupid! It was JT that bastard was after last night—not me. He thought I was JT, because I was with Shanna and on JT's horse. Someone has to warn them! Word's probably already got around town that Van Alstyne's henchman shot the wrong man. They'll know Dan and JT rode out here, and they'll set up an ambush to get them on their way back to town!"

"Oh, my God!" Shanna gasped. "Or they might go to the plantation, thinking to catch them there. That rider last night didn't stay around to see where we went after he shot you. And . . . oh, Lord. Everyone in town probably knows the whole story by now—about JT being Toby's father and . . . and the wedding."

"Now do you see why I have to get out of this goddamned bed?" Cody snarled, flinging back the covers and managing to sit on the side of the bed.

"Leave him be," Pappy said as he came into the room, carrying his black bag. "The man would rather kill himself than let his family be harmed, and can't say as I blame him. Help him get dressed, you two."

"He can't. Pappy, he's not able to ride," Shanna pleaded in a stricken voice. "We have to go instead."

"Do what I said, child," Pappy ordered. He dug in his bag, pulling out a bottle and holding it out to Cody. "Here, son. Not too much, just a sip. It'll dull the pain enough for you to do what you have to do. I'm gonna strap that arm down, though, so you don't start the bleeding again. You'll have your right arm free for your gun."

Pappy gave Shanna a stern look, then tossed a glare at Zerelda. "Go hitch up the wagon, woman!"

Zerelda hurried from the room, and Shanna quickly grabbed Cody's denims from the chair, along with a clean shirt Bessie had brought over. She slipped the denims over Cody's feet, while Pappy wrapped another bandage around Cody's arm to hold it against his chest.

A few minutes later, Cody stumbled out the front door of the cabin, his arm across Pappy's shoulders and his gun belt strapped to his hip.

"What . . . what was in that bottle, Pappy?" Cody said as Pappy helped him down the steps to where Zerelda waited in the wagon.

"Opium," Pappy said shortly. "It's addicting, so don't expect me to give you any more when you're in pain from all this strain on your shoulder. And be careful with that gun. The opium's gonna affect your awareness of just where things are."

"I'll be careful."

Pappy helped Cody into the wagon bed, then took the rifles he had ordered Shanna to retrieve from a closet in the living room. After Shanna scrambled in beside Cody, Pappy handed her one rifle and walked to the front of the wagon.

"Get down, woman," he ordered Zerelda. "You're not gonna take a chance with our baby by going with us!"

"I've got another child over there at Cody's," Zerelda informed him in a no-nonsense voice. "Susie's there, and I'm just as good a damned shot as you are. Get in here, old man, so we can get going."

Chapter Thirty-two

JT grimaced in pain when Susie parted his hair and wiped the scalp wound with antiseptic. "Damn, Susie, that hurts worse than the cut!"

"Shut up. You can't see to shoot with blood running in your eyes."

JT glanced at Dan, who stood by the kitchen window, next to the shattered door. They had managed to prop a chair under the doorknob, giving them a barrier to the bullets slamming into the house. Dan's rifle spoke periodically, sending his own fire in the direction of the barn.

"Dan, did you get any of them yet?" JT asked. "How's your arm?"

"Arm's fine," Dan replied. "It's your turn to get patched, so you can get your ass up here and help. And, yeah, I got one who stuck his head out the door on the haymow. Don't think he's dead, but he won't give us any more trouble."

JT finally pushed Susie away and picked up his rifle from the table. "You get on back in the parlor with Bessie and the kids now," he ordered. Hopping over to take his place beside Dan, JT aimed his rifle out the window. A shadow flickered from one side of the open barn door to the other, and JT smiled grimly at the man's scream of pain after he shot.

"Looks like they'd think to shut that barn door," he said to Dan.

"That's what worries me. They've got something in mind."

"Well, we can't do anything about it until we know what it is. Sorry 'bout your arm. You wouldn't have got hit if you hadn't had to help me up the steps."

"Just be glad we saw those bastards coming in time to make a run for the house. Otherwise, they'd be in here and have hostages."

"You get a count on them yet?"

"Five or six left, with the two down. Van Alstyne's got plenty of money to pay that many men. Probably all rounded up by that son of a bitch, Bobby. Van Alstyne's out there, too. I saw him when they scattered off their horses and took to the barn."

"Don't sound like him, coming out here himself to do his dirty work."

"Doubt if he's in his right mind," Dan said with a glance at JT. "Knowin' his wife's ex-lover is back in the picture, plannin' to marry his daughter. The telegraph operator told me there's been a lot of wires going out to Kansas City over the last few weeks—written in some gibberish he couldn't understand. I don't think Van Alstyne ever went back to New York. I think he stayed in Kansas City, keeping tabs on what was going on around here."

"Yeah, probably so." JT took a quick shot at another shadow inside the barn, but heard no sound to indicate the bullet found its mark.

Bittersweet Promises

JT worked the lever on his rifle to push another shell into the chamber. "You think your deputy's still alive over there behind that horse trough? Crazy fool. He should have stayed hidden when he saw us ride in with that gang of men on our tails."

"He was only doing his job, trying to cover us so we could get in the house."

A shot rang out from the direction of the horse trough and Dan jerked his head around. Immediately his eyes swung back to the barn as a man screamed and fell from an upper story window.

"He's still alive," Dan said with satisfaction. "I think that was that bastard, Bobby, that fell. But now those men know my deputy's alive, too."

"You in the house!" a voice yelled. "Send out Randolph and we'll let the rest of you alone. He's the one we're after!"

Dan's rifle spoke the answer to the demand. "Go to hell!" he called, following up his shot.

"You've got women and kids in there!" the voice hollered back. "We can fire the house. Won't none of you get out! We're not leaving without Randolph!"

"You have to get close enough to do it first!"

"Damn it, Dan," JT said. "We can't hold out in here forever. It'll be dark in a few hours, and they can sneak up and set the fire, pick us off when we run out. If I could just talk to Van Alstyne for a second. . . ."

"Yeah, and tell him what? You know something about him he don't want known? Maybe something his wife told you? Hell, man, they've got the upper hand, and anything you say to Van Alstyne will just make him more determined to kill us. And the women and kids, too, for overhearing it."

"How'd you figure that out?"

"I saw you through the window, giving Mrs. Samuel

something in an envelope. Heard what you told her, too. Lawman's got to be able to listen to two conversations at once sometimes—figure out from the evidence what the options could be."

"Liberty's lucky to have you for a sheriff, Dan."

"They'll have to find a new one if we don't figure a way out of this." Dan swung over to the window and shot again without taking much of an aim. His eyes widened when he heard a scream.

"You gonna tell me what was in that letter, in case you don't make it through this and I do?" he asked JT, after JT nodded a grim acknowledgment of Dan's shot.

"Van Alstyne was financing blockade runners for the South during the war. Diedre overheard him talking to someone one night—man with a Southern drawl. She found the records after that, when she searched his desk. She never wanted to turn him in at first—didn't want the scandal on Shanna's or Toby's heads—but she made sure she always knew what was in those records. A lawyer friend of hers in New York has part of them now. Diedre stole them before she died and gave them to him, to keep until I showed up."

"Man must have been a good friend."

"That's all he was—a friend." JT shot Dan a warning look. "A *good* friend."

"I understand, JT. And I reckon Van Alstyne could still be tried for those crimes, if they came to light. At the very least, his business would go to hell when word got out he was a traitor."

"That won't happen if he agrees to give up any claim on Toby. I'm the only one who can put my hands on the proof needed."

"Cut the fence wire," Cody demanded in a raspy voice. "We can't take a chance on going up the road. That line of trees behind the barn will hide us until we get close enough to see who's shooting which direction."

Pappy reached behind the wagon seat and lifted the lid on a wooden box. He pulled out a pair of wire cutters and jumped down from the wagon seat. Standing beside the fence post, he snipped a wire, jerking his arm back when the string whipped away. He cut the other two strands, then climbed back to his seat.

"You get back there with Cody and Shanna now, Zerelda. Behind the seat."

"And leave you up here to draw their fire?"

"I've thought of that, woman. I can guide these horses just as well from behind the footrest. 'Sides, they probably ain't gonna see us at first, with those trees in the way. Go on. Now!"

After waiting until Zerelda climbed carefully over the wagon seat, Pappy scrunched his body behind the footboard. He grabbed his rifle and propped it beside him, then slapped the reins on the horses' backs.

"Get up there!"

The wagon bounced over ruts in the partially plowed field, the newly turned earth absorbing the sounds from the wheels and the horses' hooves. Cody checked his rifle and wiped a sheen of sweat from his forehead, blinking his eyes against the wavering images in front of him. Damn, why couldn't that drug kill his pain without affecting his vision! Pappy had done the best he could, though.

Cody noticed Zerelda check her own rifle and watched Shanna try to follow suit. "Don't, Shanna," he said quickly when he saw the hammer click back on the rifle she held. He gingerly took the gun from her, his fingers well away from the trigger guard as he lowered the hammer.

"Look, Shanna, you don't want that hammer back unless you're ready to fire a shell. And we aren't ready for that yet."

Shanna laid the rifle down when Cody gave it back. Reaching into her skirt pocket, she pulled out Susie's derringer.

"Maybe I better just use this."

"That thing's only got a range of about ten feet," Cody informed her. "You best be closer than that when you shoot, unless you've got a good aim on your arm."

"We're at the trees now, Cody," Pappy said in a harsh whisper. "I'm gonna sneak up there to see what's going on."

"We're all going," Zerelda said as she climbed from the back of the wagon.

Pappy sprang out of his hiding place and grabbed Zerelda's arm when she walked to the front of the wagon. He had to lift his head to look at his much taller wife, and he gave her arm a firm shake. "You're going to stay behind the largest tree and protect yourself. If I catch you so much as sticking a toe out from behind it, I'm gonna drag you back to this wagon and take you home!"

"I can't see to shoot unless I look where I'm aiming, Pappy," Zerelda said, attempting to pull her arm free. "Come on, they need our help up there."

Pappy's fingers bit into Zerelda's arm, refusing to loosen their hold. Shanna helped Cody from the wagon as the two stared at each other.

Zerelda dropped her eyes first. "All right, Pappy," she said meekly.

Pappy grabbed his rifle and offered his arm to Cody, who stumbled a couple times before they finally made their way through the trees to where they had a clear view of the Garret place.

A rifle spoke from the kitchen window and a head dropped back to shelter.

"That was Dan," Pappy whispered.

"Are you sure?" Cody whispered back, though they were way too far from the action for anyone to hear them.

"Damn it, boy, there ain't a thing wrong with my eyes! Got some other parts of me that still work, too!"

"Sorry, Pappy," Cody apologized. "That opium you gave me...."

"Told you that would happen. Now, let's think this out. If Dan's in the house, I 'magine JT is, too. Probably the women and kids are there, or else Dan wouldn't be shootin' at the barn. Wouldn't want to risk hittin' one of their own. And I don't expect there would even be any shootin' at all, if those bastards in the barn had any hostages."

"Makes sense," Cody agreed. "The ones in the barn probably think they can just hole up there until dark, then sneak up on the house. They don't know anyone else realizes what they're up to."

"We're gonna give you one last chance!" someone yelled from the barn. "Send Randolph out and we'll leave!"

Two simultaneous shots rang through the kitchen window, along with one from behind the horse trough by the corral.

"Yep," Pappy said. "That's JT and Dan. And the feller over by the horse trough must be that deputy. He's not shootin' at the house—he's aiming at the barn."

Pappy stepped out for a brief instant and waved an arm. The man behind the horse trough raised a cautious hand and returned the gesture.

"We need to get closer," Cody said. "Let's try for that wagon over there. I better warn you, though, it's loaded with manure. The women can cover us if we get spotted. Or at least, Zerelda can."

"Both of us will," Shanna spoke up, and Cody looked over at her to see her rifle again in her hands. "I've figured out how to work this thing, with Zerelda's help."

"You sure?" Cody asked.

"I might not hit anything, but I know how the bullets

get out. I can at least aim it and pull the trigger."

"You might just hit someone, Shanna. It's not a pretty feeling to shoot a man."

"Toby's in that house," Shanna shot back grimly. "I'll do whatever I have to in order to get him out of there safe."

"All right," Cody agreed. Crooking his rifle in his arm, he wiped his hand once again across his eyes. "Let's go, Pappy."

"Wait a minute." Zerelda leaned over and kissed Pappy. "Be careful, honey," she whispered softly.

"I will, darlin'," he replied. Then he asked Cody, "Can you make it that far?"

"I'll make it." Cody looked at Shanna, and she pressed her fingers to her own lips.

"Be careful. Please, Cody," she whispered after she blew the kiss at him.

The weeds in this unplowed section of Cody's field sheltered them as the men moved in a crouch down the trail made by previous wagon trips. The two women pointed their rifles toward the barn, their hearts in their mouths as they waited for a shout indicating someone had spied the men. Breathing out a unified sigh of relief when Cody and Pappy made it to the wagon undiscovered, Shanna and Zerelda relaxed their fingers on the rifle triggers just a hair.

Cody and Pappy had a clearer view of the kitchen window now, but the barn was set off enough to protect the door from their rifle shots. They were close enough to hear a commotion inside the barn, though—a horse neighing shrilly.

"Goddamn it, get it outside and head it toward the house!" a man yelled.

"Who?" another voice screamed back. "I'm not leading that damned horse out in front of those guns!"

"Jesus!" the first voice hollered. "It's spreading in

Bittersweet Promises

here! Scare that goddamned horse out of here!"

Shots rang out, and a wild-eyed horse pulling a wagon filled with flaming hay burst through the barn door. Cody dropped to his knee. The horse galloped straight at the house, neighing and plunging in terror.

Cursing his one-handedness, Cody aimed the rifle and pulled the trigger. The horse swerved when the bullet creased his neck, heading away from the house, toward the gate.

"The horse'll burn up with that damned wagon, Pappy!" Cody shouted. "I can't see well enough. Shoot him!"

The horse bucked in its traces, then reared in senseless fright, its front hooves pawing the air in panic. Overbalanced, it fell backward. A second later, it surged to its feet, traces broken, and galloped out through the gate, leaving the wagon burning well away from the house.

"Pappy," Cody said. "I heard them say the barn's on fire. They'll be coming out. Get ready."

"Damn," Pappy said as both men moved to the front of the wagon, trying for a better view of the barn door. "You got any more animals in there?"

"No. Jed's boy turned them out to pasture, like I always do, when he did chores this morning. I saw Brownie and Starlight in the far corner when we crossed the field. The plow horses and cow, too."

Smoke boiled from the opening and two men emerged, choking and holding their hands in the air.

"Don't shoot! There's a couple wounded men in there. We have to get them out!"

The men ducked inside and returned, each pulling a body by its feet. They stopped when they cleared the smoke, dropping their burdens and gasping for air as they raised their hands again.

"Tell the rest of them to come on out, unless they want to die in that barn!" Dan shouted from the kitchen window. "We won't shoot, if they leave their rifles behind!"

"You heard him," the first man to get enough breath shouted toward the barn.

Three more figures emerged, hands high in the air, except when they reached down to wipe their eyes. Cody and Pappy stepped from behind the wagon, covering them with their rifles as they approached the barn.

"Damn it," Dan mused inside the house. "Where's Van Alstyne? I don't see him."

"Be all right with me if he fries in there," JT said.

"Cody!" Dan called. "Watch yourselves! There's one missing!"

Cody immediately started around the barn toward the rear door, though he didn't see how anyone could possibly still breathe in there. Flames already shot from the roof, fueled by the dry hay inside. A gust of wind blew smoke and cinders in his eyes at the same instant he heard a horse gallop out the rear barn door.

Shanna raised her rifle as the man galloped toward her and Zerelda. Suddenly giving a start of recognition, she swung her rifle barrel, bringing it up under Zerelda's gun, knocking it up and sending Zerelda's bullet into the air.

"Don't! For God's sake, don't!" Shanna screamed when Zerelda shot her an astonished look and tried to take aim again. "That's my father!"

Zerelda lowered her rifle and allowed the man to ride away unchallenged. Van Alstyne never noticed the two women standing in the trees, but Shanna kept her gaze trained on him until he disappeared from view.

"I . . . I thought I hated him enough to see him dead," Shanna said with a sob. "But I couldn't let you do it."

"I understand, Shanna. And you did the right thing." Zerelda attempted to take the sobbing woman in her arms, but her bulky stomach hindered the embrace.

Bittersweet Promises

Shanna gasped in amazement when Zerelda's stomach moved under her breast. "Z-Zerelda," she choked, her tears drying as her head sprang up. "Are . . . are you all right? You aren't going to have the baby right now, are you?"

At Shanna's worried look, Zerelda burst into almost hysterical laughter. Smoke from the burning barn drifted toward the two women, but neither of them took any heed as they bent their heads over the distended stomach.

Shanna touched Zerelda's stomach, and a tiny bump against her palm softened her face in awe.

"For goodness sakes, no, I'm not in labor, Shanna," Zerelda managed to say. "He's just moving—telling me he's all right and he enjoyed his first adventure with his ma."

"The baby? The baby's moving? Is that what I felt? Does he do that much?"

"Lots. Sometimes too much, 'specially when I want to sleep. Here. Give me your hand again."

All thought of her father's escape left Shanna's mind when the mound rolled under her hand and she caressed what felt like a miniature head.

"Oh!" Shanna's head shot up. "If you and your baby are all right, we better get to the house and check on the other children."

"We've already seen them, and they're fine, Shanna," Cody said as he and Pappy approached the two women.

Shanna whirled and ran to him. "Cody! What about you, then? Let me help you back to the house, so you can lie down." Wrapping an arm around his waist, Shanna pulled Cody's good arm over her shoulders, urging him to lean against her.

"JT and Dan kept everyone in the parlor, out of danger of flying lead," Cody explained as they walked away from the trees. "Bessie and Susie have the kids busy helping clean up the mess in the kitchen—you know how Bessie is about keeping her kitchen clean. Everyone's fine, honey. The barn's gone, though. All we can do is let it burn."

"And the rest of those men?"

"The deputy's guarding the ones who can still walk, while they make sure the grass around the barn doesn't catch fire. The wounded ones, including Bobby, are tied up out by the gate until Dan returns. Pappy'll fetch his bag and tend to them."

"My father got away, you know."

"I know, darlin'. Dan went after him as soon as he caught a horse. He won't get far. Dan's not going to let him go unpunished."

"He'll deserve whatever he gets. Cody, he . . . he rode right at us. Zerelda had her rifle up, but I couldn't let her shoot him."

"He's your father, darlin'," Cody said, as though that explained everything. And it really did.

JT stepped from behind the apple tree on the edge of the yard, where he had been waiting for their approach. Realizing JT had to have overheard his endearment to Shanna, Cody stopped in his tracks, his fingers clenching on Shanna's shoulder.

For one, heartbreaking second, Cody and Shanna's eyes met; then Cody slowly loosened his fingers. Dropping his arm, he straightened, quickly masking the grimace of pain the movement brought to his face.

"She was only helping me into the house, JT," Cody said in a flat voice.

"I understand, Cody," JT replied.

Cody gave a curt nod, then stepped away from Shanna and started toward the house.

"Where you going, old pard?"

Cody halted, his back to them both. "To the house, JT. I can make it on my own."

Bittersweet Promises

"Well, now," JT drawled, "I reckon that's the damnedest lie I've ever heard. Since when did you start spouting lies, Cody?"

Cody's fingers twitched on the hand hanging by his holstered six-gun. Slowly he turned.

Keeping his own hand well away from his six-gun, JT leaned on his crutch and met Cody's glare.

"Stop it!" Shanna cried. "Both of you. I. . . ."

"Shut up, honey," JT said in a mild voice, never even glancing at her. "Sorry, Cody," he continued, a wry quirk to his mouth. "Just force of habit. I won't call her that again."

"JT. . . ." Cody studied his friend's face, a look of understanding slowly dawning in his eyes. "You're right, old friend," he said. "I can't manage without her."

"Didn't think so," JT said with a chuckle. "She's *your* darlin'. Always has been—always will be."

"But Toby!" Shanna choked.

"Well, now, I fully intend to be a part of my son's life somehow, Shanna," JT said, finally glancing at her. "I'm not about to head back to my hermit life."

"Do you want me to leave, so you can talk to Shanna alone, JT?" Cody asked quietly.

"It's not necessary, old pard."

Shanna took a hesitant step toward JT. "Are you saying you'll let me keep Toby to raise, even if you get custody?"

"Won't be any need for a custody hearing, Shanna. Your father won't be able to take Toby away from you while he's in prison. And that's where he's headed, at least for a few years, as soon as Dan catches him. He and his men attacked unarmed women and children and wounded two peace officers. Dan recognized Van Alstyne among the attackers, so you won't even have to identify him in court, even if you did see him ride away."

"I'm glad." Shanna breathed out a sigh of relief. "I don't think I could do it. I didn't know just how hard it was to hate someone totally, until I thought Zerelda was going to shoot him. But. . . ."

"And if he gives you any trouble later on," JT broke in, "I've told Dan all he needs to know to stop him. Someday, maybe I'll tell you, too."

JT reached out a hand and gently ran a finger down Shanna's cheek. "I want to thank you, Shanna, for coming into my life. For bringing me my son and giving me back my self-respect—for hauling me out of my self-pity and making me realize what love really is."

He dropped his hand and motioned for Cody to come closer. "You take care of her, old pard. I hope you know just how damned lucky you are."

Cody clasped JT's extended hand and nodded his head, clearing his throat against a lump. "I'll remember, JT. And if Toby grows into half the man his father is, he'll be a son we can both be proud of."

"Thanks, Cody. Now," he said after a final squeeze to his old pard's hand, "Shanna better get you into the house to bed, then discuss finishing that wedding dress with Susie. Maybe I'll talk to you later about being your best man. I've still got a hankering to wear my suit to a wedding."

JT settled his hat more firmly on his head and limped toward the house.

Shanna watched JT leave with a mist shadowing her eyes and swiped at a tear creeping down her cheek. "Oh, Cody, how can I ever repay him?"

"I think you already have, darlin'. Didn't you hear what he said?"

"Oh, that." Shanna waved a dismissing hand. "He wouldn't have stayed out there in the mountains forever. He's got far too much to offer the right woman someday. Look at the wonderful child he fathered. Sooner or later, some lucky woman would have found him and healed him."

"I don't have a hell of a lot to offer you, Shanna," Cody said, leaning against the apple tree in an attempt to keep Shanna from noticing his sway of pain. "But what I do have is yours to share."

"Oh, Cody, I'm not talking about material things. Cody! You need to be in bed. Here. Lean on me again."

"Huh-uh. Not just yet."

"Darn it, Cody," Shanna said with that delightful little stamp of her foot. "Then at least let me help you sit down. Do you want me to run to the house to ask Bessie for some laudanum for the pain?"

"Don't want neither—to sit or for you to leave. Man ought to be on his knees when he asks a woman to marry him, but since I don't think I can manage that and be able to get back up, the least you can do is hang around while I do the askin'."

"Oh," Shanna said in a tiny voice.

"Will you, Shanna? I love you with everything I have in me to love with. Will you marry me, City Girl—grow old with me out here in the country?"

"Yes! Oh, yes, Cody. I love you. I never thought this could happen, but all I've ever wanted since I realized how much I loved you was to be your wife. But. . . ."

"Damn it, Shanna, quit with the buts and come here!" Despite his waning strength, Cody swept her against his chest and buried his face in her hair when she clung tightly to him. "We can discuss the details later. Right now, you better kiss me, while I can still kiss you back."

Shanna tipped her face up and obeyed. A long moment later, she felt Cody's lips slacken as he tried to muffle a grunt of pain.

"Please, Cody," she said in a worried voice when he loosened his arm. "Now will you go lie down?"

"Guess I better." He draped his arm across Shanna's shoulder and allowed her to help him across the yard. "I sure hope this shoulder's at least partly healed by next Sunday. Since all the invites are out anyway, we might as well go ahead with the ceremony then, just with a different groom. But even if the shoulder's still sore, it's not going to stop our wedding night."

"What do you mean?" Shanna asked as she helped him up the porch steps.

"Remember, darlin', I told you there were different ways to do things."

"Different ways to do what on a wedding night?" Toby asked from the open doorway.

"Toby," Shanna gasped. "Toby, are you all right?"

"Yeah, we're all fine, Shanna. My dad took care of us. Different ways to do what?" he repeated as JT gave a chuckle behind him and laid a hand on his head.

"Hush and let me get Cody to bed," Shanna said with a violent blush as JT urged Toby out of the doorway so she and Cody could pass.

Cody's laughter rumbled through the kitchen as they walked across the floor. "You hush, too," Shanna said as they entered the hallway.

"Guess that's one of those things she's gonna talk to me about someday when I'm older," Toby said with a grin at JT. "But she forgot that I've got a dad to answer questions now. What was she talking about, Dad? Huh? Just between us men."

JT groaned and leaned against a porch post, his own cheeks slowly heating up. "Well, son. . . ."

Epilogue

Spring, 1871

"I can't believe how gentle that horse is with Toby," Shanna said as they stood in the backyard and watched Toby saddle Starlight. "Why, he'll hardly even let you ride him."

"Stud, City Girl," Cody said, wrapping his arm around Shanna's thickening waist, his eyes twinkling as he glanced at the blush on her cheeks. "Toby's riding over to JT's again, so Starlight can take care of a couple of his mares that are ready to breed. City Girl, you still have a few things to learn about the names for the farm animals."

The screen door slammed and a small figure raced by them, legs pumping as he ran toward the corral.

"Wait, Toby!" the little boy called. "I'm done with my homework now. Aunt Bessie said I could go with you!"

"Joshua Garret!" Shanna called. "Where do you think you're going?"

The four year old skidded to a stop. He looked at his mother, then gazed yearningly at the corral.

"I've done my lessons, Mommy," he said as he trudged back to Shanna. "I said all my ABC's right and counted all the way up to a hundred for Aunt Bessie. You said at breakfast that I could have some free time today after lessons."

"Josh, Toby's going over to JT's to...."

"Go on, Mommy," Cody said with a laugh. "Tell our son why Toby's taking Starlight over to the Lazy T."

"Oh, I already know that, Daddy," Josh said. "He's gonna let Starlight make babies with Uncle JT's mares. Toby said I could go with him on Chessy if I got my lessons right in time. Please, Daddy."

"Joshua Garret!" Shanna gasped. "JT doesn't let you watch while the horses ma-make ... babies!"

"It's called matin', Mommy." Josh's small face puckered in a frown. "An' no, he ain't ... hasn't let me watch yet. He said maybe next year, when I'm five."

Josh screwed up his face even further and centered his eyes on Shanna's stomach. "Mommy, did you and Daddy get the new baby started by...."

Cody's laughter roared, covering up Shanna's choke of embarrassment. "You better get going, son," Cody said when he could speak. "Toby's leading Chessy out for you to saddle. Just be sure that you and Toby get back before dark."

"We will, Daddy," Josh yelled, already running toward the corral.

"Next thing you know, JT will have Josh training those horses, right along with Toby," Cody said with a smile. "I'm glad you helped JT buy his old home place back and start his horse farm."

"Toby's the one who talked JT into letting him be a part of the horse farm with his share of our mother's inheritance," Shanna reminded him. "I'll bet Toby's the youngest half owner of a horse farm in the state. And it's turned into a good investment for him, with both Starlight and the other horse . . . stud . . . JT has. But," Shanna grumbled, her cheeks still flushed. "It all makes me stop and wonder sometimes. These children know more about how animals reproduce than I did until after I was married!"

"Not quite, darlin'," Cody said softly as he turned her in his arms and bent his head. "Remember that night in the barn? I'll never forget that you told me you loved me that night."

Cody's lips covered hers, and Shanna sighed in surrender as she returned his kiss. Cody jerked his head up when he felt a movement against him and tenderly ran his hand down Shanna's stomach.

"That's the first time I've felt this one move," he said in wonder. "It never ceases to throw me for a loop every time. Are you feeling all right?"

"Wonderful," Shanna replied. "Just like last time. I still have this crazy craving for fried fish, though, like the ones we had beside the lake that evening."

Someone cleared a throat behind Cody, and Shanna glanced around to see Melinda standing there.

"If you two would quit smoochin' for a minute," Melinda said, "I was gonna ask if I could go catch Mom some fish. Pappy told me yesterday the fish were biting over by his place. And I was gonna take Archie with me, if Mrs. Samuel will let him go."

"Melinda," Cody said with a frown. "What in the world do you have on?"

Melinda looked down at herself and turned a wide-eyed, innocent gaze on her father. "Just a pair of Toby's old trousers. I can't go tramping through the field to the creek in a dress."

Shanna stifled a giggle and touched Cody's arm. "She's right, darling. The last time she came back with her skirt pricked and torn from briars. The denims make much more sense."

Melinda turned away and called over her shoulder, "Thanks, Mom. Aunt Bessie said to tell you she's taking a nap!"

Cody stared after his daughter until she emerged from the barn a moment later, a cane pole over her shoulder and a bridle in her hand. Melinda climbed through the corral fence, and Brownie immediately trotted up to her. After slipping the bridle over the mare's head, Melinda leaped aboard bareback and urged the mare over the railing on the far side, clearing the fence with inches to spare and galloping across the field beyond, braids bouncing on her shoulders.

"Where in the world did my spoiled princess in ruffles and lace go?" Cody asked in a forlorn voice. "What will the neighbors think, when they see her in those pants?"

"That little princess is still there under the tomboy," Shanna soothed. "Just give her a couple years or so, until she starts discovering boys."

"Oh, Good Lord," Cody groaned. "I don't know which is worse—a tomboy or a princess I have to stand guard over with a shotgun."

"Well, keep in practice, because I've got a feeling this one will be a girl, too. I'd like to name her Diedre after my mother, Cody. We can call her Dee Dee while she goes through her tomboy stage."

"Um-hum. Whatever you want, sweetheart."

"Cody, are you listening to me?" Shanna tugged on his sleeve until Cody looked down.

"Huh? Listening? Yeah, I was listening to the silence. Do you realize we're alone here—at least for the next two hours."

"No, we're not. Bessie's in the house."

"Asleep. But I wasn't thinking about the house. I was thinking about the haymow."

"Oh, the haymow," Shanna said in a dreamy voice. "I haven't been in the haymow in years, not since the new barn was built. Is this haymow as nice as the old one?"

Cody swept her into his arms. "Let's go see what you think of it," he growled.

Author's Note

Though Cody, Shanna and their families live only in my imagination, the James/Samuel family lived near the fictitious site of the Garret Plantation. Zerelda, Pappy, Jesse and Archie are buried, along with various others from their family, in the Kearney, MO, cemetery. The details of Zerelda's life, blended in with Shanna's, are as near to historical fact as research can make them, though over 100 years of mystique and legend sometimes blur facts.

Zerelda was indeed pregnant at the time of my story, with her last child, Archie, who was to die 12 years later in the infamous firebombing of the Samuels' cabin by the Pinkertons, during which Zerelda lost her hand. Though I can only imagine the heartbreak Zerelda James Samuel must have gone through, I'd like to think she may have had friends like Shanna and Cody to help see her through her trials.

COMING IN FEBRUARY!
TIMESWEPT ROMANCE
TEARS OF FIRE
By Nelle McFather

Swept into the tumultuous life and times of her ancestor Deirdre O'Shea, Fable relives a night of sweet ecstasy with Andre Devereux, never guessing that their delicious passion will have the power to cross the ages. Caught between swirling visions of a distant desire and a troubled reality filled with betrayal, Fable seeks the answers that will set her free—answers that can only be found in the tender embrace of two men who live a century apart.

_51932-1 $4.99 US/$5.99 CAN

FUTURISTIC ROMANCE
ASCENT TO THE STARS
By Christine Michels

For Trace, the assignment should be simple. Any Thadonian warrior can take a helpless female to safety in exchange for valuable information against his diabolical enemies. But as fiery as a supernova, as radiant as a sun, Coventry Pearce is no mere woman. Even as he races across the galaxy to save his doomed world, Trace battles to deny a burning desire that will take him to the heavens and beyond.

_51933-X $4.99 US/$5.99 CAN

LOVE SPELL
ATTN: Order Department
Dorchester Publishing Co., Inc.
276 5th Avenue, New York, NY 10001

Please add $1.50 for shipping and handling for the first book and $.35 for each book thereafter. PA., N.Y.S. and N.Y.C. residents, please add appropriate sales tax. No cash, stamps, or C.O.D.s. All orders shipped within 6 weeks via postal service book rate. Canadian orders require $2.00 extra postage and must be paid in U.S. dollars through a U.S. banking facility.

Name_____
Address_____
City _____ State_____ Zip_____
I have enclosed $_____in payment for the checked book(s).
Payment <u>must</u> accompany all orders. ☐ Please send a free catalog.

TIMESWEPT ROMANCE
TIME OF THE ROSE
By Bonita Clifton

When the silver-haired cowboy brings Madison Calloway to his run-down ranch, she thinks for sure he is senile. Certain he'll bring harm to himself, Madison follows the man into a thunderstorm and back to the wild days of his youth in the Old West.

The dread of all his enemies and the desire of all the ladies, Colton Chase does not stand a chance against the spunky beauty who has tracked him through time. And after one passion-drenched night, Colt is ready to surrender his heart to the most tempting spitfire anywhere in time.

_51922-4 $4.99 US/$5.99 CAN

A FUTURISTIC ROMANCE
AWAKENINGS
By Saranne Dawson

Fearless and bold, Justan rules his domain with an iron hand, but nothing short of the Dammai's magic will bring his warring people peace. He claims he needs Rozlynd—a bewitching beauty and the last of the Dammai—for her sorcery alone, yet inside him stirs an unexpected yearning to savor the temptress's charms, to sample her sweet innocence. And as her silken spell ensnares him, Justan battles to vanquish a power whose like he has never encountered—the power of Rozlynd's love.

_51921-6 $4.99 US/$5.99 CAN

LOVE SPELL
ATTN: Order Department
Dorchester Publishing Co., Inc.
276 5th Avenue, New York, NY 10001

Please add $1.50 for shipping and handling for the first book and $.35 for each book thereafter. PA., N.Y.S. and N.Y.C. residents, please add appropriate sales tax. No cash, stamps, or C.O.D.s. All orders shipped within 6 weeks via postal service book rate. Canadian orders require $2.00 extra postage and must be paid in U.S. dollars through a U.S. banking facility.

Name_____
Address_____
City _____ State_____ Zip_____
I have enclosed $_____in payment for the checked book(s).
Payment <u>must</u> accompany all orders.☐ Please send a free catalog.

HISTORICAL ROMANCE
HUNTERS OF THE ICE AGE: YESTERDAY'S DAWN
By Theresa Scott

Named for the massive beast sacred to his people, Mamut has proven his strength and courage time and again. But when it comes to subduing one helpless captive female, he finds himself at a distinct disadvantage. Never has he realized the power of beguiling brown eyes, soft curves and berry-red lips to weaken a man's resolve. He has claimed he will make the stolen woman his slave, but he soon learns he will never enjoy her alluring body unless he can first win her elusive heart.

_51920-8 $4.99 US/$5.99 CAN

A CONTEMPORARY ROMANCE
HIGH VOLTAGE
By Lori Copeland

Laurel Henderson hadn't expected the burden of inheriting her father's farm to fall squarely on her shoulders. And if Sheriff Clay Kerwin can't catch the culprits who are sabotaging her best efforts, her hopes of selling it are dim. Struggling with this new responsibility, Laurel has no time to pursue anything, especially not love. The best she can hope for is an affair with no strings attached. And the virile law officer is the perfect man for the job—until Laurel's scheme backfires. Blind to Clay's feelings and her own, she never dreams their amorous arrangement will lead to the passion she wants to last for a lifetime.

_51923-2 $4.99 US/$5.99 CAN

LOVE SPELL
ATTN: Order Department
Dorchester Publishing Co., Inc.
276 5th Avenue, New York, NY 10001

Please add $1.50 for shipping and handling for the first book and $.35 for each book thereafter. PA., N.Y.S. and N.Y.C. residents, please add appropriate sales tax. No cash, stamps, or C.O.D.s. All orders shipped within 6 weeks via postal service book rate. Canadian orders require $2.00 extra postage and must be paid in U.S. dollars through a U.S. banking facility.

Name_____
Address_____
City _____ State_____ Zip_____

I have enclosed $_____in payment for the checked book(s).
Payment <u>must</u> accompany all orders.☐ Please send a free catalog.

FROM LOVE SPELL
FUTURISTIC ROMANCE
NO OTHER LOVE
Flora Speer
Bestselling Author of *A Time To Love Again*

Only Herne sees the woman. To the other explorers of the ruined city she remains unseen, unknown. But after an illicit joining she is gone, and Herne finds he cannot forget his beautiful seductress, or ignore her uncanny resemblance to another member of the exploration party. Determined to unravel the puzzle, Herne begins a seduction of his own—one that will unleash a whirlwind of danger and desire.

_51916-X $4.99 US/$5.99 CAN

TIMESWEPT ROMANCE
LOVE'S TIMELESS DANCE
Vivian Knight-Jenkins

Although the pressure from her company's upcoming show is driving Leeanne Sullivan crazy, she refuses to believe she can be dancing in her studio one minute—and with a seventeenth-century Highlander the next. A liberated woman like Leeanne will have no problem teaching virile Iain MacBride a new step or two, and soon she'll have him begging for lessons in love.

_51917-8 $4.99 US/$5.99 CAN

LOVE SPELL
ATTN: Order Department
Dorchester Publishing Company, Inc.
276 5th Avenue, New York, NY 10001

Please add $1.50 for shipping and handling for the first book and $.35 for each book thereafter. PA., N.Y.S. and N.Y.C. residents, please add appropriate sales tax. No cash, stamps, or C.O.D.s. All orders shipped within 6 weeks via postal service book rate. Canadian orders require $2.00 extra postage and must be paid in U.S. dollars through a U.S. banking facility.

Name_____
Address _____
City _____ State_____Zip_____
I have enclosed $_____in payment for the checked book(s).
Payment <u>must</u> accompany all orders.☐ Please send a free catalog.

FROM LOVE SPELL
HISTORICAL ROMANCE
THE PASSIONATE REBEL
Helene Lehr

A beautiful American patriot, Gillian Winthrop is horrified to learn that her grandmother means her to wed a traitor to the American Revolution. Her body yearns for Philip Meredith's masterful touch, but she is determined not to give her hand—or any other part of herself—to the handsome Tory, until he convinces her that he too is a passionate rebel.

_51918-6 $4.99 US/$5.99 CAN

CONTEMPORARY ROMANCE
THE TAWNY GOLD MAN
Amii Lorin

Bestselling Author Of More Than 5 Million Books In Print!

Long ago, in a moment of wild, rioting ecstasy, Jud Cammeron vowed to love her always. Now, as Anne Moore looks at her stepbrother, she sees a total stranger, a man who plans to take control of his father's estate and everyone on it. Anne knows things are different—she is a grown woman with a fiance—but something tells her she still belongs to the tawny gold man.

_51919-4 $4.99 US/$5.99 CAN

LOVE SPELL
ATTN: Order Department
Dorchester Publishing Company, Inc.
276 5th Avenue, New York, NY 10001

Please add $1.50 for shipping and handling for the first book and $.35 for each book thereafter. PA., N.Y.S. and N.Y.C. residents, please add appropriate sales tax. No cash, stamps, or C.O.D.s. All orders shipped within 6 weeks via postal service book rate. Canadian orders require $2.00 extra postage and must be paid in U.S. dollars through a U.S. banking facility.

Name_____
Address_____
City _____ State_____Zip_____
I have enclosed $_____in payment for the checked book(s).
Payment <u>must</u> accompany all orders.☐ Please send a free catalog.

AN HISTORICAL ROMANCE
GILDED SPLENDOR
By Elizabeth Parker

Bound for the London stage, sheltered Amanda Prescott has no idea that fate has already cast her first role as a rakehell's true love. But while visiting Patrick Winter's country estate, she succumbs to the dashing peer's burning desire. Amid the glittering milieu of wealth and glamour, Amanda and Patrick banish forever their harsh past and make all their fantasies a passionate reality.

_51914-3 $4.99 US/$5.99 CAN

A CONTEMPORARY ROMANCE
MADE FOR EACH OTHER/RAVISHED
By Parris Afton Bonds
Bestselling Author of *The Captive*

In *Made for Each Other,* reporter Julie Dever thinks she knows everything about Senator Nicholas Raffer—until he rescues her from a car wreck and shares with her a passion she never dared hope for. And in *Ravished*, a Mexican vacation changes nurse Nelli Walzchak's life when she is kidnapped by a handsome stranger who needs more than her professional help.

_51915-1 $4.99 US/$5.99 CAN

LEISURE BOOKS
ATTN: Order Department
276 5th Avenue, New York, NY 10001

Please add $1.50 for shipping and handling for the first book and $.35 for each book thereafter. PA., N.Y.S. and N.Y.C. residents, please add appropriate sales tax. No cash, stamps, or C.O.D.s All orders shipped within 6 weeks via postal service book rate. Canadian orders require $2.00 extra postage and must be paid in U.S. dollars through a U.S. banking facility.

Name _____
Address _____
City _____ State _____ Zip _____
I have enclosed $_____ in payment for the checked book(s).
Payment <u>must</u> accompany all orders. ☐ Please send a free catalog.

FUTURISTIC ROMANCE
FIRESTAR
Kathleen Morgan
Bestselling Author of *The Knowing Crystal*

From the moment Meriel lays eyes on the virile slave chosen to breed with her, the heir to the Tenuan throne is loath to perform her imperial duty and produce a child. Yet despite her resolve, Meriel soon succumbs to Gage Bardwin—the one man who can save her planet.

_0-505-51908-9 $4.99 US/$5.99 CAN

TIMESWEPT ROMANCE
ALL THE TIME WE NEED
Megan Daniel

Nearly drowned after trying to save a client, musical agent Charli Stewart wakes up in New Orleans's finest brothel—run by the mother of the city's most virile man—on the eve of the Civil War. Unsure if she'll ever return to her own era, Charli gambles her heart on a love that might end as quickly as it began.

_0-505-51909-7 $4.99 US/$5.99 CAN

LEISURE BOOKS
ATTN: Order Department
276 5th Avenue, New York, NY 10001

Please add $1.50 for shipping and handling for the first book and $.35 for each book thereafter. PA., N.Y.S. and N.Y.C. residents, please add appropriate sales tax. No cash, stamps, or C.O.D.s. All orders shipped within 6 weeks via postal service book rate. Canadian orders require $2.00 extra postage and must be paid in U.S. dollars through a U.S. banking facility.

Name_____
Address_____
City _____ State _____ Zip_____
I have enclosed $_____in payment for the checked book(s).
Payment <u>must</u> accompany all orders. ☐ Please send a free catalog.

TIMESWEPT ROMANCE
A TIME-TRAVEL CHRISTMAS
By Megan Daniel, Vivian Knight-Jenkins, Eugenia Riley, and Flora Speer

In these four passionate time-travel historical romance stories, modern-day heroines journey everywhere from Dickens's London to a medieval castle as they fulfill their deepest desires on Christmases past.
_51912-7 $4.99 US/$5.99 CAN

A FUTURISTIC ROMANCE
MOON OF DESIRE
By Pam Rock

Future leader of his order, Logan has vanquished enemies, so he expects no trouble when a sinister plot brings a mere woman to him. But as the three moons of the planet Thurlow move into alignment, Logan and Calla head for a collision of heavenly bodies that will bring them ecstasy—or utter devastation.
_51913-5 $4.99 US/$5.99 CAN

LEISURE BOOKS
ATTN: Order Department
276 5th Avenue, New York, NY 10001

Please add $1.50 for shipping and handling for the first book and $.35 for each book thereafter. PA., N.Y.S. and N.Y.C. residents, please add appropriate sales tax. No cash, stamps, or C.O.D.s. All orders shipped within 6 weeks via postal service book rate. Canadian orders require $2.00 extra postage and must be paid in U.S. dollars through a U.S. banking facility.

Name _____
Address _____
City _____ State _____ Zip _____
I have enclosed $_____ in payment for the checked book(s).
Payment <u>must</u> accompany all orders. ☐ Please send a free catalog.